M000084287

Stonebearer's Betrayal

JODI L. MILNER

Immortal Works LLC
P.O. Box 25492
Salt Lake City, Utah 84125
Tel: (385) 202-0116

© 2018 Jodi L. Milner
jodilmilnerauthor.wordpress.com

Cover Art by Ashley Literski
strangedevotion.wixsite.com/strangedesigns

Formatted by FireDrake Designs
www.firedrakedesigns.com

All rights reserved, including the right to reproduce this book or portions thereof in any form whatsoever. For more information email contact@immortal-works.com or visit www.immortal-works.com/contact

ISBN 978-1-7324674-4-6 (Paperback)
AISN B07HDJDZK1 (Kindle Edition)

To Joe, who encouraged me to find magic every day.

Chapter 1

O nly sixteen days remained before Katira's coming of age ceremony, and she prayed for more time. She'd spent eighteen years of her childhood without giving the passing moments a single thought, and those moments were running out.

Katira shifted aside her well-worn quilt an inch at a time, trying not to make a sound as she readied herself to sneak out of bed. Elan promised to meet her outside the gate when the moon passed behind the highest peak across the valley.

The bed frame creaked as she sat up. She held her breath, not daring to move or lie back down. On the other side of the small room, the heavy slumber-laden breathing of Mamar and Papan continued unchanged.

Over the years, Elan had begged her to sneak out dozens of times. Each time he asked, Papan's warnings of dangers in the woods echoed through her head. Papan spoke of things out there that wanted to hurt her. Going with Elan not only went against her father's rules, it scared her.

Back then, there was always the promise of another chance.

Not anymore. Elan insisted that it would be unseemly for her to participate in that year's coming of age ceremony without ever having set foot in the woods. She needed to have this small adventure to proclaim her entry into adulthood. It was expected. All the other youths did it. Even clumsy Gonal, her father's smithy apprentice, had been rabbit hunting with his older brothers. Or so he said.

Then again, the other youth didn't have Papan as their father. They wouldn't be forced to carry water until their hands bled as a lesson in responsibility.

She pushed the rest of the blanket aside. Nothing could make her change her mind. Not now. Today marked her eighteenth birthday. She was an adult. If she wanted to leave the house and go to the woods, she could do so without permission. She would have to face her fears and there was no one better to do it with than Elan.

The frozen floor chilled her toes even through her thick woolen socks. She slipped out of the room and nudged the door closed. She took a moment in the kitchen to collect herself, breathing in the scents from the fragrant herbs and flowers Mamar had hung to dry from the thick beams holding up the thatch roof.

A dark orange petal of sanaresina had fallen and lay on Mamar's worn work table. Katira crumbled it between her fingers and collected the fragments in her cupped palm. It smelled of pepper and camphor. She had helped Mamar prepare medicines ever since she was strong enough to lift the heavy mortar and pestle. After the ceremony, Katira would officially take her place as Mamar's assistant in the shop. As assistant she would be allowed to care for her own patients and earn the respect she had seen given to her mother.

Katira's stomach rumbled. Had this been a normal morning, she would have kindled the kitchen fire and warmed the breakfast porridge.

She dared a glance toward the closed bedroom door. Guilt wrapped heavy around her like a blanket. Not enough to stop her, but enough to make her pause. A tingle of worry crept down the back of her throat. Papan wasn't one to make up stories. What if there really were things in the wood that wanted to hurt her?

Katira wrapped a thick green scarf around her neck and over her head, carefully tucking in the stray strands of hair. Her stomach fluttered at the hope of Elan giving her a compliment about how she looked. Mamar had helped her pick out the green scarf the week before, saying it complimented the chestnut browns in Katira's hair.

The barest pink of morning crept over the peak of the mountain to the east, spilling across the tops of the jagged rock as she eased the door open and slipped outside. A breeze whirled sparkling circles around the corners of the stone cottages in the isolated village. Frost glittered on the edges of the new fallen leaves.

Elan leaned against the low garden wall surrounding the healer's cottage. A thick woolen cap pinned down his golden curly locks making the ends stick out at all angles. Katira tried to stop the grin from spreading across her face and failed. Perhaps he would let her run her fingers through his hair to fix it. Her face grew hot imagining how it would feel. She pinned her hands behind her back. There would be no hair touching. Not yet, at least.

Elan's coat hung large on his lean frame, a hand-me-down from his older, much bulkier, brother. He hated it. But to her the coat was charming. It whispered the possibility of him folding her inside it with him, should she get too cold.

Elan's lips quirked into a half-smile as she neared. He poked at the scarf and his fingers grazed the side of her neck, sending a scurry of shivers down her back. "You sure you'll be warm enough?"

She tugged the scarf straight again. If he was going to act like a silly child, so could she. "You sure I won't kick you when your back is turned?"

Elan chuckled and pulled a cloth bundle from one of his coat pockets. "Here, take this," he said. "Happy birthday."

Katira gave a tiny gasp before she could stop it. She untied the twine and peeled back the folds of cloth to show a hunting knife tucked snugly inside its own leather sheath. It was much like the one

Elan always wore on his hip. Beneath the knife was a richly oiled leather belt. She drew the blade free and rested it on her palm. From tip to pommel it measured no longer than the length of her hand. "It's a bit small, don't you think?" she teased as she compared it to the much more impressive blade resting at his hip.

Elan bit his lip and pushed his hands in his pockets. Knowing him, he must have spent hours stitching and polishing the leather of the sheath and belt.

She leaned into him, nearly unseating him from the low wall. "I love it. It's perfect."

He lifted the belt from her hand and wrapped it around her waist, fastening it with a rougher than necessary tug. "You're welcome." He let his hands linger on her waist a second longer than necessary before letting them fall away. Katira hoped he would find a reason to put them back.

This close to him, Katira could smell the leather polish that had worked into his hands from his father's shop along with the earthy scent of his skin. She longed to bury her face in his chest and breathe him in.

Elan slipped his hand into hers and they walked through the quiet lanes. The skin of his hands was always chapped and sore from working the tanning vats. She had offered him a healing salve before, something to take the pain away. He never accepted it, telling her that hands like his proved how hard he worked.

A sparrow burst out of a nearby tree, making Katira jump. Papan's warning made every shadow hold a monster.

"Are you still scared about going?" Elan asked.

"A little." Katira swallowed down the lump of fear. "It's silly, I know."

"No. Not silly. I promise." He tucked an errant curl back under his cap. "What do you think is out there?"

"You'd laugh if I told you."

"Try me."

"You know how Schoolmaster Aben taught about wielders?" She

gave a half-hearted laugh. "Evildoers who don't age and can control the elements themselves?" Wielders weren't real. Everyone knew that. "I used to imagine they prowled the forest, waiting for young girls to put under their spell."

Elan wiggled his fingers at her. "Better watch out. Maybe I'm one of them. Maybe I'll place you under a spell to make you think I'm handsome."

"Stop that." Katira laughed and swatted at his hands. The tension she had been holding between her shoulders melted away. "Do you believe wielders exist?"

He kicked at a pebble. "I've read the books. The few books they keep at the school, at least. They must have at some point. But I can't imagine them being around anymore."

They passed the last home of the village. The only thing separating them from the woods was the waist-high stacked stone wall that kept the sheep out of the village proper. "Why's that?"

"They can't have children. They can die if they get hurt enough. The books agree on that much. Seems like they would have all been killed off by now." Elan gave her hand a reassuring squeeze before letting go to open the gate. "Unless they look like rabbits, I've never seen anything magical out here."

Elan led her up an old well-worn deer trail heading north away from the village. Katira let the fresh cold air fill her lungs. Fallen leaves crunched beneath their feet and perfumed the air with their crisp scent. The wind carried the promise of snow. Her worries of what she might find outside the village floated away and a new freedom buzzed through her.

A large blackberry bush rustled ahead. Katira's heart leapt up into her throat and she darted behind Elan. He put a finger to his lips and motioned her to look. Inside the thorny branches, a plump gray rabbit cleaned its face with its paws. Katira put her palm to her chest to stop her heart from pounding.

Just a rabbit, nothing more.

"Stand over there," Elan whispered, pointing past the bush. "If it runs, grab it."

Katira picked her way to the other side, careful to not step on any twigs. It wasn't fair. She didn't see Elan jumping at each rustle of a bush or at each flapping of a bird's wings. If he could catch a rabbit, so could she.

She crouched at the other edge of the bush, hands held out ready to catch their prey.

Elan gave her another smile and a slight nod. He stretched his arm forward and lowered his hand until it hovered over the quivering animal. The rabbit licked its other paw and scrubbed away at a long soft ear. Katira shifted on the balls of her feet and the rabbit froze in place, nose twitching. Elan lunged forward to grab it and missed. The rabbit scrambled away in a flurry of feet and fur.

"Get it, quick!" Elan shouted with boyish glee.

Katira grabbed for the fur at the rabbit's neck a fraction of a second too late. It slipped through her fingers like water and shot away through the trees.

"By rock and ruin," she cursed as she brushed off the leaves clinging to the hem of her skirt. "I was so close."

Elan was sure to say something reassuring. He always did. She opened her mouth, ready to fire back a sassy reply, but snapped it shut again when she noticed he'd turned his back to her. He stood rigid, intent on something else to the side of the trail.

"What is it?" she asked, squinting to make it out.

He held out a hand. "Shhh."

"Don't you shush me," Katira scolded. She picked her way back around the bush and to his side. "What? Is there another rabbit?"

He remained still. Focused. "That's no rabbit. Listen." His voice was barely above a whisper.

Katira strained to hear something, anything, unusual in the direction he was leaning. Her heart pounded harder at Elan's sudden seriousness. She would not let her fear win. "What am I listening for?"

"The woods went silent."

She slapped his shoulder. "Stop trying to scare me. It's not funny." Katira tugged at her scarf and tried to ignore Papan's warning echoing in her head again. "So what if it's quiet? Does it matter?"

He shifted his hand closer to his knife. "Quiet means danger."

If he was pulling a prank on her, she wouldn't play along. She crossed her arms under her chest and stuck out her lower lip, trying to elicit a laugh.

Elan glanced at her but quickly looked away. He didn't even crack the tiniest of smiles.

This was no joke.

"Does this happen often?" Katira asked, fingers reaching for the hilt of her new knife, grateful for the small amount of added protection it offered.

"No." He freed his own knife from his belt. "That's what has me worried."

A shadow flickered off to the side of the trail, making no more sound than the whisper of dry leaves.

Elan gripped Katira's arm, pulling her back. "We're leaving. Now."

"I don't understand, what's happening?" The sudden change in Elan confirmed her every fear about the woods. Papan was right. She wasn't safe here.

"We're being hunted." He pushed her down the trail. "Run."

She needed no urging. She ran. Tears blurred the path and trees around her. She wanted nothing more than to be home. The pounding rhythm of Elan's footfalls raced behind her.

Loose stones and raised roots littered the trail. Katira fought to keep from tripping. Branches whipped at her face and caught in the fibers of her coat. Her breath burned in her lungs. A flat stone rolled beneath her step, sending her sprawling forward. Elan caught her arm and kept her from slamming into the dirt.

"You okay?" he asked, breathing heavily.

She struggled to put words together. In this horrible place, every shadow held a monster. Every sound meant a new danger.

Elan placed a hand on either side of her face, so she could see nothing but him. "Shhh. It's okay. I'm here." He wiped a tear off her cheek. "Breathe."

She stared into his crystal blue eyes, willing herself to get lost in them, willing her heart to slow.

"There, that's better." He pulled her into a hug. "I think that's enough excitement for one day. Let's go home."

She nodded her agreement and let his soothing scent calm her.

A low hissing growl came from a thick patch of scrub oak not twenty paces away. Katira's stomach dropped to her feet. She didn't dare move for fear of making a sound. A menacing presence filled the air.

Elan muttered a curse and twisted to face the sound, his knife ready.

"They've blocked the way," he said, the firmness of his voice left no room for argument. "Stay behind me. Watch your side of the trail."

Katira bolted to her feet and pulled the small blade from her belt. Her experience with knives was limited to kitchen duties. She could clean fish and break down game animals. It wasn't much, but it was better than nothing.

Another low hiss came from the trail ahead of her.

They were surrounded.

"Now what?" she asked, gripping her knife tighter.

He shifted his feet, preparing to face whatever might come. "If it comes close to you, stab at it, kick it. Do what you have to do to keep it away."

The tall bushes on either side of the trail twitched. A dark shadowy shape darted from one patch of scrub oak to the next. Katira squinted, but the harder she strained to see it, the more blurred and indistinct it became. The small flame of her fear exploded into a roaring fire of panic. This was no normal animal.

The shadow lunged forward. Its needle-like teeth gleamed in the dim light. Katira screamed and slashed at the thing, swinging her arm wildly. Behind her, Elan yelled and stabbed at another shadow leaping up at him from the other side of the trail. No matter how desperately she tried to fend off her attacker, her blade passed through it like smoke.

A blinding flash lit the area beneath the trees. The shadows shrieked and darted away, back beneath the undergrowth. Papan barreled through the brush, hair wild, shirt unbuttoned. He held his long hunting knife clutched with both hands as if it were a sword, ready to fight. Clear blue light cut radiant patterns across his bare chest, down his arms, and extended down the blade of his knife.

"Run, Katira!" he commanded. "Get away from here!"

Katira stumbled back away from him. The newcomer wore her father's face, but what she saw couldn't be possible.

A shadow snarled and lunged for Papan's thigh. With one clean stroke he struck it with the glowing blade and flung its limp body into the undergrowth. Another creature charged from the other side, leaping at Papan's face. He moved like a dancer, bringing his blade up in a smooth arc and through the creature's side.

Papan turned and lifted Katira to her feet. Next to her, Elan stood clutching his knife in front of him. His face had gone white. Papan grabbed Elan's shoulder and gave him a shake. "Take Katira to safety," he ordered. The tone of his voice demanded unquestioned obedience. "They won't follow you if I'm here."

Elan stammered and blinked. "But, Master Jarand—" he began.

"Go!" Papan sidestepped another shadow creature, bringing his blade down into its back.

Elan caught hold of Katira's hand and pulled. The blue glow of her father's blade flashed brighter as it struck another of the dark creatures.

Katira couldn't look away. Wielders were a myth, stories used to entertain children. No one could truly wield magic. She had to be dreaming.

A pair of shadows broke free from the rest. She tried to warn Papan, but they moved faster than any words. One streaked for his neck, another toward his legs. He pivoted, catching the first shadow in the flank. The second wrapped around his calf, sinking in its teeth. He hissed at the pain before grabbing it and flinging it away. Its formless body struck a stout pine trunk with a thud.

Katira broke free of Elan's grip, fear forgotten. Papan was hurt. He needed her.

"Stay back." Her father scanned the undergrowth. "There's one more."

Her senses sharpened, every sound of the wood echoed in her ears. Something shifted to her left, too far for Papan to reach. "It's here," she whispered. The image of the terrible needle teeth of the first creature came unbidden to her mind. Her fingers squeezed the hilt of the tiny knife. "What do I do?"

"Stay still." Papan stepped toward her with a wince. "I won't let anything happen to you."

He couldn't reach her in time. The creature would strike before Papan took another step. She held tight to the handle of her tiny knife. It was all she had.

The shadow prowled into view, a dark smudge with four slender legs. Its dark shining eyes locked on her. It crouched, like the winding of a spring. Shadow muscles rippled as it prepared to lunge.

Elan pivoted, knife in hand. Five steps too far away.

The shadow leapt.

Blue streaks raced down her father's arms as he punched the ground. Lightning shot forward, catching the shadow and throwing it back into the clearing. Its shrieks pierced the air. Katira clapped her hands over her ears. Blue light webbed around the shadow and grew brighter until the creature crumbled into dust.

Elan raced to Katira's side and stood ready to protect her. His wide eyes darted around the wood. "Are you okay?"

"I think so." She loosened her grip on the knife and slid it back into its sheath. "I think they're gone now." She expected her hands to shake, for her heart to beat a fierce protest against what had happened. Instead, she found a strange peace.

"Bless the Stone." Elan exhaled and pulled her into his arms. His whole body trembled as he held her. Katira wasn't sure if it was with fear or relief. She returned his embrace until he pulled away. It was the least she could do.

"I should help Papan. He's hurt." Katira peeled away from Elan and turned toward her father.

"No." Elan caught her arm. "You saw the light, his marks. He's a wielder. He shot a bolt of light straight at you." He swallowed hard. "He could have killed you."

Katira refused to believe it. Wielders weren't real. There had to be another explanation. "No, he stopped that thing. He saved me. Didn't you see it?"

Elan pressed his lips tightly together and glanced over at Papan. "I know you saw the light. He used magic."

"I don't know what I saw." Katira twisted her wrist free. "All I know is he saved us from something horrible." She took another step back toward Papan.

Elan skirted around her, standing in her way. "My father needs to know. As head of the town council, he'll know what to do."

Papan made no attempt to come closer. "Please," he called to Katira. "Don't leave." His breathing had grown labored and the color had left his face. All Mamar's teachings screamed to Katira that something more was wrong than a simple bite wound.

Rays of early morning sun broke through the tops of the trees filling the wood with rosy light. It seemed wrong to Katira for the morning songbirds to announce the end of the night. The darkness of Elan's words stuck to her.

"You can't trust anything he will say to you." Elan smoothed her hair and placed a kiss on the top of her head. "He will enchant you to believe anything. He will erase your memory of what you've seen here."

Papan lowered himself to the ground with a grimace and tore the fabric of his pant leg, revealing a bloody wound. "What they've taught you isn't true. You don't need to fear me."

Elan's words worked their way in. There was no denying it.
Katira saw the light. She saw the glowing marks across Papan's chest
and arms. She wanted to go to him, and at the same time wanted to
run. Moments ago, the father she had trusted, the humble blacksmith,
had changed in her eyes. He had used a forbidden power. He was not
who he claimed.

He was a monster.

The thought hit her with more force than the magical blast that
ignited the last creature. A cold chill pierced her through, turning her
stomach. Everything she had known about her father and her whole
life with him, unraveled before her eyes.

"We must go." Elan tugged her arm. "It isn't safe to be here." He
took her other hand in his and led her, one step at a time, down the
path and back to the village.

While her feet carried her along behind him, her thoughts
refused to leave the clearing. There were too many questions and not
enough answers. Did she really see what she had seen? What were
those things? Should she have stayed?

They walked in silence. When they entered the village square,
Elan stopped and turned to her, his eyes wide as if he had realized
something terrible.

"What is it, Elan?" She tightened her hold of his hand.

"If he's a wielder then he's not your father. He can't be."

Katira gasped. The thought was too horrible to consider. "How
could you say such a thing?"

"Hear me out. Wielders can't have children. All the denying in
the world won't change it."

Her mouth went dry. She wasn't ready to accept this. "There
must be some other explanation."

"I'm not saying this to hurt you. It's better for you to know, don't
you think?"

Katira's world was a spinning top. Stories she had brushed off as
superstition were coming true. Truths she had never thought to question were lies. She hugged her arms to herself. "I don't know what to

think anymore."

KATIRA HUNG behind Elan as they approached his father's leather shop, situated at the edge of the village so the reek from the tanning vats wouldn't foul the air. Elan's father, Master Lucan, stooped over a vat with his large paddle, stirring and lifting a pelt, inspecting its progress. Elan's older brother, Andril, worked at a large frame on the other edge of the yard, scraping away the fur from a stretched skin with a long, curved blade.

Elan's father set aside the paddle and crossed his bare sinewy arms over his chest. Judging by the look on his face, he had a word or two for Elan, and not pleasant ones either. "You'd best have a good explanation for this. Sneaking out before dawn? With a girl? I thought better of you than this."

Elan squared his shoulders to answer. "I told you I was going for rabbits last night, I didn't lie. I promised Katira I'd take her with me."

"You know how her parents feel about her leaving the village." Master Lucan leveled his stare at Katira and shook a finger in her face. "I'm surprised your father hasn't come pounding on the door yet, young lady."

Elan laced his fingers into Katira's. His rough skin, borne from long hours working the vats, spoke silent volumes of strength. "There's something more important we need to discuss with you." He glanced toward his older brother. "In private."

Informing Master Lucan about what they saw felt like treason to Katira. Her insides prickled thinking she might be bringing trouble for her family. Papan was a good man, he didn't deserve this. She put her free hand on Elan's shoulder and prayed for the courage to stop him before it was too late.

"Don't you go changing the subject." Master Lucan picked up his paddle and gripped it in his hands. "If it's about you asking to wed

Katira, there's no need for privacy. Anyway, that's between you and Master Jarand. Everyone else in town knows."

"No, it's not about that." A charming blush crept into Elan's cheeks. He gave Katira's hand a squeeze. The moment didn't last. "We saw something you need to know about. About Master Jarand."

Master Lucan's tilted smile faded to seriousness. "If you are implying wrong-doing then you'd best be careful. Master Jarand is a respected man in this town and a friend. I won't stand for idle gossip or trouble making."

"No, sir. I understand how serious this is."

Katira squeezed at Elan's shoulder, but couldn't bring herself to speak. Yes, her father was a good man, but he had also lied to her and the town. Didn't that deception deserve some sort of punishment?

"I'll be the judge of that." Master Lucan said with a jerk of his thumb toward the small cooking fire at the side of the tanning yard. "I have a feeling this might take a while. Might as well be comfortable." Elan and Katira followed him as he wound his way past several vats. He stopped at one and dipped in his paddle to lift out a large hide.

Katira gagged as the smell of rancid fat filled the air, opening her mouth to breathe to lessen the foul assault. She wouldn't embarrass herself by doing something as childish as plugging her nose. Definitely not in front of Master Lucan.

When they reached the fire, Master Lucan sat on a large upended log and warmed his hands.

Elan shifted from foot to foot before sitting on a fat log bench opposite his father. Katira joined him.

"Well?" Master Lucan poked the fire with a stick. "You have my attention. Out with it."

Elan twisted his hands into knots in his lap. "Master Jarand used magic. We both saw him." Even though Katira knew what was coming, the words stung like a lashing from a whip. She flinched at the sudden pain. Stonemother have mercy on her.

Master Lucan stopped his poking and looked Elan straight in the eye. If he was surprised, he didn't show it. "Now why would he go do something like that?"

Katira stared openly. She had expected a much different reaction from the village high councilman. This was a serious accusation. How dare he not treat it with the attention it deserved?

Elan's brow furrowed, and he exchanged a glance with Katira before continuing. "There were these things in the wood. Weird dark things set on attacking us. He came out of nowhere and cut them down."

Master Lucan pushed the stick into the fire and let it burn. Katira wished she could push her jumbled up feelings into the fire the same way.

"He saved your life then?" Master Lucan laughed to himself and stroked the short hairs of his greying beard. "I suppose I should go thank him then. Is that why you came to tell me?"

Elan unknotted his hands. His mouth worked open and shut. "Well, yes. I suppose so." He stammered at the sudden change in the conversation. "But the magic, I mean, that's wrong isn't it? Aren't wielders forbidden here?"

"We don't judge a man by what he is, but by his actions. Master Jarand did something for the greater good. He deserves your gratitude."

"I don't understand. He's a wielder, capable of destroying the whole town and everyone in it. He could bring a blight over the crops, could bring the pox. Why would you want someone like that to stay here?" Elan paused. The furrows in his brow went slack. His mouth fell open. "You knew, didn't you?"

"There are forces at work here you have yet to understand." Master Lucan stood. "It would be best if you dealt with him directly. I've made promises I don't intend to break. Stay here. I'll go fetch him."

"What?" Elan exclaimed. "I don't want to speak to him."

Master Lucan didn't acknowledge his son's outburst as he crossed the yard in wide, purposeful strides.

The weight of Elan's words halted Katira's racing thoughts. It wasn't like him to act fearful toward anyone. As soon as his father had left the yard, Elan jumped to his feet and paced, muttering to himself about how it wasn't right for her father to stay in hiding, about the dangers he brought to the village.

Katira had never seen this frenzied side to him and she wasn't prepared to accept it. Especially not from someone she intended to wed.

She blocked his path and stopped him short. "How can you say such things?" she demanded. "You don't even know if they're true."

Elan met her eye for a moment before dropping his gaze to his balled fists. "I mean what I say." He kept his gaze averted but softened his tone. "It's wrong for him to hide in the town. The people have a right to know and decide if he should be here."

She punched him in the arm. "If they are anything like you, they'll have him hanged before they listen to a word." Papan was kind and gentle. He deserved far better than Elan was willing to give.

Elan rubbed at his shoulder. "That hurt."

"It was supposed to." She turned away from him and sat on a log bench on the other side of the fire. This was not the Elan of her childhood. She wanted that Elan back.

Elan sat next to her and set his hand on her knee. She slapped his hand away and scooted further down.

"Katira, I didn't mean—"

She cut him off. "Promise me not to do anything stupid. He may not be my true father," the thought made her throat tighten, "but he raised me, loved me, and has done nothing but good in this place. I will not allow your fears to ruin him."

Elan removed his cap and ran a hand through his hair. "I would never hurt you. I hope you know that."

She sniffed. There was nothing more to be said. They sat in silence, contemplating the fire before them. The warm red flames danced in patterns so alive, so natural compared to the cold blue light Papan summoned.

Elan had to add another piece of firewood to the flames before Master Lucan returned. He led Papan and Mamar around the vats and stretching frames. Papan walked with a halt in his step, his leg wrapped in a fresh bandage.

Katira ran to Mamar's arms, wanting nothing more than for her to take all the hurt away.

"I was so scared." Mamar's words tripped over themselves as she pressed Katira into her chest. "Why did you leave like that? We warned you about the dangers in the woods. Why would you risk yourself?"

Papan reached for her, but she shied away. Knowing what he was, what he had done, the lies he had told ... how could she ever trust him again?

Master Lucan stepped into the circle and took a seat, settling into his role of high councilman. He spoke with practiced authority. "I've brought Master Jarand and Mistress Mirelle here so we can settle this matter in a civil way. This is the time to resolve all differences and put this matter to rest." He looked at each person in the circle before settling his sights on Elan. "You started this, son, you must confront them."

Elan made an awkward shuffle and stood. It took him a moment before he found his voice to address Papan. "What were those things? What are you?"

Papan sighed and leaned forward, resting his elbows on his knees. Katira had never seen him in any other role than a humble village blacksmith, quiet and hard working. During a single morning he had transformed. He wore the steely calm face of a warrior. She searched the hard planes of his face as he sat there by the fire, hoping to find a hint of the father she knew. He was gone.

"What you saw was a shadow hound - a twisted creature escaped from the mirror realm. Had it bitten either of you, you would have been dead in minutes." Papan glanced to Katira, pain reflecting in his eyes. "I couldn't let that happen."

Katira's attention shifted to the bandage on her father's leg. "It bit you. I saw it. I don't understand."

Papan unbuttoned his sleeve and rolled it up past his elbow. Pale white lines marked his skin and wove their way up his fingers and up his arm. "These are the marks of the Khandashii, the power both Mirelle and I hold. I've kept them hidden for all these years to protect you. With it, I can cleanse my blood of venom."

Mamar pulled back her sleeve and showed her wrist. The lines were there, as clear as chalk on a slate. For Katira's whole life they had been there, right before her eyes, and she had never paid them any attention more than she'd give a scar or odd birthmark.

Seeing those marks now, this time clearly, made Katira's stomach twist and her breath catch. She was ready to accept that Papan had been concealing the truth. But for both to have hidden this secret for so long? She pressed her fingers to her temples to keep from being sick.

Papan reached out to steady and comfort her like the hundreds of times he had done in the past. She shifted away, terrified at what those hands were capable of. He left his hand outstretched for a moment longer before tucking it into his lap. His calm warrior face cracked, revealing the humble blacksmith once again.

Mamar placed a reassuring hand on Papan's arm. "I'm so sorry you had to learn the truth this way," she said to Katira. "We were going to tell you when the time was right, when we both felt you were ready to know. We never meant to hurt you, only protect you." She tugged her sleeve back down. "You deserve to hear the whole truth."

Katira braced herself. She knew what was coming and she did not want to hear it. Elan had tried to warn her, to prepare her for this moment. If anything, it made the anticipation worse. A shiver buried itself deep within. Even if her life was a lie, it was a nice one, much nicer than learning the truth.

"I guess there is no easy way to say this." Her mother took a steadying breath before continuing. "You are not our natural child." She pulled Papan's hand into her lap and held it tight as she struggled to find the right words. "Your parents were killed when you were a baby. You had no other family. We took you in. Raised you as our own." Mamar touched Katira's knee. "Loved you as our own."

Katira's hands balled into tight fists. The shiver inside her grew long icy tendrils. Papan tried to catch her attention, but she refused to meet his eye. "Why hide this from me?" She didn't bother to conceal the pain their words had brought her. "Don't you think I'm old enough to understand?"

"It was not an easy decision to make," Mamar said. Her voice, which usually maintained its authoritative calm, now pinched with emotion.

Elan shifted closer to Katira and set his hand next to hers. She ached to take it, to let its warmth fight off the chill of this new truth she struggled to accept.

"All I want to know," Elan started, "What we all want to know ... Is the village safe with you around?"

Mamar cleared her throat and dabbed at the corner of her eye. Her authoritative calm returned, as if she were addressing one of her patients. "Those who have this power are still men and women. They have the freedom to make their own decisions. Just like you."

Elan stiffened. "How can we be sure? You don't deny you are dangerous. You could kill us all this moment if you wanted to. You wouldn't even have to lift a finger."

Master Lucan held up a hand and glared at his youngest son. "Elan, don't be absurd."

"He's right. We could," Papan said. "But we won't. Just as you won't stab me with the knife hanging from your belt. Simply because we wield something that can be used as a weapon doesn't mean we will. We've sworn an oath to protect the people of this world."

"Protect them from what?" Elan held his hands forward, as if preparing to deflect their words away. His eyes narrowed.

"From themselves mostly." Papan turned a thumb tip sized stick between his fingers. If Elan's outburst irritated him, he didn't show it.

"There are other things - unnatural things. Like what you saw in the wood this morning."

The fire cracked, sending a bright ember tumbling across the dirt. Master Lucan nudged it back into the fire with the toe of his boot. "Jarand," he said. "What would you have us do? I know you to be a good man and Mirelle a good woman. However, if the village were to learn the truth, I'm afraid things might get ugly."

Papan tossed the stick into the fire and watched as the flame licked around it. He then straightened and met each of their gazes. The warrior had returned. "I would ask all of you to not speak of this to anyone, both for our safety and for that of the village. There are those out there who would cause problems if they knew."

Master Lucan's brow wrinkled. He took a long look at Elan as if weighing the impact of his words before saying them with a nod. "As always, you have my word."

Katira didn't want to agree. She didn't want them to think she accepted this new truth. She crossed her arms over her chest, hugging herself for reassurance, as she stared into the fire.

"Katira," Papan said softly. "We have to know we can trust you. This knowledge is harder on you than anyone else and I'm sorry. One day you will understand. I swear it."

She gripped the end of her scarf until her knuckles ached. Her father's small stick turned black and fell beneath the larger pieces of firewood. She was that stick, held and admired and then tossed into the flames to be consumed.

"Please, Katira," Papan pleaded. "This is for the safety of the whole town. If word gets out that we wield the power, they'll force us to leave or try to kill us. There are those in the world who'll burn this town to the ground if they suspected a Stonebearer was being harbored here." A flash of pain crossed his face. "It's happened before."

Katira could no longer see the small stick. It was lost. "You are asking me to forget what has happened? Forget who you are? I can't do that."

"No, we are asking you to help us." Mamar leaned in, forcing Katira to look her in the eye. "That's what good people do. They help each other. You can help us by keeping this secret safe."

Katira tried to push away. She didn't want to see the love and honesty written on Mamar's face, but Mamar wouldn't back down until Katira gave her an answer.

"I won't tell," she said reluctantly. "But it doesn't mean I'm not upset."

Papan let out a sigh. "Thank you." He turned his attention to Elan. "I know what they teach. You're old enough to form your own opinions. Listen to your heart. Let your feelings guide your decision. As you consider, remember, if the village hears of this, of us, we'll have to leave and Katira will come with us."

Katira gasped, her father's words stabbing hard. "You can't make me."

Papan stood and fixed his shirt to cover his markings. "I'm afraid you don't have a choice." He spoke softly. "There are things beyond our control that can't be changed."

Elan stood to face Papan, fists balled, back straight. "Can't you see how much this hurts her?" His protest echoed across the yard. Andril looked up from the scraping frame.

"I'd rather see her hurt than dead because of foolishness," Papan snapped.

Elan flinched back. "I won't agree to this."

Papan pressed his lips together and glanced to Mamar. She nodded. "Then it is settled," he said. "We'll be gone by tomorrow morning."

Katira was falling, burning out of sight. She would be lost, forgotten forever.

Papan held out a key in his palm. "Lucan, the healer's cottage and my forge is yours along with whatever else we leave behind. We travel light."

Elan's mouth hung open. Katira silently pleaded with him to

agree, so she wouldn't have to leave. After all that had happened, she wasn't sure if she could bear it.

Elan swallowed hard. "I'll agree. Don't leave because of me."

"Can I trust you?" Papan's hand closed around the key and he returned it to his pocket.

Elan kept his eyes trained on the fire. "I'm doing it for Katira, not for you." He stepped closer to Katira. "For her, I'd take your secret to the grave."

"Thanks all the same." Papan gave a slight bow of his head. "I've grown accustomed to this place. I'm not ready to give it up."

Mamar looked to Katira. "I need your help in the shop today. I imagine you have questions. Will you walk back with us?"

Katira shook her head. She wasn't ready to be alone with them yet. "No, I need time to think."

Master Lucan stood and patted Katira's shoulder before turning to face her parents. "Give her time. I'll keep an eye on her until she's ready to return."

Chapter
2

Regulus Tauricen heaved himself against the worm-eaten timbers of yet another storeroom door with a grunt. Quests were for younger men, not him. He rubbed at his shoulder to soothe away the ache. Whoever wished for immortality had no idea what they were asking for. Even with the power of the Khandashii sustaining him, his back hurt and a deep-seated fatigue always itched in his bones.

He missed the comforts of the warm library at Amul Dun. What he would give to be surrounded by thousands of beautiful books and studying about ancient Dashiian magic again. Anything would be better than crawling through dank catacombs.

But when High Master Ternan gave an order, it must be carried out. Something of this importance couldn't be trusted to a younger man, or so his master had said. The Disk of Shaldeer had to be found. With the knowledge bound within its crystalline depths, they might learn how to lock the shadow creatures back in their own realm once and for all.

Regulus and his apprentice, Isben, had been searching the ruins of Khanrosh for ten days. Ten long days of digging through rubble, breathing dust, and crawling through collapsed tunnels. Regulus gave the door another shove. Instead of opening, the wood gave away with a thud, sending him sprawling to the floor in an eruption of dust. Whatever had been behind the door tottered and fell with a mighty crash.

Isben ducked his head through the opening with a lantern in hand. A feather pen perched behind his ear and a dark smudge of ink trailed from the corner of his mouth to his chin. He had been instructed to memorize the seven axioms of King Darius. Regulus suspected he might have been writing another story instead.

Isben snatched the pen and stuck it behind his back, but not before Regulus had taken note of it. "I heard the crash. Are you okay?"

"I'm fine, thank you." Regulus clapped his hands against the new layer of grime on his sleeves. Dust clung to his tailored vest and stuck to the sweat around his neck, making him itch. "How many doors is that?" he sniffed, sucking in some dust. The resulting sneezing fit raised another cloud.

When the fit subsided, Regulus caught sight of Isben doing his best not to laugh. He flicked at the layer gathered on the boy's shoulder. "It's not like you look much better. I've seen snow calves with less powder on them." He turned back to the newly opened room and squinted to see what was inside. "Now, how many is it?"

Isben nudged back a sheaf of dirty blond hair from his face. Regulus looked at his own hands. After long days of digging through the ruins, they both could use a hot bath and a good scrub.

"Seventeen, Master. Four more than yesterday." Isben yawned and hurried to cover his mouth. Days working underground had made it impossible to tell the time. "Are you sure you want to continue? It's awfully late."

"It's not your place to question me." Regulus plucked the lantern from his hand. "You'd do well to remember that." He swung the light ahead of him and tested his footing on the rubble of the broken door.

"No, I'm not done for the night. Not until I've searched this room. I feel good about this one."

The flickering lantern projected dancing shadows across the jumbled floor of the abandoned store room. Shelves, some leaning haphazardly against walls, some lying in pieces, filled the dark dusty space. Shattered bottles littered the ground, their contents long since crumbled to powder, leaving the air with a bitter taint.

Regulus didn't dare tell the boy he felt the Disk's call ever since they had descended into the lower level. It wanted to be found.

"Would you like to give it another go?" Regulus asked. The boy had been reluctant to use his power ever since he conjured up a fireball that singed off his left eyebrow. Blessed Stonemother knew he needed the practice.

"No, go ahead." Isben slunk back. "It would do me good to watch one more time."

Regulus pressed his lips together to suppress his irritation. "You'll learn faster by trying."

Isben shuffled his feet. His gaze wandered from one shelf to the next. Fireballs weren't the only possibility when a poorly formed glyph collapsed. Once, the boy transformed the rain over his head into a rancid, foul slime which refused to wash away. "Next time, Master. I promise."

"I'll hold you to it. You know I will." Regulus clucked his tongue. He didn't want to push the boy. Not when the Disk's call haunted his thoughts. The sooner he found it, the sooner he could break free of its touch on his mind.

He tugged the focusing stone free from the cord around his neck and bound it into his palm. Crafted from milky green motherstone, this stone gave immortals like himself the name Stonebearer. It made using the power an art instead of a barbaric practice.

Deep within, the Khandashii surged within its bonds, eager to be awakened. He rolled up his sleeves, exposing the intricate coils and circles lining his skin. With a steadying breath, he braced himself for the pulsing burn of the power as it raced through his every nerve and sinew. Possessing the power meant understanding and accepting the agony of using it. Pain was the price all Stonebearers had to pay to use their gift.

Isben moved back to the safety of the doorway and watched.

When the initial ache passed, Regulus raised his hands and brought each delicate glyph into existence. Ribbons of light flowed from his stone, guided by thought into four distinct patterns. He formed the Finding Glyph first, an arrow bent into a spiral, before setting three refining glyphs about its edge instructing the Finding Glyph where, how, and what to search for.

At his unspoken command, the cluster winked into a point so bright it made his eyes water. The point trembled and burst to life, throwing out brilliant streamers in all directions over shelves, debris, and the floor.

Regulus let his hands fall to his sides, too tired to even rub at the ache in his neck. The glow on his arms faded, leaving him and the boy in the halo of the lantern once again. If the Disk had not called to him, he would have stopped hours earlier. Each glyph drained him of power. This relic compelled him to push himself harder and work far longer into the night than he should.

A single streamer returned and danced in an anxious circle. Regulus's breath caught in his throat. After so many failed searches, he wasn't sure if he could trust his eyes. A beacon only formed when it found something.

"Is that what I think it is?" Isben's voice trembled.

"Would you look at that? And to think, you didn't believe me when I thought we were close." Regulus gave a dry chuckle. "Here it goes. Be ready to chase it."

He touched the circle of light and the streamer shot away, zigging its way through the debris. They raced after it, climbing over and around the fallen shelving. At the back of the storeroom, the streamer shot under the shelter of a broken table.

Isben skidded to a stop and crawled into the cramped space with the lantern. There, the streamer bounced, marking four points on the floor before vanishing. He reached for where the beacon touched.

"Stop!" Regulus commanded. "Don't move."

Isben froze in place, his hand hovering inches from the dirt.

Dealing with ancient magic was an uncertain business, something the boy should have known. Regulus summoned a series of small glyphs to test for any residue of latent magic and sent them circling around Isben and the surface of the stone. The glyphs enabled him to see otherwise invisible threads and snares of magic placed to protect the relic. To his relief he found none.

"I didn't mean to scare you." Regulus patted Isben on the shoulder. "Can never be too cautious."

Isben let out a pent-up breath. "Maybe warn me next time?"

Regulus's bushy eyebrows bunched together in annoyance. "Consider yourself warned. Don't go mucking about relics until the area's clear. Got it?"

Isben scooted over to allow Regulus to squeeze under the broken table and set the lantern between them. "How can you be sure it's safe now?" The boy wasn't convinced. "No one has dealt with ancient magic for ages. What if there is something you haven't thought of?"

"Honestly, Isben. Who's the master here?" Regulus turned his attention toward the area the beacon marked, cutting off further conversation. Being so close to his prize after searching for so long made any thought of small talk impossible. It *wanted* him to find it. Its call embedded itself into his mind like a splinter.

He examined the dust covered floor where the beacon stopped. The pattern changed here. One long rectangle stood out among the other angular square blocks. He swept the dirt away with his hand, revealing sky blue crystalline curves and lines carved into the surface.

"There's a symbol of some sort here." Isben pointed to the surface and shifted the lantern closer, making the crystal glitter.

"These are runes of the older Dashiian magic. This might be the one." He cheered and beckoned to Isben with an outstretched hand. "Quick! My tools."

Isben hurried back to the hall and returned with the leather satchel. His fingers fumbled with the buckle several times before he was successful in opening the bag. By the time he fished out the long, thin prying blade, Regulus had to keep himself from ripping it out of his hand.

"Do you think the Disk is still intact?" Isben nibbled at the edge of his nail, something Regulus only caught him doing when his nerves got the better of him. "Because if it is, won't it protect itself?"

Regulus tightened his grip around the mason's blade. "No harm can come to us as long as we don't do anything foolish. I checked it. It's safe enough." Regulus set the tip of the tool in position and worked the thin mason's blade down the slit between the stones. Within moments, the edge of the block lifted free.

"Hold the lantern here." Regulus pointed to a spot above the hole. "I need to see this."

Isben hesitated before scooting a few feet closer. The lamp light spilled over the opening. Dust and cottony fibers of spider cocoons choked the space. Regulus slipped his finger under a fold of stiff, brittle cloth and lifted out a bundle the length of his forearm.

He laid the parcel on the ground next to the hole and unwrapped the cloth to reveal a flat square ironwood box. More crystalline runes danced in an elaborate ring across its surface. A cunning lock rested in a delicate metal collar around its edge.

Isben leaned in, keeping more distance than necessary between them. Several moments passed as they both took in the sight. The burnished black wood shone like glass. The flow of the words created such a perfect symmetry it held them both in a trance.

Isben broke the silence. "What does this one say?"

Regulus ignored the question. He didn't want to be bothered yet. Irritation prickled his throat when Isben asked again.

"I'm not sure." He wiped the sweat from his brow. "We'd best figure it out."

AFTER BEING UNDERGROUND ALL DAY, the fresh night air tasted as good as clean cold water. Regulus drank it in and let it fill him. A broad, starry sky shone through the gap of the great hall's barrel-vaulted roof. Ages ago, war left Khanrosh broken and empty. Thick grime covered the elaborately tiled floor. Weather-faded tapestries hung along the walls between the remaining slender fluted columns. No one wanted to live with memories of so dark a past.

A series of small offices lined the sea-facing side of the hall. Ages ago, when this hall thrived, the heads of each of the Stonebearer orders had their own space to conduct business. The plaster and paint had long since flaked away. Stained glass lay in pieces across the floor. This late in the season, brisk, salty air blew in through the broken windows. The building might be crumbling, but Regulus's memories remained vibrant.

The Golden Age of the Stonebearer never should have ended. The war should never have been allowed to start. He was young then, and foolish enough to think his opinion didn't matter to anyone. Even now, hundreds of years later, he wondered, if he had said something, would it have been enough to make a difference?

They made camp in what once was the Head Seeker's office since it felt the most like home. Regulus had spent many years summoned in and out of that office. That, and it was one of the few rooms with a serviceable fireplace. Over the days of their stay, Isben had taken it upon himself to make it as comfortable as possible - cleaning out rubble and finding furniture enough so they could work and rest. He was a good and thoughtful boy. That was, when he wasn't buried in his stories.

Regulus set the box on the table and pulled a worn leather-bound notebook from an inside vest pocket. On the other side of the room, Isben busied himself with stacking kindling to start a fire. After all those hours in the catacombs, Regulus wished the boy would hurry. The cold had eaten its way to the bone.

The relic inside called him again, wanting Regulus to run his fingers along the crystal curves, to touch the runes. At their makeshift camp he felt safer, more secure, than while in the dank passages below. Should he allow himself to become enthralled, nothing bad could happen. He brushed the surface of the box and the Disk's song filled his head with promises. He needed to open it to fulfill them.

A jolt of motion broke him free of the reverie. Isben held tight to his elbow.

"Master?" Isben shook him again.

Regulus jerked and inhaled with a sharp gasp. It took a second for his eyes to focus. "What? What is it?"

"You didn't answer me. It was like you were asleep with your eyes open."

A cheerful fire burned in the fireplace and the first tendrils of steam rose from the cooking pot. Time had passed and Regulus hadn't noticed. If he told the boy about the relic's strange hold on him, he might try to put a stop to it. Regulus couldn't risk it. "I don't know what you mean." The relic tugged again. He itched to turn back to it. "I'm fine."

The boy didn't look away. "Are you sure?" The intensity of his gaze made Regulus uneasy. "You haven't eaten all day. Do you want dinner?"

"No, I'm not hungry." Regulus shooed him away. "You go ahead." From the corner of his eye he could see the boy watching him, wary. He would have to wait until Isben wasn't around to touch the box once more. Instead, he leafed through his notebook, searching for any mention of the runes dancing across the lid of the box. They seemed so familiar. It bothered him he couldn't remember.

The lantern's weak flickering light and his own cramped handwriting made deciphering the pages of the notebook a painstaking process. The deeper he searched, the clearer one fact became. This wasn't the relic Master Ternan sent him to find. The histories described the fabled Disk of Shaldeer as resting in an unmarked box crafted from the purest white marble. This relic didn't match the description.

So many questions. What had they found? Why was it calling to him? More disturbing still - how could the esteemed Master Ternan make such a mistake?

After an hour, Regulus knew he didn't have the patience or focus while the relic continued to call. The craving to touch it interrupted his every other thought. He set down the notebook and moved over to his chair by the fire. Maybe with a moment of rest he would remember where he saw those markings before.

Isben had fallen asleep slouched in the other chair with a plate still in his hand. The fire burned down to coals. Regulus tossed on another log, sending a constellation of bright sparks into the air.

Isben straightened and cleared the sleep from his throat with a cough. "Sorry, I should be doing that."

"I thought you were asleep."

"I didn't mean to—" Isben stumbled to his feet and reached for another log, his plate clattering to the floor.

"Don't you fret about it. I've lived alone long enough to know how to feed a fire." He added another stick. "I don't mind."

"What about the Disk?"

Regulus fanned the flames urging the new stick of wood to light. Another cascade of sparks leapt into the air. "It has me puzzled. I don't think it's what we seek."

Isben froze as he reached for the dropped plate. "What is it, then?"

"I'm not sure. We need to test it. It would be a waste of precious time to bring this to the tower if it holds nothing useful." Regulus walked back to the table and bent closer to the archaic lock, running his finger over the keyhole. "We must get it open."

"You don't mean to test it here, do you?"

"Here's as good as anywhere." Regulus gestured to the circle of runes carved into the floor. "That old warding ring will be useful to us."

Isben slid his toe over a rune. "We could be back at the tower in a matter of days. Surely it would be better to test the relic with the proper protections in place."

"And appear the fool if it's nothing?" Regulus grunted. "I won't give Master Ternan the satisfaction of rubbing my face in it." He set his hand back on the box. The relic inside filled him with song once more and carried his mind to a soft quiet place.

Isben asked him something. Regulus could see his mouth move but couldn't make sense of the words. He shook his head to clear it.

"Master, when will you test it?" the boy asked again, louder than needed.

Regulus's mind rushed through the possibilities. If he tested it, he could immerse himself in the relic's song without Isben worrying about him. Waiting would only drag out the torment of not knowing. His mouth worked wordlessly for a moment before he found his voice. "I'll test it once I get the box open. Tonight, if possible."

The boy turned toward him with a jerk. Regulus knew this wasn't what he wanted to hear.

"Why so soon? What's the rush?" The boy tried to sound casual, as if he didn't care when the test happened and failed. This relic scared him.

"I might as well. I won't rest until it's done." The relic wouldn't let him.

"Let me help you." The boy's voice no longer wavered.

"You may watch. However, I can't allow you to help. Not yet. You're not ready." He patted Isben's shoulder. "Besides, if something should happen, I'll need you to go for help."

REGULUS SHOULD HAVE SEARCHED his notes longer. His rational mind fought against him as every nerve twitched to be closer to the mystery relic. It wasn't in his nature to be impulsive. The relic gripped his mind, and he needed to know why. He needed to study it further. The box had to be opened.

He unrolled his soft leather tool kit on the table and pulled out two thin metal picks. Dirt crusted the lock and jammed the tumblers in place. It would take time and focus to clean and oil it before it would open.

The relic sang to him as he worked, eager for him to finish. He scraped at the keyhole. With each touch, the urgency to get it open increased. His heart pounded in his chest and beads of sweat gathered on his brow. It wasn't long before his hands trembled with anticipation.

He tried to force the lock, sending the pick skittering across the hard, stone floor. He cursed and pushed himself away from the table to fetch it.

The relic's song faded the further he moved away. His thoughts grew clearer. The fire's warmth drew him close. He hadn't realized how cold he had become until he tried to warm his hands and they stung.

Could this still be the Disk of Shaldeer? Perhaps the original box had shattered and needed to be replaced. If this was the sought-after relic, why didn't Master Ternan warn him of its strange pull?

Isben returned, his arms bristling with branches for the fire. His eyes darted to the box. "Trouble with the lock, Master?" he asked as he stacked his load on the hearth.

Regulus shrugged away the doubts welling up in his mind. His hands trembled from the relic's song. He clasped them to his chest, hoping Isben wouldn't notice. "It's proving more difficult than I expected. I plan to try again in a few minutes."

"If you'd like, I could fry up this last sausage while you finish."

Regulus waved him off. "Nothing for me. Perhaps later." He scooped the pick from the floor and returned to the table. As he touched the box again, another surge of desire washed through him, strong enough to make him catch his breath.

A few more careful pushes with his picks and the lock released.

He opened the box, revealing a thick midnight blue cloth. Beneath the cloth, the relic's perfect circle of translucent green motherstone glowed in the flickering candlelight. Voices beckoned to him from within.

While gazing at the disk, Regulus's power surged against its bonds, aching to be released. Runes circled the edge of the disk and spiraled smaller and smaller towards its center. Trying to read them made Regulus feel as if he were falling.

Isben appeared at his side, shaking his arm once more. It took a few moments to break free. The relic held his attention with a firm grip. When he looked away, he felt it pulling him back.

"What's the meaning of this, Isben?" he snapped and pushed the boy away, immediately regretting the action. He rubbed his forehead, his hand coming away slick with sweat. "I'm sorry, boy. I lost myself for a moment. What's wrong?"

"It's you, Master. You were about to do something with the relic without preparing yourself, without giving me your instructions." The boy's ruddy face had gone pale. "It had a hold of you."

Compared to the Disk's song, the world around Regulus had lost its vivid color. He felt hollow, incomplete. Every nerve craved to return and answer its seductive call. If it weren't for Isben and the responsibility he felt for him, he wouldn't hesitate. Isben's presence helped him remember why they were doing this in the first place. He steeled himself against the call of the disk and forced himself to step away.

"These relics are powerful, this one especially. I didn't expect it to draw me in as it has. It's calling to me even now." Regulus stepped further away from its influence. "When I do use it tonight, I'll need you to keep watch. My body will be entirely defenseless as my mind enters the relic. The connection between my mind and body is my hand on the relic. If the connection is broken, I will not be able to return to my body when the time comes to leave. Your duty is to maintain my contact with the stone."

Isben hugged his arms against himself. "And if something goes wrong? How will I know?"

"This is a simple test. I plan on entering, looking around, and returning. It shouldn't take long."

"But, what if?"

Regulus rested his crossed arms on the back of the rickety wood chair. His thoughts veered away from even considering anything going wrong. The boy needed an answer. "If I don't return after a few hours, go into Fordzala and seek help. You know who I trust. Whatever you do, you are forbidden to come after me. That's an order and I'm asking you to swear on it." He looked up at Isben.

For a moment Regulus thought he might protest. The order demanded obedience even if the boy didn't like the situation. Isben pinched the green apprentice stone hanging around his neck. His eyes closed. When they opened, Regulus saw grim acceptance there. "If this is how it must be, then I swear."

WITH ISBEN'S HELP, Regulus cleared the floor around the large warding circle. A series of runes lined its inner edge, each invoking a different protection for the Stonebearer within its bounds.

Having Isben there gave Regulus the resolution he needed to withstand the longing. He could only hope it would be enough once inside.

"Isben," he called.

The boy looked up from warming his hands. "Yes, Master?"

"It's time."

Isben tossed another log on the fire and gave it a poke before joining him next to the circle on the floor.

"Stay on the outside of the circle, no matter what." Regulus walked along the outer part of the circle and pointed to its edge. "The only time you are allowed to cross it is if my hand slips from the Disk.

If that happens you must only touch me. Don't touch the Disk or even the box. Once activated it might draw you in as well." He glanced up to check if the boy was paying close attention. One misunderstanding could trap them both within the relic for an eternity. To his relief, Isben listened as if his life depended on it. In some ways, it did.

When Regulus finished, Isben shifted back and forth on his feet. They had butted heads in the past, over much less serious things. The boy had learned so much since those early days, had matured past an irksome youth to a dependable young man. Even so, he had a backbone and a stubborn streak. Regulus worried he might put up a fight.

"I don't like this." Isben stepped between Regulus and the relic. "You should take this to Amul Dun and use it under their protection."

"You know why we can't." Regulus stepped around Isben, but the boy moved to block his path. "People are dying. At least a dozen a week." He held out his stone, a constant reminder of his own duty, of the oaths he had taken. "Finding the Disk of Shaldeer might be the key to put an end to it. Any delay means more death." He let the stone fall back to his chest and moved to step around Isben once more. This time the boy let him pass.

"It's just ..." Isben pushed his foot at the floor and didn't look up when he spoke. "This all feels wrong."

Regulus took the boy by the shoulders. "I'm hard to kill. All Stonebearers are and you know it. I'll be fine." He gave a reassuring squeeze. "Trust me."

"Promise?" When Isben finally met Regulus's eye, a shimmer of a tear reflected in the fire light.

Isben had reached his twentieth year earlier in the fall, and yet in that moment all Regulus could see was the boy from his memory five years back, a terrified child found in the back of a slaver's wagon. The High Lady Alystra felt Isben needed a father figure more than a teacher, and Regulus needed someone to fill the emptiness he had carried since his last apprentice had passed his tests those many years ago.

He couldn't promise Isben nothing would happen. The boy had been lied to enough in his short life. "I'll do my best. That's all I can offer."

"Doesn't make me feel any better." Isben dragged a heavy wooden chair from its place by the fire to the edge of the circle and straightened its half-broken leg before sitting in it.

Regulus removed his heavy cloak and draped it over the work table. The linen shirt he wore underneath did nothing to stop the cold air from piercing through, making his skin prickle and his breath catch.

The boy's concerns and worries had done nothing to soothe his frayed nerves. He wanted the whole unsettling business to be over. He unbuttoned and loosened the collar around his neck and bound his stone to his palm.

He placed the box on the floor in the center of the circle and knelt, head bowed, hands resting on his knees. He bid the fullness of his dormant power to wake and loosed it from its bonds. It roused within him, stretching and flexing like a vine. Tendrils of power pierced their way through him. He gritted his teeth to stifle a groan of pain threatening to escape. The lines of the Khandashii on his hands and arms glowed.

Filled with the power, the relic's beckoning for him became sharper and more urgent. It pulled at the depths of his mind and stirred within him an even deeper, more terrible longing. He pushed the feeling aside and did his best to ignore it. He had to stay in control, stay focused on the task at hand.

He opened the darkwood box. The Disk glowed brighter in the presence of his power. With the fingers of the hand holding his stone, he touched the relic's surface. The runes flickered to life and pulsed, spinning in a slow dance. With great care, he formed the glowing glyph 'enter' in the air before him.

The glyph flashed as it took hold and funneled into the Disk around his outstretched fingers. The Disk grew warm, and the light grew brighter. A lacy net of power flowed up and whirled around him. His awareness of the room dimmed until he saw nothing but spinning runes, felt nothing but the heat of the power. The sea of runes rushed toward him and he fell toward a great black nothingness. He wanted to scream but he couldn't draw breath. Blackness engulfed him.

As his vision returned, he stood in a waking dream. Deep gray ceremonial robes from the Tower replaced the dirty clothes he wore in the catacombs. Immense fluted columns surrounded him, circling the base of a dome so high a cluster of clouds floated between it and the floor.

The space stretched on and on behind the columns, further than he could see. Everywhere he looked, he found evidence of both ancient and familiar Khandashiian lines worked into the ornate mosaic floor and inscribed into the bases of the columns.

At his feet, a twin to the relic rested in the center of the floor. He took note of its position beneath the arch of the massive dome. If he wanted to leave, he would have to return here.

Nothing around him revealed a single clue about how to access the wealth of knowledge that was supposed to be stored within the relic. He assumed there would be a library with shelves holding collections of books and scrolls. He assumed wrong.

Somewhere in the vast space another presence lurked. He felt for his stone, which now hung from a fine chain around his neck, and pressed it between his fingers. It served as a reminder of his identity and his purpose.

The relic's song charged the air with living, breathing energy. It reignited the fire of want within his chest. Perhaps the song embodied the knowledge held within the Disk and all he had to do was ask what he needed.

A woman's throaty laugh echoed in the hall behind him. The sound sent a chill of fear racing through his blood. He turned to face her. Long black hair cascaded down her body to her waist. A crimson silk dress clung to her every curve, making her appear as if she were painted in blood.

A demoness.

Nothing could prepare a man for facing a demoness, especially one as appealing as this. Regulus cursed to himself. Isben's intuition had been right.

She didn't speak but purred. The sound made his hair stand on end. "What an unexpected pleasure. After so many years I was starting to think you Stonebearers had forgotten me."

It took Regulus a moment to find his voice. When he did speak, it was thick and raspy. "Who are you and why are you here?"

"Some call me Wrothe."

Regulus's mind reeled. Every seeker knew of her and her treachery. This Wrothe, this Archdemoness, was a master manipulator. She used her influence to turn the world of mortals against those who wielded the Khandashii. She planted the seeds of distrust and malice into the hearts of men, twisting their views of the Stonebearers from benevolent peacekeepers, to workers of evil. And now he faced her in this space, unprepared, unprotected. He stepped back, closer to the relic embedded in the floor.

"You seem conflicted." She drew closer. Close enough for Regulus to see the unnatural blackness of her eyes. "Perhaps I can help you feel more at ease. Tell me, why are you here?"

Everything about the demoness enraptured Regulus - her face, her voice, even her smell. He struggled to remember why he entered the Disk. Every part of him wanted her in his arms, her touch on his skin.

No.

He couldn't allow it.

Regulus gripped his stone tighter and forced himself to remember his purpose. "I came seeking knowledge of eras past. Disks like this one are said to contain it."

"And what do you need it for?" She closed the distance between them in the space of a breath. Regulus didn't see her move.

He stumbled back, another step closer to his escape. He had to get out. Even if he could find the knowledge hidden in the Disk, it would be impossible to make a record of it with her in the way. "The mortal and the mirror world have grown too close. Shadow creatures curse the land." The words came unbidden as if she summoned them from his brain. He couldn't stop them. "It is my duty to stop it and restore order. I, and others, believe the key lies within the ancient magic."

"Ancient magic, hmm." She smacked her lips together. "Sounds dangerous."

Again, she came closer, so close he could smell her skin. The desire to touch her filled his senses. He forced the thoughts from his mind. "I can see coming here was folly. Permit me to leave."

"Demons like myself are remnants of the old world. The old magic runs through us." She held up a hand, revealing dark lines that mimicked his own. "Perhaps I can be of assistance to you after all."

The thought shot through Regulus like lightning. He knew demons had connections to ancient magic, but the thought of seeking out a demon bordered on insanity. Face-to-face with one, the possibility stretched before him.

He turned toward her, stone still in hand. He could not risk falling into her trap like so many before him. "If you answer my questions, what would you ask for in return?"

She brushed his ear with her lips. "Freedom," she breathed. The word made his whole body tremble.

"I can't offer you that. Not after what you did."

"You're not in a position to be making deals. I'll take what I want, and I'll use you to get it. You need me."

Another wave of desire passed over him. He struggled to work the moisture back into his mouth. "No. I don't need you. I need information." He forced out the words, his voice felt leaden and heavy. "I'll find another way."

"You seem conflicted." Wrothe crossed to his other ear. He could feel the warmth of her breath. "Perhaps if you put your little rock away, I could help you relax."

As she spoke, his grip loosened around the stone, as if his hand had a mind of its own. Hundreds of years of captivity made her bold, desperate even. He curled the hand holding the stone into a fist and gripped it with the other until his nails cut crescents into his palm. "Stop it, Wrothe."

"Why? You are enjoying this as much as I am."

A thrill of pleasure shot through him and he trembled. Had he been a weaker man it would have been enough to convince him to give himself to her for the eternities. He refused to be weak. Instead, he flared the power within him causing the markings on his arms to radiate bright purple light as he rose up against her. The pain brought blessed focus. Wrothe's eyes flashed a dark angry red.

"I told you to stop," he said. "If you cooperate I'll not use this against you."

"Oh, I have no intention of cooperating." She trailed her finger over his collarbone. "But, for fairness' sake, what can you offer me in exchange for your precious information?"

The longer she stayed next to him, the more effort he needed to form a single thought. Again, he pushed his focus away from her and to the stone in his hand. He could make one promise that might be enough to tempt her. "Once the mortal world is safe, I would return to you here in the Disk. You would have me for your own."

She laughed. "You would give your life for this quest? I would let you keep your life if you set me free."

He flinched as another wave of longing seized him, making his breath catch. "I can't do that. You're too dangerous."

"For someone willing to give everything, you are not in a good position for bargaining." She turned and strutted toward a throne hidden in shadows. "You are either very brave, or very foolish. I admire that. Perhaps we can come up with some kind of arrangement." She draped herself over the throne and clapped her hands. "Come children, we have a guest."

Dark shapes darted in and out of the edge of his vision. Shadow creatures emerged from the corners of the great space. They kept their distance from him, cringing away from the light of the power he held at the ready, as they joined their mistress.

Impossible. How could shadow creatures exist here in the Disk? Regulus's mind filled with theories. Demons were creatures of the mirror realm. Could Wrothe summon them at will?

In her presence, these creatures appeared as he imagined they existed in the mirror realm. Instead of shadows, they had long delicate limbs and silken tawny coats. This many in one place made him wary. One word from Wrothe and they would rip him apart.

There could be no arrangement. She wouldn't aid him without being granted her freedom, taking his life, or both. He had to escape this place, to access the relic in the floor and leave. Twenty paces. If he made a mad dash, he might make it before the shadow creatures reached him. If only he could get closer without arousing her suspicions.

He stepped closer to the relic, never taking his eyes from her. A long-bodied creature hissed at his feet and scooted further back. "Tell me," he said, stalling for time. "What sort of agreement are you considering?"

Wrothe sighed, her one hand rested between the twitching ears of a great black wolf whose eyes glowed a sinister yellow. "If you're unwilling to free me, then it comes down to you." She stroked the wolf as she studied him with hungry eyes. "Let me have you for my own right now."

"Would you seal the breech between our worlds if you had me?"

The demoness leaned forward and looked him over the same way a butcher would inspect a side of meat. Regulus had the eerie feeling she wasn't just looking at him but inside him as well. "Oh, yes. In time I would remove it. Does this mean we have a deal?"

Regulus's heart pounded in his ears. Her influence wrapped around him like fine soft wool and it took all he had not to say yes. "Not yet. If I let you have me, I'd require you to be bound to your promise. You'd have until the end of winter, no later."

Wrothe slumped back into the chair in mock defeat. "Anything else?"

"No."

Even slouched in the great chair, she looked both dangerous and inviting. "What makes you think I'd agree to this arrangement?"

"I'm offering something denied to you for centuries. It would be fair if you did something in return."

Wrothe stood, her inviting gaze melted into a sinister grin. "I have a better idea." With a flick of her finger the wolf bounded toward him, its massive teeth bared. An army of shadow creatures followed close behind.

Regulus summoned the glyph for an energy bolt, the only fighting glyph he knew, and punched the tile at his feet. The white streak shot across the floor and into the mass of fur and scales racing toward him. His head swam as the glyph sucked energy from him. He was a seeker of knowledge, not a fighter. Damaging glyphs cost him more energy than he could spare. Wrothe screamed in anger as scores of her creatures fell smoking to the floor.

The great wolf strode out of the blinding flash, unharmed and angry. The shimmer of a protective ward reflected in the dying light of Regulus's blast. Regulus couldn't risk draining his energy for another shot. He needed everything he had to defend himself against Wrothe if he couldn't reach the Disk in time. He turned and ran, feet pounding on the tile.

The wolf gained ground faster than any animal Regulus had ever seen. With a growl it leapt up at him, catching him in the shoulder and knocking him to the floor. Regulus roared in pain as massive teeth grated against bone. He kicked at the wolf's belly to knock the beast off. It dug in deeper. Lights flickered at the edge of Regulus's vision as the pain caused every muscle to stiffen. It couldn't end like this.

With one final effort, Regulus gathered the tattered remnants of his flagging power and prepared to blast the wolf away. The attack might not harm the beast, but the force would throw it off far enough for him to reach the relic. Before he could summon the glyph, the wolf leapt free at some unheard command. Regulus seized the opportunity to claw his way across the few remaining feet. His wounded shoulder screamed at the effort.

Wrothe stood between him and the Disk, hands on her hips. The wolf returned to her side. Blood stained its jowls, making it look even more devilish. Regulus refocused the power he intended for blasting the cursed wolf out of his way on her. The glyph refused to form.

Her influence overwhelmed him, this time with such intensity it brought a new pain driving deep into his skull. He gathered himself for one final effort and formed the glyph, slapping it into the tile, enveloping her in a halo of white light.

To his horror, she laughed. The light wavered around her and she reached out her hands to drink it in. Her whole body trembled in ecstasy, her eyes pressed shut, her head thrown back.

Regulus took advantage of the distraction and dragged himself toward the Disk once more. It took every ounce of muscle to keep moving forward.

He reached for the relic. Wrothe kicked his hand away. Her touch made his senses scream as if he were a bow being pulled too tight. Part of him wanted to snap, the other refused. With inhuman force she shoved him onto his back as if he were nothing but a toy in her hands.

"You didn't think I would let you leave, did you?" she asked as she pried at the fingers of his hand holding his stone.

Regulus refused to answer and fought at her touch. He couldn't let her take his stone. Without it he couldn't form the glyph to escape.

She pushed her influence toward him again and this time, he couldn't resist. His fingers weakened, and his body grew heavy. With growing horror, he found he could no longer move. He was helpless against her. She plucked the stone free and studied it in her open palm. Its color faded to a dull cold gray, lifeless in her hands.

"The stone is of no use to you, Wrothe," he gasped.

She closed her hand around it and clucked her tongue as if he were a child. Her hand glowed as the stone flared to life and her lips twisted into a wicked smile. "Oh, isn't it?" When she opened her hand, the stone glowed blood red.

His eyes widened. She had corrupted the stone. It was impossible, unheard of.

"Please, Wrothe. I beg you—"

Before he could finish, she pressed the stone against his chest. It burned into his flesh like a coal. The dream world shrank and folded around him until he could only make out the determined scowl on her face. His struggles against her made the world tilt and pitch violently. The burning pierced through his chest and ran to follow the pathways of his power. The power itself changed within him, twisting and turning into some dark thing, unrecognizable as his own.

As she ravaged his power, she attacked his mind. She pushed at his consciousness until it began to crack from the strain. He wouldn't let her breech this final boundary. She could have his body, but his mind was his.

They fought for what seemed an eternity, his mind against hers. When his strength failed, he screamed as his mind tore. From inside his head he heard her laugh. The sound brought a dread chill. The thought of her merging herself with him disgusted him so much, he wanted to scratch away his skin and bleed her out.

The longing to escape bubbled to the surface from deep inside. Regulus wasn't sure if it came from him or her. With great effort, he brought himself to his knees. His shoulder oozed blood that soaked through his shirt. Blistering burns ran the length of his arms and joined together where she had pressed the burning stone into his chest. With a grunt he pulled it free. The hall echoed. Wrothe and her minions had vanished.

If he reentered the real world, the monster would follow. He couldn't let Wrothe back into the world, not through him. His hand moved against his will. She forced him to move. An exit glyph sprung forth unbidden. Light sprung from the relic as it drew him in. He prayed the strain would kill him.

Chapter 3

Darkness.

Regulus clung to the nothingness separating the mortal world from Wrothe's prison. His strength trickled away, consumed by each second he forced the relic to hold his mind in limbo. Wrothe struggled within him like a fish gasping for air. If he died before reaching the other side, Wrothe would die, too.

His grip slipped from the void. The Disk itself pushed against the unnatural intrusion. His consciousness slammed back into the confines of his body with such violence, it knocked him to the ground. The Disk's light winked out. He reached for it. He could force her to return, force the Disk to claim him.

A pair of arms held him back. A voice pressed on him, insistent. He couldn't make sense of it.

He opened his eyes.

Isben hovered over him and pressed a wadded-up shirt to his wounded shoulder. Horror filled his wide eyes. "Master! What happened? Please," he begged, "speak to me."

"Disk. Must return." Regulus reached out again. Stars clustered in the corners of his vision. Desperation gave him the strength to free one arm from Isben's grasp. She burrowed deeper into his mind. Another minute and she would take control.

"Stop fighting me." Isben kicked the box out of reach. "Let me help you!"

The box and the relic inside it slid across the floor. Regulus couldn't reach it in time. His consciousness wavered as Wrothe continued to rip and tear through the barriers he pushed in her way. He didn't have the strength to fight her.

One option remained. He had to make Isben understand. He blinked away the darkness constricting his sight and gripped the boy's arm.

"Isben ... you must ... kill me."

The boy met his gaze. His movements were frantic, desperate. "Please, Master. I can't do that. Anything but that."

Regulus couldn't hold on any longer. The darkness fighting to claim him crashed through and he fell into oblivion.

MEMORIES FLITTED BY, like feathers floating on the breeze. Regulus grabbed one and cradled it in his palm. As it brushed against his skin, his mind filled with the sights and smells of a crisp fall day. A pretty girl in a wide brimmed hat sold him an apple and gave him her smile for free. He valued the smile far more.

He reached for another memory and flinched as he found himself on a battlefield. The metallic smell of blood rose from the bodies at his feet. Men shouted as their weapons crashed, mere mortals pitting themselves against the fiery blades of Stonebearer Guardians.

From within the tumult came a familiar throaty laugh. The vision of the man standing beside him wavered and bent until it transformed into Wrothe's sleek form.

She regarded the battlefield with disdain. "Men are weak. They deserve nothing more than to be controlled, like animals."

"These were good men. You tangled with their reasoning, warped their sensibilities, forced them to fight us." His hands balled into fists as the memory continued to unfold. "They didn't have to die."

"Don't get sentimental." She crouched next to the dead man at her feet and pushed back the visor on his helmet. "You miss the respect the lines on your skin once earned you, nothing more. These men were nothing to you." To emphasize her point, she slapped the dead man across the face. His head snapped to the side.

Bile rose in Regulus's throat at the sight. "If it wasn't for you, we would still have it." He swallowed it down and steadied his voice. Allowing anger to win would give her more power over him. The vision faded.

She stepped closer and her influence poured over him, filling his mind with the desire to please her. They stood, surrounded by the feathers of his drifting memories. She reached for another.

He snatched the feather away from her outstretched hand. These memories belonged to him. She had no right to intrude. She reached out again.

"Stop." He slapped her hand away. "Have you no decency?"

"I don't think I've been accused of that before." An impish smile quirked on her lips. Damn her, she was enjoying this.

She reached again.

As Regulus moved to stop her, he realized she had no interest in his memories. She wanted information. His mind contained secrets powerful enough to bring down the entire Stonebearer Society. He couldn't let her have them.

The drifting memories darted away from her touch. Colors and shapes organized into furniture and walls. Memories assembled themselves into books and flew onto shelves. The once shapeless mindspace transformed into the place Regulus knew better than any other - the Tower archives. It seemed fitting to pattern his mind after it.

"A library?" Wrothe smirked. "What makes you think this will keep me from learning your treasured secrets?" She plucked a book from the low table by her side. The title read *The Taste of Bacon.* "If anything, this will make it easier to find what I need."

Regulus chuckled. "You will find nothing useful. I will make sure of that." He snapped his fingers and hundreds of doors and locks sprung into existence. The click of each lock rattled through the silence.

Wrothe snarled as she turned around, taking in the sight of the secured library. "You won't win." She set her fingers against the nearest door. A glyph sprung into her other hand and she sent it burrowing into the wood. Lines of black crawled out from the center, spreading like a cancer.

Regulus winced as a sharp pain pierced his chest. He reached for his stone. If his mind couldn't contain her, his power certainly could.

Nothing happened. His power refused to respond.

"If you make this hard for me, I'll make it torture for you." Another glyph formed at her fingertips and split into dozens of pieces, flying to the surrounding doors. Dark, piercing tendrils spread over each surface, eating their way deeper into the wood.

Pain erupted from dozens of points on Regulus's body. His knees buckled from the sudden shock.

She pulled his stone from his hand and held it close to his face. It shone blood red. The sight made him shiver. "Your power is my power now. I draw strength from you and you weaken. Your pain is for nothing. Give in."

Wrothe summoned another splintering glyph, and another. Regulus collapsed to the floor, unable to stay upright.

IN THIS ODD DREAM SPACE, time held little meaning. Wrothe didn't stop, didn't slow. Locked doors and shelves of the library crumpled one after another as she consumed Regulus's knowledge at a furious pace.

Each door Wrothe attacked brought another wave of agony.

Regulus conjured up more doors to slow her, knowing it would prolong his torment. As the hours passed, his focus slipped more and more often. His thoughts grew hazy and dim. Nothing else existed but this library, Wrothe, and the unyielding pain.

Despite his efforts, she had wormed through enough of his memories to learn how to bring the Stonebearer Society to its knees.

A faint shimmer of power touched at the corners of the dream space. The long lines of shelves wavered at the edges. Someone reached for him from the outside world. Not Isben. He would have recognized the unique ripples of the boy's fledgling power. Someone else wanted him awake.

Regulus pulled at his own power once more. He needed to repel them, push them away. Once awake, Wrothe could start working her plan. He couldn't let her have the chance.

Again, his power wouldn't respond and instead his efforts rewarded him with a new wave of crippling pain.

Wrothe closed the book she had been studying with a snap. "Keep trying. The more you try, the more my power digs into you. You're making it easier for me."

Regulus gathered his strength and pushed himself to standing. His knees shuddered with the strain. He removed the book from her hands. "You will be stopped. I swear it. I won't give up."

She smiled her impish grin at him again. "That's nice. I hope your friends are as pathetic as you are. I've rather enjoyed making you mine. I'm sure taking them will be just as pleasant."

Her words ignited his anger once more. No one threatened Isben or the Order. Not while he lived.

"They are not yours to have," he said through clenched teeth.

The shimmer of light from the outside world pressed in again, this time shining through the cracks between the exposed books and around the seams of the weakening doors. Voices broke through. The sensations of his physical body returned, jarring his strained senses. He gripped the blanket in his fists and his whole frame trembled at the new onslaught of pain.

"What's going on?" Isben's familiar voice sounded worried.

"He's starting to wake," said a woman's voice. Isben must have gone for help. "It won't be long now."

"Can't you do anything for him?" Isben asked.

"I've healed what I can," the woman answered. "The rest is up to him."

Someone slid a warm hand into Regulus's and held it close. "Please, Master. I'm here. Wake up. You're safe now."

Regulus squeezed back, reassuring Isben as best he could. He opened his eyes a fraction to see the boy leaning close. Two others stood nearby. His vision hadn't cleared enough to tell who they were. Wrothe stirred within him and so did her hunger for a fresh kill.

"You're not safe. Get away from me." His words came out as a hoarse whisper.

Isben leaned closer. "What's wrong?"

Regulus pushed the boy back. "Keep your distance. I can't protect you against her."

Isben's eyes went wide, and he waved the woman over. She hurried closer to Regulus. Close enough for him to make out the kind eyes and tidy black braid of his trusted friend, Catrim of the Plains Sept of Stonebearers. Isben had done well to fetch her. She'd saved his skin in the past. She could help him.

"Hey, old goat," she said softly. "What have you done to yourself?"

When Regulus attempted to speak, Wrothe seized control. "Oh, this? It's nothing. Ran afoul of a shadow creature. He got the best of me." From within, Regulus's shouts echoed inside his head. He had to tell them Wrothe had him. The demoness had to be stopped.

Catrim's brow knitted together. "There was a shadow creature in the relic?" By her tone it was clear she had doubts.

Wrothe forced his face into a smile. "Yes, a great wolf. I nearly didn't make it out alive."

"That explains the shoulder." She tucked in a loose end of the bandage wrapping his chest and shoulder. "It doesn't explain why your stone was burned into your hand, or why it turned black."

Too many questions. Too much suspicion. Wrothe snarled and gripped Catrim's hand. Unbidden power flowed through Regulus and shot up Catrim's arm. The woman's eyes rolled back as she stiffened. Her frantic heartbeat filled Regulus's head and part of Wrothe's oily dark presence slid free from him and buried itself into Catrim's mind and body.

Catrim staggered back, her head in her hands. Her companion, a sturdy man named Tash, rushed forward and grabbed hold of her before her knees gave out. All color had drained from her face.

"No, no, no, it can't be," Regulus moaned. "This can't be happening." He would have punched at the bed in frustration had Wrothe left him with even the smallest shred of energy. She took the power she needed to possess Catrim straight from his life force, leaving him weak as a newborn. It wasn't fair. Catrim had no warning, no way of fighting against the Archdemoness, and now Wrothe had her. His friend was dead. She just didn't know it yet.

Isben returned to his side. "What was that? What's going on?"

"She's escaped," Regulus said between gasps. "She must be stopped." He tried to sit up again. Tash had to be warned.

"Lie still. You're not well." Isben pushed him back into the bed.

The boy needed to understand the danger. This demon could destroy them all should she wish it. "I must speak to Tash. Must warn him about her."

"What are you talking about?" Isben tugged Regulus's blanket smooth. "Lady Catrim worked for nearly two days to save your life. You're confused. You need rest."

Regulus raised his unsteady hand in front of his face to see the Khandashiian lines running across the back. With Wrothe gone, the corruption of his power might be gone as well. Instead of white, they burned black under his skin.

Regulus drew in a sharp breath, let his head fall back, and shut his eyes. "Why didn't you kill me?" he mumbled. "This wouldn't have happened had you done as you were told."

Isben flinched back as if stung. "How could I?" He wrapped his arms tightly against his chest and sat on the floor next to the cot. "Please, Master, what are you talking about?"

Soft voices from the other side of the room caught Regulus's attention. Catrim sat on the edge of the other cot, talking to Tash.

Regulus spoke so only Isben could hear. "Listen carefully. There was a demon imprisoned within the Disk." Wrothe stirred enough to prevent him from naming her. Even after possessing Catrim, she still had power over him. "Her captivity has driven her mad. She used me to escape. She has possessed Catrim. The woman isn't to be trusted. Tash must be warned. He's in great danger."

Isben watched Catrim as she talked with Tash. "What will happen?"

"I'm not sure. Keep your guard up when she's around." Regulus coughed.

Isben poured a glass of water and offered it. "What about you? Are you okay?"

"Okay enough." Regulus poked at his bandaged shoulder. "I told you I was hard to kill, didn't I?" He didn't dare speak of Wrothe's control over him or his power. The boy didn't need to worry about that. Not yet.

Isben rubbed his brow between two fingers. "What are we going to do?"

"She won't give up. We can't either."

Catrim returned to his bedside with Tash following close behind. Isben shifted out of her reach. One of his hands drifted to the apprentice stone beneath his tunic, the other to the short knife he wore on his belt.

"I don't know what came over me." Catrim reached forward once again, the same way a healer would when using a delving glyph. "What's important is making sure my healing weaves are still in place." Regulus caught a hint of a sinister smile and a trace of darkness in her eyes.

He pushed her arm away. "That's not necessary. I'm fine. If you wouldn't mind, I would like a word with Tash, alone."

She crossed her arms underneath her breasts. "Whatever you have to say to him you can say to me."

Regulus paused, choosing his words carefully. "I was going to tell him to take extra precautions. Shadow creatures have been seen near the capitol." As he spoke he watched Tash. He had to know if Wrothe cast her influence over him. If she had caught the man in her web, no warning would help him. He would be defenseless against her. Sure enough, Tash moved as if in a daze.

Catrim set a hand on Tash's arm and cleared her throat. "Speaking of Fordzala, we must return. We left our shop in the care of a friend and we've been gone too long. The provisions we brought should last several days. We'll return with more at the end of the week."

"Can't you stay for at least another day?" If Regulus could keep Tash close, he might have a chance to break through enough to warn him. "The boy is an excellent helper, but he's no fighter or healer, at least not yet. I'd feel better if you spent another day here with us."

"Don't be silly." The woman who was once Catrim clucked her tongue. "You don't need three nursemaids to feed and tend you. You're well protected here. I'll have Tash set extra wards to keep anything dangerous away."

"Please, Tash, I would much rather you stay. One more day?" Regulus pleaded in a last effort to get them to reconsider. The man moved away as if he hadn't heard. Catrim collected her pack and headed for the door. Tash hoisted his pack onto his back. His movements were stiff, like a jointed puppet. For a moment he hesitated as if he might have sensed something amiss.

Catrim drew closer to him and a strange smile spread across his face. His shoulders relaxed. "You'll be fine, Regulus. We cannot afford to be gone from our post this long. We'll return in a few days. I promise."

"Tash. Stop." Wrothe fought against what Regulus was about to say. A red-hot burning flared within his skull. "She's hiding a demon." Each syllable he uttered brought more pain.

Tash paused in the doorway and looked back. For a second, Regulus thought he saw the man's eyes widen as the thought took hold. It didn't last. Catrim called from the hall and the man's face relaxed once more. He left without a word.

Regulus gripped the edge of the cot, angry at his own helplessness. "She'll kill him."

The door shut with a dull thud, leaving Regulus stuck with a serious problem. How to save a man who has fallen under a demon's spell?

He could sense her. Wrothe's hunger had grown even more desperate.

Time. He needed more time. He wanted to rush after them and stop her. It didn't matter if she struck out at him. Regulus was willing to take a blow or two if it woke Tash from her trance.

Isben stood staring at the closed door.

"Help me up." Regulus said. "We have to go after them."

The boy blinked, confused. "What?"

Regulus gestured to himself. Every moment lost gave Wrothe the time she needed to turn against Tash. "Me. Up. Now!"

Isben hurried back to the bed and helped him to sit up. The effort made the room spin around Regulus. He gripped at his shoulder. It felt like it was splitting open.

"Are you sure?" Isben untangled Regulus's legs from the blanket. "You're too weak to even light a candle. What do you intend to do?"

Regulus removed his stone from the cord around his neck and bound it to his burned hand with a grimace. "Something stupid. Get me out that door."

Isben obeyed. The whole ordeal had the boy anxious and fearful. His hands trembled as he lifted Regulus to standing.

They didn't have to go far to find Catrim and Tash. The sounds of talking and the occasional giggle echoed in the silence of the great hall where the pair had stopped to feverishly exchange kisses. Tash's shirt and coat had been discarded, revealing his lean muscled torso and the intricate pattern of lines playing across his chest and up the sides of his neck.

He worked at the laces on the front of Catrim's bodice, growling like an animal each time his hands slipped.

Isben stifled a groan. His cheeks darkened several shades of red as he looked away. "So much for her being dangerous," he said under his breath.

"Quiet." Regulus put a finger to his lips. "If I'm right—"

The sounds of passion changed to sounds of a struggle. At first, he thought they had taken their advances to the next level. Then a grating cry escaped Tash's throat followed by sounds of gagging.

Catrim pinned Tash to the wall by his neck, his feet dangled and kicked above the debris-strewn floor. His face turned purple as he fought to remove her hands from his throat. Streams of power poured off Tash in arcing halos. Regulus shivered as he watched Catrim drink them in. She had done the same to him while within the relic. The memory was far too fresh.

"Stop, Wrothe!" Regulus shouted.

Wrothe ignored him. She reveled in taking her prize. Tash's struggles slowed. With each passing moment Catrim's features grew more sinister, her once gentle smile hooked into a familiar impish grin.

Isben tugged at Regulus's arm to get him to leave the terrible scene. His efforts distracted Regulus's focus, yet they gave him an idea. "Isben," he said. "Throw a rock at her."

Isben's eyes went wide. "I don't think that's a good idea."

"Quickly, boy. Before it's too late."

Isben snatched up a chunk of masonry the size of his fist and lobbed it at the demoness, striking her in the arm. Wrothe hissed at the unexpected pain and whipped around to face them, dropping

Tash. His body fell to the ground with a horrible thud. He didn't move. Regulus couldn't tell if the man breathed.

Wrothe's eyes shone even darker as she sniffed the air.

Regulus pushed Isben down behind a fallen pillar. "Stay out of sight."

Her eyes locked on Regulus's. "How dare you interfere?" The words pierced the air in a shriek. "He wanted me to take him. He begged for it."

Regulus leaned on the fallen pillar, too weak to stand. "He had no choice."

She knelt by Tash's side and stroked his cheek. "It's not my fault his mind is weak."

Tash stirred. He was alive, much to Regulus's relief.

Strange glyphs flew from her hands and into the man Catrim had loved.

Regulus reached for his power out of instinct. He would do anything to save a friend.

"If you try to stop me, you'll suffer." She didn't turn when she warned him. She didn't need to.

Regulus didn't care. He let his power fill him. Instead of leaping to his command, it struck back at him from within, filling his veins with molten fire. He watched on in horror as Tash's white lines of the Khandashii burned to black. The stone hanging from his neck darkened from milky green to blood red. With one final glyph he gasped and sat up. His brown eyes had turned coal black. All traces of kindness were gone, leeched out of him and replaced with a feral cruelty.

The demoness caressed Tash's chest. He gazed up at her, hungry for her every touch.

"You are mine and will do exactly as I say," she said

"Yes, my queen," he replied, his voice filled with fervent desire.

"It seems poor Master Regulus has lost his mind. He murdered your dear Catrim and will kill again. You will return to Fordzala and bring your fellow Stonebearers here to contain him until the Tower can bring him to trial."

"Yes, my queen." Tash answered without any pause for thought. He hurried to put his shirt back on and left the hall without looking back. The real Tash would have balked at the request, would have fought against such horrible lies.

Regulus balled his fist around his stone, not caring about the pain it caused him. His wounds were temporary. They would heal. Tash and Catrim were as good as dead. Wrothe would destroy both of them. All of this was his fault. If only he had trusted more in Isben's suspicions all of this might have been avoided.

One fact remained. He had freed the demon and his friends had paid the ultimate price for it. He couldn't take any chances. Wrothe had to be exterminated, and Regulus knew just the man he could trust.

He sank down next to the boy. The confrontation left him winded. Through their strange bond, Regulus felt Wrothe's strain from enslaving Tash so soon after possessing Catrim. She couldn't attack again until she regained her strength.

Regulus slid the heavy signet ring from his finger and pressed it into Isben's hand. Even untrained, his apprentice would be a valuable source of power. He had to get the boy away from Khanrosh before the demoness came for him. "Go for help."

"I can't leave you." Isben pushed the ring back. "She'll kill you."

"I'm anchoring her to this world. She can't kill me." He caught his breath. "Even if I was strong enough to run from here, I'd be too easy for her to find." He pushed the ring into Isben's hand once more. "Go find help."

"I'm an apprentice," Isben said. "No one will listen to me."

Every second they wasted was a second Wrothe gained. Regulus felt each second slip away and into her hands. He had to convince Isben, and quickly. "What is the first thing I ever taught you?"

The boy stammered as he thought. "To do nothing is death."

"Correct." Regulus nodded his approval. "You listen here. We're not defeated. Not while we're still alive." He swallowed down the wave of pain and weakness. "Go north. You have youth and speed on your side. You can travel quickly and without drawing notice. Seek out Jarand Pathara up in Namragan. Show him this ring and he'll believe anything you say."

"General Pathara? I thought he went into hiding." Isben closed his fingers around the ring and held it close to his chest.

"He did," Regulus said, the strain of speaking wearing him down. "That's why it's crucial for you to take the ring to him. He has no reason to believe you otherwise. Tell him everything. He'll know what to do." He let his head rest against the column.

"What about you?" Isben's voice tightened around the question. "What if I fail?"

"Don't let yourself think about that. Focus on what must be done." Regulus pointed back toward the office. "Take my cloak. It's thicker than yours. It gets cold up north. My coin purse is on the table. Take it, too. You'll need money to travel and to eat."

Wrothe's rage bubbled to the surface of his mind. She must have sensed him plotting. His punishment would come and he would take it. If he could distract the Archdemoness for even an hour, the boy would have that much more time to get away.

Isben returned and knelt at Regulus's feet with the items clutched in his arms. "Promise me you'll be okay."

The boy had said those same words before Regulus entered the relic, and again he could make no promises. "I'll do what I can." He pushed Isben away. "Take the back stair to the cliffs. Quickly!" The sound of Isben's footsteps faded as the boy skirted the edges of the hall and disappeared into the shadows. Regulus offered a silent prayer to the Blessed Stonemother the boy would not come to harm. For the moment, Isben was safe.

He pulled free the short knife he kept tucked in the top of his boot. Maybe, by some miracle, he could stop Wrothe before she hurt anyone else. The thought of killing Catrim weakened his resolve. Would she have done the same thing had their roles been reversed? Would she have plunged a dagger into his heart to stop a greater evil?

Footsteps crossed the hall toward him. He tightened his grip on the hilt and braced himself for the task.

"Well, then. What have we here?" Wrothe's words flowed over him, warm like fresh cream. His body hungered for them.

He couldn't give in. He needed to fight. He couldn't let her have her way. His grip on the knife loosened, and he fought to remember what he intended to do with it. It must have been important.

"That's better," Wrothe purred. "Put it away. We're friends, remember?" She came closer and plucked the knife from his hand and set it on the floor, out of his reach. She'd changed so much already. Catrim's appearance had faded away. Her hair fell in sheets, jet black and smooth as a raven's wing. Her kind face sharpened until it resembled a bird of prey, all angles and sharp dark eyes.

Regulus's thoughts came as if forcing their way through mud. "What do you want with me?"

She stroked his stone hanging from its chain and it grew warm with her touch. "Where is that little brat of yours?"

He clenched his teeth to keep the details of Isben's quest from rolling out. He couldn't allow her to know. Not yet. Every hour he could hold out would keep the boy safe.

"Come now. Don't make this harder than it needs to be." She leaned closer, her breath caressing his cheek. He wanted to touch her, to feel her skin against his lips.

He needed a distraction, something to pull his mind far from her. He focused his attention on the core of his power. Perhaps with enough study, he could relearn how to access it. Wrothe had figured out how to corrupt it. It stood to reason there could be a way for him to reverse it.

She slapped him across the face. He tasted blood. "Your power is no longer yours to use. The next time you try, I'll punish you. Now, where is that boy of yours?"

Punishment or not, he reached deep within once more. There had to be a way. It was his power. Her tinkering could not change fact.

"I warned you." The demoness reached toward him, her hand resembling a claw. The power within him surged forth in a ragged torrent, uncontrolled and wild, and streamed to her. She drank it in. The lines on her arms shone, not in the clear light of the Khandashii, but with a sinister sickly darkness.

He didn't have much power to give. He reached toward her, pleading. "Stop, Wrothe. I'm nothing to you dead."

She took one more pull, leaving him with barely enough to remain awake. "I've changed you. Don't waste your time and energy pleading for mercy. I can keep you alive for as long as I please."

"You've lied about everything else." He panted, waiting for the pain to subside. "How can I believe you?"

"We're bound. You'll know when I'm telling the truth."

Regulus stopped and directed his attention inward. Her words resonated within him. She was right, although it sickened him to think they were this close. "Why do this?"

She knelt in front of him. "Stonebearers like you imprisoned me. They need to pay."

Her influence seized him, filling him with a terrible longing. His mind reeled and in his weakened state he found her hard to resist. He wanted to serve her, to do her bidding.

"Join me." She cradled his face in her hands. "Those close to me will become powerful beyond imagination."

Regulus wanted to be in those arms, to be hers. With one colossal effort he reached for his power once more. Although it would no longer do his bidding, it served as a reminder of who he was, what he was, and what she was as well. He clutched the stone in his palm until his fingers went numb.

"I will never be yours." he said through his clenched teeth.

"We'll see." She laughed and several glyphs leapt into her hands.

Chapter 4

Katira shifted the basket hanging from her elbow to serve as a barrier between her and the press of the crowd as she worked her way through the displays of lush fall apples and goose-necked winter gourds. She stepped out of the way of the portly baker carrying a tray of hot apple tarts fresh from the oven on its way to his table of breads and pies.

Ever since Katira had learned the truth about her parents, the sounds in the village had changed. Everywhere she went she swore the whispers followed, telling her the life she pretended to live was a lie. The joyful shrieks of children playing used to make her smile, now they summoned visions of shadow hounds lurking around every corner. Every farmer's wife that met her eye wore a suspicious smile and children darted through the tables like shadows. The market used to remind her of happy get-togethers with friends and good food. Not anymore.

Elan's family remained true to their word. No one knew the secret she held. No one had reason to suspect anything had changed. Still, holding this large of secret felt like a banner had draped itself over her shoulders, announcing to everyone the truth about her so-called family.

Around the square, people climbed ladders to hang brightly colored flags for the harvest festival. Tomorrow morning the square would flood with people from all the surrounding villages. A cluster of musicians practiced a fast jig on the large stage in the corner.

Two weeks had passed since the incident. Katira spent each day since grinding herbs and roots into powders while ignoring Mamar's attempts to talk to her. One day she might find the courage to open the door she slammed shut between them, but until then, her pride kept the door locked tight. They'd lied to her for eighteen years. It wasn't something she could forgive in a day. Or even a week.

Elan pretended nothing changed between them. She wouldn't be fooled. Ever since they witnessed her father use a forbidden power, ever since Elan demanded her father be sent away, a wall stood between them. Talking with him no longer fascinated her. When they went to touch, each caress had become clumsy and awkward. The thrill of a secret kiss or even a whispered word from him had faded.

Maybe it would be better if her family did leave.

The smell of fresh brook trout wafted up from its wrapping in her basket, reminding her she needed to hurry home.

The warmth of the cottage welcomed her as she opened the door. Mamar sat in quiet conversation with a patient sitting on the cot in the corner. Village Elder Cornish had lost his sight years ago. His hearing, never good, had grown worse over the recent months. He came and visited with Mamar at least three times a week with one problem or another. She'd tried every herb and poultice for his swollen knees and various sores before learning the real reason for his visits. He was lonely and needed a friend.

Katira slipped past Mamar into the kitchen where the cooking pot hadn't been prepared. The steady beat of Papan's hammer working at the forge echoed through the walls. The potatoes and greens hadn't been washed. Dinner would be late, and she would have to make it.

Again.

It wasn't that Katira minded cooking the evening meal. She found the simple tasks of washing and cutting and seasoning food calming after a busy day. She used to never think twice about it.

That was before.

Ever since things had changed, since she learned she wasn't blood kin of Mamar and Papan, she questioned everything. Had she not been there would they have hired a girl to help them? Did they only keep her around to take care of errands and household chores?

Did they even love her?

Sometime between refilling the heavy pot over the fire with water and scrubbing the potatoes, Elder Cornish had gone home. Mamar plucked a bushel of greens from the basket on the table. "Thanks for getting this started. I thought he would never leave." She unbundled the greens and plunged them into the wash basin. "That's a nice fish. You have to argue old Bean for it?"

Katira scrubbed at another potato and didn't answer.

"You know who's pregnant? She came in today ..." Mamar baited her with a conspiratorial smile. "It's quite the scandal."

"Whatever happened to respecting the privacy of your patients?" Katira muttered and grabbed another potato.

Mamar sighed and roughly chopped the greens before tossing them in the steaming pot. "Whatever happened to your sense of humor?"

Katira shrugged and continued with her work. It felt wrong to joke with the woman standing next to her. After all, Mirelle wasn't truly her mother. She was a woman who might be hundreds of years old. How could she understand what Katira felt when it had been lifetimes since she'd been there herself?

"We can't go on like this forever." Mamar wiped her hands on the cloth hanging over her shoulder. "I'm the same person I've always been. I've mothered you, protected you, and taught you. No matter what you think of me, that's not going to change." Mamar's tone remained sincere. She wiped the chopping block clean and patted Katira's shoulder. "I'm going to tell Papan to finish up his work and clean up. Can you handle the fish?"

Katira waved her away. Cleaning a fish was far easier than cleaning a deer carcass and she had done plenty of both. She tasted the broth and made a face. Mamar had forgotten to add the salt.

The small window above the washbasin opened into the smithy behind the cottage. Katira peered out, unable to help her curiosity. Papan leaned against a thick post supporting the roof of the workshop working a polishing cloth over the fine steel of a new knife. These past two weeks had changed him. He acted more agitated, always scanning his surroundings, always moving.

Gonal worked at tidying up the shop and hanging up the heavy tools on their hooks. A hammer slipped from his hand and clattered to the floor. He bumped his head on the heavy work table going after it.

When Mamar entered the shop Papan knocked on the table to get Gonal's attention, causing him to smack his head once more. Papan excused him for the evening and Gonal gave an awkward bow before hanging up his apron and leaving the shop.

Mamar leaned into Papan and he wrapped his arms around her. They fit together like two pieces of well-crafted iron, like they were made for each other. Once, Katira hoped she would find a love like theirs.

But now?

If she and Elan couldn't resolve the rift between them ...

She blinked back the tear threatening to form. Enough tears had been shed already. Crying over fish wouldn't solve anything.

Papan peeled off his sweat-stained shirt and Katira averted her eyes. She shouldn't watch. It was improper. She returned to slicing the fish into stew-sized chunks, but her thoughts couldn't leave what was happening on the other side of the wall alone. Her father only removed his shirt in private. She couldn't remember a time she had seen him with it off. He was hiding his marks. She knew that now. Hiding them from her, from Gonal, from the prying eyes of the village.

She wanted to see his marks now. Needed to see them. She lifted her gaze back to the window. The sight should have scared her. Had she seen it a month ago, it would have. Now she could appreciate them for their striking beauty. Each line started at a finger and then wove itself into an intricate pattern up his arms. It reminded her of the fine embroidered vines she had spent hours sewing into the sleeves of her Harvest Festival dress.

She tossed the fish into the pot and returned to the window. The lines weren't the only thing marking his skin. Thin white scars criss-crossed his whole body. A thick ragged scar crossed his ribs. Had he turned, she was sure there would be more. These weren't scars from working a forge. Burns left wide puckered stripes. If she were to guess, they were scars from something sharp, like a knife. There were so many. Where had they come from?

She set the heavy round table with bowls and cups and checked on the bread and soup before looking out the window again. Papan had washed in the rain barrel and put on a clean shirt, something Mamar always insisted on before their meals together. He buttoned up the shirt and tugged the sleeves straight.

Turning away, Katira ladled hot fish soup into each of the bowls and set the warm loaf on the table. Her parents returned as she set out the last cup. Papan took a cautious sip of soup from his spoon.

He turned to Katira and winked. "Perhaps we should allow you to do all the cooking."

Mamar swatted at him with the towel from her shoulder. She pressed her lips together to keep from smiling. "And perhaps we should have you do more cleaning."

It was a comfort to see them smile and laugh. Part of Katira wanted to laugh along like she had so many times before. However, the rest of her couldn't shake off the feeling of not belonging. She stayed quiet and stirred her soup.

Papan's face drooped. The laughter faded from his eyes. "It's not that Mamar can't cook. Her thoughts are usually elsewhere." He scooped up a chunk of fish and ate it thoughtfully. "I don't mind, unless the meat is too burned."

Mamar shot Papan a dirty look and picked up her spoon. Even at this humble meal she sat straight and took small bites.

The front door swung open. A gaunt man, dirty from travel and smelling of stale sweat, stood silhouetted in the light from the street lantern.

Papan leapt to his feet, placing himself between the stranger and the table. He gripped the stone at his throat in a motion Katira now recognized as part of using his magic. The stranger stepped into the room and shut the door behind him.

"Put it away, Jarand." The stranger gestured for Papan to sit back down. He sounded almost bored. "I've been away too long if you can't recognize me." He removed his wide brimmed hat and set it on Mamar's work table, followed by the long overcoat. The ratty red scarf at his throat stayed

"Bremin!" A huge smile broke across Papan's face. "By the stars, what brings you to this part of the world? Last I knew, The High Lady had you walking across the entire Lower Peninsula." The two grasped each other's hands and slapped each other's backs like old friends.

Papan pulled a chair from the worktable and brought it over to the table. "Come sit. I bet it's been awhile since you've had a hot meal."

Katira looked to her mother for some clue if this stranger was welcome or not. Mamar leaned forward at the table. Her sharp eyes searched the man up and down the same way she would assess a patient. She didn't seem alarmed in the least at the stranger's intrusion, nor did she stand to greet him.

"It's good to see you too, Mirelle." Bremin snatched a piece of bread from the table and inhaled its scent.

"Hello, Bremin. It truly has been too long." Mamar greeted him with a slight nod of her head. Not completely unfriendly, but nothing like the greeting Papan had given the stranger. "Why are you here?"

"I'd love to tell you I was here because I was in the area." He loosened the scarf at his neck a fraction. Katira thought she saw wielder's marks, but she couldn't be sure.

Bremin joined them at the table. "Truth is, I come with news."

Mamar stood to find another bowl and spoon to serve their guest. Manners first, as always. "No one comes to Namragan on a whim. Are you well?"

"I'm fine, Mirelle." Bremin lifted both his arms revealing a shirt in dire need of washing. "See? You can stop looking. There are no extra holes in me. However, a hot drink would be most welcome. Is it me or does the cold get colder every year?"

"It wouldn't feel as cold if you fattened up a bit." Papan clapped a hand on his belly, well-muscled from his days at the forge. "Staying in one place for a while does have its benefits."

"My work is far more important than knowing where my next meal is coming from." Bremin looked at the bowls of stew and then to Papan. "Is it safe?" he asked in a quiet voice.

"It's not like what they serve in Fordzala, but it'll do." Papan answered, giving Katira another wink.

Mamar set a steaming bowl in front of Bremin along with a mug of ale before returning to her seat with a huff. Katira swore she caught the hint of an eye-roll.

Bremin ripped off a hunk of the bread and dunked it into the soup. He closed his eyes as he ate, as if he hadn't eaten in days. He took a deep drink of his ale and sighed. "Much better." He pinched at his shirt with a disgusted shudder. "I'll deal with washing up later. I imagine I'm quite a sight." He then turned his attention to Katira. "Before settling down to business, who is this young beauty?"

"Do I need to tell the High Lady you are flirting, again?" Papan raised an eyebrow and crossed his arms over his chest.

"I never do more than smile, you know that." Bremin took another swig of ale. "I can't believe you told on me the first time."

"Bremin, I'd like you to meet our daughter, Katira." Mamar held out a hand. "Katira, Bremin is an old friend of your father's." A wry smile quirked the corner of her mouth. "Very old."

Bremin set down his mug of ale and his spoon. "My goodness, I'd almost forgotten." He leaned toward Katira. His smell drifted along with him. "Tell me, how old are you my dear?"

Papan scoffed and slapped the table. "Since when did you start forgetting things?"

"I came of age a few weeks ago." Katira answered, determined to be a part of this discussion. She might not have been speaking to her parents, but she hadn't spoken to anyone new in years. Living in a small village had its drawbacks.

Bremin let out a low whistle. He glanced at Mamar and Papan before studying her again. "Has it been that long? It seems not long ago when I heard you'd taken her in." He stopped himself short. "Does she know?"

"I'm right here." Katira couldn't stand being ignored, especially when she was the topic of conversation. "Do I know what?"

"She knows about us," Mamar answered. "About what we are. But not much else."

Bremin froze, his mug at his lips. He set it down. "When did this happen?"

Papan gestured with his mug toward the forest. "Less than two weeks ago. She was attacked by a shadow hound. I had to stop it." He took a swig of ale as if what he said was the most ordinary thing in the world.

Bremin dropped the hunk of bread he had been holding into his soup causing it to splatter onto the table. "There are shadow hounds here already? That's part of the news I wanted share with you. Sightings of the creatures have increased. Alystra wants the border towns protected."

Papan set his mug on the table and leaned back in his chair. "I hoped it was an isolated group. Do you think more will come?"

Bremin nodded grimly. "I know they will, and after them even worse creatures. If the barrier isn't closed, it won't be long before they are unstoppable."

Papan huffed. His forehead creased. "I thought the seekers would have found a way to fix that by now."

The turn in conversation made Katira uncomfortable. She didn't understand anything about shadow hounds and magic, nor did she want to. These things were forbidden. If they were going to discuss the doings of wielders, she shouldn't be there.

She stood to leave.

Mamar slipped her hand into Katira's, stopping her. "Stay," she said. "It'll help you understand who we are."

Bremin cupped his hands around the mug as if unsure where to start. "That's the other reason I'm here. Stonebearers have gone missing from the capitol. They say Catrim has been murdered."

Mamar gasped. She pressed her hands over her mouth. "When did this happen?"

Bremin held up a hand to calm her. "No more than ten days past."

Papan leaned across the table, his meal forgotten. "You're not telling us something."

Bremin tapped the table as he considered his words. "I have read three separate reports from my sources in the capitol. All three say Master Regulus is involved, perhaps responsible."

Papan stood, sending his chair toppling behind him. "He would never do anything like that. It's not possible."

Bremin continued, unaffected by her father's outburst. "Tash's shop was found abandoned on the first day of Drent. There was no sign of a struggle. Both he and his companion were simply gone. Soon afterward, rumors poured in about Master Regulus going insane and killing Catrim."

"Then it's a rumor." Papan picked his chair up from the floor and set it right. "I refuse to think this is the work of my master. There has to be another explanation."

"That's why I'm here." Bremin fished the bread out of his soup and took a bite. "Of all the order, you're the one closest to him. You might have some insights that will help us learn the truth and bring this matter to an end."

"What does the High Lady say about all this?" Mamar hadn't moved since Bremin had shared the news of the murder.

"She needs this resolved as soon as possible and kept quiet to preserve his good name." Bremin pressed his hands together and brought them to his lips. "It won't do any good to start a panic. She has given me the order to bring him in. If he resists, he is to be killed. If he has gone insane, he is a danger to us all."

The news hung in the silence of the room like a specter. Papan sank into his chair once again. "Then we must find him first. If he has lost his mind, he deserves a chance to find it again."

"When do we leave?" Mamar asked.

Papan didn't wait for Bremin to answer. "First light. Every minute we delay puts him in greater danger."

The words seized Katira by the throat and pinched it tight. How could they decide to leave so easily? What about what she thought?

"That's not fair!" she protested.

Mamar ignored Katira's outburst and folded her hands on the edge of the table. "It's too fast. There are things that must be done. The festival begins tomorrow. We can pack up and leave in the commotion of the day after. That will give the two of you time to set out a protective ward for the town." She turned her attention to Katira. "And it'll give you a chance to give Elan a proper farewell. We'll be gone for a few weeks at most."

"Waiting a whole day is foolishness," Papan paced the narrow space between the table and hearth. "It'll only take a few hours to set wards. We can be done and gone before midday tomorrow. Elan's family knows the truth about what we are. We need to leave anyway. A festival is a breeding ground for rumors."

"Regardless, we will leave the morning after." Mamar shot back. "We will not be sleeping in these woods, not with shadow hounds around."

Katira gripped the braid hanging over her shoulder until her knuckles went white. "I don't want to leave."

Papan put his hands on his hips and sighed. "You don't have a choice."

"I'm of age now. I can do what I choose, and I choose to stay here while you are away." She turned to Mamar, hoping to find a more sympathetic ear. "Someone needs to stay and run the shop. You can't leave the village without their healer, not with winter coming. Like you said, it'll only be a few weeks."

Mamar turned away from Papan and Bremin, a deep crease marred her forehead. Katira had never seen real worry on her face before. "There are many women in this village who know their herbs. They can manage for a while." Mamar took hold of Katira's hand and held it in hers. "Don't you want to see the world beyond this valley?"

Katira pushed the toe of her boot against the wooden floor and considered her reply. Whining would make her sound like a spoiled child. "It's not that I don't want to explore. I do. I don't want to leave Elan. Not now, not after everything that has happened."

"I know you don't, but this is important." Mamar patted her arm. "Imagine how proud he'll be of you. You'll be the only one of your age who has seen the sea. That's got to count for something. By the time we go, I'm sure part of you will be excited to come along. Until then, let's not let this darken our remaining time here."

"No." Katira shook her head and backed up toward the door. "This isn't fair. You can't make me agree to this!" If they wouldn't talk to her, Elan would. She grabbed her cloak and ran out.

∿

On the evening of the Harvest Festival, the sun painted the autumn sky in gold and pink. Katira kicked at a pebble and watched it bounce across the cobblestone to where it stopped at the base of the fountain in the center of the town square.

Soon the square would be cleared, and preparations made for the

traditional dance. She followed the pebble's course to the wide edge
of the fountain and sat down. For months Katira dreamed of this
night being her special night. Mamar had found buttery yellow cloth
as soft as rose petals on the trader's cart that summer. During the
evenings of the past months she had spent every minute working on
her dress.

Katira ran her hand over the delicate embroidery running in an
intricate pattern down her sleeves. As she had stitched each vine and
flower, she allowed herself to imagine Elan kneeling at her feet
bearing a proposal crown woven from slender evergreen boughs and
decorated with vibrant fall flowers. Evergreen symbolized the long
and happy life they would have together. Red fall roses were for
strength in adversity. Feathery white woodsmoke seedpods were for
the hopes of future children. She and Elan would spend the whole
evening dancing and talking and exchanging soft kisses with the
support of the whole town behind them.

The chance of building up a life with him kept slipping through
her fingers one tiny thread at a time. In her mind, it had been so
perfect. She would be so happy.

Not anymore. Elan wouldn't propose now. Not with her leaving
in the morning.

"Why so sad?" asked a gruff voice.

Katira barely glanced up, longing to be left alone. Bremin had
done nothing to dress up for the night's activities. The same long
tattered coat hung on his gaunt frame. The same red scarf bunched at
his throat. He leaned against the edge of the fountain next to her and
watched people as they walked by.

"Just because you're a friend of my family doesn't give you the
right to pry into my business." She sniffed. She knew she was being
rude. She didn't care.

The corner of his mouth turned up in a half smile. "Feisty one,
aren't you? Good, it will serve you well in your life."

"It's doing me loads of good right now." She threw her hands in
the air. "They're making me go with them and I hate it. I'm sure

no one dragged Papan away when he was about to propose to Mamar."

"What, Jarand?" Bremin chuckled to himself. "I don't know if anyone could drag that lout anywhere he didn't want to go."

Katira wasn't in the mood for joking. "You know what I mean. He's probably never had something he truly wanted with all his heart and then was refused it."

Bremin grew serious, all traces of mirth extinguished. "Oh, now, I wouldn't say that. There's more to Jarand than you could ever imagine." He bent down and picked up the pebble at her feet and studied it. "That man has been kicked around more than he lets on. He doesn't talk about it much, but it doesn't mean he hasn't had his share. More than his share if you ask me." He set the pebble on the wide edge of the fountain next to her.

His tone caught Katira by surprise. The memory of Papan's scars flashed into her mind. "I'm sorry," she said, tucking a stray bit of hair behind her ear. "I shouldn't have said that. But ... do you think he's being unfair?"

"Lass, it isn't usually my place to say whether another man's thinking is right or not. But with this particular situation I'm afraid his decision is for the best." Bremin pushed his hands into the deep pockets of his coat and squinted into the sunset. "If I was in his boots I'd be forced to do the same thing."

"But why?" Katira picked up the pebble and rolled it between her palms. "Why can't I stay here? Is this his way of saying he doesn't approve of Elan?"

"No." Bremin pursed his lips and gave a small shake of his head. "Elan is a fine boy. He would be the pride of any daughter's father."

"If it's not him then ..." she paused, the realization hitting hard, "then it must be me."

"Like I said lass, it's not my place to say. You'll understand when it is time. Not before." Bremin looked back at her. "Making you come has nothing to do with them trusting you or not, so you can put that out of your mind."

"That's what Papan said." Katira slipped the small pebble into the pocket sewn into the side of her skirt. It felt wrong to toss it away. "Why must the both of you talk in riddles?"

Bremin adjusted his scarf, the smile returned. "Because that's what we do best." He pushed himself up from the edge of the fountain and straightened his coat. "I believe you are expected." He glanced toward the other end of the plaza, her eyes followed.

There, walking across the plaza, was Elan. He wore a crisp linen shirt the color of wheat with a finely tooled leather vest over black embroidered trousers. He must have spent hours on his vest - the work was extraordinary. With a pang, she knew he had made these to celebrate their special night together, just as she had made hers.

Bremin tipped his hat at Katira and wandered over to where the tables for the evening's feast would take place. Elan joined her at the fountain and sat by her side. For a moment they gazed into the final colors of the sunset together.

Elan broke the silence first. "I can't stand the thought of not being able to ask for your hand in front of the town tonight." His voice sounded unsteady as if he wasn't sure what to say. "It would have been so perfect. I had planned for the musicians to play your favorite song for us to dance to. I even collected the branches for your crown. We were going to be the happiest couple at the festival."

"I know." Having him there, that close, and knowing both of their dreams had been shattered, made it feel as if her hopes for the future were being ripped into pieces. She wove her hand into his. "It's not fair. I should be allowed to stay." As much as she didn't want to, tears fell down her cheeks.

"Hey, it's okay. Don't cry." Elan cupped her chin in his hand and wiped the tears away. "We're stronger than this, remember? It's only a few weeks." He pulled her into his arms and held her close. "When I do propose, it will be special. I promise. You'll get your day."

He stroked her hair and let her cry. For that moment, the world consisted of Elan and warmth and comfort. He waited until the shaking stopped, until the tears dried before continuing. "You deserve happiness. I want to be the one to give it to you." He brought her hands to his lips and placed a gentle kiss on each of her fingertips. "You look so beautiful. Forget about tomorrow. Tonight, let's pretend we are the happiest people here."

She let her head rest under his chin. He smelled of leather and soap. "I would love to."

~

ELAN LED Katira into the throng of dancers. The music lifted her spirits, and she lost herself in it. All her worries of the past few weeks evaporated into the air with the rise and fall of the drumming beat.

It had been so long since she had seen Elan smile. At first, she wasn't sure if it was real. His feet tapped and kicked in time as though the rhythm held him captive. He led her in twirls and jigs all around the dance floor. When the song ended, they found themselves laughing and out of breath.

A pack of young children, the oldest no older than seven, giggled and pointed at a couple on the dance floor stealing a kiss at the end of the song. Katira laughed at the sight. It gave her an idea. She snuck in and planted a kiss on Elan's cheek while he wasn't looking. The children cheered.

Elan's mouth dropped open, a mix of mock surprise and some real. Not to be outdone, he pulled Katira in close and gently pressed his lips against hers. All thoughts of children turned to dreaming of the day when she and Elan would have their own beautiful babies.

Elan led her from the dance floor to a quiet patch of grass, breathless from more than just dancing.

After a moment of quiet, the fiddler began a melancholy song, one of remembrance of times past. The song spoke of a battle, where good fought against a mighty evil. Mountains moved. Seas tossed themselves on the land. Great blasts felled those defending their homes. Cities fell and the dead outnumbered the living. When all felt lost, a great light shone from the sky and the evil hoard disappeared, never to be seen again.

Katira couldn't help but think of Papan's scars again. The great war had happened over a hundred years ago. Could he have been a part of them? The possibility stretched before her with a chill. Was he part of the evil hoard or one of those who defended the good?

She sought Papan out in the crowd, spying him near a stall selling fragrant roasted meats. If he was listening to the song, it didn't seem to affect him. His jaw didn't knot in anger, or his eyes crease with remembered pain.

"It's like you've seen a ghost." Elan put himself between her and sight of her father, interrupting her chain of thought. "What's on your mind?"

"I'm thinking about the song." She smiled and pushed the thoughts of her father away. One day she'd have to ask him about his past, but not tonight. "How about a treat? I've smelled honey-glazed walnuts all evening."

Elan gave a low and completely unnecessary bow. "Your wish is my command, my lady."

"Stop it!" She laughed and swatted his shoulder.

"Anything, my lady!" He bowed again. His grin crossed from ear to ear as he darted off to the vendors carts.

A hand gripped Katira's elbow and she jumped.

Papan broke into his most innocent grin. He had clearly witnessed Elan's ridiculous display. "I wanted to see if you had everything you needed for tonight. It will be getting colder. You might want to go get a shawl."

"By the stars above! I'm old enough to take care of myself," she exclaimed, trying to still her racing heart. If he could pretend nothing was amiss, so could she. "What about you? Mamar expects you to find her a gift. Have you gone looking yet?"

The merriment drained from her father's face. She caught sight of a brief flash of panic. "I was planning on going as soon as I had seen you."

"Liar. Do you need ideas?" Katira asked.

"No. Of course not. I know just the thing." He glanced to the vendors' carts and back again. "For good measure, though, tell me what you were thinking she'd like."

Katira rolled her eyes. "There are some lovely combs for her hair on a table halfway down that way." She pointed toward a line of carts.

"Really?" His gaze followed to where she pointed. "Are you saying I shouldn't get her a new mortar and pestle then?"

"Trust me." She fought to keep from sighing. Were all men this clueless?

Elan returned, candied nuts in hand. He didn't look up until too late and stopped inches from running headlong into Papan's broad form.

"Evening, Master Jarand," he said, somehow making it sound like an apology.

"Good, you're back." Papan rested his arm heavily on Elan's shoulders. Elan nearly wilted under the sudden weight. "I want to ask you both a favor."

"Anything." Elan's eyes widened, fearful what her father might ask.

"Promise me you'll both stay here in the square. There are plenty of rowdy men cavorting around tonight. Nothing but trouble, if you ask me." He leaned in closer. Elan paled, looking as if he would be sick. Papan jerked a thumb in Katira's direction. "Keep an eye on Katira. Make sure she doesn't receive the wrong kind of attention."

"Yes, Master Jarand." Elan nodded vigorously. "Of course."

"You have my thanks. Enjoy your evening." Without another word Papan turned and walked away.

"Sorry about that." Katira helped herself to a handful of nuts. "Some habits die hard. Can you believe he wanted to remind me to get a shawl?" She shivered, a cold breeze teased up her skirts and beneath her hair enough to set goosebumps to prickle her arms. Curse the man for being right.

Elan reached into a pocket and pulled out a small parcel, handing it to her with a shy smile. "Before I forget, I have a gift."

Katira untied the strings, letting the paper fall away to reveal a bracelet woven from fine strands of leather. She had never seen anything else like it. The strands twisted and turned and wove between each other to create a series of elaborate and beautiful knots. "Elan, this is beautiful. You must have spent hours on it."

He tied it to her wrist using another elaborate knot, taking her hand in both of his. "This way," he said, "while you are away seeing the wonders of the world, you'll think of me."

A rush of heat raced under Katira's skin. She didn't need a bracelet to keep him in her thoughts. He wormed his way into her every waking moment without it. She would treasure the bracelet because he had made it just for her.

She traced the path of a strand, admiring his work. "I have something for you as well. Come, it's at the cottage."

Together they ran and laughed through the crowd drawing angry shouts and yells from those they bumped as they passed. Katira wove her way through the swarms of people, neatly dodging the town's portly ale maker and his massive jug of personal brew as she went.

They reached the smithy cottage out of breath, stopping at the low garden wall, laughing and falling into each other's arms. In that brief second, she could imagine a lifetime with him.

Katira twisted from Elan's arms with a mischievous smile. "Wait here. I'll be right back." She hurried inside the dark of the cottage, looking back to see if he was doing as he was told. Being near him made her feel like a raging springtime river choked with ice and swollen with the runoff - both invigorating and painful.

Something shifted in the deep shadows near the door to the forge. Her joy came to a halt and she stilled, frozen with fear.

She wasn't alone.

~

Before Katira could scream, two dark figures surged forward. One clamped a hand over her mouth while pinning down her arms. She kicked out as hard as she could, striking a shadow. A hand struck her across the face, a crack of pain bolted through her skull.

Her captor's voice spat in her face. "Stonemother twisting twat, I outta put a blade in you!"

A second blow sent Katira's senses reeling and knocked the fight out of her.

"Stop it!" the man holding her pleaded. "Hitting her won't do any good."

Before she could regain her bearings enough to strike out again, they tied a foul-tasting cloth in her mouth and bound her hands and feet with rope.

She fought against her bonds. Her elbow caught the edge of a heavy bowl. It smashed to the floor.

"Katira!" Elan yelled into the darkness as he rushed through the front door. Wind slammed the door behind him and flung open the door leading out to the forge. Katira's captors wasted no time hauling her out the door and over the low sheep wall where a pair of horses stood waiting.

"Take your hands off her!" Elan shouted, grabbing an iron from the workbench and charging toward them.

Katira sagged in relief.

The shorter of the two men released his grip, letting her legs fall to the ground. "This has nothing to do with you, boy. Turn around. Forget what you've seen." He pulled back his coat to reveal a line of slender knives.

The taller man lifted her and tossed her like a sack behind the saddle of the first horse, her head hanging low. Her cheek pressed against the horse's hip. He turned to face Elan. "Don't be foolish."

Elan would not back down. "You'll give her back this instant."

The taller man continued. "Please, you have no idea what you're dealing with." Compared to the shorter man, he sounded timid and reluctant.

"You can't have her!" Elan lifted the iron rod over his head and ran at the men.

The shorter man moved in a blur, flinging one of those slender blades with deadly precision. It buried itself deep in Elan's chest, knocking him backward to the ground.

Katira screamed behind the gag. A raw primal cry bit at her insides and threatened to tear her sanity into lifeless shreds.

They had killed Elan.

She sobbed, knowing there was nothing she could do except watch him die as they rode away.

Chapter 5

Jarand hung back at the edge of the dance floor, waiting for the right song, the right time, to ask Mirelle to dance. He had promised her one dance, as he did every year, and he intended to do his best for her.

He was an excellent dancer, despite his reluctance. The rhythmic steps and precise timing resembled the fighting forms he'd devoted over a century of his life mastering. War had consumed another three decades. Ever since the last battle, the one that broke him, he couldn't dance a step without memories of terror and blood. Jalan's Gap had left more than his friends dead. It had left him clinging to life alone in the middle of a battlefield. He reached for the sword that wasn't there, needing something to steady him as his heart raced.

The fast-paced jig faded to a waltz, much to Jarand's relief. The tension that had been building between his shoulders eased a fraction. On a good night, he could manage a waltz. He collected his courage and turned to ask, only to find a young woman about Katira's age whispering in Mirelle's ear. The girl huddled under a finely woven blue shawl as if hiding something. Jarand pressed his lips together. The moment had been perfect, and now he had to wait. He prayed the girl would finish quickly, before the waltz ended.

Whatever her predicament, it was none of his business. Situations like these made him glad he worked in metals. Iron didn't ask questions and never found itself in embarrassing situations. For all the fire and the heat, iron was free from the folly people entangled themselves in.

Mirelle finished giving her advice and the young woman melted back into the crowd, head hanging low like she wanted to disappear. Whatever Mirelle had said had not pleased her.

He seized his gathered courage as it threatened to flee and threaded his arm through Mirelle's, tugging her close. "Would you like this dance?"

"I thought you'd never ask." She leaned in close to him as he led her onto the dance floor between other couples swaying in time to the music.

Jarand breathed in the scent of wild sage and lavender in her hair. The knot of tension melted away as he let her presence soothe him.

She bumped against the wrapped package hidden in his coat. He had entertained giving it to her before asking her to dance in some grand romantic gesture. With the moment lost, he brushed the thought aside. Neither of them liked attracting undue attention. He would find a quiet moment later.

She pressed her head against his chest. "I was hoping to watch Elan and Katira dance once more before the evening ended. Have you seen them?"

"Less than an hour ago. Poor Elan still jumps when he sees me." He laughed to himself and swung Mirelle in a slow circle. The folds of her dark dress opened like a flower. She glowed with joy. He would dance with her all night to see her that happy.

"I trust Bremin's found himself a deep pint of ale and a gambling table by now," Mirelle murmured when they closed the gap between them again.

"He's bound to be around here somewhere." He scanned the

gathering crowd for signs of a red scarf but saw nothing. "It would be easier if he didn't tend to blend in quite so easily."

She squeezed his arm. "You're tense."

"Master Regulus is like my father." The accusations Bremin had made poked at Jarand's mind. Murder, insanity, betrayal - it didn't feel right. "I pray whatever trouble he's gotten himself into isn't serious."

"We'll get to the bottom of it. I promise." Mirelle circled her arms around his neck. If ever there was a quiet moment between them, this would be it. He pulled the paper-wrapped package from his coat, stopping their dance even though the music still played.

Mirelle unwrapped the package to reveal the intricate Ashandi knot comb he'd picked up from the stand Katira had pointed out. Her breath caught and spots of color spread on her cheeks. "It's lovely." She pulled him in for a kiss, her lips gently pressing against his.

He took the comb and slid it into her hair above her coiled braid.

Her eyes sparkled in the lantern light. "How do I look?"

"Like a queen." In that moment, the stars grew dim compared to her radiance. He drew her into his arms, determined never to let her go.

The dance flowed and Jarand allowed himself to relax into the motion, sweeping Mirelle with him. The music swelled through him as they stepped in time. Memories of his last battle flickered on the edge of each turn. His pulse quickened. Panic nibbled away at his newfound happiness. He pushed the nightmare away.

He would finish the dance. For Mirelle.

A sound at the edge of the crowd caught Jarand's attention. He stumbled over a step as he strained to see what was going on.

"What is it?" Mirelle asked.

"Something's wrong." He squinted in the dark. "Someone's shouting."

Mirelle's forehead creased as she listened. Her grip around Jarand's arm tightened and her eyes went wide. "Sounds like Gonal."

Jarand's apprentice wormed through the crowd, tripping and

shouting as he went. A path soon cleared, and the awkward boy stumbled straight toward them. Jarand's stomach clenched.

Gonal's face dripped with sweat. His thick frame wobbled as he tried to compose himself to speak. "Mistress Mirelle, come quickly. It's Elan. He's hurt." He frantically gestured for them to follow as he turned back the way he had come.

Jarand turned to Mirelle, unsure if he heard correctly. "Did he say Elan?"

Mirelle nodded, her eyes speaking the same fear that sliced through Jarand's strained nerves. She untangled herself from his arms and hurried her way through the crowd. Jarand sped after her.

Katira had reached the age when her power would manifest itself any day now. It was often a violent and dangerous process. Without them to guide her, she could easily hurt herself or others. She might have hurt or even killed Elan by accident.

Of all the secrets they had to keep from Katira, this one was the worst. They had raised her knowing one day they would have to explain the real reason they had taken her in. Eighteen years ago, the seed of her power had called to them, drawing them to the ravaged town and helping them find a baby girl among the burnt remains of the houses. That seed had protected Katira when the rest of her family perished in the flames. That seed was destined to grow until the Khandashii filled her. She was destined to be a Stonebearer.

They rushed through the crowd. Bremin joined them as they wove their way past startled onlookers.

"Where have you been?" Jarand demanded.

"It's a festival. Where do you think?" Bremin shrugged, trying to keep up with Jarand as he ran. "What's going on here?"

"Something's happened to Elan."

Free of the crowd, Gonal broke into a dead run straight toward the cottage. "Hurry, he's out back!"

Jarand sprinted after him, letting his feet fly.

When they reached the back of the cottage, the darkness pressed so close only the barest of details could be seen. The edge of the heavy table, the dull glow from the dying fire, the trees and brush beyond. When Jarand's eyes adjusted, he spotted Gonal crouching. There, splayed on the dirt next to his panting apprentice, Elan lay as if dead.

Mirelle pushed past, rolling up her sleeves. She knelt next to the two boys, reassuring Gonal he had done the right thing.

Elan groaned and muttered something.

The boy lived.

Jarand heaved a sigh of relief. "What is he saying?"

Gonal straightened, his face splotched with red. "They took her. He made me promise to make sure you understood." He shuffled his feet, as if what he had to say scared him. "Katira's been taken."

The icy knot in Jarand's stomach exploded and for a moment the ground felt as if it tilted beneath him. Memories of fire and desperate screams filled his mind.

Bremin slapped his shoulder hard. The stinging pain brought him back to the present.

"We will go after her," Bremin said. "We'll bring her back."

Mirelle turned toward them. Even in the dark, Jarand could see her hands trembling. "Gonal, go fetch Master Lucan. Tell him what's happened." Her voice quaked.

Gonal ran off with a nod, back towards the festival.

With Gonal gone, Mirelle turned to Bremin and Jarand, the pinched sound of distress clear in her voice. "How could this have happened? We were so careful. Why would anyone take her?"

Bremin knelt on the other side of Elan. "We'll get her back, I swear it to you. First, we must tend to the boy. Can he be saved?"

Mirelle sniffed and returned her attention to Elan. She pointed at the spreading stain on his chest. "He's taken a blade. He's cold, and he's gone into shock. I'll do what I can, but I don't know if he's strong enough to survive this. We need to take him inside."

Jarand scooped up the boy in his arms while Mirelle hurried ahead to light the lamps inside the cottage. He laid the boy on Mirelle's long work table, taking care not to jostle him too much.

Mirelle set straight to work cutting away the shirt and the leather vest.

"There's been a struggle in here." Bremin pointed at the scuffs in the floor, the broken bowl, and the toppled baskets near the wall by the door to the forge. "They must have been lying in wait for one of us."

"Someone would have to be a fool to think they could get away with this, especially if they knew who we really are." Jarand paused and opened himself to the air around him. If they used the power, there would be a residue.

He found nothing.

"Enough," Mirelle demanded. "We'll deal with that later. One of you get the fire going. The boy needs warmth."

Elan's breathing had grown shallow and labored and the edges of his lips had turned blue. Even Jarand, who knew little about healing, knew those weren't good signs.

The front door to the cottage flew open with a bang and Lucan rushed in, eyes wide and chest heaving. "What's happened?"

Jarand stepped in front of him, blocking his path before he could disturb Mirelle. "He was attacked. Gonal found him out back."

Lucan pushed against Jarand. "Confound you! Let me go to him," Lucan begged.

Jarand held him fast. "Mirelle is trying to save him. Let her work."

Lucan's struggle against Jarand's grip slowed and stopped. He lowered his voice, speaking only to Jarand. "Will he live?"

"I've seen worse," Jarand said. He tried to give a reassuring smile. "Your boy is strong-willed."

At the table, Mirelle and Bremin spoke in murmurs as she peered into Elan's eyes and felt his pulse. She shifted her focus to Lucan. "Your son is lucky. Had Gonal not found him when he did, he would have passed. As it is, he's not safe yet. The blade is making it impossible to stop the bleeding. It must come out."

Elan groaned and halfway opened one eye. "Pa? Is that you?"

Lucan shoved past Jarand and to the boy's side. "I'm here, son. I'm here." He pulled the boy's hand to his cheek.

"Took her ... Katira ... save her." The boy muttered as his eyes rolled back.

Lucan jerked his head up and turned to Jarand. "Is this true? Have they taken your girl?"

"Yes." Jarand wrung his hands together. Every part of him screamed to leave and track down the fool who dared touch Katira. "I think Elan was protecting her."

"You must go after her." Lucan set his jaw. "Why are you still here?"

Jarand glanced to the table, to Elan. The knife would have to come out. "Mirelle might need my help."

"It's okay. I'm here." Lucan gripped Jarand's shoulder. "Go find your girl."

Bremin nodded his agreement from the other side of the table. "We don't know what these scoundrels are capable of. The sooner we catch them, the better."

Jarand looked to Mirelle. He hated leaving her alone when things were going wrong, when lives were at stake.

"Go. Now. I'll be fine." She hurried through her workshop gathering bandages, hooked needle, and sinew. "I'll find you when Elan is out of danger."

Jarand lifted a floorboard and pulled out items from the secret compartment underneath.

Bremin toed a long scabbard. "Do you really think a sword is necessary?"

Jarand buckled a baldric across his chest and hung the great blade at his hip. "A sword is always necessary. I'm not taking any chances." The weight on his shoulder, the solid steel of the hilt, brought back memory upon memory, his training, his victories, his defeats. With it, he felt invincible.

Mirelle arranged all her tools on a tray and double checked to see if she needed anything else. Removing a blade was risky business. If she wasn't properly prepared, it could kill Elan. She wouldn't forgive herself for that.

Lucan hadn't moved from Elan's side. With Jarand gone, he'd have to help whether he liked it or not.

Jarand's apprentice shifted on his feet. Mirelle had forgotten the boy had returned. Good. He could be of use as well. "Gonal, guard the door. No one comes in unless I say so."

He slipped out the door with a nod.

She carried the tray to the table. "Lucan, I need you to pull the blade."

The man blanched white. He looked like he might be sick. His gaze darted to her, then back to Elan, then to the door where Gonal had just left.

Mirelle bent so they were face-to-face. "Jarand's not here to help me, Lucan. It has to be you."

Lucan squeezed his eyes shut, taking a deep breath and letting it go. When he opened his eyes, Mirelle saw the no nonsense face he wore during village council meetings. "Tell me exactly what to do."

Mirelle's gaze lingered on him for a moment. He would do his best if it meant helping his son. She hoped he wouldn't faint. "When I'm ready," she said, "you'll pull the blade straight out in one smooth slow motion. Then you'll set it down here on the tray and get out of my way."

Lucan wiped the sweat off his face. "Okay. I can do that."

Mirelle gathered a stack of cloths in her hand and stood at the head of the table. "I'm ready. Nice and slow."

He positioned himself next to the boy's shoulder and wrapped his fingers around the slender handle. With a muttered prayer, he gently pulled the blade free. Elan screamed and arched off the table before falling still. Mirelle pressed the cloths into the wound to stanch the flow of blood. Lucan turned his head away and braced himself against the table with both hands.

"He shouldn't bleed this much." Mirelle grabbed another stack of cloth. "A vessel has torn."

Elan stopped breathing.

Lucan gripped the edge of the table, he looked ready to collapse. "Can you do something?"

Mirelle knew what he meant, what he left unsaid. Could she use her power to save Elan?

"I'll save him," Mirelle said to Lucan. "But I'll have to use my stone. Will you permit me?"

Lucan glanced toward the door and back. "Anything, yes. Please, Mirelle, save my son."

There was no time to waste. Elan's heart was giving out. Mirelle pulled her stone free and summoned her power. It filled her with its sweet ache. She gripped the table as the fire of the power burned through her. It had been so long she wasn't used to the pain like she once was. Her hands and exposed forearms glowed in the lantern light.

Mirelle pulled back the blood-soaked cloths and placed her hands on either side of the wound. Threads of power danced, seeking out the torn vessel and quickly knitting it back together.

Elan still wasn't breathing. She moved a hand to his chest and formed a life glyph. It was a desperate choice. The glyph transferred a portion of her own life energy to Elan's heart, strengthening it. Elan gasped and breathed on his own again. The dusky blue around his lips faded. His heart beat stronger.

The damage caused by the blade still needed to be repaired, but the boy would live. She returned her hands to either side of the wound. Threads of power wove complex patterns over the skin before sinking in. With each layer the wound shrank until it was nothing but an angry puckered red scar.

She released the power, and the glow faded from her hands, arms, and neck. Her hands fell away to her sides. The life glyph cost her, but it had saved him.

It was worth it.

"That was closer than I would have liked." She rubbed her neck and closed her eyes. "He'll need to stay quiet for the next few days. But after that he will be fine. I'll bind his shoulder. The less he moves it the better."

Lucan stirred in his chair. He still looked pale. "Will he recover?"

"There is a small chance the vessel I repaired might break." She took a damp cloth from the tray and wiped away the blood from Elan's skin. "Stonebearer healing can piece everything back together, but the body needs time to make those connections strong."

Lucan returned to the table and caressed Elan's face. Mirelle wished she could feel the same relief of knowing her child was safe. Katira was out there. Jarand had not returned.

"How long do you think it will be before he wakes?"

"A few hours at least. It's hard to say." She wrapped Elan's shoulder with a roll of bandaging linen, tying his arm snugly across his chest. When she was finished she pointed to the nearby bed in the corner of the workshop. "He can rest there until you're ready to take him home."

Mirelle sank into a chair and rubbed at her eyes. They felt as if they were full of grit. Lucan carried Elan to the bed and covered him with one of the quilts he found there. Mirelle watched on, aching to be tucked into a soft warm bed herself.

She stroked the stone at her neck. Jarand felt far away, further than she expected.

Lucan touched her shoulder. "Are you okay?"

She had closed her eyes. She didn't mean to. Power healing used Khandashii. Those in the healing sept had a natural affinity toward glyphs that put broken things back together. Putting Elan back together wasn't what made her tired. The life glyph did. Had he been a fellow Stonebearer, she could have used Khandashii energy to strengthen him. Since he wasn't, she had to grant him the only thing that would save him—her own life energy.

"I will be in a little while." In time she would regain what she had lost, but not for days.

"Is there anything I can do for you?" Lucan kept looking at her as if he half-expected her to fall off the chair. "Something to drink, perhaps?"

Before Mirelle could reply, someone tripped and muttered a curse near the front door. She knew she had forgotten something. Gonal had been standing guard all this time. "Could you tell Gonal he can go home now, with my thanks?"

Lucan smiled and nodded. The familiar voices of Lucan's family poured in from the open door. Mirelle overheard Lucan quietly asking them to go home, that Elan was too tired for visitors. While he was right, she knew they must be worried sick.

"It's fine Lucan, they can come in," she called from the chair, not bothering to stand.

~

PINES AND BRAMBLES caught at Katira's hair and scratched at her face and arms as she hung face down over the rump of her captor's horse like a sack of grain. She fought as long as she could against her bonds until sweat slicked her back and blood dripped from her wrists.

They carried her through the darkened forest for what felt like years. Each step of the horse sent a jolt through her stomach and ribs, bringing wave after wave of nausea. Her festival dress offered little warmth in the fall night air. She could no longer feel her feet for the cold.

Every time she shut her eyes, she saw the shock on Elan's face as the knife struck him, saw him stagger to the ground crying her name, reaching for her. Each blink brought a fresh stab of panic of him bleeding out behind her home, dying alone on the ground. How could she live knowing he died trying to save her?

She pushed the thoughts from her mind once again. He would find a way to survive. He had to. He wouldn't give up. Not on himself, not on her.

Night closed around her, bringing with it threads of doubt that knotted and tangled in her mind. A web of hopelessness wove itself around Katira and when her resolve failed her, she allowed the darkness of grief-fueled sleep to take her.

When she woke, crisp morning light filtered through the tall pines

A river murmured not far from where they rode. She wracked her brain to picture the map on the wall back at the school house. If her memory served her correctly, it showed only one river leading south from Namragan, the Kanth. Should she have the chance to run, it would lead the way back home. Her captors would have to stop eventually to eat and allow the horses a drink. After the long night's ride, the poor beasts' sides heaved in exhaustion and their coats were foamy with sweat.

She twisted in her bonds to have a look at her captor in the light. Mamar always said a man's face spoke volumes about his character. Instead of finding the cruel face she had imagined, she found a boy so like Elan it brought a new stab of sorrow. Except instead of blond curls, his hair was a shade darker and hung straight in poorly cut chunks. When he looked back at her, he had the face of someone who had been beaten down, who had failed. Under any other circumstances, she might have trusted him.

The other man rode a short distance ahead. He sat slumped in the saddle, like a man who didn't care what anyone thought. His black greasy hair hung in strings nearly brushing his shoulders. This was the man who threw the blade at Elan. The man who had struck her.

When the boy saw Katira was awake, he turned to the man riding ahead. "Master Surasio, may we stop?"

"Why?" The reply came short and sharp.

The boy glanced back at Katira again before patting his mount's neck. "The horses will serve us better if they've had a chance to rest for a while."

Master Surasio swore and spat before pulling on the reins. She hated him for what he did to Elan. Seeing him up close made her hate him even more. He sneered at her and spat again, missing her head by a fraction. The limp shirt hanging from his slouched shoulders spoke of a carelessness and filth running clear to his soul.

"This isn't about the horses, is it?" He kneed his mount closer until Katira could smell sour rancid sweat. "It's about your own aching backside and grumbling stomach. Not to mention the girl. Don't pity her." He ran a probing finger down Katira's back and through her hair. Her stomach clenched. Despite the frigid morning air, a cold sweat broke out on her face and neck.

"Don't do that," the boy said. "You're scaring her."

Without warning, the younger man tensed and gasped in pain, doubling forward and gripping the reins until his fingers blanched white. Surasio watched with a sick grin, taking great pleasure in the young man's suffering.

The fit passed after several long minutes, leaving the young man breathless and slumped forward in the saddle.

"Watch your tongue and remember your place." Surasio flicked the reins on his horse, urging it forward. "We'll stop after we've crossed the river and no sooner. I don't want to hear another word from you until then."

"Yes, master," the boy answered in a whisper.

Katira's body trembled in the chill of the early morn. Lying against the warm rump of the horse helped, but not nearly enough. She needed to get warm and soon.

After another hour, they crossed the river and into a deep copse of trees against the side of the mountain. Surasio swung off his horse and took a few strides before stopping to take a piss like a foul little troll.

The boy loosened the ties securing her behind the saddle and those binding her feet. "My name's Isben." He spoke so only she could hear him. "If I let you down will you promise not to run?"

Katira would have promised him her first born to get her feet back on the ground. She nodded, her mouth too dry to speak.

He unknotted the last rope and lowered her down to the ground.

Her legs buckled, and her feet burned as the blood slowly returned. She would have fallen had Isben not been holding her fast.

"Take it easy," he murmured. "Let me help you." He set her arm over his shoulder and wrapped his other arm around her.

Each step brought piercing white-hot bolts up her legs. She hated feeling like a newborn calf hobbling across the small clearing. Everything hurt. Her whole body felt as if it had been beaten with a stout log. Running would have to wait until she could trust her legs again.

"You've had a hard night," Isben said, looking at the ropes in his hands with disgust. He tossed them aside. "What's your name?"

The anger and fear knotting Katira's insides loosened a fraction. However, when she tried to speak, only air came out. She coughed and shook her head.

Isben returned to the horse for a waterskin and handed it to her. She fumbled to hold it with her cold-deadened hands.

He lifted the skin to her mouth, the gesture gentle and careful. "Here, let me."

The water tasted stale, but it was welcome and cool. "My name's Katira." She took another drink, this one longer. "Why are you doing this, Isben? Where are you taking me?"

Isben glanced toward where Surasio slouched against a boulder smoking a pipe. "My master sent me to ask your father for help. I got caught by that foul beast of a man. He forced me to do this."

Isben reached for her hands and held them between hers. The heat from his hands stung. "You're frozen." He tugged his cloak from his shoulders and wrapped it around her.

She pulled it close as best she could with bound hands, the warmth welcome after the long cold night. The stomach-wrenching dizziness from the ride subsided and her feet, although sore, no longer felt as if they were being sliced open with hot knives.

Isben pushed bread and a wedge of cheese into her hands. "Eat this. It might be a while before we stop again."

Two distinct swirls marked the top of the small loaf. Katira recognized Mama Thanes' handiwork from the many times she'd bought her goods. Mama Thane had made these festival morning and had been so pleased how they turned out. A lump formed in her throat and indignation washed through her with each bite she took.

How dare they take her away from her home and her life? How dare they hurt Elan? She forced herself to be calm again and wiped her cheeks dry. No solution ever came from allowing panic to run wild. She had to escape. Both Surasio and Isben had their backs turned. She had to try.

She had traveled to the neighboring town, Gibbon's Rock, a handful of times with Papan. He had friends there, people he traded his wares with, and she knew many of them. On a good traveling day, it took until early afternoon to get there if they set out at first light. Judging from the lay of the land and the time her captors spent picking through the forest, the small town couldn't be far.

Surasio groaned and scratched himself. He was the more dangerous of the two. Something about him bothered her more than his outright loathsomeness, something familiar in the way he stood. She didn't like it, whatever it was.

She tested her legs. They were wobbly, but they would support her. She would not show that pig Surasio weakness. The ropes had rubbed the skin at her ankles raw. While Isben repacked the saddle bags, she tested the knots at her wrists and found them sloppy. It would be short work to loosen them.

She discreetly untied the rope and glanced back toward Isben. Too many questions remained unanswered about him. Why did he need Papan's help? Why would Surasio capture him? Was he even telling the truth?

On the other hand, he had been kind to her. He'd tried to protect her. What would happen to him if she ran? She took a deep breath, held it, and then let it out. If she could free herself, she couldn't be concerned about such things.

Isben wandered over to the edge of the river and stooped to wash his hands and face. Surasio had his back to her. She slipped free of the ropes and darted into the woods, as quiet as a fallow deer.

With luck, she would make it close enough to Gibbon's Rock to attract someone's attention. Without it, her escape attempt would cost them time and give those searching for her a chance to catch up. Papan would never give up until he found her. Mamar wouldn't let him.

The freedom she felt as she darted through the lumbering pines made running feel more like flying. Her legs found strength the more they moved. The ground became a blur. She heard a shout from behind her and pushed herself harder. Chimney smoke rose above the tree line ahead. Gibbon's Rock was close.

A horse crashed through the underbrush behind her. Isben shouted her name, begging her to stop. She couldn't. He couldn't catch her, she wouldn't let him. Each step she ran further away was a victory.

Another crash came at her from the side. Surasio leapt from his horse and tackled her to the ground. They rolled until he sat on top of her and twisted her arms behind her back, pushing her face into the dirt.

"I wish you hadn't done that," Surasio said through his teeth. Anger oozed from him in waves. "Now someone has to be punished."

Isben leapt down from his horse. "Please, Surasio, don't hurt her!"

"You've got some nerve." Surasio shouted at Isben as he hoisted Katira to her feet. "What, did you forget to check the ropes? How did she get free?"

"No," Isben said. "I did nothing. You can't expect her not to try to escape. Look at who raised her."

"Don't bring him into this." Surasio raised his hand and Isben collapsed, writhing in pain.

"This is how you will pay for your mistake girl," Surasio said, his voice oily and slick. "You will watch him die."

"No, stop it!" Katira cried out as she watched on in horror. "What are you doing to him?"

"He's bound to me and my mission. Any failure on his part

means pain." Surasio prodded Isben with the point of his boot. "The worse the failure, the worse the pain."

Isben's eyes rolled back in his head. His ragged shouts grew weaker.

"Please, stop," Katira begged. "He had nothing to do with my escape."

"Promise me you'll never try to escape again." Surasio sneered. "Or I'll kill him."

Katira couldn't watch someone else die because of her. "I promise! Please, stop. I won't run again, I swear it."

With a wave of Surasio's hand, Isben fell still. A trickle of blood ran from the corner of his mouth to the ground. He gasped to regain his breath, his eyes pressed shut. Katira wished she could help him as he groaned and rolled to his feet, staggering with his first few steps.

"Give me your hand, girl." Surasio held out his grimy hand toward her. He had something gripped in the other. "Should've done this before."

Katira stepped back. Whatever the troll wanted, she wanted no part of it.

Surasio directed his hand toward Isben, his threat clear. "I said, give me your hand."

Katira held out her hand and turned away, not daring to look at what horrible thing Surasio might do.

"No. Master Surasio, you don't need to do this." Isben gripped the pommel of his saddle to steady himself. He sounded too tired to fight, yet he spoke out. "She's promised to obey."

"Shut up, boy."

Isben cringed waiting for whatever punishment Surasio dealt to strike him. It didn't come.

Surasio's attention was fixed on Katira. He seized her hand and a golden web of light extended from his fist. It formed a glittering cage around her. Someone so filthy had no right to create something so beautiful. Katira flinched as the web drew closer.

The threads of the cage clung to her skin as they touched her, burning as they went. They wove themselves over every inch. She fought to keep them from touching her face. Surasio gripped her arm as she squirmed against the unwelcome invasion. Her whole body burned where the glittering strands touched as they settled deeper and deeper, burying themselves into her flesh. She screamed as the pain overwhelmed her senses.

"Obey me and you won't hurt like this again." Surasio was so close flecks of spit hit her face when he spoke.

Surasio released his grip and let her fall to the ground. The pain faded. She had pressed her eyes shut when the torment grew unbearable and now she didn't want to open them, fearing to see her own blood and burns from Surasio's net.

"It's okay." Isben set his hand against her back. "Open your eyes. It isn't real."

Katira blinked and studied the backs of her hands. No burnt lines marred the skin. No web of blood crossed the palms. She pulled up the sleeve of her shirt. Nothing. "What was that?" she asked.

"Death oath." Isben pulled her sleeve straight and helped her to her feet. "He put one on me as well. Don't fight against it." Isben took a steadying breath. "It can kill."

JARAND WATCHED on as Bremin made quick work reading the different foot prints and marks in the dirt by the dim light of the moon. While Jarand prided himself on his own tracking skills, being with Bremin was being in the presence of a master. The man observed, analyzed, and acted before Jarand could spot his first trail sign.

"There were two. Both had horses." Bremin held out a lantern over a point on the other side of the low sheep wall separating the forge yard from the encroaching wood. "The larger of the two took Katira with him on his mount. Looks like she gave him a hard time of it, too."

Bremin straightened. "Remind me who your enemies are around here."

"Haven't attracted any. At least, none that I know of." Jarand's thoughts went back to the cottage, to Elan stabbed and bleeding, to Mirelle saving him. "Elan knew the truth about us. He wasn't happy about it, but he swore on his love to Katira he wouldn't tell."

Bremin snorted. "He didn't actually say that, did he?"

"It was along the same lines." Jarand examined the boot prints at his feet. "If he accidentally let his tongue slip around the wrong people at the festival, it might explain all this."

"A Stonebearer hater in a neighboring village then. We better get the horses in case I'm right." Bremin turned toward the small stable to the side of Jarand's cottage and called back. "I'm usually right."

Jarand turned to follow when the first pulse of Khandashii rippled through the air. If Mirelle had to use her power, the boy was in mortal danger. His steps faltered. She needed him. He should be there. Anyone within a league with the smallest inkling of power would have felt the pulse.

"Don't even think about it." Bremin led his bridled horse out of the pen and looped the reins to a post. "Mirelle can take care of herself." He ducked back into the pen for his blanket and saddle.

Curse Bremin for always being right and figuring it out faster than he could.

Katira needed him more. She was young and scared. She needed her Papan.

Jarand bridled his horse, stroking the tall stallion on the nose. The horse snickered and searched his pockets for carrots. "Easy there," Jarand said to the steed. "You can have a whole bushel of carrots after this."

"That's okay," Bremin said wryly. "I don't care for carrots that much. Now ale, I could do with a nice ale." He cinched the last strap. "There a break in this wall?"

"This way." Jarand pulled himself into the saddle, eager to be on the move. Beyond the wall, the moon didn't pierce the darkness under the canopy of the tall pines.

Bremin leaned out from his saddle and held out the small lantern in front of him. He followed the trail of hoof prints and broken branches like connecting dots on a map, quickly and with practiced efficiency.

Jarand strained to see the clues as they passed, something to ease the knot of uncertainty building in his throat. The kidnappers hurt Elan, they could easily have hurt Katira as well. And now Mirelle wasn't with them. He pushed the thoughts away. He couldn't allow himself to be distracted by all the unknown possibilities or he would miss the world in front of his nose.

If they didn't return to the cottage in a few hours, Mirelle would come find them.

"Stay close," Bremin called from further ahead. "Don't bother trying to find what I'm seeing, you'll just get lost. We don't have time for that."

Lucan's family had come and gone. There had been so many questions, and too many of those questions Mirelle didn't have answers for yet. Trying to comfort them brought a dull ache behind her eyes. She needed that comfort for herself. Her daughter was gone, possibly hurt, and she couldn't leave until she was sure Elan would live.

Lucan pressed a warm mug into Mirelle's hands. She took a sip of the hot broth and let its heat soothe her. Each passing hour made it clear—she needed to go to Jarand. If anything happened, she would be too far to help them.

She pressed her stone between her fingers, allowing it to transport her awareness to Jarand. He hadn't turned in his course, hadn't stopped.

They hadn't found Katira yet.

"Lie down." Lucan took the empty mug from her hands. "I'll watch him for a while."

"No." She draped the blanket over the arm of the chair and stood up. A wave of dizziness forced her to grip the back of the chair. "I need to get ready to leave."

She went over to Elan. The color in his cheeks continued to improve. He breathed the slow, easy breath of sleep. She placed her hand on the skin of his neck and summoned her power once more. A single delving glyph wove in and around the wound, showing her what the eye couldn't see. To her relief, nothing had started to bleed again. Her healing held strong.

Lucan stood by the fire staring into the embers. "I would have you stay. Not just for Elan." He turned to face her. "I don't like a lady like yourself leaving into the woods in the middle of the night. There have been too many ill happenings already. If you wait until morn, I'll take you if you feel you need to go."

"It's my daughter. I can't rest until I know she is safe." Mirelle placed a traveling satchel on the kitchen table. "Besides, by morning they will be leagues away."

"How?" He glanced to where her stone hung on its chain, as if unsure if he could ask. "How can you know where he is?"

"Jarand and I are a bonded companionship." She touched the stone. "Our stones are two parts of the same whole. With it I can always find him and know if he's safe. As can he with me."

"Can you do the same with Katira?"

"The Khandashii is a fickle thing. It doesn't let you bond with anyone except the one who is your match." She tucked the stone beneath her shirt. "He's traveled half the way to Gibbon's Rock. There's no sign he's turning back." She plucked the key from its hidden hook in the kitchen. "Hold on to this. If we don't return ..."

He pushed it away. "You will."

"Nothing is certain. This is a precaution, nothing more." She pushed it back. "I need to gather a few more things. Could you saddle my horse for me?"

He sighed. "I don't like this. But if it were my daughter I'd do the same. I'll bring your mare out front."

"You're a good man, Lucan."

With Lucan gone, Mirelle carefully wrapped the blade they removed from Elan and tucked it into her satchel. Jarand would want to see it. He knew his metals, knew the craftsmanship of the local metal workers. He would know where it came from.

JARAND AND BREMIN continued hour after hour, searching out the marks left from Katira's captors. Each hour, Jarand's uncertainty grew for her safety. The sun crawled over the horizon and made its slow climb into the sky. Around midmorning, Bremin whistled from across the river. "Here. They stopped here for a while."

Jarand pushed through a thinner patch of brush to the boulder strewn edge of the river. Had it been spring, the runoff would have churned the water until it ran fast and white, too deadly to cross. This late in the fall the river grew tired and lazy as it wandered down its course. Still, Jarand mounted his horse. Anything to keep the water from spilling into his boots. On the other side of the river, in a clearing filled with long grass, Bremin examined a short length of rope. He pulled free a long dark hair caught in the fibers.

Jarand jumped down and examined the hair. "It's hers."

Bremin handed him the rope and continued to search out more signs of Katira's passing through.

"Why would they leave this here?" Jarand ran the rope through his hands. "If this was the rope they used to bind her, she must have tried to get away." He followed a series of footprints, one small set and one larger. "Yes. She tried to run here, I'm sure of it."

"The tracks lead this way." Bremin followed the marks in the ground as they led away from the clearing. He pointed at the dirt. "Something happened here. She was caught."

"Show me." Jarand jumped down and leaned forward to examine the tracks Bremin had found.

He pointed to a larger set of footprints. "At first I thought she was being chased by one, but here's a second set of feet. He must have flanked her from the side"

The air held a strange energy. It throbbed against Jarand's temples. He opened himself to the power. Green tinged flecks of light floated in the air, too scattered to make out what they might have been. "Power was used here. Looks like bender work." Jarand scanned the surrounding forest to see if there was something out of place. Benders changed the nature of things, turned wood into stone, water to wine. As long as the elements were present, they could create whatever they wanted.

"Odd. Can't think of what a bender would be doing out here." Bremin stroked the short hairs of his beard. Then he stopped mid-stroke. "There is one explanation, and it's not one you're going to like."

"I'll be the judge of that."

"Benders can change people's minds." Bremin paced. "It's been forbidden for centuries. They can remove memories, compel people to do things, nasty business."

"Are you saying this scum might have done something to Katira's mind?"

"All the more reason to get moving." Bremin dabbed at the dirt with his fingers and rubbed them together.

"What? What is it?" Jarand gripped both hands around the hilt of his sword, anchoring himself to what was real and not the horrible things his mind wanted him to believe.

"Blood. Hours old. Not enough to be a serious wound."

The sight of the blood stoked the smoldering fire within Jarand into a blaze. He had to get her back. Every minute they wasted meant another minute where she would be further away and harder to find. He swore and kicked a nearby tree.

"Easy, Jarand." Bremin said. "If we go any faster we risk losing the trail. They'll most likely continue to travel south and then either make for capitol or take another crossroad." He set his foot in the stirrup and swung onto his horse.

"If that's true, they'll have to pass through both Cerro's Cross and Burk's Gap." Jarand looked toward the south. "Those hills are well patrolled. They wouldn't do well to try to sneak around. Our best bet is to make for the crossroads."

"Taking the main road will save valuable time." Bremin took a swig from his flask and wiped his mouth with the back of his hand. "Unless they aren't going south."

Jarand pressed his stone between his hands. Mirelle had left the cottage hours ago. "How far is the road from here, you reckon?"

Bremin swung around and studied the narrow valley. "Not far. Half a league." He turned back to Jarand. "Why?"

"Mirelle is close." Jarand nudged his horse toward the road. "She might have learned something more from Elan." He kicked the horse into a run and didn't wait for Bremin to follow.

At the road, Jarand spotted Mirelle heading his way at a ground-eating pace. Her cloak and dark hair whipped out like a flag behind her. She slowed as she drew closer.

Jarand jumped down to grab hold of the bridle on Mirelle's horse. "You didn't ride the whole way like that, did you?"

"Of course not." Mirelle patted the mare's neck. "Ananda needed a good run, and I knew I was close. I know how to take care of her, thank you very much."

Bremin jumped down and joined them. "Did the boy survive?"

"Honestly, Bremin." Mirelle removed the satchel from around her neck. "After saving your skin so many times, you doubt my abilities?"

Bremin shrugged. "Healing Stonebearers is one thing, healing mortals is another. He didn't look good when we left."

"He'll be fine." She unwrapped the blade from her bundle and handed it to Jarand. "Here, this might be of interest to you."

Jarand took the blade from her hand and held it in the sunlight.

This blade had been made from quality iron by a master blade crafter. The folds of metal on metal were fine and even. And familiar.

"This is a Fordzala blade," he said with certainty. "No one around these parts would have one. It's rare enough to find a throwing knife around here, let alone a good one." He passed the blade to Bremin.

"I had my suspicions. That's why I brought it." She reached into the satchel once more and handed bread to each of them. "What have the two of you learned?"

Jarand opened his mouth to tell her the bad news, but Bremin beat him to it. "There's a rogue bender involved. We think he might have used forbidden glyphs, possibly on Katira."

Mirelle's back stiffened and her knuckles went white as they gripped the reins. She swayed in the saddle. When Jarand reached up to steady her, she clung to his hand. Touching skin-to-skin opened their awareness to each other. He felt her shock, exhaustion, and fears race through his mind. He tried to find his calm, his strength, for her to lean on. It was the best he could do for her.

When she opened her eyes again a moment later, her rock-solid steadiness had returned. "What are we waiting for?"

Jarand held fast to her hand a moment longer. There was something else. The exhaustion radiating from her was more than what he'd expect from the loss of a night's sleep, more than what she would have needed to work healing glyphs. "There's something you aren't telling me. What is it?"

She squeezed his hand and bent to kiss it. "He was dying. I had to. Don't be upset."

Jarand studied the pattern of energy pulsing through her and cursed to himself. Of all the fool-brained things to do, she had gone and given the boy her life energy. Under any other circumstance, he'd bundle her off to a warm bed and make her stay there for a day or two. However, there would be no warm bed for either of them for what could be days.

He returned the gentle kiss and his throat tightened with worry. "Will you be okay?"

A fire burned in her eyes. Nothing would stop her. "As long as you're with me, I'll be fine." She released his hand and sat tall. "Let's go save our daughter."

ELAN'S SHOULDER throbbed and when he opened his eyes he couldn't see any more than shapes and shadows. The unfamiliar bed carried a fragrance that stirred his foggy memory. Vague images swam before his eyes, a struggle, horses, shouting.

Katira.

He bolted upright in the bed when the realization slammed hold. Knife-like pain sliced through his chest and shoulder. He clutched at the bandaging, panting.

Katira needed help.

"Easy there, Elan. Take it easy." Familiar hands gently pushed him back down on the bed. Pa lit a candle from the dying embers of the fire. Neat bundles of herbs hung in rows across the ceiling. He was in Katira's house, in the cot where Mistress Mirelle cared for her patients.

Elan's mouth felt like it had been stuffed with wool when he tried to speak. Pa held a cup to his lips. Elan took a sip, then cleared his throat. "Is she safe?"

"I wish I knew. Master Jarand began tracking those fools the first second he could. If anyone out there is going to find her, it'll be him. How's the shoulder?"

"It hurts." Elan winced when he touched the bandage. "How long have they been gone?"

Pa stretched and peered out between the shutters of the nearby window. "I reckon Mistress Mirelle left two, maybe three hours ago. Master Jarand's been gone since before midnight." He ran his hand through his hair. "I thought I nearly lost you. If Mistress Mirelle wasn't here, you would have died."

Elan closed his eyes at the memory. The agony when his father pulled the blade, the sense of something tearing inside, of his own hot blood gushing over his skin. Thinking about it made his stomach turn.

"There's more." Pa's mouth worked wordlessly before continuing. "I let her use her power on you. I couldn't stand the thought of watching you die." He wiped at his eyes and crossed his arms over his chest. "Not when something could be done."

Elan shivered. He'd seen what the power could do, had watched it dissolve one of those shadow hounds into dust. That same power had touched him, had fixed what had torn inside him.

Had saved his life.

He should have been grateful, but all he could feel was sick. His father had allowed an evil to touch him. Even if it had done a greater good, what would the cost be? Would Mistress Mirelle now have a claim on his soul?

Elan let his head fall back onto the pillow. A bundle of sanaresina hung above his head. Its peppery smell brought his thoughts back to Katira. "What of Katira? Is there any news?"

"Before Mistress Mirelle left, she said Master Jarand and his friend had tracked Katira south toward Gibbon's Rock." Pa held his hands out as if he didn't quite believe it himself. "Something about the magic lets them keep track of each other."

More pressing questions filled Elan's head. "Why would they take Katira? She's just a girl."

Pa arched an eyebrow. He leaned over to check the bandages and was pleased with what he saw. "If someone wanted to hurt me, the worst thing he could do is threaten my children. It's the same for any parent." He sat back down into the chair next to the bed. "I believe someone wants to punish Jarand and Mirelle for being what they are. They're using Katira as bait."

It wasn't fair. Katira shouldn't have been a part of this. She deserved safety and security. "Do you think she'll be okay?"

"Both Jarand and Mirelle are capable. Whoever did this will pay." Pa stifled a yawn. "As for you, it would be best if you went back to sleep. Mistress Mirelle says for you to stay quiet for a few days while you finish healing."

The thought of sleep was inviting. How nice it would be to slip back into its warm embrace where the pain of his shoulder could fade away for a while.

Elan couldn't let himself drift back to sleep, not when Katira was in trouble. Master Jarand and Mistress Mirelle had left town. He had to do something. He tried to talk some reason into himself, but he couldn't stop worrying. He had to go after her. He couldn't rest until he knew she was safe. He'd promised to protect her and he had failed. He had to prove to Master Jarand and himself that he was willing to do what was needed.

Pa blew out the candle and the room plunged back into darkness. The chair he sat in was close enough Elan could hear him breathe. Elan waited for those breaths to slow, waited for him to sleep before he slipped from the bed. Only a tiny shaft of morning sun shone through the shutters like a thread of white against the floor. He couldn't go anywhere until he found his shoes, shirt, and coat. At least they had left his pants on.

Years of hunting deer had taught him to be silent and patient. They had tied his right arm tight across his chest, making it hard to maneuver through the space. A neatly stacked pile of his things rested on top of a chest. He had almost made it to the door when the boot he had stuffed under his arm fell free and thumped to the floor.

Pa grunted and opened one eye. "Where do you think you're off to?"

Elan stopped cold. He had hoped to make a clean break - no fighting, no justifying his actions until after, when everyone returned safe and sound. It was always so much easier to ask forgiveness when the deed was done than to plead for permission. "I'm going after Katira. If I don't, I'll never forgive myself."

Pa crossed his arms over his wide chest. "You're hurt. Besides, she's involved in wielder business now and that's not where you want to be. Jarand and Mirelle are decent folk. But there are those out there that aren't." His father slid the pile of Elan's belongings closer to himself and rested an arm over it. "The stories about all the wicked deeds from these people didn't spring from the imagination of some bard. There are some of them who use their power to get what they want. If they want you dead, they'll not hesitate to kill you."

"I'm going whether you like it or not." Elan fetched the boot that had fallen. He had to grab the back of a chair to steady himself. His strength wasn't half of what it should be, but he wasn't going to let it stop him. "I don't have time to argue. I know the risks." There would be time for rest later. The longer he took to leave, the greater the head start they would have, and the harder it would be to catch up. "I won't give this up." He swayed a fraction. "Don't make me fight you."

"Fight you? Why would I fight you? First, I'd win. And second, I'm letting you go." Pa sounded resigned as he said it. "Promise me to stay out of the way of the wielders. Even with the best intentions, they can be trouble."

Elan stopped short, his next argument halted on the tip of his tongue. Did his father say he could go? The change startled him so much he dropped into the chair.

"What?"

"Knowing you, you'll make off whether I grant you permission or not. I'd rather you have my help and come back safe, than not and perhaps not be prepared for the trip."

"Really?" Elan asked, unsure of what he was hearing. Somehow leaving without permission was more thrilling than having it granted. He began to second-guess himself.

No, he needed to go. Katira needed him as much as he needed her. How could he say he loved her and wanted to spend the rest of his days with her if he wasn't willing to go to her rescue?

"What will you tell Ma?"

"Let me deal with your mother. But promise not to do anything foolish. If you don't come back, she'll skin and tan my hide." He sighed and there was a hint of a smile in it. "Now, what will you need for your journey?"

Before Elan could answer, Pa began gathering food stuffs. By the time Elan struggled into his boots and coat his father had returned with a packed saddle bag. Elan's trusted horse, Rivan, snorted and puffed in the chill of the fall morning.

With one good arm, Elan gripped the pommel and swung into the saddle. The motion pulled at his hurt shoulder and he stifled a groan. The fresh wave of pain was enough that thoughts of quitting stabbed his mind.

His father held the bridle and stroked Rivan's nose. "Stay to the main roads. Find shelter at night. Don't let anyone take advantage of you. They have a few hours on you, but chances are they will have to stop in the towns sooner or later."

"I know, Pa."

"Master Jarand is well known. They can tell you if he's been through. If you get in trouble, tell them you're my son. It'll open doors if you need them. That said, do something stupid in my name and you'll have to answer to me."

Elan cleared his throat. It had to be hard for Pa to let him go. "I'll return as soon as I can." Before he turned to go, Pa tossed him a small pouch. Elan caught it with his good hand.

"You'll need coin once your supplies run out. That should last you for a while if you use it wisely."

Elan hefted the pouch. It must have held all the coin they earned at the festival. "I can't take this. It's too much."

"I'm not giving it to you. I'm lending it. I fully expect you to return home and work it off."

"I will, Pa. I promise." Elan tucked the bag into his coat pocket and rubbed Rivan's neck. Without another word he trotted off, leaving his family and all he knew behind.

Chapter
6

Regulus suffered Wrothe's torture for almost two weeks - enough to learn his place, but not enough to break him. This time he'd deliberately pushed her too far, hoping she would lose control. He had to test his theory that he was her anchor to the mortal world. He pushed his awareness through their connection and prodded at her thoughts and memories. If he could uncover another clue to how the connection worked, he might learn how to break it.

It was worth dying for.

"You meddling fool! I warned you!" Wrothe screamed, raising her arms and summoning glyphs of ancient magic Regulus didn't recognize. Her anger filled the seeker's office and pressed against the walls, pinning Regulus to the floor.

Light from dozens of glyphs flashed from her hands. He braced for the blow to land, for death to come. He wanted it to come. Her power pierced him in hundreds of places, spearing him through with white-hot daggers. The torture would leave no mark, but while it lasted it held him in a vise of pain. Perhaps this time her anger would be enough to end him. Dark mist clouded his vision. Death's release hovered a whisper away from his grasp. He yearned for its touch.

The burning light vanished.

Reality slammed back into place.

"Let me go!" he pleaded between gasps.

Wrothe knelt next to his head and stroked his jawline with the tips of her fingers. "Why do you fight so hard against me?" The rage in her voice melted into a seductive purr. "I could make our time together blissful, if you'd simply give up."

After the pain, the pleasure she forced on him jangled his nerves. His fingers curled and uncurled desperate for release. "Why won't you kill me like the others?" He envied the Stonebearers Tash had lured away from Fordzala. Most didn't suffer more than a day.

"I've seen your mind." Her probing finger followed the edge of his ear and across his forehead. His whole body quaked as she pushed her influence to the limit. "You know why I keep you alive. We're bound, Stonebearer. I can't inhabit a body of flesh without first rooting myself in a host." She cut off the flow of pleasure, leaving him panting and hollow. He could move again. "I prefer that the host be willing, but desperation brings compromise."

"Your desperation will bring your downfall." He jerked away from her touch. "If not through me, then through someone else."

A cruel smile curled Wrothe's lips. "Oh, what little you know. As we speak, more of your fellow Stonebearers are turning to me, looking to me for a future."

"You will be stopped." He spit out the words, not caring if she hurt him again.

She crossed the room to the window and breathed in the sea air. "If you're referring to that brat you call your apprentice, Surasio sent word last night. He captured the boy along with that girl you've been hiding from me."

Regulus's already jumbled world fell off its high shelf and smashed against the floor. Surasio, that soulless, honorless, oath-breaking slime had no right to call himself a Stonebearer. If Isben and Jarand's girl had fallen into his hands ...

Regulus prayed the scum of a man brought them both back unharmed. If he knew Surasio, they'd be lucky to come back alive.

THE LANDSCAPE CHANGED with each passing hour, smoothing out as if a giant had taken the edges of the land and pulled them, flattening the jagged rocky peaks to gentler rolling hills. The tall spine of the Pathara Mountains stretched up high behind them to the north reminding Katira how far they had traveled from her home.

In the hours since her escape attempt, Katira's thoughts kept tangling themselves in knots. Isben had tried to answer her questions, but she heard the exhaustion in his voice, saw it in the way his head hung low. There would be time for answers later. She rested her head on Isben's back as they rode, glad he was there. Glad she wasn't alone.

It wasn't until the sun hung low in the sky that Surasio veered his horse off the road and through a break in the trees to an abandoned campsite. Heavy clouds gathered to the south. A breeze picked up, swirling the leaves at their feet and bringing the smell of wet stone and earth. Isben straightened in the saddle, alert with the sudden change.

Katira willed her speeding heart to slow. Any change opened new possibilities. She leaned close to Isben's ear. "What is it?"

"I'm not sure." He glanced around. "I think we're close to Cerro's Cross." He shaded his eyes with a hand. "Yes, there." He pointed down where the road led. "You can see a corner of the wall from here."

Katira squinted to see where he was pointing. The village wall back home was only high enough to keep out the sheep. She used to walk across their tops, pretending she was a traveling acrobat. What Isben pointed to was no wall. It was an immense barrier taller than the two-story inn on the edge of Namragan's square.

Isben nudged her. "You're staring. Have you ever left Namragan before?"

Katira clamped her mouth shut. "Only to visit the neighboring villages. Why do you ask?"

"If you're impressed by this, Fordzala is going to knock your buttons off."

Surasio dismounted and tied his reins to a low hanging branch. "Girl, clean yourself up." He pulled a pipe from a coat pocket. "I don't want people thinking twice when they see you."

Katira nodded her obedience. This wasn't a matter worth fighting over. She could only imagine what a mess she looked like. She had spent hours brushing and braiding her hair into sleek knots for the festival only the night before. Her yellow dress now hung wrinkled, torn, and stained. Grime streaked her sleeves.

Isben reached up to help her come down from the horse, and she was grateful. The long ride paired with the even longer night before left every inch of her sore. It would be foolish to trust her own legs.

Isben pulled strips of bandaging linen from a saddle bag and gently wrapped her scabbed wrists and ankles. She didn't dare look at the damage caused by the ropes. Somehow not knowing helped it not hurt as much. Had she been home, Mamar would have applied sanaresina salve to help them heal.

Isben handed her a cloth and a flask of water. "To clean your face," he explained. "I might even have a comb somewhere."

She gave a hollow-hearted laugh. "I imagine I'm quite a mess."

He dug in the saddle bag once more. "Let's say you've seen better days."

Katira did her best to clean herself up. Washing her face helped her feel human again. She tried to run the comb through her hair, but her arms were too sore to do any good.

Isben took the comb from her hand without a word. By his confident strokes, it was obvious he'd done this before. Katira tried to remember if there was ever a time Elan had done the same. A memory surfaced of the time he stole the comb she had borrowed from Mamar and refused to give it back. They were children then and Elan had loved nothing more than to make her cry.

Thinking of Elan was like placing a heavy weight on her chest, crushing her slowly, robbing her breath. He might be dead and here she was remembering when he was a naughty little boy. It all felt so wrong.

The practiced way Isben worked the knots from her hair soothed away her worries. She closed her eyes and imagined she was home with Mamar in front of a cheery fire.

"My little sister has long hair like yours." Isben stopped to pick out a twig that had become ensnared. "When my mother was too busy I'd help her comb it sometimes. She loved it. I can braid, too. I'm sure that's not something you hear every day." He resumed the rhythmic motion of combing. "In fact, if you take the crossroad east from Cerro's Cross it's only a two-day ride to my home."

There was something more he wasn't saying. "Did something happen to her?"

"No. Not to her. I had to leave." The comb stilled. "When the town learned I was different, I was sold into slavery. Had my family fought against the town's decision for me to be sent away, their farm and home would have been burned. Possibly with them in it."

"Different? How?"

He resumed combing once more. "My master - not Surasio, the one who sent me to Namragan - used to be your father's master. Your father is one of the greatest generals the Order has ever known."

Katira whipped around to face him, the motion causing her hair to yank the comb from his hand. "You must be confusing him with someone else. He's no general. He's just a blacksmith." The image of her father's scars surfaced in her mind and she paused. Could it be possible?

Isben's mouth hung open for a moment before he clamped it shut. He collected the comb from where it had fallen and gathered her hair into his hands once more. "I shouldn't have said anything. If he hasn't told you, it's not my right to talk about it."

Surasio trudged back into the clearing. The man had changed his shirt and patted down the stringy tufts of greasy thinning hair. Judging by the smell, he hadn't bothered to wash.

"Get her up. We're going." Surasio untied the reins of his horse.

Isben reached for her hands to help her to her feet. "Do you think you can ride?"

Katira wasn't sure, every muscle ached. "Suppose I can't talk him into letting me walk, can I?"

Isben's eyebrow rose an inch. He glanced over to see if Surasio was watching. "Probably not. The good news is once we're inside Cerro's Cross, I'm sure we're stopping. Everything will feel better with a decent night's sleep. I promise." He lifted her onto the back of the horse once more and patted her leg. "There's not much further to go."

Back on the road, the entirety of Cerro's Cross came into view. As they drew closer, the walls grew higher and higher making Katira blink to be sure what she was seeing was real. She felt so small in comparison. The gates hung open like jaws of a huge beast, ready to eat her.

The low hanging dark clouds opened as Katira was consumed by the city. She strained to see through the mist one last time at the road behind her, hoping in the distance she would see the familiar outline of her father riding toward her.

The road remained empty.

Even with the rain, the streets of Cerro's Cross bristled with people running in different directions. Hawkers cried their wares under the protection of awnings. Weary workers carried heavy baskets on their hunched shoulders. Children ran through the mess, dodging carts and horses in a game.

They turned off the main road. Katira lost sight of the gates. The tiny flicker of hope that somehow her father would find her in all of this was snuffed out in the maze-like passages. She held tighter onto Isben's waist.

Isben tilted his head back. "You okay?"

She didn't answer. She didn't know what to say. This was all so new. Part of her was eager to see everything, to experience the world. The other part couldn't stop thinking about going home and feeling safe again.

He pressed his hand over hers, it was warm and reassuring. "I'll do whatever I can to protect you, I swear it."

"I know," she heard herself say and was surprised she believed it.

As they rode on Katira caught sight of a leatherworker polishing a saddle the same way she had seen Elan do in his father's shop. The smell of polish summoned the memory of Elan falling to the ground, of his cries. She flinched and pressed her face into Isben's back, pushing the pain of the memory away.

Dark fell soon after. Lamplighters on long stilts tottered from lamp post to lamp post with their shielded candles and their paper straws, filling, trimming, and lighting as they went. The last of the hawkers fell silent leaving an eerie quiet where it once was too loud. The rain muddied the crisp smells of harvest spices with smells of the wet ground.

"When we stop, don't attract notice." Isben's breath tickled her ear. "Surasio won't have any reason to bother either of us until morning."

They followed the filthy man down a dark narrow passageway leading to a row of shuttered and locked stores. A single lantern hung next to a broken sign. Surasio slammed his fist against a wide door and a child no older than ten peeked out. "Still room?"

The child took a quick look, nodded, and held up five fingers.

"You'll take three and you'll like it." Surasio argued back. "You little stable maggot."

The child flinched away from Surasio's fist and opened the door, his hand outstretched for his coin.

Katira opened her mouth to say something to protect the child. Isben held up a hand to shush her. Surasio had already gone inside the inn without paying.

"Don't worry." Isben jumped down. "Surasio should have bargained more. It's kind of expected here. If he's not more careful, a stable kid like this is likely to stick a thorn under his saddle." Isben helped Katira down. "Not that I would mind seeing him getting bucked off tomorrow, but it won't do anything for his mood."

He fished around in a coin purse tied to his belt and held the payment out for the child. "Listen here, you know and I both know he should have argued you down to two coins. It wasn't fair." The child nodded and jutted out his lip. "I'll give you your three, but those horses better be fed and well brushed. They've worked hard."

Inside the inn, the keeper led Isben and Katira through the dark cramped commons area to an equally dark cramped room. There was no window, no fireplace. It might as well have been a closet. A single bed filled most of the space with only a narrow channel of floor to one side of it to let a sleeper in or out.

The unfamiliar bed smelled of pipe smoke and old straw. It didn't matter. After so many hours of travel Katira could have slept anywhere if it was flat and didn't move.

She was asleep before she could even take off her boots.

THE ROAD STREAMED across the bounding hills, dipping and turning as it traveled along the foothills. The leaves on the trees erupted in a riot of reds and golds, all vying for Jarand's attention. Under other circumstances, he would have stopped and taken in the view. With Katira in danger, he could think of nothing other than racing toward their destination.

Long rides made for long thoughts. Bremin rode ahead, his head hanging lower with each passing hour. Mirelle rode at his side, her normally straight back rounded with exhaustion. Her hair had fallen loose of the comb Jarand had given her during the dance the night before and hung limp to the sides of her face.

If the task had fallen to him alone, Jarand would have given the stallion his head and let him run fast and hard. Bremin insisted on maintaining a more reasonable pace for the long journey. It took all Jarand's self-control not to throttle the man.

Jarand thought he saw the glimmer of a tear on Mirelle's cheek. He steered his mount so their knees were almost touching. "Want to talk about it?"

Mirelle stared off into the distance, toward the next town. "I can't help thinking this is somehow my fault."

A sharp stab of anguish echoed through their connection. Jarand longed to hold her in his arms. Anything to ease her guilt, make her feel secure. While riding he could only offer his words. "You can't allow yourself to start down that path. We can't change what we did or didn't do."

Another echoed stab lanced through their bond, this one laced with anger. "Does thinking that make you feel better?" Mirelle snapped. "Will your maxims get our daughter back?"

"No, Mirelle. I suppose not." No apology would soothe her. He knew better than to try. Underneath all the anger and guilt, Mirelle was near collapse. She needed rest. Fighting with her would help no one.

Jarand's own aches from long hours tracking in the chill air wormed their way into his back and behind his eyes. The power of the Khandashii lent him the strength to go on, but it wouldn't last. His discomfort gave him a measure of hope. Katira's captors would tire as well. No one could keep up this pace forever.

Heavy thunder clouds hung overhead making the road dark. The world held its breath, waiting for the storm. He didn't relish the thought of being caught in the downpour and pulled his cloak closer to his throat.

Bremin slowed and squinted his eyes at something behind them. Jarand turned in time to see a horse and rider round a bend in the road.

Jarand loosened his sword in its sheath and pulled his stone into his hand. From the corner of his eye, he saw Bremin and Mirelle do the same.

The rider came closer and Mirelle lowered her hands. "By rock and ruin, it's Elan."

Jarand raised an eyebrow. Mirelle wasn't one to curse. He removed his hand from his sword, Elan was no threat. "What's he doing here?"

"I was worried this might happen." Mirelle sat straighter to see Elan better.

"The boy has no idea what he's dealing with here. He should go home." Bremin grumbled. "He'll get in the way."

Jarand agreed with a nod. "His father won't forgive me if he gets killed out here."

The boy rode up to the three of them, breathless and barely hanging on to the reins. His arm was still bound across his chest. "I'm coming with you," he demanded when he finally caught his breath.

Jarand nudged his mount forward, but Mirelle stopped him with a hand. "Let me handle this."

She rode until she was side by side with the boy and spoke to him in a low voice.

At first the boy listened. Then his face scrunched in anger. Mirelle tried to soothe him, but he grew more and more upset.

"I don't care," he shouted at her. "I'm coming and that's final."

"Enough, fool boy!" Jarand hollered. He gripped the reins tighter to keep himself from walloping the boy. "Wasn't the blade in your chest enough to teach you these men are dangerous? You aren't any good to Katira dead."

Elan set his jaw, but there was uncertainty in his eyes. "Master Jarand, I'm no fool. I don't have the experience you have, but it doesn't mean I'm useless." His last few words grew more garbled. He paled, and his eyes rolled back. He slid from the saddle in a dead faint. Mirelle grabbed his free arm, preventing him from striking the ground at full force.

"Damn." Bremin said, resigned. "I guess we can't exactly leave him here, can we?"

"And we can't take him back either." Jarand turned to Mirelle who had jumped down to help the boy. "How is he?"

"He pressed himself too hard to catch up to us." Mirelle prodded at him. When he didn't stir right away, she pressed her hand to his chest. Her marks flickered briefly.

Elan gasped and sat up straight. "What happened?"

"You fainted," Bremin said with a chuckle.

Elan stood up and steadied himself against his horse's flank. "I wouldn't."

"Aye, but you did, son." Bremin adjusted his scarf. "You were talking and then pitched right off your mount. Perhaps you might want to reconsider joining us now?"

Elan brushed off the dust on his pants with his good hand. The motion made him wince. He gripped his bandaged shoulder. "I'm coming."

Bremin rolled his eyes at Jarand and turned his mount back down the road. "Persistent little imp, isn't he?"

"I have a feeling we're only seeing the beginning of it." Jarand said under his breath before turning to Elan. "You can come. As long as you promise to do exactly as you are told."

Elan cocked his head. His eyes narrowed as he studied Jarand and then Mirelle and Bremin who had turned to leave. "Really? You mean it?"

Jarand leaned back as he snapped the reins to get moving. "Don't make me regret it."

"I won't. I promise." Elan gripped the pommel with his good hand and set his foot in the stirrup.

Mirelle brought her horse alongside Jarand's. "I don't approve of this."

"I don't either. But if I forced him away, he would have followed or found his own way." Jarand peeked back to see if Elan had managed to get astride his horse. "This way I can keep track of him, keep him safe as best I can."

"This is too dangerous," Mirelle hissed. "What if he gets killed? Katira would never forgive us."

"We owe it to Katira. This might be her only chance to give him a proper farewell. She deserves that much."

Chapter 7

Katira awoke covered in sweat. Her heart raced. The nightmare clung to her.

A man murdered Elan. His desperate yells filled her head. Rough hands tied her to a horse.

She rubbed at her eyes and face and waited for her heart to slow. Her body ached, and she craved a few more hours sleep. A layer of dirt rubbed loose beneath her fingers. An unfamiliar smell filled the air. She sat up and searched for the familiar outline of the doorway and the corner of her parent's bed. Even through the darkest night she could always see the window. There was no window.

That was no nightmare.

A sound next to the bed prickled her skin.

She wasn't alone.

A sliver of light gleamed under the door, enough to see the rough shape of a person sleeping on the floor. Isben lay curled up beside the bed with his coat pulled up high around his neck. His head rested on one arm, like a child. The sound of his teeth chattering in the chill air of the room filled the darkness.

The bed had a single blanket and not a thick one either. She ran her hands over the scratchy wool, wondering if she should give it to him. Something else weighed down the top of the thin blanket. Her fingers touched the soft thick folds of fine cloth.

Isben not only gave her the bed and blanket, but his cloak as well. The gesture warmed her heart and made her smile.

Without a sound, she gathered the cloak and tucked it around him before curling herself under the blanket and drifting back to sleep.

A few hours later, rough hands shook her awake. She smelled Surasio before she saw him. Isben grunted as the man kicked him in the stomach.

"It's morning. We're leaving."

Isben hurried to his feet before he could be kicked again. "Yes, Master."

"You have two minutes." Surasio left as soon as he had come, slamming the door behind him.

Katira sat up with care. The abuses of the day before made each muscle and each rib throb with deep bruises. The simple task of putting on her boots hurt too much.

"Sit there a moment. Let me do it." Isben whispered. He slid on her boots and deftly laced them up. "Do you think you can walk?"

"Barely." Katira tried to smile, but a grimace won. "If he keeps this up he'll need a bucket to carry what's left of me."

"At least you're up to telling jokes." Isben bent to tie his own boots. "I told you a night's sleep would do wonders."

Katira picked up the cloak which now lay in a pile on the floor. The thought of him tucking her in the night before made her cheeks warm. "Here's this. Thank you."

He draped the cloak over an arm and swatted at the dust it had picked up from the floor. Katira spied a touch of color rise in his face. "It was nothing. I should be thanking you." He draped the cloak across her shoulders. "You should wear it again. I insist. I have my coat. The cloak's not mine, anyway."

Katira pulled the cloak around her and fastened the clasp at the neck. "Are you sure?"

Before he could answer, heavy footfalls announced Surasio's return. Isben hurried and opened the door to show they had done as he asked.

"Well?" Surasio shoved his arm down his pants and fished around, adjusting his bits far too much for any decent person. "Get going."

At his command, both Katira and Isben sped into the hall and out of the dirty little inn. The light of morning didn't improve Katira's impression of the place. The thick matted layer of straw covering the floor reeked of mold and vomit. Crusty plates and half empty ale glasses dotted the tables. She was glad they were leaving so quickly. Eating there would poison them all.

Walking brought the good kind of hurt. Her tight muscles loosened. Her stomach rumbled so loud it stopped Isben midstep.

"I'd best find us both some food or you might decide I might make for a tasty morsel."

Katira chuckled at Isben's attempt at a joke. "Food does sound good."

The first light of morning barely touched the sky in the distance. They entered the stable and Surasio went to work saddling his horse. The stable boy from the night before was nowhere to be seen. When Surasio fought to buckle the belly strap of the saddle, the horse shied away and tossed his head in fear. Katira silently hoped the horse would kick the vicious worm of a man in the head.

Isben wasted no time getting his mare ready. He stroked her nose and patted her flanks as he worked. His calm confidence reminded Katira of when she watched her father shoeing horses.

Surasio shoved past, leading his horse behind him. "Follow me."

"Master?" Isben started, keeping his eyes on his hands as he finished fastening the last buckle. "Will we be stopping for supplies?"

"Supplies?" A devilish glint shone in Surasio's eyes. "I suppose we could pick some things up as we leave."

Isben exchanged a worried glance with Katira.

They had no choice but to follow Surasio as he wound back through the winding streets of Cerro's Cross and to a run-down grocer's shop. He tossed the reins over a post and indicated they should do the same.

"Inside, now," Surasio ordered. His smug grin sent shivers cascading down Katira's skin.

Inside the shop, crates and baskets littered the floor. Dust, dirt, and traces of vermin filled every corner. The smell of animal urine and rot made Katira's eyes water.

An elderly man shuffled out from the back room and over to a stool behind a cluttered counter. "Awful early, sir." He plucked a pipe from the mess on the counter and stuck it between his rotting teeth. "What can I do for you?"

Surasio detailed a short list for the man, mostly food stuffs. Katira's appetite disappeared. Nothing from this shop could be less appealing.

"Anything else for you, sir?" the shopkeeper asked.

Surasio shot a silencing look toward Isben and Katira before returning his attention to the man. "Information. What news from Fordzala?"

The shopkeeper lit a twist of paper from a smoking lamp and held the flame to the bowl of his pipe. "Nothing too unusual. People are angry about something. The guards have been mandated to deal with it." He took a deep draw and blew out a cloud of smoke. "Like I said, nothing new."

"Could you be more specific? My business takes me there. Surely there's more you could tell me." Surasio flashed a coin in his palm.

The shopkeeper leaned forward on the rickety table, his bulk causing it to shift precariously. "Between you and me, I think those vile wielders have something to do with it. People don't just disappear."

"Funny you should say that." Surasio reached for the stone hanging from the chain around his neck.

Isben's breath caught in his throat. He stepped further away from the two men at the table, bringing Katira with him. "Don't watch."

"Don't watch what?" She strained to peer around Isben.

"Just don't." From the look on his face, he meant it.

Lines of light shone from Surasio's arms - the same lines she had seen on Papan, the lines she had seen when Surasio placed the oath on her. The old man backed away, his hands spread out before him like a shield. A symbol formed and hung in the air between them for a split second before piercing the shopkeeper's chest.

The old man gasped and clutched at his chest before staggering backward and falling to the ground. Katira lunged forward. She could help him, save him.

Isben grabbed her and held her tight. "There's nothing you can do," he murmured. "Surasio stopped his heart."

The old man twitched and fell still. Surasio bent over him and plucked his coin along with a handful of others from the man's coin pouch.

"Take whatever supplies you need." Surasio rifled through the dusty boxes on a shelf and selected a handful of items. "This old fellow doesn't mind a bit."

Katira couldn't move. Surasio turned and left the shop showing no more remorse than if he had stepped on a spider. The sight sent a chill down her spine.

"He killed him." She hugged her arms to her chest. "How could he do that?"

Isben turned her away and led her out of the shop. "It's against the code. He's not allowed to kill with the power unless his life is in danger. And even then, there are strict rules."

Katira swallowed hard hoping to push down the horror she had witnessed. It dug in deeper, turning her stomach. "We've got to do something about this, fight him. He has to be stopped."

"Someone will, in time. When other Stonebearers learn of this, there will be no mercy for him." Isben clenched his fist in frustration. "He doesn't deserve the stone he wears."

RAIN SOAKED through Jarand's coat and dripped from his beard. The downpour had lasted three long hours, drenching them and churning the road to mud.

Elan's head hung lower and lower over his chest as evening progressed. Jarand watched the boy from the corner of his eye. Having him fall off the horse again would slow them down. Worse, if he broke open his wound, Mirelle hadn't regained enough of her strength to heal him again.

"Remind me how much you love this daughter of yours?" Bremin asked as he wrung the water from his scarf.

Jarand hoped the question was in jest. "Are you complaining? Sleeping in the rain is far worse than riding in it."

"It's not that. We're being watched."

Jarand swung his head around and scanned the road behind them and to either side. Mist swirled around the feet of their horses and formed odd shapes in the darkness.

"Are you sure you're not jumping at shadows?" Jarand loosened his sword in its scabbard.

"I think there are shadow hounds around." Bremin touched the knife at his belt.

Jarand sucked air between his teeth. Shadow hounds were the last thing he wanted to deal with. "How sure are you?"

"Sure enough to suggest finding a defensible position."

The warning came too late.

A low growl came from the bushes ahead. Jarand jumped down from his horse and pulled his sword free.

"What is it?" Mirelle asked.

"Hounds." Jarand put himself between the dark tree line and the group. "Stay back with Elan while I deal with this. Bremin, you too. This isn't safe for you."

Bremin jumped down and pulled his knife free. "I'll make that decision for myself, thank you."

A shadow streaked out from the trees, bounding toward them. Jarand took hold of his power and formed the glyph to bring his blade awake. The steel shone brightly in the dark and the hound shied away at the sudden light.

"There are at least two more. Stay alert." Bremin held his glowing knife at the ready.

The hounds wasted no time. They dodged in, jaws snapping, moving fast. Jarand dispatched one with a clean upward stroke, sending the body sailing off to the side of the road. Bremin lunged forward, stabbing one in the chest.

A flash of light burst from behind them. A hound smoldered not far from the front of Mirelle's mount. The horse shied away at the smell.

Bremin raised an eyebrow. "I love that woman."

"So do I." Jarand grinned and set the point of his sword down in the mud.

A snarl came from the shadows. A hound leapt up at Bremin, latching onto his forearm. Bremin shook it free with a yell.

Jarand chopped it in half before it hit the ground. He squinted through the mist. "Is that the last of them?"

"I think so." Bremin grimaced and grabbed at his arm.

Jarand quickly wiped his blade clean and slid it back into its scabbard before grabbing hold of Bremin's arm and tearing back his shirt to reveal torn skin. "Have you ever been bitten before?"

Bremin cringed and looked away. "I haven't had the pleasure. Damn, that venom burns." His face paled as his head dipped. The venom worked through his body quickly, aided by the pounding of his heart.

"Can you deal with it or do you need Mirelle's help?" Jarand caught Mirelle's attention and gestured for her to come closer.

He waved her off. "Better if I do it. Save her for when we really need her."

Bremin found a low stone to sit on. The marks on his arms flared and the area around the bite glowed a dull red. He groaned and gritted his teeth.

"What's he doing?" Elan asked, all traces of sleep gone.

"He has to cleanse himself from the shadow hound venom." Jarand answered, readying himself to move quickly. "It'll only take a minute. That's not what I'm worried about, though."

Elan's eyes grew wider. "Then what is?"

The marks faded and Bremin released a pent-up breath before pitching sideways in a dead faint. Jarand caught him before he fell in the mud.

"This part." Jarand grunted as he supported Bremin's weight. "He faints when he uses the power. No one quite knows why. The more he uses, the more dangerous it is for him. When he wakes, he won't remember what happened."

"Should I check him?" Mirelle asked.

"He didn't use that much." Jarand watched his friend closely for the signs indicating he was starting to wake. A full minute passed before Bremin blinked and shook his head.

He took one look at his arm before blanching and turning away. "Do I want to know why I'm bleeding?"

"Shadow hounds." Jarand took a roll of bandaging linen from Mirelle's outstretched hand and wrapped and bound the wound. "We dealt with them."

"And one bit me? That's a pity. I liked this shirt." He scanned the ground, quickly assessing the scene. "Did I kill any?"

Jarand pulled the sleeve back over the bandage. "One." He scanned the dark mist at the edge of the woods. The sooner they reached the city, the better. "We best keep moving."

"Agreed." Bremin flexed his arm and wiggled his fingers. "There's no use hanging around these parts." He pulled himself into his saddle with a grunt. "How many did you get?"

"Two." Jarand grinned and swung into his saddle.

"Show off."

They reached Cerro's Cross in the small hours of the morning, hungry and tired. Bremin jumped down from his mount as they passed through the gate and tossed his reins to Jarand. "Go find a place to get warm and dry until dawn. I have some searching to do."

Jarand tossed the reins back in Bremin's face and jumped down. "If you believe I'm going to go tend horses while you search for traces of my daughter, you're wrong."

Bremin looked Jarand over from head to toe. "You draw attention. It's best if I go unnoticed." He didn't wait for Jarand to respond before handing him the reins once more and turning and leaving.

Jarand squeezed the bundle of reins in his hand the same way he wanted to wring Bremin's neck. Shouting at Bremin in the middle of the street would prove the man's point all too well.

"I can't believe this." Jarand led both horses to a nearby hitching post.

Mirelle stroked his back. "You trust him. That's what you always say. He's best at finding information. Let him do his work." She straightened the high collar of his coat. "Admit it, you leave quite the impression. Normal folk don't carry big swords."

"Fine," he grumbled. "Bremin's right. But I don't have to like it."

Along a side street they found an abandoned stable attached to the back of a broken-down building. Jarand tested the door and found it unlocked. Rats scurried away from the door as it swung open, disappearing into the piles of garbage stacked along the walls. Rain trickled in from breaks in the roof. A ladder led to a shallow loft.

He led the horses in and Mirelle and Elan followed close behind. "This will do for a few hours. Looks like there's hay up in the loft. You two get some rest."

"You need rest, too." Mirelle said.

"I'll be up once I've cared for the horses." He didn't want to tell her he couldn't sleep. His mind churned with worry and wouldn't let him rest even if he tried. At least caring for the horses would let him work and use his hands. He could lose himself in the rhythm of brushing and feeding for a while.

Mirelle climbed the ladder. Elan followed her, too tired from the long day's journey to argue. Scarcely more than a day had passed since they found him bleeding behind their cottage at Namragan. Jarand had to admit the boy's determination impressed him. He hoped it would be enough for the days ahead.

After feeding and watering the four horses, Jarand lost himself in the calm repetition of brushing out their coats.

The stable door opened with a small squeak. Bremin stepped in and shut it behind him. "You didn't rest, did you?"

"Neither did you."

"I know my limits. Do you know yours?"

Jarand tucked the brush into the saddle bag, ignoring Bremin's question. "Did you find anything?"

"We just missed them." Bremin fished around in the satchel Mirelle had left with her horse and pulled out an apple. "They holed up in a rat's nest of an inn and left at first light. I reckon they are only a few hours ahead of us."

Jarand had only one question, and he was afraid to ask it. He had to know. "Is Katira okay?"

Bremin grew serious. "Hard to say. She's alive. That's the best I can tell you."

Jarand hefted a saddle in preparation to leave. "Anything else?"

Bremin swallowed down a bite of apple. "A shopkeeper was found dead a few hours ago. I'm getting the feeling it wasn't natural."

Jarand's guardian nature flexed, eager to put this law-breaking Stonebearer in the cells deep beneath Amul Dun where he belonged. He wanted nothing more than to make him pay for what he had done.

He rested his hand on the solid metal of his hilt. "We best go check it out."

～

OUT ON THE main street of Cerro's cross, it was early enough that only the tradesmen had started their day. A baker haggled with the man who sold the firewood next to his cart heavy with everything from kindling to uncut logs. Livestock lumbered along in the street, heading to the butcher's market. A cloth merchant organized his bolts of cloth into a dramatic rainbow of color.

No sign of the rain clouds from the night before remained. The sky shone an eye piercing blue.

Jarand, along with Mirelle and Elan, did their best to keep up with Bremin as he worked his way through the street. If it wasn't for his red scarf, Jarand would have lost him.

It didn't take long for Bremin to find his target.

Most shopkeepers prided themselves on keeping a tidy, well-organized shop. This one didn't. Jarand scrunched up his nose at the smell even before he stepped in the door.

Mirelle turned to Elan as she stepped over the threshold. "You don't have to see this. Perhaps you should stay outside."

Elan set his jaw into a firm line, looking so much like Lucan it made Jarand shake his head. "I'll be fine."

Jarand pushed down a sigh and stepped inside. Fool boy's stubborn pride would get him killed some day.

Bremin knelt behind a counter ready to collapse under a pile of rubble. A body sprawled next to him.

Elan hung back in the doorway. "Why haven't they removed him yet? People know he's dead. Why wait?"

"Those who have families and coin to nag the pastors and gravediggers are attended to first. I doubt this fellow had either. It might be hours yet before they come." Bremin studied the patterns in the filthy floor and pointed out the boot prints. "It's good news for us. Hardly anyone has come in to disturb the evidence."

"What have you learned so far?" Mirelle asked.

Bremin scooted to one side and motioned Mirelle to join him. "Bodies aren't my specialty. Perhaps you should look."

Mirelle studied the corpse, peeling back an eyelid and looking in the mouth. Jarand could see her checking things as if she were checking off items on a list.

"No marks showing signs of a fight or struggle. No bruises. No bleeding in the mouth. He's not the healthiest fellow. His poor diet would have killed him in a year, maybe two."

She unbuttoned his shirt and studied the skin covering his chest. "It was either his head or his heart. Anything else would have taken too long. There would have been more struggle, more things in the shop kicked around." She pointed to a spot on the chest. "There. See the raised skin? The clean edge? That's a glyph welt."

"If that's true, there should be Khandashii residue floating around here." Jarand added.

Bremin cocked an eyebrow. "Then you should check."

"Right." Jarand opened himself to the power, allowing the pain to fill him as it stretched and flexed. A subtle ripple in the air centered around the body. Jarand wasn't skilled at reading past signatures, but this one rang clear. A single precise green tinged glyph had been used.

"This is bender work."

Mirelle covered her mouth as if she might be sick. "But that means ..." She tapped on the corpse's chest and gagged. "His heart was turned into something else."

"We could open him to see," Bremin suggested. From the sly look on his face, Jarand wasn't sure how serious he was.

"Absolutely not," Mirelle shot back. "That's disgusting."

Elan clamped a hand over his mouth and hurried out of the shop to empty his stomach.

Jarand raised an eyebrow at Bremin. "You did that on purpose."

"Of course I did." Bremin stood and brushed the dust from his hands. "What's the use of having him around if we can't have a bit of fun?"

"Stop it, boys." Mirelle wasn't having any part of the joke. "This has to be our man. I can't think of two benders going rogue. Which means Katira was here in this shop."

Jarand examined the footprints in the dust and filth. Those near the door had been ruined but a clear set of prints stood out in the dust deeper in the shop. He pointed. "These smaller prints. They look like hers."

"Is there a way to be sure?" Mirelle stooped to look.

Elan had returned. He looked green and refused to even turn toward the body on the floor. He bent to get a better look at a print. "They're Katira's. I fixed her boot not a month ago. There was a split in the heel and it needed to be replaced. This print's heel is a sharp square with two edges rounded, like the ones I make." He scanned the floor, looking for something more.

"Here." He pointed at another small print. "This one all four of the corners are blunted, more worn. She was here."

"What can you remember from the night she was taken? Could you describe the men?" Bremin asked.

"I didn't see much." Elan rubbed at the bandage beneath his shirt. "There were two men. The one who threw the knife had a foul temperament and was short. The other was younger. I don't remember much more."

Bremin swore under his breath. "If this is who I believe it is, then we're in for trouble. I can guarantee it."

Jarand's strained patience snapped. "Out with it."

Bremin met his eye, deadly serious. "It's Surasio. It has to be."

Over the years Jarand had had several dealings with the man, none good. The thought of that foul beast having his hands on Katira made Jarand's blood run cold.

"We go straight to Fordzala." Jarand brushed the dust from his hands. "Rats like him prefer big cities. He's holed up there for ages. With luck we can break up his nest and get Katira back."

Bremin traced a map in the dust on the floor and rested his finger on a point in the center. "He has to make it through Burk's Gap. Between here and Fordzala, it's the best place to hide. I'm willing to bet he stays there tonight."

"Doesn't explain why he would want Katira." Elan scooted further away from the dead man. "Doesn't it seem odd to anyone else that he would take her?"

Jarand was about to ask Elan to leave the discussion. He didn't belong there, and they had work to do.

"He's right." Mirelle added. "Namragan is small and isolated, hard to get to. What would his reason be for going that far from his usual haunts?"

"To get to Jarand." Bremin reasoned. "It has to be. Jarand's made powerful enemies over the years. That's one reason the two of you went into hiding in the first place, isn't it? Perhaps Surasio finally scraped together enough information to find you."

Jarand rested his hand on Mirelle's shoulder. If this had been meant as a trap for him, then it was his fault it had happened. "Why didn't he attack me? Why her?"

Bremin crossed his arms over his chest and tilted his head. "No bender in his right mind will attack a guardian. Least of all you. You'd rip him to pieces. He wants you drawn away from your home, put off balance, and made to be tired and worried." He gestured south. "Taking Katira is the perfect way to do that."

KATIRA LOOKED BACK, past the walls of Cerro's Cross, past the low rolling hills, and strained to see any hint of the dramatic mountain peaks marking her way home. They had come so far. All the black rain clouds from the night before had bunched up at the base of her mountains, covering them in a thick white blanket.

Isben told stories and jokes as they rode, each one falling flatter and flatter until he gave up. Katira couldn't laugh. She couldn't stop thinking of the flash of light leaving Surasio's fingers and how the shopkeeper crumpled to the floor. It had been a stupid, pointless death.

"Do you want to talk about it?" Isben asked after a long silence, all traces of humor gone.

"Why?" she asked. "Why would he do something like that? It makes no sense."

"He was showing us he's in control."

Katira scoffed. "Showing me he could torture you with a wave of his hand wasn't enough? Making it so he could do the same to me wasn't enough? What will he do next? Drown a basket of kittens?"

Isben reached up and snagged a brilliant red leaf from an over-hanging tree branch and examined it.

Overhead, the sky shone a brilliant blue, far too cheerful to dwell on Surasio's foul deeds. "Tell me about where we are headed next," Katira said, determined to change the subject.

"It will be the biggest city you have seen so far, although not a fraction of Fordzala. It has great walls as tall as ..." He scanned the surrounding countryside and pointed toward a slender pine pushing through the forest canopy. "As that tree over there."

Katira craned her neck to see the top. "You're joking. Why would they need a wall so big?"

Isben shrugged. "To keep invading armies out. Burk's Gap is a trade hub between the Southern Road and the Great East Passage, anything going anywhere passes through it." He handed her the leaf. "It's under Fordzala's protection. Too much at stake if crime gets out of hand. The standing guard there don't like people like Surasio, so this might be interesting."

"Wouldn't it be nice to see him dragged away?" Katira mused to herself. Something Isben had said that morning tickled the edge of her brain. She'd meant to ask him about it. "You said this wasn't your cloak. Did you steal it?" She was only half-joking. He didn't seem like the stealing type. Or the kidnapping type, for that matter.

"No, I didn't steal it. It belongs to my master." He fingered the edge of his open coat. The further south they traveled, the warmer the air became. "He made me take it when he sent me north."

"Where is he now?"

"Near Fordzala. There are ruins outside of the town. We were working there before he got himself into trouble." Isben tightened his hold on the reins and stiffened in the saddle. Whatever happened in those ruins had shaken him more than he was letting on.

She laid a hand on his shoulder, remembering how scared she was when she first learned about Papan's abilities. Having Elan to talk to made it bearable. "Would you like to talk about it?"

Isben dared a look toward Surasio and shook his head. "Not with him around."

Katira steered the subject back to safer territory. "Is that where we are going, the ruins?"

Isben nodded. "I believe so."

They continued to talk as the hills rolled by punctuated by an occasional field of wheat or ranch. Thin streams of smoke rose from homesteads hidden in the trees.

Isben nudged Katira as they rounded a curve in the road. "Look ahead. You can see Burk's Gap and its outlying villages. We should arrive before nightfall if I've judged the distance right."

Katira looked up to see what he was talking about. "Will he stop there for the night, even with the guard?"

"Knowing Surasio, he's got a friend or two hiding somewhere. It's safer and easier to stop in the city than to risk a night on the side of the road."

They continued to ride. Katira watched as the city loomed closer and closer until it grew impossibly large, far bigger than Cerro's Cross, and she'd thought that had been huge. Men patrolling the top of the wall looked no bigger than ants marching back and forth. A line of carts, horses, and people waited to enter.

To her right, an elderly man and a sour-faced woman who might have been his daughter sat on a rickety cart filled to bursting with sacks of grain.

Ahead of Surasio, a stunning woman draped in bright red sat atop an equally impressive midnight black mare whose coat had been brushed until it shone. A dark veil covered her head so only her eyes could be seen. A man wearing a coat bearing the insignia of a dagger and an hourglass led the horse. He walked shoulders back, head high, scanning the road.

Isben saw the question forming before Katira had a chance to voice it. "She's a mystic. People pay her well for a glimpse of their future. Judging by her clothing and guard, she's been quite successful."

"Can she really?" Katira had never seen such a sight in Namragan. She tried not to stare. "I mean, if I asked her a question about my future, could she answer it?"

A crippled man hobbled past with a crutch, begging for coin. Isben tucked his coin purse inside his coat, well out of reach. "If you supply enough coin, she will tell you anything you want to hear."

Ahead, a woman walked the line of carts and horses selling bread from a large basket balanced on the top of her head. Isben waved her over and bought two rolls for each of them.

"But can she actually do it?" Katira asked between bites. Bread tasted so much better after being hungry all day. "I mean, does she have a way to see the future?"

"Most can't. It's a hoax. The same as the fellow selling magical cures from his wagon up ahead." Isben used his loaf to discreetly point at the man hawking elixirs from the seat on the front of his cart. "However, there are those who can among Stonebearers. It's a rare talent. What would you want to know?"

Katira continued to stare in the mystic's direction. "I need to know if Elan survived. Would she know something like that?"

"Hard to say." Isben ripped off another piece of his roll. "If you had something of his, perhaps. But like I said, most mystics aren't the real thing."

Katira traced her fingers around the knots of the bracelet Elan had given her. It wasn't something of his, but he had worked on it for hours and hours. Perhaps it would be enough.

She sighed and tucked the bracelet back under her sleeve. It was no use even thinking about it. Surasio would never let her talk to anyone, let alone a strange mystic.

The massive gates of Burk's Gap loomed ahead. The same as before entering Cerro's Cross, Katira turned back toward the road, clinging to the hope that perhaps out in the distance she might see Papan coming for her. The knots of people waiting for their turn to enter the city blocked her view. If Papan was back there, she would have no way of knowing.

Thoughts of escape crossed her mind. She could jump down from the horse and dart into the crowd. With the confusion of all these people, buildings, alleys, and dark corners and crannies, she could disappear. In the commotion of the crowd it would be impossible for Surasio to follow, she was sure of it.

If it wasn't for the death oath, she would try. There had to be another way. Perhaps she could get a guard to suspect him, see his marks.

No. If that were to happen Surasio would trigger the oath on them both and let them die in the street before he allowed himself to be taken.

The familiar metallic ping of a hammer on an anvil broke through the wave of sound filling the city. Katira whipped her head toward it. For a moment, she imagined her father standing there, working over a piece of glowing hot iron. His wide shoulders and capable hands shaping and crafting something useful.

This man worked bare-chested, his skin shining with sweat from the heat of the fire. His skin bore many white puckered scars from where the metal had burned him. Unlike Papan, though, this man did not bear the marks of a wielder.

She wanted it to be Papan. Stonebearer or not, he had cared for her, he had taught her. He would come for her.

Until then, she would search out a way to beat Surasio.

REGULUS DIDN'T RECOGNIZE the man Tash had brought in for Wrothe. The neatly trimmed beard and close-cropped hair, paired with his distinct high-collared long coat, showed he came from the Eastern Flame Order of Stonebearers. Regulus cataloged the identifying information away. If he survived this endless ordeal, he would make an accounting of all Wrothe's foul deeds.

Wrothe held the man immobile with her power and plunged a stone blade into the thick muscle of his thigh. He screamed and the lines along his arms and chest flared bright before he fell quiet, panting with shock.

"You think you can resist me?" she asked, her voice tender and soft. "Try resisting this for a while. You'll change your mind."

Regulus refused to cover his ears or hide himself away from the horror. He forced himself to watch on as fellow members of the Society suffered, as if by suffering with them he could absolve himself of the relentless guilt.

Wrothe had stolen knowledge from his mind the same way a thief stole jewels. With it, she knew where to find his network of friends and fellow Stonebearers.

It took three days of prying, of torture, before she broke through the barrier he built to keep her out, revealing his most guarded and shameful secret. In a misguided effort to protect the innocent people of the world from shadow creatures, he'd created a weapon that rendered Stonebearers powerless.

The High Lady Alystra had made him swear on his stone not to tell a soul. And now these weapons had fallen into the hands of Wrothe. Weapons she now used on the Stonebearers she'd taken.

Regulus pleaded with the demoness. "This is a waste of time," he said. "You know what will happen, why continue?"

She wrenched the blade free. The man cried out again through grit teeth. Regulus cringed as he heard the point break within the wound. If it remained, the man had only a few days to live. If only Regulus had control of his own power, he could do something, anything, to save the man.

"Unless you have a better way to convince your fellow Stonebearers to join me, keep silent." She studied the broken edge of the bloodied blade and set it back into the small chest with the others. "Besides, your expertise of these weapons leaves much to be desired.

I need to know the extent of what they can do to your fellow immortals."

She had killed three Stonebearers already. No doubt more would die before she was satisfied.

Tash stood in the corner of the cramped cell and stared into space. He had done his job and had lured the man to Wrothe. When instructed, he would leave and find another.

The man on the stone table fought to use his power. They all had. Regulus watched on as the glow of his lines flickered and failed. As with the others, the man's efforts were rewarded with fresh agony as his power fought against the elements in the blade fragment and refused to obey him.

With the task done, Wrothe left the cell. Tash followed her without a word, like a trained dog. Regulus would have to follow before too long as well. The binding she had placed on him never allowed him to wander too far from her. He had a moment, no more. He ripped a strip of cloth from the man's discarded cloak and bound the wound. At least it would stop the bleeding.

The man flinched away, confused. "Why are you doing this? What is this madness?"

"What is your name?"

"Davin Holyoak of Trinium." He sucked air through his teeth in a long hiss as Regulus pulled the bandage tight. When the pain subsided, he studied Regulus for a moment before the realization dawned on him. "Tash said you lost your mind, that you killed Catrim."

"Lies. That monster is all that's left of Catrim, I'm afraid." Regulus stifled a groan as the need to hurry after Wrothe grew stronger. "I can't stay. If you want to live, don't fight her. Give her what she wants. If you're convincing enough, she might leave your mind intact."

"You can't be serious."

"No more need die. Not for the likes of her."

Davin grasped the stone around his neck. "I hold to my oaths. I won't be disloyal to the Society."

"This threat is beyond what the oaths were meant to protect. You can't protect our ideals if you're dead." The binding to Wrothe began to burn. His time was up. "Save your strength, you'll need it."

"Wait!"

Regulus hurried from the room before Davin could say more, letting her pull direct him to where she had gone. The ruin's dungeons dug deep into the stone of the surrounding hills. At the end of each hall, a row of windows opened out toward the sea. Iron torch brackets hung empty, marking the way into the darkness of the other end of the hall.

Since Isben left, Tash had brought nine Stonebearers to the ruins, including Davin. One of these Wrothe had ensnared and turned into another mindless drone like Tash. She locked the surviving five down in the cells. Regulus could hear their groans as he passed.

Cold fingers of guilt dragged Regulus into a deeper despair. He hoped Isben could succeed somehow, but the odds were stacked against him. Fordzala had been drained of its protective force. The surrounding towns would lose their Stonebearers in the space of a week.

Regulus beat his fist against the dank stone wall. If he could unlock his power from Wrothe's grasp, he could do something to save them.

Chapter
8

Night fell long before Jarand and the others reached the closed city gates of Burk's Gap. Two rounded mountain slopes rose on either side, making the town look as if cupped in a giant hand. Homes and businesses grew up the hills, hugging the slopes like lichen.

The high walls meant to keep the city safe were now an impassible barrier between Jarand, Mirelle, and their daughter. Surasio most likely hid behind those walls with Katira. Entering Burk's Gap meant readying for an attack.

Memories of another battlefield rushed into Jarand's mind. Bodies of the soldiers who fought at his command piled at his feet. The enemy pressed in. Even with his great sword, with his skill, he couldn't keep them back. A blow nearly cut him in half. He squeezed his eyes shut, pressing the vision of flames and blood away.

Mirelle laid a hand on his shoulder, helping him come back to the present. She always knew when the memories hit, when the nightmares came. "That time is past," she said. "Stay focused on what is important."

Jarand forced himself to draw slow, steady breaths and think of

Katira, and how she needed him. The memory withdrew, releasing its sharp claws. He patted Mirelle's hand, letting her know the terror had gone.

Two uniformed men slouched off to one side of the gate, talking and laughing to each other. A brazier full of coals glowed at their feet, painting their faces a devilish red in the flickering light.

When Jarand and the others drew closer, one guard straightened and stepped into the road. He held a long pike against his shoulder like he didn't want to be bothered using it. Jarand wondered if he even knew how.

Before Jarand could say a word, Bremin hopped down and approached the man. His easy smile and good humor had the man smiling and laughing within minutes. Bremin placed a pouch of coin in the man's hand and, before long, they were being escorted through a concealed door behind the gatehouse.

On the other side of the door, Bremin tipped his wide brimmed hat at the guard. "Next time I come through, we should have a nice drink together."

"Aye. That we will, Master Bremin." The guard touched the brim of his hat in a friendly salute.

Further down the main street, Jarand brought his horse up alongside Bremin's. "Friend of yours?"

Bremin grinned. "Is now. Having a few guards on my side comes in handy, especially in the larger cities. Whenever I get into trouble, I have somewhere to turn for help."

"Let's hope we don't need your friends anytime soon."

"Suit yourself." Bremin tugged at his scarf. "I'm serious about settling down and getting myself a stiff drink with that fellow the second this is over."

Mirelle nudged her way between the two men. "Please tell me one of you has a plan. I don't savor wandering from inn to inn for the rest of the night."

Bremin scratched at the hair under his hat. "I know two of the innkeepers here, and one owes me a favor. I think it's time to pay him a visit."

"What about other Stonebearers?" Mirelle asked. "Surely the companionship here would be of assistance."

"Here? Haven't been any for years. The hate in this town runs deep for our kind. Makes it too dangerous to maintain a presence. However, there are pairs in both of the next towns. They keep tabs on the place. I'll contact the pair in Sulsudy in the morning. They keep informed about things in Fordzala and might have news concerning Regulus." He tugged on the reins and clicked his tongue to move his horse forward. "We'll visit Mara's Wheel first."

Jarand went cold at the mention of his master's name. Regulus had been the father Jarand needed as a bull-headed youth. His master was in trouble, these rumors were a cry for help. The High Lady had personally tasked him to find him and learn the truth. To delay acting on her orders risked putting his loyalty to her and the Order in question.

She would have to understand. He wouldn't abandon his daughter, not now, not when she was so close to coming into her power. Not when she was in danger. Once she was safe, he would continue after Master Regulus, but not before.

They continued down the central road, crossing through the deep shadows between the streetlights at either side. This place would be cheery in the daytime. Baskets full of flowers hung from the light posts. This late at night, their bright yellows and reds faded to dusky blues and grays. The few people dotting the street hurried about their business, none giving them a second look as they passed.

At the inn, Bremin dismounted and tossed his reins over the rail out front, not bothering to tie them. Jarand did the same and tromped up the wooden stairs behind him.

Bremin turned and stopped him with a hand. "It's better if I go alone."

Jarand pushed the hand away. "This is my daughter we're talking about. I'm coming with you."

Bremin stood, blocking Jarand's path. The only way past him was through him. "Someone needs to stay out here and keep an eye on them." He cast his eyes over Mirelle and Elan, who both looked ready to fall asleep in their saddles. "I wasn't joking about having problems in this place."

"Don't be long," Jarand grumbled, "or I'll find a reason to come in after you." He glared as Bremin entered the inn alone.

Mirelle patted her horse's neck before dismounting and lacing her arm through his. "Have patience. You've told me many times how much you value his skills."

Jarand didn't want to have patience. He wanted to find Katira. "What if they ask Bremin something about Katira he doesn't know?"

"You'll drive yourself crazy." She pulled him close and leaned her head against his arm. "You're not yourself right now. You need to rest."

He wrapped his arms around her, taking much needed comfort in her presence. "I can't. Not until she's found."

Elan slid awkwardly from his saddle, holding tight to the pommel with his good hand. He stumbled when his feet hit the ground. Judging from his stiff-legged walk, the ride had been hard on him.

Mirelle crossed the porch over to him. "How are you feeling?"

Jarand paced along the porch, watching the road. Unease prickled the back of his neck.

"I'm fine," Elan said, his voice sounded too quiet compared to the noise coming from the inn.

"If you plan on traveling with us, you need to tell me the truth." Mirelle pressed. "Now, how are you?"

The boy ran his fingers along the edge of his coat. "I've never been this far from home before. I didn't think it would bother me, but the further we go, the more out of place I feel." He spoke slowly, each phrase hanging in the air before he said the next.

She adjusted a wrap around his arm. "How about your shoulder?"

"It aches, although not as bad as before." He gave it a shrug and winced. "I can't stop thinking about Katira. Do you think they've hurt her?"

Jarand attempted an understanding smile. "The sooner she's found the better, for all of us."

A wormy fellow who smelled as if he had had a few too many drinks stumbled his way toward them, a hateful sneer on his face. He shrank back a step when Jarand straightened to his full height to face him.

"We don't like strangers around here. State your business," the man slurred.

Jarand lifted the corner of his coat and placed a hand on the hilt of his great sword. "It's of no concern to you, be on your way."

The man leaned in closer. "Oh, but it is. It's my duty to ensure no unwanted folk pass through here. Show me your arm."

"And if I refuse?"

"You wouldn't want to do that." The drunk tilted his head toward the street where four other men waited in the shadows.

"Are you threatening me?" Jarand asked, keeping his voice deadly calm. He withdrew the blade a fraction.

Just then, Bremin stepped out the door talking and laughing with a jolly innkeeper wearing a pristine white apron. The man pressed a loaf of bread into Bremin's hands, insisting he take it. When they saw Jarand towering over the drunk, they stopped laughing.

"Gargan, you slime," the innkeeper bellowed, all traces of laughter gone. "I've told you to never harass my customers or I'll tell your mother."

The man cowered back. "They look suspicious. I had to be sure."

"You look suspicious." The innkeeper poked Gargan in the shoulder and he stumbled back a step. "Perhaps I should tell the guard what you've been up to. It's been weeks since they've put someone in the stocks. I've saved some rotten potatoes to throw just in case."

Gargan cringed. "No, ain't needed. I'm gone already." He turned and slunk back into the alleyway where the other shadows waited.

The innkeeper turned to Jarand and extended a hand. "Master Sopan at your service. A friend of Bremin's is a friend of mine. Sorry for Gargan there, he's always been a bit strange around newcomers. You'd best be careful, though. He and his friends can be persistent."

Bremin raised an eyebrow. "Potatoes? Isn't it supposed to be tomatoes?"

"Potatoes hurt more, smell worse, and cost less. It's worth it." Master Sopan smiled and adjusted his apron around his thick middle. "I'm serious about watching your back around here."

Jarand agreed with a nod. "Thank you for the warning. It's always a pleasure to receive a warm welcome."

"The pleasure is mine." Master Sopan returned his attention back to Bremin. "Promise me the next time you're in town you'll stay and enjoy a meal. It's been too long since we've shared a table." He gave a hearty chuckle. "I wish you all the best in your endeavors." He turned and hurried back into the inn.

Bremin divided the warm loaf Master Sopan had given him among the group. Jarand inhaled the fresh-baked aroma. It smelled like heaven.

"I have good news," Bremin said around a mouthful of bread.

Of all Bremin's traits, withholding news like this was his worst. Jarand crushed the chunk of bread in his hands. "Speak, man!"

"She's in an inn up on the west side of the town. Sopan's narrowed it down to two for me." Bremin adjusted his scarf with a triumphant smile. "We can be there within the hour."

JARAND CAREFULLY CONSIDERED what they knew as their small group followed Bremin up the hill on the west side of Burk's Gap. Bremin had insisted they leave the horses behind with the innkeeper since this place had a reputation for horses to go missing even in broad daylight.

If Master Sopan's information was right, Katira would be in one of two inns high in the grimy fingernails of the city. The further they ventured from the main street, the darker the passes became.

"Can Master Sopan be trusted?" With so much at stake, Jarand couldn't bear the thought of being misled or delayed.

"I don't think he would intentionally lead us astray." Bremin's gaze darted to the shadows of the alley ways as they passed. His hand hovered near the hidden sheath where he kept his long knife. "His loyalty earns him good coin. He'll be rewarded when this is over. It's the others who have me on edge. Gargan and his friends have been untold trouble in the past."

The man's unease unsettled Jarand. He bound his stone to his palm and checked his sword. "What kind of trouble?" Using power here would attract the unwelcome attention of the guard, but if it meant the difference between life and death, he would gladly risk it.

"Trouble enough for the Tower to remove the companionship stationed here for good."

Mirelle pulled her cloak tighter around her. She would never admit to being afraid, but this place unnerved her. Her unease whispered through their bond.

When they reached the first inn, Mirelle and Elan hung back in the shadows while Bremin darted to the stables. Jarand peered through the window. At this late hour, only a handful of patrons occupied the great room. An elderly fellow snoozed in a rocking chair by the fire while three men tossed dice at the heavy round table in the center of the room. Bremin returned, shaking his head. "No sign of them here."

The other inn hid deep within streets snaking higher up the hill. They took a few wrong turns before stumbling into its small courtyard. No light peeked through the shuttered windows. A single tin lantern hung at the front door. Sour smelling piles of refuse littered the gutters running alongside the walk.

A stiff mountain breeze whistled its way up the hill, carrying with it an icy chill which bit through their clothes. Elan shivered and Jarand could hear his teeth chattering.

Bremin waved from the side of the inn next to the entrance to the stable. A stable boy snored on a pile of dry hay inside the door and didn't notice when they crept inside. They found a pair of ragged and tired horses still wearing saddles in the last two stalls. Dried sweat matted their coats.

Elan touched the first horse's flank with a gentle hand and the horse snickered and twitched its ears. "These look like the horses I saw."

Mirelle produced a tiny light and willed it to hover at the tip of her finger. She ran her hands along the edge of the saddle and down to the stirrup. She pulled a long strand of dark hair from a metal buckle. She clasped the hair in her fist and held it tight against her chest. "She's here."

Jarand marched toward the door, stone in hand and sword drawn. Elan followed close behind. Bremin stood in their way, folding his arms across his chest.

Jarand raised his sword. "Let me pass."

Bremin did not flinch or cower away. He stood firm and stared Jarand down. "We can't go in there without a plan. It won't do us any good to get her back if it gets us all killed."

Jarand saw the somber conviction in his eyes and lowered his sword. "Damn you. Don't make me wait. Not another minute."

Elan stared, the dark hollows under his eyes visible even in the dim light. "Why are you afraid of them?" he asked. "As wielders, can't you use your magic to deal with them?"

Bremin turned his attention to Elan. "Stonebearers, boy. We prefer to be called Stonebearers. Wielders are those crazy people who didn't train in the towers. Although there aren't many, they are dangerous. Those who survive at least. Most end up getting themselves killed." He adjusted his coat with a jerk. "The power can only help so much. If we are outmaneuvered, they will win."

Jarand clenched his teeth. Being so close and being stopped pulled his nerves tight enough to snap apart. "What do you propose we do?"

"We wait them out. Fighting tonight is madness. We all need rest." Bremin gestured to the stall next to him and the pile of fresh clean straw. "Bed down here in an empty stall. We'll take turns keeping watch and then surprise them when they come for their mounts."

Mirelle leaned her head against Jarand's shoulder and rested her hand against his neck. Her awareness merged with his. She wanted Katira back just as badly. Exhaustion poured from her in waves. She worried about him, that he would be hurt in the coming confrontation. Asking her to fight like this was foolishness.

He wrapped his arms around her, allowing her presence to calm him, allowing her to draw strength from him. She led him to a pile of straw and pushed him down into it.

"Let me help you," she said softly and lay next to him. "You haven't slept in days." The lines on her arms glowed gently to life.

"Save it for when someone needs it," he whispered as he pushed her hand away.

"You need it. I won't take no for an answer." She locked her arms around his neck and pulled him close. Glyphs danced around them and Jarand felt his cares drain away as Mirelle's soft lips caressed his skin.

Sleep weighed him down like a chain pulling him into the depths.

JARAND WOKE to the sound of voices outside the stable doors. He blinked the remnants of sleep from his eyes. A sliver of morning light shot through the crack of the closed stable door. Judging from the angle of the light, he must have slept several hours. Mirelle slept soundly in the hay next to him, warm under her cloak. He laid a hand on her shoulder and whispered in her ear. She woke without a sound and rose swiftly and silently. After being with him on so many campaigns, she was ready for anything at a moment's notice.

Bremin had taken his position at the edge of the stall wall, his hand resting on his long belt knife. Jarand crouched next to him. Mirelle knelt to rouse Elan, who groaned as he woke and clutched his shoulder.

The door swung open, widening the sliver of light into a broad shaft. A short man wrapped in a tattered coat spat as he entered.

"Keep quiet or I'll be forced to punish both of you," he said to someone behind him. He kicked the stable boy. "Get your lazy bones moving and bring us our horses."

The lad yelped and scrambled back into the stable, rubbing at his hip. Jarand caught him and yanked him down into the hay where Mirelle clamped a hand over his mouth. The boy's eyes went wide with fright.

"Shhh. We won't hurt you." Mirelle murmured.

Jarand stepped into the puddle of light from the guttering lantern and rested the point of his great sword in the dirt in front of him. Surasio slouched by the door as he waited for his horses. Katira and another man stood close behind. Scratches covered her face, and she wore sloppy bandages at her wrists. Her head hung low.

She was there. She stood on her own two feet. Despite all the evidence of danger they had collected, she appeared as if she had taken no serious injury. He would get her back and all the fear and anger would be over.

"How dare you?" Jarand said to Surasio with a snarl. "Have you no honor? Have the vows you have sworn meant nothing?"

Katira raised her head when she heard his voice, her mouth falling open in disbelief.

"Papan!" she cried out, reaching for him. The young man with her gripped her shoulder tightly, holding her back.

"Katira," Jarand said, nearly breathing her name. "I'm here. It'll be okay."

Surasio's lips pulled back, bearing his teeth. "What do you know of honor? You've spent nearly two decades hiding in a tiny village in the woods. Things are changing for people like us." He reached for his stone, preparing to fight. "How do you know you are on the right side? A new age is starting, Jarand. Those with the power will no longer need hide to in the shadows."

"You owe a refund to whoever bought your soul, you worthless worm." Jarand stepped forward, taking grim satisfaction as Surasio shied back.

Jarand stiffened his grip around the hilt, feeling the strength in his arms. He opened himself to the power and let the sweet ache fill him. It would be a pleasure to rid the world of this vermin.

Surasio dragged Katira in front of him like a shield.

The young man who had been holding Katira met Jarand's furious gaze with one of steady determination laced with fear. He held out his hand, low and to the side where Surasio couldn't see. Jarand squinted. The boy held a ring. It looked familiar, but he was too far to make out the details.

Surasio pulled a knife from his belt, drawing Jarand's attention again. He set the blade against the skin of Katira's neck. "Leave or I will cut her."

Jarand's fist gripped his sword tighter. Elan lunged forward, a guttural cry escaping his lips.

Bremin caught Elan and forced him back. "Whatever you were promised for her," Bremin said, "we can give you more."

Surasio laughed. "You can't give me a fraction of what I've been promised. Bring me my horses. Now." He pressed the blade against her skin. She whimpered and stiffened as a bright red bead of blood welled up.

"Don't hurt her." Jarand stepped back and lowered his blade. The vile man stood too close to Katira for Jarand to blast him into pieces without harming her. He had to get her away.

Jarand sheathed his sword and held up his hands. "Fine. I'll get them. Put the knife away." He stepped back to the stall of the first horse and unlatched the gate.

"What are you doing?" Elan asked in disbelief. Jarand ignored him.

Surasio smirked. "That's better. Now the second."

"Not until you put away the knife."

Surasio released Katira and pushed her into the arms of the young man. He flipped the knife in his hand, the handle smacking into his palm, before he slid it into its sheath.

Jarand unlatched the gate to the other horse's stall and led it into the wide hallway of the stable, slapping its rump to get it moving. It startled and jumped forward, bounding toward the open door. Using the running horse as a distraction, Jarand summoned a force glyph into the air and slammed the stable door shut. The horses reared and screamed at the crack of sound. He cast another, more focused glyph directly at Surasio, throwing the man to the floor.

Surasio deserved no quarter. Jarand drew his sword and charged at him. Nothing would please him more than running the man through.

Surasio threw his own broad bolt of energy, striking Jarand hard and sending him stumbling back. It threw Bremin and Elan to the ground. Mirelle stayed concealed behind the low wall with the stable boy, safe for the moment.

"Take her. Get out of here. Hide. I'll find you." Surasio shouted to the young man holding Katira as he gained his feet. The young man gave a curt nod and dragged her toward the door and whistled for the horses to follow. Katira kicked and screamed against him, her voice hoarse and desperate.

"Cooperate girl, or else." Surasio held out his hand toward Katira. Despite his warning she continued to fight. He closed his hand into a fist and Katira cried out and crumpled to the ground. The other man scooped her up and carried her out of the stable as she thrashed and screamed.

"Stop!" Jarand hollered. "What are you doing to her?"

"Protecting my assets." Surasio summoned another series of glyphs into his hands. The stable door slammed shut blocking Jarand's view. Surasio launched his glyph into the bale of straw next to Jarand and it exploded into flame.

Jarand threw himself away from the blast, summoning his own glyphs to fire back. A bender wasn't going to win, not today. Not when it meant losing Katira again.

THE DEATH OATH seized Katira in its fiery net, cutting and burning deep within her. Its strands wrapped around her neck, squeezing her throat shut. She couldn't breathe. Isben held her tightly in his arms and carried her away. The pain overwhelmed her senses, pressing her eyes shut, drowning out sound.

Cold air hit her face. The net loosened and fell away. She took a ragged breath. She could hear again. The agony faded. Her muscles spasmed against her will with remembered pain.

"Don't fight it." Isben pressed his hand to her cheek, his eyes wild with fear. "It will be okay. Just breathe. It will pass."

She took another breath. The tremors calmed. She reached up to hold his hand.

"Good, let it go." He smiled and folded her into his arms. "It's over."

"They came for me." She struggled to stand. "I have to go back."

Isben held her fast. "He'll kill you. You know that."

Oath or no oath, she couldn't allow Isben to take her away again. She slammed her foot onto his. His hold loosened enough for her to break free and run back.

The stable erupted into flame. The blast of heat threw them both to the ground.

"No!" She crawled to her feet. Her family was in there. She had to do something.

Isben grabbed her wrist. "We have to go. It's not safe here."

"I won't leave them." She twisted at his grip, but he held firm.

His eyes pleaded. "Please Katira. You've seen what Surasio can do."

"Yes, and now he's doing it to my family. I can't let that happen."
She yanked at his grip again.

Isben forced her to look him in the eyes. "Listen. Your father is a
Stonebearer Guardian, a warrior. If anyone puts that dog down, it
will be him. He can't do that if Surasio has you to use as a shield." He
glanced to the horses. "The best thing we can do is get far away. Far
enough to where Surasio can't find us."

Katira stopped fighting. "Don't make me leave," she pleaded.
"Not now. Not when they are so close."

"If Surasio comes out and we're still here, he will kill us both and
he will make your family watch." Isben walked her to the horses, his
head bowed. "I can't watch you die," he added in a low voice.

Katira looked at the two horses. He was right. She hated Surasio
for making this be their best choice. If she had to leave, she would do
it on her terms. "If we have to go, we will make it hard on him. I'll
take his horse. We'll go faster that way." She patted the nose of Surasio's horse and gathered the reins.

The two of them sped away from Surasio, away from the pain of
being a captive, away from the fear of not knowing what was next.
The early morning streets blurred past, and an assortment of shouts
from vendors and tradesmen echoed in their wake. Freedom coursed
through Katira's veins. She would find her family again. She would
go home. She would be whole again.

THE FLAMES to Jarand's left sent waves of blistering heat through the
small stable. Mirelle covered her mouth with the fabric of her sleeve
and coughed. They couldn't stay in there, not while the fire spread
and smoke choked the air. Surasio bolted toward the door.

Jarand couldn't let him get to Katira, not again. Not after coming
this far to save her. Another glyph flew to his fingertips, he sent it
flying overhead, slamming the stable doors shut before Surasio
could exit.

"We will all burn in here, Jarand. Is that your plan?" Surasio shouted over the noise of the fire. The man formed a complicated series of glyphs between his hands.

If it was to be a battle, Jarand would be ready. He summoned a blade glyph to give his sword an edge capable of cutting through anything. An armor glyph prevented anything from piercing his skin.

"Bremin, be ready." Jarand swung his sword in graceful arcs, preparing to engage with Surasio. "On my signal, get everyone out while I distract him."

Surasio threw his green glyph into a pile of straw the fire hadn't touched. One limb at a time, a massive straw golum assembled itself and stood ready to strike Jarand down. Impressive work for a bender, but it wouldn't be enough. Jarand leapt into the air and swung his sword, removing one of the golem's arms.

"Go, Bremin. Get them out!"

The golem reeled back as the arm reformed. Sweat coated Surasio's face and his filthy shirt. He couldn't sustain the beast for long. Jarand darted in, slashing and cutting, anything to keep the beast's attention from the others as they made their way out the door. As soon as he cut, the golem repaired itself.

Bremin darted past, pulling the stable boy along by his arm. Elan hurried behind them, wide eyes fixed on the beast. Mirelle wasn't with them.

Jarand allowed himself to get too close. A straw fist caught him in the side of the head, jarring him off balance. The sudden shock of the blow combined with the flames brought back memory upon terrible memory of war and blood. He shook his head, trying to break free. This was not the time to allow his past to claim him.

The golem charged forward, arm raised for a crushing blow. Mirelle leapt forward, stone in hand, and slammed down a shield glyph. The golem smashed itself against the shield.

Surasio staggered back and dropped his arms. The golem came apart, falling into a pile of straw once again.

Jarand narrowed his attention to the present. He focused on

Mirelle by his side, the solid metal in his hand, and the raging fire of the power burning through him. With a yell, he charged Surasio, intent on cutting the man in two.

Instead of facing the attack, Surasio turned and ran out into the street. Jarand gave chase. This needed to end quickly. The longer the fight lasted, the more chances Surasio had to hurt someone. Jarand had no doubt he would kill bystanders if they got in the way.

Jarand didn't see the flash of power as Surasio flung a melon-sized rock. It struck hard enough to send Jarand flying back onto the cobblestones. He gasped in pain as his ribs cracked and the breath was forced from his lungs.

Mirelle rushed forward, hovering over him as she formed a new shield. Jarand struggled to his feet and pulled her behind him. A stone broke against the shield and Mirelle lost her hold on the glyph. It disappeared. "Get out of here," he shouted to her.

"I won't leave you," she shouted back.

Jarand needed to end this. With blade ready, he advanced towards Surasio again, this time resolved to bring him down. If it was a fight the man wanted, Jarand would give it to him.

A line of blood ran from a cut above Surasio's eye, making him blink. Summoning a golem had drained him. It was a fool move. The only glyphs he could have strength for were simple force bolts. He threw bolt after desperate bolt at Jarand to keep him back. The bolts bounced off Jarand's sword as he continued to charge forward.

Surasio released a bolt straight at Mirelle. Jarand made a mad lunge to block it, leaving him exposed. Surasio threw another bolt, catching Jarand in his damaged ribs and driving him to the ground again.

Jarand hurried to his feet, ignoring the pain that fought to take his breath away. He formed the series of glyphs that would bind Surasio and keep him from summoning more glyphs of his own. He only needed one clear shot to bring the man down.

Surasio's shoulders hunched forward. He rested his hands on his knees to catch his breath. The man's expression changed from desperation to wicked triumph as he held out his upturned fist. Whatever he held in his hand promised nothing good. Jarand dropped his seizing glyph and threw a shield in front of himself and Mirelle as Surasio shot a stream of shining darts at them.

The darts punched through his shield like paper, bouncing off Jarand's glyph armor as they whizzed past. Mirelle had no such protection. The darts struck her. She fell to her knees.

Jarand's anger exploded in a burst of heat and fury. He didn't care if this man burnt to ash. He charged forward, an angry death glyph forming before him as he went. Moments before its release, Surasio disappeared in a blinding flash.

Jarand's glyph snapped closed with a sharp crack leaving the air shimmering with heat. He howled and threw his sword clattering to the ground. Surasio was a bender, not a traveler. He shouldn't have been able to spirit away, not when Jarand was so close to striking his victory.

Through the smoke and chaos came a sound that sent a cold chill up Jarand's spine.

Mirelle's labored breath.

He ran to her side.

Her hands shook against his chest. Her body spasmed with pain. "Jarand, you have to stop the bleeding."

Bremin raced back into the courtyard with Elan close behind, red faced and panting.

"They were too fast. We need the horses." Bremin glanced around, confused. "Where is he?"

Jarand was too busy tending to Mirelle to answer. The darts had struck her in more places than he dared count.

Images bolted through Jarand's head - bloody hands, screaming, helplessness. He forced the nightmare away and knelt to scoop her into his arms and held her close. Mirelle needed him. With his head resting against hers, he opened himself to her and allowed himself to feel her pain. He had to know where she was hurt, and how serious her wounds might be.

The first rush of sensation stole his breath. The darts had plunged deep, cutting as they went. Once the initial shock of pain faded, he found the five different points where she had been hit. Three had stuck deep into muscle. Another passed between her ribs, punching a hole in her lung that was filling with blood. The last lodged deep in her belly.

"I'm here. Hang on. I won't let anything happen to you." He prayed he could keep his promise.

Compared to Mirelle, Jarand's abilities were limited to breaking and defending. He had learned a handful of glyphs to treat battlefield injuries and even then, he never had the talent to do it well.

She must have sensed his hesitation. She placed a hand over his. "Do what you must."

With stone in hand, he cast the rudimentary glyphs he knew to staunch the flow of blood at each point. She gripped his arm as he worked, face pale, teeth clenched tight. She needed so much more help than he could give her. He hoped it would be enough to buy her time to find someone who could.

Elan hung back while Bremin knelt next to them. "How bad is it?"

"I've done what I can." Jarand's voice betrayed the fear he was trying to keep at bay. His hands were wet with her blood. "She needs a real healer and soon. Is there anyone nearby you trust?"

"Lady Lucia in Sulsudy. She's helped me in the past. It's a two-hour ride." Bremin turned toward Elan. "Get the horses, boy. Tell Master Sopan we're in a hurry."

"Of course, sir. But—" Elan paced in the street as if he might bolt at any second.

"But what? Go. Now."

"But Katira ..."

"No one's forgetting anyone." Bremin stood and gripped Elan by the shoulders. "We can only deal with one emergency at a time."

Elan froze, finally seeing Mirelle for the first time. "By the Stonemother. I didn't know."

"Go!" Bremin barked.

Elan hurried out of the courtyard, bounding like a scared young rabbit.

Jarand held Mirelle closer and pulled her cloak around her.

"I can't do this," he said. "I can't leave Katira to that filth." Threads of desperation pierced him through. Katira needed him. Mirelle needed him. He couldn't save them both.

Bremin placed a comforting hand on his shoulder. "We'll get her back."

Jarand wished he felt as confident as Bremin sounded. "He Traveled. He's a bender. He shouldn't have been able to do that."

"It will cost him. That's good for us. He can't push as hard, at least for a while." Bremin rummaged around in the pockets of his coat and withdrew a vial of dark liquid.

Jarand pressed his eyes closed. The whistles of the guard sounded in the distance. "Do we know which way they went?"

"South. I'm sure of it. Lucia's is on the way." He uncorked the top. "Here, Mirelle. Take this. It'll help."

"What is it?" Jarand asked, eying the vial with uncertainty.

"It dulls pain." Bremin touched the top of the vial and brought a drop of the liquid to his mouth. "I've used it plenty over the years. It's safe."

Jarand gazed down at Mirelle's face. Her eyelids fluttered between half open and shut as she swallowed the medicine. He couldn't bear the thought of losing her. The sooner the darts were removed, the better.

Chapter 9

J arand rode as fast as he dared with Mirelle clutched in his arms. Each bouncing gallop brought her more pain and nothing could be done for it except to keep pushing forward. Each jolt ground Jarand's broken ribs. He sought the place deep within himself that let him push aside pain. He would live, he could wait. Mirelle couldn't. Elan and Bremin followed close behind.

They arrived in Sulsudy midmorning amid the bustle of other travelers and tradesmen. The streets crawled with life. Children darted between wagon wheels and around horses, laughing and shouting as they went. Shopkeepers organized their trays of wares and chatted to their neighbors. The whole town smelled of spice, damp stone, and fresh baked bread. The chaos of the marketplace meant fewer people would take notice of Jarand and he was glad for it.

Bremin stepped up his pace to ride alongside Jarand. "How is she?"

Mirelle had been too quiet on the ride. Her life continued to drain away. Jarand pulled her tighter into his arms. "Not good. Where does this Lucia live?"

"Not far." Bremin led them to a cottage with bundles of herbs hanging from the eves. The heavy smell of river sage hung in the air. An old shoe propped the door open.

Bremin rapped on the doorframe. "Lucia!" he called, stepping through the door. "Lucia, we need you."

From the back of the house came a tall gaunt fellow wearing a much-worn leather vest over an equally worn tunic. Angular Khandashiian lines peeked above the collar of his shirt.

"Bremin, what brings you here this late in the season?" The man looked him over.

Bremin waved him off. "I'm fine. Mirelle is the one who needs help."

The tall fellow leaned out of the door. His smile vanished when he saw Jarand carrying Mirelle. "Bring her in. By rock and ruin, what happened here?"

Mirelle barely stirred as Jarand slid down from the horse. "You're going to be fine." He tried to smile.

Mirelle said nothing. Jarand set her on a cot in the corner as Lucia bustled into the room wiping her hands on the cloth hanging from her shoulder. Her greying hair was pulled into a loose knot on the top of her head. Had her lines not been peeking out from beneath the edges of her sleeves, Jarand would have thought she was nothing more than a kindly grandmother.

"Okay, boys. One of you tell me what happened."

Jarand found himself too upset to talk, leaving Bremin to tell Lucia everything. Lucia looked over Mirelle as she listened, gently examining each wound.

"It's a pity I wasn't there when it happened, although from the sound of it I wouldn't have wanted to be. You did well, Jarand. These will scar. Not much I can do about that. I imagine there's quite a bit of damage beneath needing to be cared for, which explains why she hasn't rebounded." She tugged her stone free from under her shirt. "Let's see what can't be seen."

She placed a hand on Mirelle's chest and closed her eyes. Several small glyphs danced over each wound, weaving around and through. When the glyphs finished, Lucia frowned.

"Darts you say? Did you happen to gather any?"

Bremin reached into one of his many pockets and pulled out three small diamond-shaped darts. "I haven't had a chance to examine them myself. Something about them bothers me and I can't quite put my finger on it."

Lucia picked one from his palm and held it up to the light. "Strange. I haven't seen anything like this before. It almost looks like stonebane, which would explain why her own power hasn't helped her heal yet." She licked the edge of a dart and then spat. "There's something else as well. Whatever it is, I'd feel better if the darts were out."

Jarand gripped the edge of the cot. He wanted nothing more than for Mirelle to be healed and free from pain. "Please be careful."

Lucia summoned her power once again, this time focusing on the wound in Mirelle's belly. The lines on her hands shone, and the glyphs wove themselves in dizzying circles. A sheen of sweat formed on her forehead as she worked. Talan, her companion, stood close.

Anxious minutes passed. Jarand would not, could not let anything happen to Mirelle. Bremin found a nearby chair and sat, resting his head in his hands. Mirelle's eyes sprung open, her body stiffened, and she flailed out to push Lucia away.

Jarand reached for Lucia's outstretched arm. "Something's wrong. Stop!"

Lucia pulled her hands back, the light vanished. "What child? What is it?"

"It's burning!" Mirelle cried as she arched from the cot.

"Do something! Help her!" Jarand begged.

Lucia shook her head. "Whatever I do might make it worse. It's like nothing I've seen. When I touched it with the power it changed. I'm afraid if I do anything more it will cause more damage."

Bremin ripped back the fabric of Mirelle's dress, exposing the skin. Dark purple streaks slowly spread from the wound. "By the Stonemother's throne, it's a poison."

The color drained from Lucia's face. Her mouth worked soundlessly before she found her voice again. "Take her to Head Master Firen at Amul Dun. If anyone can help her, it's him. This is beyond me." She pulled a thick blanket from the shelf behind her and handed it to Jarand. "There is a traveling post nearby, do you know it?"

Jarand's world stopped. He stood frozen unable to cope with the sudden change. Poison? Lucia pushed the blanket into his hands. He wrapped it around Mirelle and scooped her back into his arms. "Yes, I know it."

She urged him toward the door, "Go. Talan will come with you to make sure there are no delays."

The gaunt man buckled on a belt with a long knife and pulled on his cloak.

Outside the healer's house, Bremin searched through his pockets and handed the vial of dark medicine to Jarand.

"She needs this more than I do. No more than four drops every two hours."

Jarand gripped Bremin's arm in silent thanks. "Go after Katira. I'll come as soon as I can. Take Elan with you. Keep him safe."

Bremin opened his mouth and shot a look at Elan. "I work best alone. You know that."

Jarand shifted Mirelle's weight in his arms. He couldn't wait, not a second longer. "This isn't the time to argue. Do you want to help me or not?"

"It's just ..." Bremin went pale. His gaze dropped to his feet. "Of course. Go."

Mirelle's body in Jarand's arms weighed nothing compared to the despair hanging from his heart.

Mirelle would have insisted he leave her to go rescue Katira. She would have let herself die if it meant their daughter would survive. He couldn't bear the thought of losing either of them. Trusting Bremin gave both Katira and Mirelle a chance.

Using the traveling post would exact its price on Jarand, dangerously sapping his strength. He had to take the risk. He had enough energy to reach the Mountain Tower at Amul Dun, but not much more.

Master Firen, the head of the healing order, would bring Mirelle back to health. If he couldn't help her, no one could.

Talan led the way up the meandering trail, turning and twisting through the dense brush and trees. Had Jarand gone alone, he would have lost the path for sure. He was grateful for the help.

The hair on Jarand's neck prickled. There was a presence here. He gripped his stone, still bound in his palm and opened himself to the power.

He looked out through the wood, worried at what he might find.

Talan noted the lines glowing on Jarand's arms. "What is it?"

"I thought we were being watched." Jarand let the power fade. He let his awareness return to Mirelle, if he could feel her, she was alive.

Talan continued walking. "That's because we are. We are close to the warding wall. Shadow creatures roam the other side. They haven't dared break through yet. It's a matter of time before they do. And when they do, I'll take care of them." He said as he patted his knife.

After another few turns Talan stopped at a barren cliff face. "Here we are."

Jarand squinted at the rock.

Talan smiled and stepped out of sight. Had Jarand not seen him do it, he wouldn't have believed it possible. The passageway, cut expertly into the rock, blended so well into the surroundings it was nearly invisible.

"Amazing. Is this your work?" Jarand asked as he stepped into the hidden passage.

"No." Talan ran a hand up the edge of the smooth stone. "It's been here for ages. It's why I wanted to bring you. You might never have found it if you didn't know what to look for."

"You have my thanks." Jarand gave a slight bow of his head. "If I pass this way again, I'll be sure to stop by. I owe you far more than a drink."

"I'll take your word for it." Talan tipped his hat before turning and walking back down the path.

At the end of the passage, a tiny grotto opened upward to a crescent of sky. A slender pedestal rose in the center, radiating with its own light. Its pure motherstone surface felt like water beneath Jarand's fingers.

There he knelt, setting Mirelle in his lap like a child. He pressed his stone against the symbol for the Mountain Tower at Amul Dun and summoned a traveling glyph, spending extra time to ensure he formed it correctly. The stone lit up like a beacon in the dark grotto.

The traveling post took hold of his power and drew it from him as the world spun around. Jarand held to Mirelle with his free arm, forcing the portal to take them both.

"We're almost there. Hang on." The world fell away as the two of them moved faster than thought. The post tugged more and more of his energy away from him, making him dizzy.

The brightness receded, and the scene rematerialized into the broad courtyard of the Mountain Tower. Great statues flanked either side, standing between stout pillars.

Home.

He had spent a lifetime in this place training and serving as a Guardian. Mirelle had done the same apprenticing and serving under the guidance of Master Healer Firen himself. And now Jarand brought her back to him, broken and dying.

Light faded from the pedestal and Jarand tried to stand. The effort caused his vision to dim. People ran toward him. Hands and faces swirled around him, too many to focus on.

"She's been poisoned, she's—" He looked down, her face had gone gray. He couldn't feel her through their bond. The agony of loss shot through him. He had tried so hard, they had come so close.

A white robed healer pushed through the crowd and knelt before them, his stone held ready.

"You were right to bring her quickly." A bright red life glyph formed in his hands before passing into her heart. She gasped. The relief of feeling her again through the bond brought tears to Jarand's eyes.

A second healer approached, one Jarand knew well. Master Firen's angular features made him look like a long-legged seabird. His flowing white robe gusted in the cold wind, like a pair of wings. His usual stiff, calm demeanor had been shaken at the sight of them.

"Not Mirelle! What happened?" He didn't wait for Jarand to answer. "Doesn't matter. Bring her in right away. Hurry!"

When Jarand tried to stand again, the world pitched. Master Firen steadied him and waved over another attendant. "You're in no condition to carry her."

The other attendant reached for her.

Jarand clung tighter, unwilling to let her go. "I stay with her."

Master Firen placed his hand on Mirelle's neck; his lines glowed to life. "I promise to take good care of her. I'll send someone for you right away. You look as though you need it."

The attendant reached again and this time Jarand allowed him to gently lift Mirelle from his arms and hurry her into the grand building. He watched on helplessly as they carried her away from him.

A slight figure glided up from behind him and placed a hand on his shoulder. "The last time you taxed yourself this much I had to have you pulled off a battlefield before you got yourself killed." The High Lady Alystra's words poured over him like warm water, soothing him.

"My lady." He made an awkward bow.

"Bremin sent word you were coming. What happened?"

"Surasio shot Mirelle with some sort of burning poison. It's like nothing I've ever seen." Even with the High Lady's presence calming him, saying the words aloud shoved a blade of ice into his stomach. He and Mirelle had been together for so long it was like they were two parts of the same person. Losing her would be like being cut in half.

"She needs you with her." She placed a warm hand on his chest, her fingers resting on the bare skin of his neck. "Allow me to strengthen you." She didn't wait for him to reply. The flow of her energy filled him, taking the keen edge of his fatigue away.

He attempted to stand once more, this time gaining his feet.

"That will help with the worst of it." She drew away her hand and tucked it back inside her wide sleeve. "You need rest and food soon. Come, I'll walk with you."

Lady Alystra listened on, her head bowed as Jarand related the events of the past three days. The intricate braids of her hair swung over the grass green folds of her robes of office. He expected the news to shock her, but she showed no reaction at all.

Then he understood. "This is all part of something much bigger, isn't it?"

"I'm afraid so." She sighed and looked up to the statues flanking the door leading into the keep. "There have been too many incidents over the past week to ignore. I fear this is part of a new threat. Eastern Flame reports two of their order missing and the abduction of an apprentice. The Hand of the West talks of a handful of attacks, none successful. Those from our tower have reported several attacks, and three more missing. And now we can add another abduction and Mirelle."

Jarand's back stiffened. All the evidence pointed to one fact—the Stonebearers were being targeted. "It's clear we have a new enemy, it takes cunning and a plan to coordinate that many successful attacks. The leaders from each of the towers must be summoned here and a High Council held. We must organize ourselves to strike back, and quickly. This threat must be extinguished."

The High Lady took a deep breath and let it out. "We can't. We have reason to suspect a Stonebearer is at the center of this new threat. Calling a council might very well be giving them our plans."

They arrived at the doors of the infirmary and Jarand paused before entering, afraid what he might see. For so long, he was the only one who had ever cared for Mirelle and she for him. Having to trust another, even Master Firen, made him uneasy.

"Go to her," the High Lady said. "We'll talk more later."

KATIRA STOOD high in the stirrups and raced after Isben. They sped down the Southern Road passing carts and merchant wagons as they went. Leagues blurred by.

Isben slowed the pair of horses to a walk. Tall trees burst with fall colors along the sides of the road. Ahead, a small marker indicated a hidden shrine in the wood. Isben dismounted and walked them through the trees.

A statue of a dignified woman stood in the center of a clearing. Katira jumped down from Surasio's horse. The woman held her hand out in a gesture of offering. Katira imagined the woman offering her hope, safety, and peace. After everything, she craved those things the most. It would be fitting if she found them here.

"Are we safe here?" she asked. "Can he find us?"

"We went far enough, it should be impossible." Isben caught up the reins of both horses and led them to drink from a small stream at the back of the clearing. "We should stay clear of the roads for a while, just to be sure."

Katira touched the statue's hand, wanting to feel the same serenity she saw in the statue's finely carved face. They were free. She should be happy. The bracelet Elan made her shifted on her wrist. Memories of the few moments they were in the stable were foggy, the death oath smeared over all but the barest details.

"It all happened so fast." She touched the bracelet, letting her fingers trace the path of elaborate knots. "Was Elan really there, or was I dreaming?"

"Yes." Isben didn't meet Katira's eye as he unbuckled the belly strap of his horse and removed the saddle and the blanket. "He was there."

Those three tiny words made Katira dizzy. The worry that had eaten her hollow blew away with the breeze. She felt whole again and wonderfully light, like she could dance. Elan survived. He lived. He had come for her.

Isben removed the saddle and blanket from Surasio's horse and set them over a low branch before digging out a pair of brushes from a bag. The poor horse's coats were matted with old sweat. After days of being ridden, sores had begun to form along where jutting bones rubbed against the edges of the saddle.

"Will you still marry him?" Again, Isben didn't turn to face her as he worked.

"What do you mean?" Katira took the second brush and slipped it on her hand and joined him on the other side of his horse. The familiar motions of brushing brought the calm peace she needed. "Of course I'll still marry him. Why do you ask?"

"Sometimes when horrible things happen, it can change how you think, how you feel about the world." When he met her eye, she saw a pain there she hadn't expected.

She continued working her brush over the horse's flank. If it wasn't for Isben, she would have had nothing to keep Surasio from doing whatever he wanted to her. The thought made her cringe. For that alone, Isben had her deepest gratitude. But did he have more?

He deserved an answer. He deserved to know how she felt. "I've loved Elan for years. I've always wanted to build a life with him and raise a family." Her brushing stopped. "You're right about feelings changing. I used to think I was safe, that nothing could go wrong. I was a fool."

"Do you feel safe with me?" There was a hint of hope to his voice.

Did she? He had proven himself dozens of times that he would put her needs before his, but did it make her feel safe? This was a boy she had only known a few days. Could she make that kind of decision? Her head wanted to argue the fact, but her heart stood firm on the matter. "Yes, I do."

Isben smiled and finished brushing while Katira gathered sticks for firewood. If they were going to stay for a while, they might as well be comfortable. The chill of the morning warmed to a bright fair afternoon. Isben stretched himself next to the fire and dozed in the sunshine. Katira searched the woods around the clearing for herbs and edible plants. Finding familiar plants from home made her want to return even more.

On the other side of the clearing, a brilliant speck of light hovered next to the worn statue.

Katira hurried to Isben's side and shook him awake. "What is that?"

Isben blinked and searched for what Katira was pointing at.

"By blasted rock and bloody ruin! He's found us." He scrambled to his feet and seized a stout branch. "Get back. Hide."

"No. We face him together." She grabbed a long straight branch with a pointed end. She'd never killed before, but Surasio stirred up a primal need to survive at all costs. If it meant spearing him through, she would do it.

The light grew brighter until Surasio appeared from the air. As soon as his form solidified, he fell to his knees, fighting to catch his breath. Isben charged forward first, swinging his branch and aiming for Surasio's head. Surasio held out his hand and squeezed it shut. Isben fell fast and hard as the pain of the death oath slammed around him.

Katira tightened her grip on the makeshift spear. One brave

thrust and their problems would be over for good. Surasio couldn't torment them anymore. She launched herself toward him with the pointed end of her stick aimed for the center of his back.

Surasio reached out his other hand and squeezed it shut. The oath hit Katira with such force it knocked her backward to the ground. The burning net seized her, stronger this time, each thread white-hot against bone. Isben's screams mingled with her own. She pressed her eyes shut against the pain. Threads wrapped her throat, throttled her heart.

This time the net didn't fall away, didn't fade. Katira felt her heart slow, felt her lungs burn. She forced one eye open. Isben's struggles against the oath grew weaker as did her own. Surasio knelt near Isben and grabbed him by the neck.

Katira's vision faded. Her heart stuttered. She was going to die.

Just as the last fragments of her awareness fell away, the net faded. Isben's plea from before floated into her mind. Breathe. Her body wouldn't obey. She had to breathe. A warm cocoon of nothingness closed in around her. A burst of energy struck her in the chest. Her lungs opened, she drew a gasping breath. Her heart pounded awake.

She blinked, needing to see what had become of Isben. Surasio stepped away from her and stumbled back to the fire. Had he saved her?

Isben lay deathly still. Katira crawled to his side and laid her head on his chest. She couldn't hear his heart. She pressed her lips on his and forced a breath in.

"Come on, Isben. Please."

His heart trembled. She gave him another breath.

He gasped and coughed. She fell next to him letting her head rest on his shoulder. That was close, too close.

"You shouldn't have saved him." Surasio broke the stick she had been holding and tossed it into the fire. "He'll just die later, and it will be worse."

"You did something to him, didn't you?" A new fear stabbed Katira's gut. "When you were holding him by the neck. I saw you."

Surasio shrugged and turned away without answering.

Katira studied Isben's face, looking for some clue about what she saw.

"He stole away some of my energy," Isben murmured as he rubbed his eyes and rolled onto his side.

"He can do that?"

"It's against Stonebearer law to do it without permission." He sat up with a groan. "Not like he cares."

"You'll be okay, won't you?" Katira surprised herself at how worried she was about him.

He flexed his hands. "No permanent damage. I'll be fine."

It was time for answers, Katira rounded on Surasio. "What happened to my family?"

Surasio gave a wicked smile. "I don't think they'll be following us for a while." He fished something from his pocket and held it out where Isben could see. A diamond-shaped stone rested in his palm, both ends armed with sharp points. "You know what these are, don't you?"

Isben's face darkened. He clenched his fists. "You're a monster."

"What is it?" Katira asked Isben. "Is my family still alive?" She choked on the words as if voicing them out loud would somehow seal their fate.

Isben glanced at Surasio before answering. "He's hurt someone. It might not be serious but it's enough to slow them, to keep them from following."

Katira's breath stuck in her body. "I have to go to them." She stood, not caring if Surasio tried to stop her.

Isben gripped her arm, too weak to stand. "Listen to me. If you want to protect them, keep his focus away from them. They can take care of themselves."

"Do you expect me to stand here and do nothing?" A fiery anger built up inside her. Flames licked at her mind. Although what Isben said made sense, this wasn't a time for logic. It was time to be free. She couldn't sit there knowing someone she cared about might be dying. Not again.

"Let me go!" She yanked at her hand, but his grip didn't loosen.

The fire inside her burned stronger unlike anything she had felt before. It grew and stretched through her like a living thing. She embraced the pain and fought harder against him. Lines of silver appeared on her hands as she scratched and pulled at his grip.

"Stop, Katira! You're not ready for this yet." His voice trembled. He gripped her hands. Lines on his hands shone bright against his tanned skin.

The flood of his emotion hit her hard enough to make her gasp. A swirling vortex of his desperation, need, and sorrow overpowered her thoughts. In one touch, one moment, she understood exactly what Isben felt for her. He wanted more than to just protect her, he wanted to hold her close and never let go. He wanted to brush his lips against the soft skin of her neck.

The intensity of his feelings left her shaking. It wasn't possible. She shouldn't have been able to see into his mind like that.

Isben released a slow breath and loosened his grip. "That was close."

Katira's thoughts slipped away and dark clouds crowded her vision. She fought to stay present. Something had happened, something important, she needed to know. She struggled to form the words. "What was that?"

Isben guided her back down to the ground. "It's okay. You didn't know."

Her eyes grew heavier as he spoke, and a deep fatigue settled, weighing her down. "What's happening to me?" Her words struggled to form.

"Don't fight it." Isben's words echoed through the darkness as it pulled her down. "Everything will be okay."

Chapter 10

Light spilled into the orderly infirmary from the tall windows flanking either side of the room. The healers Jarand had seen in the courtyard hurried about, taking orders from Master Firen. Beds lined both walls, each made with crisp white sheets. Three of the beds held other Stonebearers. Mirelle lay in the bed closest to the Master Healer's office. The master himself sat next to her with his hand resting on her stomach. Glints of light shone from the glyphs he summoned.

Jarand sank into the chair on the other side of the bed, glad for the chance to rest, even for a short moment. Lady Alystra's gift kept him upright. Without it he would have found himself in one of the other beds.

He gripped his stone and laced his fingers into Mirelle's, opening his awareness to her once more. If anything changed, he would be the first to know. For now, she rested under the weight of Bremin's drug. The fierce pain of the poison stayed subdued, and he was glad for it.

As his awareness spread through to her, her eyes fluttered open. "You look terrible," she whispered, her words slow and slurred.

Jarand brought her hand to his face. "We've both seen better days." As he did so, he glimpsed the blood and dirt crusted on his own hands. He couldn't imagine what the rest of him looked like. "I promise to get myself cleaned up at the first chance."

She squeezed his hand. "It can wait. Stay with me."

"I wouldn't dare leave."

Her smile came and went, warming him for a brief second. "Katira?"

"Bremin will continue to track her. He won't stop until she is safe."

"We were so close. Damn that man." She squeezed his hand tighter. "Is everyone else safe?"

"For now, yes."

The fear racing through her calmed. He forced his own fears into submission. She needed him to be strong for her. The bond worked both ways. She could feel him as much as he could feel her. His agitated mind would do nothing to help her.

One breath at a time, he sought the peace he wished her to feel. There would be time for worry and fear later. For now, it was enough to be.

The scrape of a chair sliding across the floor startled Jarand back awake. He hadn't realized he had drifted off. He straightened, surprised to find he'd bathed Mirelle's hand in his tears. She too had drifted asleep. He carefully placed her hand on the blanket, not wanting to wake her.

A thick-shouldered man in healer's robes pulled up a chair and sat backwards into it. Decades had passed since Jarand had seen Cassim. The man was companion to a fellow member of the Tower Guard, Issa. They had spent many a night together during the war.

Cassim looked Jarand over, taking inventory of what he saw the same way Mirelle did with her patients. "I came as soon as I heard you were here. What happened to you?"

"I don't want to talk about it." Jarand forced a smile and twisted to greet his old friend. The motion shifted his injured ribs, turning his smile into a grimace. "Hasn't Master Firen found a way to banish you to some remote island yet?"

"Not for want of trying. He needs me here." Cassim chuckled. "Apparently I'm a valued member of the order or something like that." His eye wandered over Jarand's body. "Speaking of, you look as if you might need fixing."

"Did Master Firen put you up to this?"

"Does it matter?" Cassim reached out, his stone was already bound to his palm. "It'll only take a second."

Jarand sighed. It would be harder to refuse than to let Cassim do his job. "Fine. But be quick about it."

A series of glyphs sprung to life between Cassim's hands. They flowed through Jarand like a warm wave, lingering near his aching side. As promised, Cassim worked quickly. In a matter of minutes, he had finished.

"Four broken ribs, a bruised lung, a mild concussion, and steeply drained reserves." The healer listed the injuries off on his fingers. "Not the worst you've had. Who'd you provoke this time?"

At any other time Jarand would have shared a smile with the healer, but he couldn't, not while Mirelle was in danger.

Cassim glanced over at Mirelle and his face grew serious. "You've never really been in this position before. Usually it's you being put back together after a campaign's gone south." He patted Jarand's knee. "We'll fix her up. Don't you worry about it."

Cassim gently poked at Jarand's aching side. "I can knit the ribs back easy enough. They'll be tender for a day or so, but leagues better than they are now. At least you'll breathe properly. As for the other things, it's best for your own power to restore them." He cracked his knuckles. "Do I have your permission?"

Jarand rolled his eyes at Cassim's mock formality. The man had been there for the better part of Jarand's battle years and had done his fair share patching him up. "You know you do. Get on with it."

Cassim set his hands on Jarand's side. Jarand gripped the sturdy wooden rail of the bed and braced himself. Healing bones always hurt more than expected and ribs were no exception. Cassim wove his glyphs with speed and precision shifting the bones back into proper alignment. Jarand forced his mouth shut to keep from yelling. With a final snap, Cassim removed his hands.

"Better?" he asked.

Jarand breathed deeply and turned side to side. To his relief the grinding of bone was gone as was most of the pain. "Much. Thank you."

Master Firen returned to the bedside, his face grave. He walked as if he carried a great weight. "We need to talk."

Cassim excused himself with a slight bow toward Master Firen.

"Can you help her?" Jarand asked after Cassim had left.

"I want to tell you yes, but the truth is I'm not sure. What I do know is those darts must be removed to prevent further problems."

Jarand picked up Mirelle's hand once more. "Lucia tried that, but it triggered the poison's release."

"It must be done without the aid of the power. Once the darts are removed, I can heal the wounds, but not before." Master Firen cleared his throat. When he spoke again, his voice was hoarse with emotion. "It's not ideal, I know. It's all I can do to preserve what strength she has left."

The fear Jarand worked so hard to suppress leapt back and wrapped itself around his throat. He found it hard to breathe. "You mean to take a blade to her?"

"I can't see any way around it."

"When will you do it?"

Master Firen shifted his gaze to Mirelle then down to his hands. He took a slow breath before looking Jarand in the eye. "Right away. I'd ask you to leave but I know you won't. If you wish to stay, you'll need to wash up. There's water and clean clothes in the chamber at the back of this room."

"I don't know if I can let you do this." Bile crept up Jarand's throat.

"She'll die if I don't."

Jarand nodded his grim acceptance and made his way down the line of neatly made beds, his terror building with every step.

In the small wash room, he removed his shirt and washed in the basin there as well as he could, scrubbing the layers of dirt and grime from his hands, face, and arms before donning a fresh shirt. He'd need a bath later, but for now this would have to do.

When he returned, the healer had set out a tray with a selection of blades and tools next to the bed. Jarand didn't dare look too closely.

Mirelle had awoken since he'd left. She spoke quietly with Master Firen. Jarand had expected to feel fear from her in the face of what must happen, but instead he felt her steely determination. Her fingers tangled themselves in the blankets as the pain returned.

Jarand sat close to her. "Has he told you what must be done?"

She extended her hand toward him. "I agree with him. They must be removed. I can think of no one I trust more to do it."

He kissed her brow, letting his lips linger against her flushed skin. "If you trust him, then I will."

Master Firen touched Jarand on the arm. "It's time. Are you well enough to put her into a deep sleep?"

Jarand's stomach clenched. Mirelle touched his face, her hand trembled. "It will be okay."

Jarand swallowed down the knot of emotion threatening to break through. With his stone ready, he placed a hand on her head and the other over her heart. He closed his eyes and slowed his breathing to match hers. Glyphs formed at his fingertips and gently pulled her down through the layers of sleep.

Her breathing slowed as the muscles, held rigid with the pain, released their grip. When he had gone as far as he dared, he sent the warmest sentiment of love and care across the bond. A flicker of feeling echoed back from deep in a place of dream and shadow.

"She's ready," he told Master Firen. "Do what you must."

≈

TIME in the infirmary crawled past as Jarand listened to each metallic tap of the instruments being lifted and replaced on Master Firen's tray. He couldn't bear to watch the man work and chose to gaze upon Mirelle's face instead.

Master Firen had advised him to break his connection to her. Enduring her pain with her wouldn't change anything. Jarand ignored him and let each heartbeat and each breath echo through him along with each burning touch of Firen's tools.

The deep sleep spared her from pain. It didn't spare him from the guilt crashing around him. He didn't protect her, didn't protect Katira. For that he wanted to feel each cut of Master Firen's knives.

There must have been something he could have done to stop Surasio before he had the chance to strike. He should have pushed harder, struck with more force. Anything to bring the foul little man down. He thought back even further. If he had kept a better watch on Katira in the first place, she wouldn't have been taken.

Flames edged up around his thoughts. Flames and the hands of the dead reaching for him. Screams echoed through his mind, tormenting him. They died because he wasn't enough. He could have saved them. He could have pushed harder. Sweat beaded on his forehead and he trembled as the past took control of his mind. *No, not now. Not when she needs me,* he begged. *Please, leave me in peace.* The dream didn't heed his plea and dug in deeper.

A cool touch at the edge of his mind dulled the heat of the nightmare. Mirelle, even in her deep dream state, reached out to comfort him. He grabbed hold of her calming presence as an anchor and forced the thoughts of Jalan's Gap back down deep where they belonged.

It wasn't fair. Even while she fought for her life, she reached out to him in his need. Jarand knew from the beginning, from the day they met so many years ago, when he knew they were meant to be paired. She would always be too good for him.

That was why he couldn't let her go.

The sun set while the healer continued to work. An attendant lit the lanterns. Hours passed before Master Firen finally set down his tools and replaced his stone back around his neck. He sat in the other bedside chair, rubbing his face. "I never want to do that again."

Jarand dared a glance down the length of Mirelle's body. All the bandaging had been thankfully covered with a blanket. "Will she be okay?"

Master Firen pinched the bridge of his nose and squeezed his eyes shut. "She's better than before. This buys us time until an antidote can be found. The poison continues to spread."

"It can be found, though? It's only a matter of preparing it?"

"I've never seen anything like this. Until I can identify what is in those darts, I won't be able to do anything." His gaze dropped to Mirelle. "If it's not something I'm familiar with, I'll have to create an antidote. The process could take weeks."

"But it can be done?"

"Yes, I'm confident in that. But that's not the problem." He took a breath and returned his attention to Jarand. "I'm afraid she won't make it that long."

Jarand heard what the Master Healer said, but his mind refused to understand. Mirelle's wounds were serious, but he hadn't doubted for a moment that Master Firen could save her. He must have heard wrong. "What are you saying, Firen?"

"If this isn't a familiar poison, she will die."

The words pierced Jarand like thousands of pins. He clenched his hands into fists at the sudden shock. He wasn't ready to accept any outcome where Mirelle didn't come out alive. There had to be something he could do, some way he could ensure they found an antidote. "I'm not letting her go without a fight."

"I know." Master Firen leaned his head in his hands. "I wouldn't expect any less from you."

Jarand had been so preoccupied with Mirelle, he hadn't noticed the deep circles beneath the healer's eyes, the halting lilt in his speech. The man was exhausted.

The door to the infirmary swung open and Lady Alystra walked in. She dismissed the other attendants with a wave of her hand before settling herself on the end of Mirelle's bed. "How is she?"

"Still in danger," Master Firen answered. "Our efforts have bought us time, nothing more. I need to study the darts to see if I have the proper antidote."

"Is the weapon used on her like what was used on the others?" She glanced across the chamber to the other occupied beds.

Jarand had seen the other three people across the room when he entered but hadn't given them a second thought. His focus had been for Mirelle alone.

"No, hers is unique." Master Firen continued, "I'm sure some elements are the same, but there are too many differences to make any conclusions yet."

Jarand took another look at the people in the beds on the other side of the room. One lay flat and still, the color had left his face. The blanket had been rolled back, revealing a thick bandage around his middle. The other two talked quietly. "How long have they been here?"

"They've all come within the last three days." Master Firen pinched at the bridge of his nose. "I haven't worked like this since the war. We knew what we were dealing with then."

"It's all happened so fast." The High Lady rested her hands on top of each other on her lap, giving an illusion of calm Jarand doubted she felt. "We're trying to make sense of it all. No one has been able to come up with a reasonable theory to pursue. I was hoping Bremin sent you with more information."

"Bremin is convinced Surasio is involved in a much bigger problem than stealing away girls." Jarand exhaled before continuing. "He seems to think Master Regulus might be involved. Has there been any news saying otherwise?"

Lady Alystra shifted on the bed. "My informants tell of rumors of him going insane, killing other Stonebearers. That's why I sent Bremin to you. You were supposed to find Regulus and learn the truth. I didn't want to believe the rumors either. But now, with these weapons being used, there's no denying Regulus's involvement."

She glanced at Master Firen and Mirelle before returning her attention to Jarand. "Master Regulus created the darts Surasio used as well as the blades used against the other Stonebearers."

Master Firen clapped his hands on his thighs, his face red. "You knew about these weapons?" He leveled an accusing finger at her. "Why wasn't I told? People are dying, Alystra, because I have no time to learn how to treat them. All of this could have been prevented."

Lady Alystra's head lowered a fraction. "It was years ago. The weapons were a mistake. Regulus knew it. He confided in me and me alone. I ordered him to destroy them and never tell a soul, not even you, Firen." Her fingers clenched at the fabric of her skirt. "If our enemies learned that a simple weapon could rob any Stonebearer of his use of the power, render him mortal, we would all be doomed."

"This isn't his doing. It can't be." Jarand fought to keep the growl from his voice. He wanted to shout, to scream. "Regulus didn't cause this, any of this. He couldn't." He gestured toward the other injured Stonebearers, feeling more helpless by the moment. "I can't see how anyone could suspect him of this."

"His weapons are being used. Master Regulus has been compromised." Lady Alystra met Jarand's eyes. He could see the pain hiding there. "He knew where you were hiding, Jarand. He knew how to hurt you most."

Jarand gripped the hilt of his sword, needing its solid comfort more than ever. "There has to be another reason, something we don't know yet. I may have been targeted, but what about the others? It doesn't make sense."

"That's why I need you to return to Bremin and get to the bottom of this." Lady Alystra straightened her back. This was her tower and she would do what was necessary to protect it. "With his informant network and your connections to Master Regulus, I'm counting on the two of you to uncover what we are missing."

Her gaze flickered to Master Firen's patients and back. "It would be a relief to know Bremin had someone watching out for him. He's been lucky through the years, but I worry with this current threat, his luck might run out."

Jarand was all too aware of Bremin's habits. The man avoided the tower at all costs, always saying he served the High Lady better out in the field. Jarand knew the truth behind that lie. His inability to use the power safely while around so many others who could had made his weakness more painful to bear. "How long has it been since you've seen him?"

Her eyes misted. "Three years."

Jarand's heart ached for the woman. Bonded companions needed to be with each other. They were stronger together. It wasn't fair the High Lady should be robbed of it. The pressures of leadership made it all the more critical for her to have someone to lean on, someone she could share the burden with. He saw it in her eyes. Bremin wasn't there to help her bend under the load. She was cracking under the strain.

Jarand loosened his hold from around the hilt of his sword and laced his fingers into Mirelle's once more. Lady Alystra needed Bremin as much as he needed Mirelle. They were two parts of the same whole. "I'd hate for anything to happen to him, for your sake. Allowing him to continue puts him needlessly in danger."

Lady Alystra pressed her lips together and blinked away the tears threatening to form. "My personal feelings aside, you need him. You said so yourself, these attacks are part of a coordinated effort. It could be the beginning of another war if we can't put a stop to it and quickly."

The thought of another war brought a chill. "We can't risk that." Jarand couldn't enter that grim world again. Especially after he had gone through such great lengths to find peace. He thought of Katira and the other youth back in Namragan. They deserved better.

If Jarand was going to help, he needed to know more. "Is there anything else you know about Master Regulus that might help?"

"He has a new apprentice. It's his first in hundreds of years. In fact, he's the first one Regulus has had since he trained you," Lady Alystra said.

Jarand chuckled under his breath. "That's odd. He's not really the master type." Master Regulus rarely took apprentices. He valued his privacy and time to work far too much to allow it to be interrupted. Lady Alystra would have only assigned one to him if she felt strongly that it was a good match.

"They needed each other. Just like you needed him all those years ago." A smile crept across her face. "With these shadow creatures growing bolder by the day, Regulus needed someone who could help him. I don't regret my decision of pairing him with the boy."

A wave of fatigue washed over Jarand. He leaned into his hand to keep from falling out of the chair.

Lady Alystra observed Jarand for a moment. Her brow wrinkled. "Bremin knows as much as I do about Regulus's comings and goings. If you have any other questions, he can answer them. Before I send you to him, you need to come with me." She stood and straightened her skirts. "This isn't something I would normally do, but considering what is at stake, it might make the difference between life and death for many." She turned, leaving Jarand to follow.

Master Firen eyed the High Lady. "My Lady, may I ask what you intend to do?"

She stopped and drew a breath. "I'm granting him rest in the arms of the Stonemother. She can restore him in hours instead of days."

Master Firen's eyes widened, he stood to face her. "You can't. We both agreed it was too dangerous to use. Too dangerous for those in the order to know about."

The High Lady silenced him with an upheld finger. "Jarand is not like most of the order. I believe he has the fortitude to resist her."

"And if he doesn't, are you willing to accept the consequences?"

"There will be no consequences." Lady Alystra turned to look at Jarand. "I will guide him."

Things were moving too fast for Jarand. One moment they were discussing finding an antidote, the next sending him back to Bremin, and now the High Lady was granting him something he had never heard of. All the while, a rogue Stonebearer was dragging his daughter across the map. "Would someone explain what the two of you are talking about? The only place I'm going is back to Bremin to save my daughter and find Regulus for a cure." His words slurred. The last of Lady Alystra's gift from earlier in the courtyard had worn off.

"No," Firen said, gaze locked on Lady Alystra. "She's right. This is the only way for any chance of success. You need this, Jarand." He gestured toward Mirelle's still figure on the bed. "And if I fail, Mirelle will need that cure. Go." He waved them off. "All of this hinges on time."

Jarand placed a kiss on Mirelle's brow before following the High Lady out of the room. He had trusted her so many times before, he needed to trust her now in his moment of need. They passed through corridors and descended stairwells until the air turned heavy and moist.

For all the years Jarand had lived in the tower, he had never been down in the deep vaults. The passageways were crafted by benders ages ago, sculpting and forming the rock into smooth halls. A series of spheres hung from the ceiling. Lady Alystra touched a point on the wall with a simple light glyph and ribbons of power chased through the wall and up to each sphere creating a line of glowing suns to guide their way.

They walked up to a heavy steel door looming at the end of the passageway. Lady Alystra strung a line of complicated glyphs into its lock. The door swung inward with a groan, opening into a room glowing with its own light. Two rectangular platforms streaked with thick milky bands of motherstone rested in the center of the room, formed with the same bender-made glassy smooth curves and lines found in the passageway.

An electric charge prickled his skin as he crossed the threshold. The glow from the motherstone grew brighter as they entered. The stone itself knew they had come. Jarand ran his fingers over the polished surface of the first platform. Waves of power churned beneath, waiting to be released, to be used. His own power stirred unbidden within him, eager to commune with the Stonemother. The markings on the back of his hand shone brightly.

His mouth went dry with uncertainty. "What is done?"

Lady Alystra walked to the end of a platform, her hands running along the surface as she passed. "Lie on the platform. Allow the presence of the Stonemother to sooth you and draw you into a dreamlike state. In the dream, do not allow her to touch you. The first time can be unnerving, and you won't want to return. I can bring you back by force if I need to. Please don't make me do that."

"What happens to those who refuse to return?"

"Your soul will remain in the dream state with the Stonemother and your body will die." She pressed her hands together and brought them to her lips as if fighting off a memory. "It's happened before. That's why this room is sealed off and not spoken of. It's too dangerous."

"Is that the consequence Master Firen spoke of, risking my life all for a few hours rest?" Another wave of dizziness hit. Jarand leaned against the platform.

"It's more than that. It is a complete renewal." She guided him back until he lay on the platform. "You aren't in any danger. Not while I'm here to guide you."

The stone, warm and alive against his back, pulsed a steady beat beneath him against which his own power thrummed. He felt a stab of panic as his power came to life without his bidding. The stone's eagerness for him to join it startled him. He sat up on his elbow and the light faded.

"Relax, Jarand." Lady Alystra placed a hand on his shoulder. "Allow yourself to be one with the Stonemother." With a gentle hand, she pushed him back down against the stone. "Let go."

Little by little, Jarand loosened the iron grip on the power he had been holding in check. He had expected pain. There was always pain when the power was summoned, but here, there was none. Once again, the complex patterns along his arms and shoulders came to life and radiated the same pulsating beat he felt from the stone.

He relaxed against the warm stone and allowed his power to mingle with it.

"Good. Close your eyes." Lady Alystra continued to instruct. She released her hand on his shoulder. "Open yourself to the power surrounding you."

With his eyes closed, Jarand could better sense the power surging through the room, through him.

"Let it wash over you and through you. Allow yourself to become lost in it." Her words came quieter as he sunk deeper into the trance.

A warm tide flowed around him, pulling him into its embrace. Burdens and worries from the last few days slid away slowly, one at a time, as if stubborn to leave him.

Scattered vistas twisted and turned in his mind and he fought to catch one, to make sense of what he was seeing. The harder he tried, the more frantic the images scattered away. He drew a slow breath and returned his thoughts to awareness of the power flowing around and through him. The images slowed and stopped. He found himself in a sheltered mountain glade. Within the glade, he could smell the lush scent of pine and hear the babble of a small creek nearby.

He wasn't alone. A woman sat near the creek trailing her fingers in the water. Her dark hair draped over her shoulders, reminding him of Mirelle. It wasn't Mirelle, though. This woman's smooth limbs stretched long, white as cream. No lines marked her arms, her neck, her chest, yet he knew she was a being of immense power. He took a step closer, daring a glimpse of her face.

"Welcome, Jarand of Pathara." When she turned, he sensed he had known her for his whole existence. They had been there, in the tranquil pine, for lifetimes together. And still, he couldn't help but gaze into her ageless face.

It held the sharpness of wisdom, of certainty. In her hawk-like eyes, he witnessed eternities. He was drawn to her as a magnet is drawn to iron.

"Do you know me?" She already knew the answer. The asking was formal, testing him.

"Yes, Stonemother. I know you." His step faltered. Her presence overwhelmed his senses. He knelt before her. It felt right to honor her in this way.

"You hurt. Is this why you have come?" When she spoke, her words filled his mind with their bell-like tones. Again, he had the sense she already knew. The asking was her giving him a chance to speak.

Visions of Katira and of Mirelle appeared in the clearing in the pine. "Yes, Stonemother. I've come because I need to help them. I need your strength to carry on."

"You have the strength. I see it in you. Your heart is strong. You give so much for others. Do you save any for yourself?" She stood from the creek bank and stepped closer. Another question, another test.

"What is strength good for, if it's not used to help another?" Master Regulus had instilled those words deep within him where they had become etched onto his bones.

The Stonemother bowed her head. His answer pleased her. "You have proven yourself. Accept my peace and lean on my strength should yours fail you."

Another presence appeared next to him. Where life itself filled the Stonemother, love and depth filled this new presence.

Lady Alystra stepped into view and placed a hand on his shoulder. "You've done well. It's time to return."

Jarand reached out his hand to the Stonemother. "May I have a few more moments?"

Lady Alystra took his outstretched hand in hers. "You can't touch her. You'll die."

Jarand lowered his arm, his heart aching. "I don't want to leave."

"I know." Lady Alystra placed a hand on his cheek. "But there is work to do."

At her touch he remembered Mirelle lying at death's edge in the infirmary and Katira screaming as they took her from the stable at Burk's Gap. The sudden pain of memory jolted through him.

He sucked in a breath and forced his mind to clear. "Take me out."

Lady Alystra wrapped her arms around him and her warmth pressed against his skin. The tide of power receded. He allowed her to pull him away, back into wakefulness. The weight of his burdens returned one by one like stones.

He opened his eyes and found Lady Alystra lying on the other platform.

Jarand ran his hands over his face. The deep aching fatigue behind his eyes had disappeared. His hands no longer trembled. He swung his legs off the side of the platform, ready and eager to go.

Lady Alystra stirred, her hands flexed. She blinked and turned her head to find Jarand. "This stays secret. Can you understand why now?"

He nodded. "Is it always like that?"

Lady Alystra nodded and sat up on the platform. "It took years to be in her presence and have the strength to leave again. It's still hard."

Something nagged at the edge of Jarand's mind. The secrecy of the room, the hushed way Lady Alystra and Master Firen spoke about it. He had a suspicion. "Stonebearers used to come here to die, didn't they?"

She sighed and ran a hand through her hair. "You always were an observant one." She stepped down from the platform. "Yes. Once they had become too tired of living, too broken, it was a blessing to let them go."

"What happened?" He braced both arms against the stone of the platform. "Do we no longer have the same right to choose when we die?"

Lady Alystra leaned against the doorframe and threaded in the glyphs to open the heavy door. "We had no choice. When the wars came, too many sought release when we needed them." She led him from the room, closed the door, and locked it. "Not everyone is as stalwart as you."

Jarand stopped mid-stride in the dim confines of the hall. "Would this help Mirelle? Restore her back to health?"

"Merely being exposed to the power, ours or that of the Stonemother, amplifies the effects of the poison. It would kill her." She sighed and allowed her shoulders to slump a fraction before steeling herself once more. "Hurry back to Bremin. He's your best bet to find Regulus quickly and get to the bottom of this."

Jarand pinched the bridge of his nose. Katira's rescue would have to wait. Every minute she stayed in enemy hands meant another minute in danger. He hated thinking Master Regulus had anything to do with Katira's abduction, but if the rumor was correct, the best way to find his daughter would be to seek him out. "Do you know when Bremin will reach Fordzala?"

"He should arrive later this morning if there are no unexpected delays. I assume he will stay at the Crescent and Star. He always does. You should find him there."

"Is there anything else that might help?"

"I imagine the city has changed since you've been there. You'll have to stay alert so you don't get lost. Last thing we need is you running headlong into the patrols." Lady Alystra opened another set of doors and they were greeted with the bright light of morning.

Jarand squinted. "I'm not going to get lost. It hasn't been that long."

"I'm serious about the patrols. These latest happenings have them jumping at shadows. They are itching to find a Stonebearer to blame it on." A piece of hair fell into her face and she tucked it back. "It better not be you." She stopped in front of the tall double doors of the tower infirmary. "I'll be waiting at the traveling post. Don't be long."

Jarand had been so intent on their discussion he didn't realize they had walked back to the familiar halls near the infirmary. He wasn't ready to say goodbye to Mirelle. He placed a hand on the infirmary door and tried to breathe around the fist gripping his heart.

The early morning sun flooded through the eastern windows of the infirmary and dust danced in the beams of light. An entire night had passed since Jarand had left Mirelle's side. He hoped it had been long enough for Master Firen to examine the darts and find an antidote.

Cassim walked between beds making his rounds as Jarand entered. Master Firen sat in his office, holding a dart carefully between the tips of a pair of slender pincers. He set it down and joined Jarand as he walked toward Mirelle's bed. "It's good to see you back to your normal self again. Do you feel better?"

Jarand nodded his reply. It felt wrong to feel completely recovered when Mirelle was in danger. He didn't want to talk about it. "Any change?"

"I wanted to give a few hours before checking, to see if any of her energy had rebounded on its own. Now is as good of time as any I suppose."

Jarand found his seat near Mirelle's head and kissed her forehead. "She feels hot."

"That would be the stonebane in the dart." Master Firen pulled up a chair on the other side. "The body reacts to it by causing fevers. Enough of it leeched into her system that it will be several days before it breaks down."

"Can't the Khandashii cleanse it away as it does other contaminants?"

"It would, if she were strong enough and if it were the only thing wrong." Master Firen lifted Mirelle's blanket and folded it back, revealing the series of tidy bandages.

Jarand swallowed down the urge to look away.

Master Firen continued. "Several other agents were used along with it—agents that react violently in the presence of both her own and anyone else's power. Lucia activated one of them accidentally." He checked the bandages with a practiced hand. "The life infusion she was given when you first arrived intensified the reaction, making the poison stronger. Cleansing her using the power would spell death."

Jarand furrowed his brow. "Doesn't delving cause damage then?"

"With a skilled hand, it can be done without triggering more. I wouldn't recommend for you or anyone outside of the healing order to try it." He pushed his sleeves past his elbows and wrapped his stone against his palm. He placed the fingertips of one hand in a circle around the wound in her belly and the palm of the other holding his stone against the skin at Mirelle's neck.

Jarand tried not to read too much into the unsatisfied grunts and scowls the man made as he went along. The process lasted several long minutes.

When it was finished, Master Firen sighed and pulled his hands away. "I had hoped with the darts gone, her own energies would rebound and break down the poison naturally. They simply haven't. Both her life energy and that of the Khandashii continue to slip away. At least we've removed the darts. No more poison can be introduced."

"What about an antidote? Have you found anything?"

Master Firen regarded him. His eyes spoke of lack of sleep. "I tested the dart for hours. There's a compound in there I've never seen before. I think it might be what's causing all the trouble."

"What does that mean?"

Master Firen looped his stone back around his neck and leaned forward on the edge of the bed. "Go find Master Regulus. He made this weapon. He would know what this compound is. He might even know how to reverse its effects. It's her only chance."

"How long does she have?" The question twisted the cold spike of fear in Jarand's belly. He refused to think of failure. Not now. Not when there was a chance.

"She's a fighter, but her body can only take so much. Considering what we've learned, I give her four days, maybe five. It's hard to say." Master Firen paused. Mirelle had been his student. No doubt having to consider her odds brought a special kind of anguish. "The damage will be considerable, and her recovery long, but I believe if the poison is neutralized she will be fine."

Jarand needed to leave, every moment he stayed meant one moment lost. "May I wake her to say I'm leaving?"

"I don't recommend it." The healer shook his head. "Pain weakens her further and we need to preserve her strength. It's the only thing keeping her alive."

Jarand's shoulders fell. He wanted to tell her he would do everything in his power to save her. He wanted to tell her not to worry about him or about Katira. He wanted to tell her he loved her. "Will you keep her asleep while I'm gone?"

"It's for the best." Master Firen patted Mirelle's leg through the woolen blanket. "Had the poison stopped its progress, I might have considered waking her so she could help search for a cure. Her knowledge of medicinal herbs exceeds my own." He chuckled at the irony but there was no joy in it. "Go, Jarand. I'll take good care of her."

Jarand lingered at her bedside. He wanted to memorize her face, so peaceful, so serene, showing no sign of the torment racking her poor body.

Surasio would pay for hurting her.

Chapter 11

Bright noonday sun warmed Katira's face. The fierce ache in her head made her moan and press her eyes shut. A pair of strong arms wrapped around her as a kind voice murmured gentle words in her ear. The soothing rock of the horse's gait brought comfort enough to drift off once more.

Dreams came. Papan came for her, rescued her. Elan held her safe and warm. They rode for home.

She didn't wake again until the sun hung low in the sky. Her thoughts were sluggish and had a hard time finding themselves. A flock of wrens erupted from a low bush as they passed, interrupting the silence. When she looked up she expected to see Elan's curly hair, or perhaps Papan's neatly trimmed beard. This was neither of them. The smell of the dust in the air spoke of large cities and busy people.

She stiffened as awareness settled about her. The rescue had failed. They had stolen Surasio's horse and ridden far away. He found them anyway. There was pain. Something had happened to her family. Isben had grabbed her, made strange lines appear on her arms. She had been so angry. And then ...

Nothing.

She remembered nothing after that.

Something must have happened.

A fierce throbbing ache cut through her head, hurting enough to make her stomach turn. Another moan escaped her lips.

Isben tugged on the reins and they stopped. "Hey. You okay?"

She swallowed and tried to work some moisture back into her dry mouth. "What was that? What happened back there?"

Isben brushed her hair from her face with his free hand, the tips of his fingers cool on her skin. "You were upset. Surasio hurt someone in your family."

She sat up, away from Isben's arms. Her hands went to her aching head. "There's more. You're not telling me something."

"Yes, there's more." Isben looked away from her and toward where the road dropped down into an immense valley. "But first—" He pointed out over the wide sloping valley falling away before them. "You woke just in time to see the best view in all of Roshnii."

They stood at the juncture between two rolling hills. Pockets of trees draped themselves over the crests and around the valley like wet felt stuck inside a basin. Ahead, the land fell away into a valley stretching open and outward past the point where Katira could see. Buildings both great and small filled the expanse of the valley floor. Walls slashed the city apart into great chunks.

An immense palace rose toward the sky at the pinnacle of the city. Its towers and spires reached so high, they seemed too fragile to stand against the slightest wind. Its white walls unfurled out of the grey of the city like the feathers of a winter dove. Beyond, the land fell away to an expanse of brilliant blue.

"That is Fordzala, the Capitol of Roshnii." Isben spoke with reverence. "There, at the peak, is the imperial palace and beyond lies the sea."

The sea, a body of water so vast it filled the sights, the senses. Katira blinked trying to see the edge of where the sea met the sky. Impossible. She had heard stories of the sea as a child and had never truly believed them. Back then, water so great nothing could be seen beyond it seemed ridiculous.

Seeing Fordzala for the first time should have filled her with wonder, with awe. Instead it stood as a clear marker for how far away she had been taken from her home. The world was so much bigger. She was so much smaller. She had come such a long way, so far from the security and comfort of Namragan. Everything was new. Seeing all this now, with her hair in knots and her dress stained and torn, reminded her of how far she was from home, of what she had lost.

"This is it, isn't it? The end of our journey is down there somewhere in all that confusion." She jumped down, needing space, needing to breathe.

"What are you doing?" Isben glanced down the path to where Surasio rode ahead of them. "If he sees you, he'll hurt you again."

It didn't matter. Surasio could hurt her if he wished, but he wasn't allowed to kill her. As gruff and disgusting as he was, he saved her back at the shrine. Isben was a different case, Surasio left him to die. Isben was the one who needed protecting, and it was up to her to do it.

"Let him. I need to walk for a while." She took the reins and led the horse after Surasio. It felt good to feel the ground beneath her feet, the life returning to her muscles as she used them. "Any news of my family?"

The road behind them and ahead of them bustled with people coming and going from the big city.

"No. But no news is better than bad news."

"How can you believe that after everything that has happened?" She hugged her arms to herself. "No news is far worse than bad news, because it means not knowing. It means wondering." She looked back to where she imagined her family might be. "It means imagining every horrible thing that could have happened."

Isben slid down to walk next to her. "It also leaves room for hope. I have to hope somehow all of this will have a happy ending, or else why keep trying?"

Katira looked out over the vast city once more. "Do all your stories have happy endings?"

"I don't see why they shouldn't." He shrugged with a smile. "Don't yours?"

"Back in Namragan, my life was a beautiful story. I thought I knew the ending. It was a good ending, too." Her thoughts went to Elan, to having a family and children of her own. "Now, I'm not so sure."

Up ahead, Surasio split off from the main road leading down to Fordzala onto a smaller path skirting the outside of the city.

Isben paused where the two paths met. "Someone once taught me that you must decide your own fate, so choose wisely." He glanced to Surasio then to Fordzala before walking down the smaller path.

"That was your master, wasn't it?"

Isben gave a sad smile and bit his lip. "Yes. I hope you get to meet him."

They walked on in silence. Katira didn't want to push him into talking about it and he didn't say more.

She looked at her hands, reddened and scratched from riding in the cold. No lines, no spots, nothing hinted at what she believed she saw earlier. She tried to summon anger for Surasio again by thinking of her family and what he had done. Nothing she did brought back that flaming heat once again. Instead her head filled with questions.

Only a handful of people dotted the Mountain Tower's court-yard. Mist collected along the ground in ghostly pools and leapt up at each step as Jarand crossed toward the traveling post.

A chill wind brought with it the smell of snow and pine, reminders of winter lurking around the corner. If Jarand could have one wish, it would be to take his family home long before the first storms came and be back in the comfort of his forge and shop.

The High Lady Alystra stood next to the traveling post. Through the mist, her grey robes made her look like a ghost. She faced away from the courtyard. When Jarand arrived at her side, her eyes were closed. She held her stone close to her lips as if praying. On the other side of that connection, through her bond, was Bremin.

Jarand stood on the edge of the circular clearing opposite her and waited, not wishing to intrude. When she finished, red rimmed her eyes. She placed a hand on the post. Her stately shoulders slumped forward. It was unusual for her to let down her guard, to remove the mask of authority, even around him. She inhaled deeply and sighed. "When all of this is finished, when you have found the root of all this trouble, I need you to promise me something."

"Anything, my Lady."

She met his eye, and he saw quiet desperation there. "Keep him safe. Bring him back to me."

Jarand wished he could promise her nothing would happen, that through all the troubles ahead he could keep Bremin safe. He didn't want to give her a promise he couldn't keep. "I'll do what I can."

The lines on her hands came to life, and she manipulated the different symbols on the post. "If I've judged the distances correctly, you should arrive at the Crescent and Star a few hours ahead of him. Be careful. Fordzala is more dangerous than ever for our kind."

She placed her stone on an indentation on the top of the post. As he watched, he couldn't help but feel jealous of the Traveler's sept. Even without the posts they could harness their power and transport themselves leagues at the speed of thought. With the posts, they traveled to the corners of the world without expending hardly any energy at all. If Jarand attempted to do the same, it would kill him.

She touched the glyph marking Fordzala and motioned for Jarand to step into the circle. Light flared around his feet and rose like a wave around him. The High Lady and the courtyard vanished as he was pulled into the network of motherstone lacing underneath the crust of the world, the life blood of the planet.

In moments, he found his feet on the ground again, this time far away from the tower, from Mirelle. He waited for the crippling energy drain to catch up to him as it always had before when he dared travel by post.

It never came. He uttered his heartfelt thanks again to the High Lady for granting him yet another gift. Without her, he would have started this most difficult part of his journey with his renewed energy gone.

The smell of salt and city rose to meet him, bringing back memories of his past, of a time ages ago when he had lived and served at the king's court. Being there without Mirelle at his side brought with it a keen sense of emptiness.

He gripped his stone and strengthened his resolve. He would save both Katira and Mirelle.

Or die trying.

Two HOURS HAD PASSED since Jarand entered the gates of the city, and he hadn't found the Crescent and Star. He stomped down yet another constricted street he swore he remembered from ages ago. This one dumped him out in the dark back alleys of the Fordzala meat market. The stench of rot crawled into the back of his throat as he hurried to find his way out through the congested maze of stalls.

A portly man carrying a pile of wrapped parcels blocked the way, forcing everyone behind him to move at his same excruciatingly slow pace. Jarand quelled thoughts of picking up the man and shifting him to the side so he could pass. Nothing was more aggravating than being in a hurry and not being able to move.

It took another hour of searching before he stumbled into the square outside the Crescent and Star. He cursed Bremin and his taste for tiny hard-to-find inns and alehouses.

Piles of garbage lined the walls. Too many of the shadows held even darker silhouettes making quiet exchanges, an unwanted kiss, a parcel, a whispered word.

Inside the inn wasn't much better. Too few lamps provided the barest light for too many tables crowding the main room. None of the other patrons paid him any attention as he crossed the space to the counter. Anonymity was one of the perks of places like this. No one wanted to be recognized, which meant everyone minded their own business. It was either that or be found in a back alley with a knife in their back.

A halo of pipe smoke hung near the hewn log ceiling smelling sickly sweet. It nearly overpowered the competing smell of stale spilled ale and sweat. Jarand leaned an elbow against the smooth wood of the counter, grateful it was kept clean. A thick shouldered innkeeper stood further down the counter, dealing with a gangly fellow who appeared to have had a few too many drinks. The man's feet kept tangling in the stool beneath him and he struggled to string his words together.

The innkeeper rolled his eyes and to Jarand's amusement, reached into the man's coat and plucked free his coin purse, selected a few, and then tucked it back in again. Another fellow with an abnormally thick brow escorted the man to the door and shoved him out into the square.

The innkeeper wiped at the spotless counter where the man had been and then made his way over to Jarand. "Sorry about that. Phil shouldn't have bothered my best serving wench. She's been known to slip nasty things into people's drinks for less." He sighed with a smile. "That's why I keep her around." He straightened. "Now, how can I ..." His voice trailed off leaving his mouth hanging open as he took a good look at Jarand. "Ah. I've been expecting you."

Jarand's insides twisted. Being recognized in the capitol as a Stonebearer meant death and he had taken all the precautions to avoid notice.

The innkeeper traced a subtle figure on the back of his hand, a symbol showing he was a friend. "Relax, Master Jarand, you're safe here. Your friends arrived an hour ago, ate, and then left again. Can I get you a plate or some fill for your pipe?"

Jarand agreed to the latter and sat in a deep upholstered chair near the fire where he could watch the door. He hated to wait, especially with so much depending on time. It wouldn't do him any good to go out searching for them. With his luck, he'd get himself lost again.

A flutist played an old ballad at the other end of the room. He knew the tune from his childhood and he let the music take him back to those carefree days, before the weight of the world descended upon him, before he knew he was different. He, like the young Elan, had fallen in love. She had flaxen hair and a smile that lit up entire towns. When he learned what he was, back as a youth, when he saw the streams of raw energy flowing from his fingers, he knew he could never be with her. It nearly destroyed him.

He knew nothing about love then. Being Mirelle's companion for almost two hundred years had taught him so much more about what love meant. It wasn't just an attraction, but a piercing desire to look after and protect. It meant making sacrifices without questioning why.

Thoughts of Mirelle brought a pang of loneliness. With her in a forced sleep, he could barely feel her through their bond. They had been so close for so long, the separation left him raw and aching. He forgot what it felt like to be alone.

Bremin and Elan wandered in before Jarand needed to refill the bowl of his pipe. From the look on Bremin's face, things were not going as planned.

Poor Elan looked as if he had been dragged around by his scruff. It was no small feat to keep up with a Stonebearer on a mission and the boy had done well. It wouldn't last. It couldn't. The boy could barely stand. For his sake, Jarand hoped their search would be over soon.

Bremin's gaze darted around the room. His face remained passive as if he hadn't noticed Mirelle's absence. Jarand wished he could do the same, wished he could put on a mask to hide the pain he felt inside.

Bremin spoke briefly to the innkeeper before heading off to a closed door on the far side of the room. Elan followed close behind. Jarand took one last long draw of his pipe before joining them.

The room could have been a broom closet. A small table filled most the space with a handful of mismatched wooden chairs filling the rest. The lamp hanging above the table needed its wick trimmed and sent tendrils of smoke spiraling toward the ceiling. Elan collapsed into a chair, practically asleep.

Jarand shut the door, taking care not to make a sound. "You two find anything?"

"They're gone." Bremin removed his coat and set it on the table before slumping into a chair in the corner.

The news caught Jarand off guard. "What do you mean, gone? You've never lost a quarry in your life."

"No, not Katira." Bremin tugged his scarf loose. "I was hoping to find another Stonebearer to assist us. You were long in coming and I didn't like the odds. There's not even one of us left in this quarter. We found their shops abandoned, looted, with no signs of struggle."

"Any word from the other quarters?" Jarand turned a chair around and straddled it, leaning his forearms across the back.

"Our kind are being hunted, and it's by one of our own. There's no other explanation. Had it been the guards or even an uprising among the people, I would have heard about it. They were blindsided. They had no warning and no way of defending themselves. No doubt the other quarters are the same. We'll lose valuable time if we stop to search each one. We need to get to the bottom of this. Not only for Katira, but for all of us."

"Where is she?"

"She never entered the city." Bremin reached in one of the many pockets hiding in his coat and pulled out a pipe. "Which leaves one place she can be. You're not going to like it."

Jarand shifted in his seat, hating what Bremin implied. "The ruins of Khanrosh."

"It has to be. There's nowhere else. Regulus has been a suspect from the beginning. That's where he's been working. She has to be there."

Jarand let his hands fall to the table with a thud. Elan jumped in his seat, startled partially awake. Jarand breathed deep. "Lady Alystra confirmed that Master Regulus created the weapon Surasio used against Mirelle. I, however, still refuse to believe he has anything to do with this. There must be some other explanation."

"He's involved, Jarand. You've got to accept that." Bremin glanced toward the door. "His name is on the lips of the commoners now. They're saying he's gone insane and is killing those close to him."

Elan leaned on the table, half listening, half dozing.

"You two getting along?" Jarand asked, jerking his chin toward the boy.

"He's a fine lad." Bremin smiled. "Although it'd do him good to take my word on some things."

If the boy had gotten himself into trouble, it must not have been too serious if Bremin could smile about it.

"He's young," Jarand offered. "He'll learn best through experience."

"Aye. As long as the experience doesn't kill him first." Bremin gave a half laugh which turned somber all too quickly. "How's Mirelle?"

The mention of her name caused a knot to form in Jarand's throat. "Master Firen can't help her. Our last hope is to track down Master Regulus and see if he devised some sort of treatment for wielders injured by his weapons. He's meticulous when it comes to his experiments. If there is a cure, he'll know of it."

Elan rubbed at his eyes. "What has any of this have to do with Katira? If Surasio been out to get you and Mirelle, why would he have sent her away when he finally had you?"

Jarand looked to Bremin, hoping the man had a good answer.

Bremin held out his empty hands and shrugged. "I wish I knew.

It should have been over at Burk's Gap. Surasio had what we thought he wanted."

Jarand scratched at his beard as he thought. "Someone out at the ruins wants me there."

Bremin snapped his fingers. "It has to be Master Regulus. If he had lost his mind, he knows no one is strong enough to bring you to him by force. But Katira is young and defenseless. By taking her, it guarantees you will follow. This might be his cry for help."

Jarand wanted to believe Bremin. It wasn't unheard of for Stonebearers to lose their minds after living hundreds of years. Sometimes the weight of a too long life was too much to bear. If Regulus wasn't in his right mind, he couldn't be held accountable for the crimes Bremin had listed against him.

"There is one other thing that might have made Katira a target, but it's not for me to tell." Bremin gave Jarand a level stare. He traced a figure on the back of his hand, like the innkeeper had done earlier. His meaning was clear. How do you tell someone the love of their life wields a power that will grant her immortality? "He deserves to know." Bremin didn't break his gaze.

Jarand took a slow breath and wished Mirelle was there. She was better at things like this. He gave Elan a level look and spoke low and concisely so the boy couldn't mishear his words. "Katira is one of us."

Elan sat in stunned silence. Jarand could see his questions bubble to the surface, then pop before he could ask them. His mouth opened and shut like a fish.

"She doesn't know yet," Jarand continued. "It was Mirelle's and my hope to be with her when her power finally manifested itself. We were assigned to keep her safe until she had matured enough to start training. That's why we settled in Namragan, so we could raise her in peace."

Elan's face reddened and his hands balled into fists. "You're wrong."

"Being angry won't change the truth." Jarand kept his voice level and calm. "I'm not telling you this to hurt you. I'm telling you because Katira will have it twice as hard when she learns it for herself." He met Elan's eye. "You need to understand so you can help her."

Elan stood from the table and pressed his clenched fists to his forehead as if he could fight free of the truth. "I don't want to understand. I want to marry her, have children, and grow old with her." He punched the wall. "She can't be a wielder."

Bremin stood and faced the boy. "Look, you both love each other. For now, that's enough. Don't do anything rash until you have no other choice. She needs you and you *will* be there for her. That's what a real man does."

Elan fixed his gaze on the door, he wouldn't meet Jarand's eye. "It would be easier for both of us if I disappeared." His words were soft, barely audible. "You should have let me die back in Namragan."

Jarand leaned forward, forcing Elan to look him in the face. "Katira needs you. You'll do the right thing by her. In person. She deserves that much."

"What will happen when all this is over?" The boy grew quiet, his voice broke.

Jarand hated knowing his words caused the boy pain. "When this is over, I'll take her to the Mountain Tower up at Amul Dun. She'll be safe there." He set his hand on Elan's shoulder and noticed the bandages were gone. Bremin must have taken care of it. "As for you, you'll need to return to your home and your family. Your father will hunt me down if you don't, and I don't relish the thought."

Bremin tapped the table before addressing Elan. "Give yourself time to think about what you've heard." He handed Elan a key. "Jarand and I have a lot to discuss. Go and rest."

The boy lingered there with his mouth hanging open. He shut it again and nodded as he rubbed at his shoulder. He held it gingerly while he stood and left the room as if he didn't trust it yet.

As soon as the boy was out of sight and the door shut, Bremin slouched in his chair and let his head fall back. "I outta whip you for making me take care of him."

Jarand found his seat once more. "What was I to do? He would have followed you anyway. At least with you minding him it might have kept you from taking unnecessary risks."

Bremin ran a hand over his face and sighed. "He's stubborn and naïve, a true northerner, really. Other than that, he hasn't been a bother. I hope I didn't scare him too much. I'm not good with kids. Even half-grown ones like him."

Jarand made a face. "Don't exaggerate. I'm sure you were fine."

Bremin absentmindedly touched his stone concealed beneath the cloth of his shirt.

Jarand gestured toward Bremin's stone with his pipe. "She sends her regards."

Bremin scoffed. "Surely she said more than that."

"She threatened that if I don't bring you with me when I return to the tower, she'll personally remove my skin one tiny sliver at a time." Jarand folded his hands over his chest. "She misses you. She needs you."

"I know." Bremin sighed. "I can't be her informant if I stay there."

"That's not the only reason you stay away and you know it."

"She's the only reason I bother to stay alive." Bremin adjusted his scarf. "We need a plan. For Mirelle's sake, we must move quickly."

Jarand welcomed the change in topic, grateful to focus on something he could act on. "What do you know of these ruins?"

"Not as much as I would like." Bremin snatched a pair of mugs from off the floor in the corner and brushed off the dust. He set them out on the table and pointed to the area between the mugs. "The main hall mostly stands, as do a handful of the adjoining buildings. Much of the greater structure has collapsed. There will be plenty of places to hide."

Jarand shifted the mug as he imagined the building. "That's not much to go on."

"We've gone on less before." Bremin snuck a sly smile under his hand. "This won't be much different from infiltrating the castle at Calenra to save Princess Althornia."

Jarand chuckled to himself. The two of them snuck into the castle dressed as peasants and bundled the princess away using only a prybar and a large basket. The guards at the castle believed her disappearance to be the work of a ghost.

Jarand peered into the empty mug, wishing there was a drink in it. "You don't think it will be as easy as that, do you?"

"No, but I can hope." Bremin tightened his belt and checked his knife. "There's no use speculating about what we don't know. And there's no reason to wait. Are you ready?"

"As ready as I'll ever be." Jarand stood and put his hand to the door. "Should we fetch Elan?"

Bremin shrugged into his coat. "No. Let him sleep."

"Knowing how hard you've pushed him, he might sleep until we return. He'll have to forgive us for leaving him out of all the fun."

Bremin set his hat on his head. "Finding his forgiveness is the least of my problems."

JARAND AND BREMIN slipped out the inn's front door as the bells tolled noon. Within minutes they reached the massive main square of the city. To Jarand's relief, it hadn't changed in the decades since he'd visited. The towering pillar and its surrounding fountain still flowed, filling the space with the sound of life. Vendors along the edges of the square set out lavish displays of fruits. Spices perfumed the air. Jarand missed this part of Fordzala most—its order, its beauty.

Namragan had the peace he so desperately needed after the wars, but it couldn't match the majesty of Roshnii's capitol city.

A pair of guards flanked the road leading to the eastern gate. They held their spears with precision, their backs straight. They would be watching like hawks for anyone acting suspicious.

The main street bustled with activity. Store owners hustled their wares under canopies in every color of the rainbow. Housewives in wide sweeping skirts walked the tables carrying great baskets on their shoulders filled with everything from food, to laundry, to bolts of cloth. Shouts to attract customers filled the air with the sing-song cadence of good-natured haggling.

A bundle of black feathers tied with a red ribbon caught Jarand's attention. He stopped for a closer look. One of the ribbons had three knots in it. A fellow Stonebearer worked here and had information he needed to pass along.

Bremin wandered back. His eyes widened when he saw the feathers. He took a cautious glance at the man arranging a tray inside the open door of the store. "Jarand, I don't recognize this man as one of ours. He might be Eastern Flame, judging by the collar on his coat."

With all Jarand had heard, both from Bremin and from the reports in the tower, a signal like this could mean valuable information. Fordzala was being emptied. Stonebearers left there would be pressed to find aid should they need it.

"If it's genuine, we are obliged to respond." Jarand surreptitiously checked his sword and his knife. So many of their number had disappeared, he couldn't help but feel uneasy. "Do we risk it?"

"I think we have to." Bremin studied a winter melon on the table in front of him. "They might have information about what's happening at Khanrosh. It might save our skins."

Jarand weighed their options. If it was a trap, it needed to be sprung or another unsuspecting Stonebearer might get caught. One that wasn't equipped to deal with problems. "It's decided then. I'll go in. You make sure I come out again."

"Be your most charming self. I'm sure you'll be fine."

"Not funny." Jarand rolled his eyes and walked toward the store, trying his best to look friendly.

The man leaned out the door and greeted him with a wave. "Welcome, sir. What are you looking for today?"

Jarand returned the greeting with his best smile and flashed the Stonebearer's secret sign with his hand over his chest. Couldn't hurt to be cautious. The man showed the correct answering sign and his smile shifted to a more somber expression. "Perhaps you should step inside."

Inside the store, several racks of different fruits lined the long table and bundles of fragrant herbs hung from the rafters to dry.

Jarand noted the lack of boxes lining the walls, the emptiness behind the counter.

"Have you been here long?"

The man shut the door behind him. "No, not too long, still setting things up as you can see."

Something shifted in the darkness deeper in the shop.

Jarand stepped to the side of the door, taking note of which way it swung in case he needed to make a quick exit. "Why did the previous owners leave?"

"They had business elsewhere. We've taken over." He shrugged as if it were nothing. "Replacements, you know."

The way the man said 'replacements' put Jarand on edge. He sized up the room. His sword would be useless in the cramped space.

"I saw your signal for help. What do you need?"

"Not much." The man's hand drifted to the heavy hunting knife at his hip. "Just your cooperation."

Jarand stepped back. Alarms sounded in his head. He needed to leave.

A tall woman with dark eyes blocked his way.

Jarand freed the dagger at his hip. His other hand went for his stone. "I'll give you a choice. Let me go or die where you stand."

The man laughed through his nose. "Hear that? He thinks he can take us."

"Maybe we should let him try?" The woman moved like a shadow, staying out of his line of sight whenever he turned. The whisper of steel told of a blade being drawn.

"You won't win this. Choose carefully." Jarand summoned his power and was grateful for the bite of pain sweeping through him, sharpening his senses.

"That's where you're wrong. We don't want to win." The man

214 JODI L. MILNER

twitched forward, Jarand sidestepped and flashed his dagger to the man's throat faster than the man could breathe. The woman vanished from view.

"Shouldn't have done that." The man gripped Jarand's arm.

The woman lunged forward, plunging her dagger into the small of Jarand's back. He smelled the cloying scent of her cheap floral perfume as his knees buckled. She wrenched the hilt sideways. The blade broke with a sickening pop inside him. A wave of agony washed over him.

He had to fight back, had to defend himself. Their deaths were regrettable, but at least they would be quick. They wouldn't suffer for their mistake. One glyph is all it would take. It's what he should have done to that beast Surasio back at the stable.

Instead of a glyph leaping to his command, it focused itself in a ball of fiery heat around his wound. The pain hit him with such force it sent him shaking to the ground.

A heavy boot kicked him in the gut. Jarand sprawled onto his back, driving the protruding edge of the blade deeper. His vision blurred. He heard rather than saw the second kick coming. Years of training guided his hands. He caught the foot and twisted it, slamming the man to the floor.

The lump of Jarand's dagger rubbed beneath his shoulder. If he could grab it ...

The man dusted himself off as he stood. "I wouldn't move if I were you. That blade is special. The more you try to access the Khandashii, the worse it will hurt you and the more permanent the damage will be. If you do as you're told, you'll be healed."

Jarand didn't care about damage at this point. "I have no intention of cooperating." His hand wrapped around the hilt of his dagger and he flung it straight for the man's heart. The man twisted away at the last second and the knife clattered to the flagstone floor.

"I've had enough of this," the man snapped at his companion. "Put him out."

"But we were told—"

"Just do it!"

In the dim light of the shop, the woman's lines glowed through the thin fabric of her shirt. Jarand shied back, he couldn't defend himself against an attack with the power, not like this.

He was as good as dead.

Chapter
12

Sun and sea breeze ruffled Katira's hair and tugged her mind away from the deep greens of the ancient forest looming ahead. She didn't want to go in there. She wanted to stay out with the sun on her face and the wind at her back.

Isben had been quiet since they turned off the main road and she could well understand why. Returning to the ruins meant facing the fears he had been hiding away during their journey.

They plunged into the cool shade and darkness of the forest. Katira squinted and tried to get her bearings. Papan's teachings surfaced in her mind. *Pay attention to your surroundings, the land will show you what you need to see.* She noted the direction the trees grew and how the forest sloped toward the city. When the wind didn't disturb the leaves, the foreign sound of crashing surf pounded in the distance. Massive stone walls loomed above the trees.

The tree-lined path opened into a clearing around the fortress ruins. A few sections of the outer wall still stood, the rest had collapsed in on itself. Surasio led them around the back of a ruined building to a sheltered area where three walls stood. A horse snickered from within a makeshift corral.

Isben leaned close to her ear. "Whatever you do, don't fight against them. Give them what they want."

The warning sent a shiver of fear down Katira's back. This was it, the moment she had been dragged toward. If this was the end of her story, she would make it a good one. She reached out her hand to Isben. He'd tried so hard. Whatever happened, she would do what she could to keep him safe. He deserved as much.

He wove his fingers into hers. The heat from his hand was a comfort against the coming trials they would face.

"When this is over, I'll give you that kiss you've been thinking about." Katira snuck him a smile. She loved Elan, that would never change, but Isben had earned an undeniable place in her heart.

Isben's face went slack and his mouth fell open for a brief second before he tried to hide it behind the redness spreading across his cheeks. "I don't know what you're talking about."

"It's okay." Katira felt her cheeks getting warm. "One more reason to get out of this mess in one piece."

They followed Surasio through a tilted doorway in one of the three walls of the corral. The roof over the narrow foyer had partially collapsed. They wound their way through piles of broken plaster and chiseled stone.

The end of the foyer opened into a vast open space. Light and shadow fell in thick bands across the broad floor. Katira couldn't see where Surasio had gone. She stopped at the margin between the two spaces, unsure if she should cross. As her eyes adjusted to the dim light, she could see frescos and tapestries. This was a place of importance, of history.

"Isben, what was this place?" she whispered. Speaking any louder felt wrong in the solemn silence.

"It used to be called Khanrosh. In the golden years of the Stonebearers, it was a citadel. King Darius ruled from his throne here in this very hall." He pointed down to one end of the hall and gave a surprised grunt. "Looks like someone found the throne while I was gone."

Katira followed his lead and strained to see through the rays of dust-speckled light. So much history had been bound up in these stones. Katira felt if she held still long enough, she would hear voices from the past.

At the end of the hall, an elaborate chair stood on an elevated platform. The sight made her breath catch in her throat as another layer of her childhood peeled back and fell away. "But King Darius is a legend. He's just a character from the stories told at the festivals, nothing more."

"You used to believe Stonebearers were a legend as well. The stories all come from somewhere. King Darius had the power. He tamed it." Isben pointed to a tapestry depicting a noble king with his arm outstretched. Light poured from his hand. "He discovered how to use motherstone to focus and tame the power."

A hollow boom echoed through the building, startling a flock of pigeons into flight from an unseen corner. Surasio stood in the light of a single torch, his hand raised to knock again.

The door opened with a creak and Surasio exchanged words with someone inside. He grunted his thanks and set his eyes on Isben. "Bring the girl."

She squeezed his hand. "We go together."

He returned the squeeze with a nod. "Together or not at all."

Inside the room, papers littered the lone table and across the floor. Along one wall a collection of odd gadgets, vials, and wooden boxes lined the shelves. Isben muttered something under his breath.

Surasio stood next to a striking woman sitting behind an ancient heavy table. Her eyes gleamed too dark for her deathly white skin and midnight black hair that fell across her body. Something about this woman made Katira want to run, to scream, but the woman's stare locked her in place.

"This is the girl under Jarand's protection?" The woman's voice poured out, thick like honey.

Surasio nodded. "Yes, Mistress."

"She's not much to look at, is she?" The woman clucked as she unfolded her long limbs like a spider and walked closer.

Katira shrank back. Her senses reeled in a panic she couldn't show. She didn't want this woman coming any closer.

Isben stood firm at Katira's back and whispered in her ear. "I won't let anything happen to you."

She wanted to believe him.

"I'm Wrothe. You will address me as Mistress, nothing else." The woman reached for Katira, her hands extending like claws. "Give me your hand. I must see for myself."

Katira pushed both hands behind her and away from Wrothe.

"Let me see your hand." Her tone took a dangerous edge.

Katira held one hand forward, hating how much it trembled. The woman gripped her wrist and placed a stone as black as night into her palm. "Close it."

When Katira hesitated, the woman forced her hand shut and held it tightly closed. Katira waited. One breath, then two. Nothing happened. A sliver of hope wormed its way into her. Perhaps all of this was a mistake and she would be free to leave.

Wrothe didn't loosen her grip, didn't shift her intense focus. A warmth awoke deep within Katira, the same as it had when she had allowed anger to take over when she learned Surasio had hurt someone in her family.

No. Another breath.

The skin on the back of her hands and up her arms tingled and grew hot. White lines appeared at the tips of her fingers and laced around the back of her hand before continuing up underneath her sleeve. The lines grew brighter and hotter until Katira was sure they burned channels into her skin. She whimpered and bit her lip, her free hand clinging to Isben's.

Isben stepped forward. "You're hurting her."

Surasio raised his arm and closed his hand into a fist. "Do not interfere, boy."

Isben cried out and crumpled to his knees. His hand slid from Katira's.

"Stop! He didn't do anything." Katira tried to pull free from Wrothe's grasp.

Wrothe's lips hooked into a wicked smile. She gripped Katira's hand around the stone while watching Isben spasm on the floor. "Oh, this is perfect! You both will be very useful."

Katira cried out as the burning pressed deeper. Each line tracing up her arm brought startling white-hot pain. Isben's face went ashen. He couldn't take much more.

"Enough. I want him alive." Wrothe's attention didn't waver as she studied the lines, studied Katira with those piercing black eyes.

Surasio let his hand fall. Katira couldn't turn, couldn't see Isben while Wroth held her captive. She listened, waiting desperately to hear Isben draw breath.

Wrothe released her grip and plucked the stone from Katira's hand. The burning disappeared, leaving her skin without a mark.

Isben gasped. He lived.

Katira hugged her arms to her chest. This time she had not imagined what she had seen. The lines were there. All the cryptic things Bremin and Isben and Papan had said to her, that 'one day' they always mentioned, that 'one day' when she would finally understand—

That 'one day' had come.

Mamar and Papan had raised her, had protected her, had taught her all these years because they knew. They knew who she was, knew what she was destined to be. Those lines she saw back at the shrine, the same lines Wrothe had forced her to reveal, weren't lines they had forced on her, they had come from inside of her.

She was destined to wield power, like her father, like Surasio.

Her knees gave out. She sank to the floor and pressed a shaking hand to her forehead as she tried to understand what possessing this power even meant. Elan knew all about wielders, had tried to teach her. Why hadn't she listened?

Isben lay curled up on the floor, his hands squeezed into fists, his eyes shut tight. Katira pressed her hand into his. She wanted to be strong for him, to be there while the shock of the death oath faded, but truth was, she needed the comfort of his grasp and knowing she wasn't alone in that room.

Wrothe leaned against the table as Surasio drew close to her. He wrapped his hands around her back and pressed his chest against her, his head tilted as if inviting a kiss. She teased at him and he grew more insistent.

"You promised me if I stopped the boy and brought you the girl you would return my affections," Surasio muttered, his voice heavy with lust. "I'm all yours, love."

"You'll receive your reward soon enough." Wrothe pushed herself free from his embrace. "There's something else I want first."

"Anything."

"Transfer both of their death oaths to me."

A strangled protest escaped from Isben's throat. Katira kept hold of his hand.

Surasio summoned his power and a series of glyphs sprung from his fingers. The lines of the net shone on their skin. Katira braced herself for the net to burn, for the agony to come.

It didn't.

The line connecting them unwound itself from Surasio's wrists and sprung over to Wrothe, wrapping around her wrists and disappearing.

"It is done, Mistress." He gave a small bow with his head. "Now for my reward."

"Patience." She held up a finger. "Ask me one more time and I will make you suffer."

Surasio stepped back, his expression reminding Katira of a whipped puppy.

Wrothe tested the new binding on her arm and flashed Isben and Katira a wicked grin. "Here are the terms of your new oath. You'll do anything I ask. You'll not attempt escape. Any disobedience will result in triggering the oath. Those who please me are rewarded. Anger me and you'll both pay in ways you have yet to imagine." She rubbed her wrists with a pleased grin. "Unlike Surasio here, I know how to use this properly. You'll beg for death after I give you a taste."

Katira's mouth went dry. However bad she thought Surasio was, this Wrothe would be far worse.

~

"Move it!" Surasio shoved both Katira and Isben across the hall. She clung to Isben's hand on her shoulder, glad for something to hold, something to think of other than what the lines on her arms meant.

A guard leaned against the wall next to an iron strapped door. He pulled a long draw from his hooked pipe and blew a jet of smoke in their direction, filling the air with the sharp odor of cheap pipe leaf. Instead of a sword, a wicked looking club hung from his belt. Scars crossed his face, one running from his left temple down to his jaw, another across the bridge of his nose.

"Another two for the dungeon." Surasio gave them both another push. "Glad to be rid of them."

The guard grunted. If he was amused, he didn't show it. He hefted the door open to reveal a set of steep twisting stairs. Katira held Isben's hand tighter as they descended in silence. From below they heard moans and coughs.

The bottom of the stairs opened into a circular anteroom barely five paces across. A lone lantern hung from a peg on a flaking plaster wall. Another huge guard with a square chin covered with a neatly trimmed beard whittled away at a piece of wood behind a rickety table. Shavings littered the ground.

He grumbled and laid down his work when he saw them. "I suppose they want you two in here as well?"

"No," the first guard said. "They've come to be your new dance partners, you dolt. Find them a cell." He gave Katira and Isben a shove before turning to leave back up the stairs.

The bearded guard plucked a set of keys from a hook in the wall before shifting his considerable bulk toward the door and hefting it open.

To Katira's surprise, light and fresh air filled the space beyond the door. A series of small windows lined the top of the far wall. Large columns supported the ceiling. Two halls branched off into the darkness on either side of the open space.

The guard walked them down a hall, pushed them into an open cell, and slammed the door. Katira stumbled into the cramped space and caught hold of the edge of the stone bed. The guard struggled with the old bar lock before sliding it into place with a bang.

Isben helped Katira to her feet. "Are you okay?"

Katira studied the dark cell. A small puddle of light spilled through the narrow bars on the top of the door revealing a windowless room with a single stone platform to serve as a bed. A rat squeaked from somewhere deep in the shadows.

"Okay enough, considering we're locked in a dungeon."

"You know what I mean." He looked at her hands. "Wrothe did something to you, what was it?"

Katira tucked her hands under her armpits. "I should be asking if you're okay. I didn't have my oath triggered like you did."

He patted himself down as if checking if he was missing any parts. "Still alive. Can't complain."

She couldn't stop thinking about the lines on her hands. It meant something so much bigger than she was ready to understand. Most fragments of her understanding led back to Elan or her father, and they weren't there to talk to. However, a few of the pieces led to the same place, Isben.

"Back at the shrine, what actually happened?" She shrugged. "You know, before I passed out."

Isben sat on the edge of the bed. He scratched at his wrist. "Your power woke up for the first time."

Katira shivered and hugged her arms around herself. "Did you know before that?"

"I had my suspicions. But, no, I wasn't sure until the shrine."

"You're one too, aren't you?" Katira stood and peered out through the bars. When she looked back, Isben held a small green stone between his fingers. The same kind of stone she had seen hanging on a chain around her father's neck.

"It's not something we talk about easily. I didn't want to scare you."

"I don't think you could scare anyone." She tugged on the door. As a blacksmith's daughter, she knew how doors and locks worked. This wasn't a lock, only a sliding bar. If she could reach it, she could get the door open. She reached her arm through the bars.

"I'm not sure that's a compliment." Isben straightened. "What are you doing?"

Her fingers stretched down. If she were a bit taller, she could touch the bar. "Exploring our options."

"If you're caught, Wrothe will torture you." He stood, a tremble of fear breaking through his voice.

"I can't wait here for the next horrible thing to come."

"Isben, is that you?" An older woman's voice called from a nearby cell. Isben leaned up against the door.

His eyes narrowed as he listened. "Lady Kala?"

"It is you! I thought I heard your voice." Cloth brushed against iron, the voice came louder. "Are you well? Have they hurt you?"

"We're okay." Isben pulled out the stone and wrapped it into his palm. "Is Master Regulus down here?"

"The first room down the other side. Wrothe keeps him there when he gets on her nerves." There was a catch in her voice. "Isben, I must warn you. He's not the same man as before. Wrothe has been cruel to him."

Isben clutched the stone in his hand and paced the cell. "He's here, Katira. I have to go to him."

"Can you do something about the door?"

"Maybe." He paused then closed his eyes and braced his hand

against the wall. The lines on his arms glowed to life. "You might want to get back. I'm not good at this."

Katira stepped back and watched on as ribbons of light flowed from Isben's fingertips. A single symbol formed in the air and fed into the door. The bar slid back. The lines on Isben's arms faded.

He swung the door open a fraction and checked up and down the hall. "We best hurry. I don't know how long it'll be before someone important comes checking."

They raced down the first hall and to the next. Isben stopped at the first doorway and peered inside. Pain creased his face.

Inside, Katira spotted what looked like a heap of rags piled on a stone ledge.

The bar on the door hadn't been slid into place. Isben slipped inside and approached the bed. He leaned close, speaking quiet words into the man's ear. When the man didn't respond, Katira came closer. With all her years of learning at Mamar's side, there had to be something she could do to help.

She examined him. His breath came shallow and sharp and his pulse raced beneath her fingers. His eyes fluttered, his muscles tensed and tightened.

"It's as if he's trapped in a nightmare." Katira sat on the edge of the stone slab bed. "We need to wake him."

"What would Lady Mirelle do?"

"Slap him."

"Really?" Isben's eyebrows shot up in surprise.

Katira looked again. She saw the blood stains on his clothes and the bruises on Master Regulus's face. "He's reliving some horror in his mind. It's a mercy to wake him. If you can't, I will." She lifted her arm to deliver the blow, cringing at the thought of hitting a wounded old man.

"Wait!" Isben caught her arm. "He's coming around."

Master Regulus blinked and his arms that had been pulled tightly against his chest, relaxed.

"Isben?" He reached out a hand and Isben held it between his. "Is it really you? I thought I heard your voice."

Isben sat on the edge of the bed. "Yes, Master. I'm here."

Katira had wanted to meet the man Isben had spoken so highly of. He had kind, wise eyes. She could see why Isben was worried for him. Now that she had seen how much that monster hurt him, she wanted to protect him as much as she wanted to protect Isben. They didn't deserve any of this.

The old man hoisted himself upright with a groan and looked Isben over. "Are you okay? Did they hurt you?"

"I'm fine." Isben reached for Katira. "We're fine."

Master Regulus heaved a sigh of relief. "I've been so worried ever since you left, ever since she set that scoundrel Surasio after you and ..." He looked to Katira as if noticing her for the first time. He turned to Isben. "Did he get you before or after you delivered the message to Jarand?"

"I'm so sorry. I was so close. He didn't catch me until Namragan and then he ... then he ..." Isben couldn't finish.

"The troll put a death oath on the both of us. Transferred it to Wrothe when we got here." Katira set her hand on Isben's shoulder. He shouldn't feel like he failed, none of what happened was his fault. "Surasio made Isben his slave. Forced him to kidnap me. He had no choice."

With effort, Regulus swung his legs over the side of the bed. "I didn't think Surasio had it in him. Death oaths were banished from practice. Any Stonebearer worth his salt wouldn't dare use them. Are you both still bound to it?"

Isben nodded.

"We'll have to find someone who can free you from it, and soon. Those things can be dangerous." Master Regulus returned his attention to Katira. "How is your father, my dear?"

The sudden change of topic jarred Katira. It took her a moment to answer. "I don't understand. How do you know my father?"

"I practically raised him as a boy. Just like I'm raising this scallywag here." Master Regulus raised a bushy eyebrow at Isben. "Didn't Isben tell you any of this?"

Isben ran a hand through his hair. "I tried. She wasn't ready to hear it."

Master Regulus patted Isben's knee. "It's okay. I imagine this whole experience has been traumatic for the both of you."

Katira's last memory of her father was him holding a great sword she had never seen before. The fire and determination in his eyes, in the way he held himself, sent a thrill through her. "He's coming. I don't think even Wrothe can stop him."

"Let's hope he knows what he's getting into." Regulus slumped forward with a groan and propped himself up with his arms. "Wrothe is a powerful enemy. Your father is strong. I hope he has it in him to withstand her. I didn't."

Isben knelt in front of him. "She's hurt you."

Master Regulus pushed him aside. "Don't worry about me."

Isben pulled out the small stone pendant from a cord around his neck. "There has to be something I can do for you."

"Put that away!" Master Regulus grabbed the stone from Isben's hand and stuffed it back down his shirt. "If Wrothe thinks you are a threat, she'll take it from you. Or worse, use it against you. It's better she assumes you are nothing more than a lowly apprentice."

"But that's exactly what I am."

"All the better to keep you safe." Master Regulus cricked his head toward the door as if he had heard something. "Go. Now. If they catch you in here, there will be trouble."

PAIN GRIPPED Jarand and held him in an iron fist the second he regained consciousness. His mind spun in circles trying to remember where he was and what had happened. All he could see were the sides of a cart. Each movement jangled the damaged nerves in his back and sent white-hot flashes up and down the length.

The blade. The trap in the shop.

It hurt to breathe. Ropes at both his wrists and ankles bit into the skin. Light streamed in from above, bright and blinding, forcing his eyes shut. Coherent thought returned one floating fragment at a time.

He had been captured.

He didn't know where he was.

He needed help.

For a moment, despair and fear threatened to overwhelm him. In his haste to find answers he had failed both Mirelle and Katira. Because of him, Mirelle would surely succumb to the poison. He prayed Katira lived, and there would be time for Bremin to rally the help to save her. Images of fire raged into his thoughts, the memories of heat licked at his arms. He couldn't succumb to his old nightmare, not now. If he did, he would lose himself to it.

One of Regulus's old teachings surfaced in his mind, "To do nothing is death." He clung to the thought. Something could always be done, but it was up to him to find it.

Voices ahead of the wagon caught his attention. He couldn't make out the words, but knowing he wasn't alone dragged his thoughts back to the present. From the bed of the wagon Jarand couldn't see much more than the sky above and a pair of crumbling walls. Birdsong and the distant whisper of wind in the trees replaced the usual jumbled noise of the city. The place seemed familiar. The smell of the fallen leaves, the way the harsh midday sun formed sharp shadows across the stone, tickled at a long-forgotten memory. He had been here before, in ages past.

The horses stamped their feet and snorted, jostling the wagon. Jarand groaned and gritted his teeth against the fresh jolt of pain. The talking stopped. The man from the shop leaned over the side of the wagon bed. His eyes widened when he saw Jarand awake.

He turned toward his companion without taking his eyes off Jarand. "Gian, I thought you said he'd be out for the rest of the day."

Hurried steps approached and the woman from the shop came into view.

"Impossible!" She bent forward to get a closer look and furrowed her brow. "He must be stronger than I thought. Doesn't matter though. Without his power, he won't be a problem."

Jarand froze at the words. He reached deep within to awaken his power. Instead of it filling him with its sweet ache, a torrent of pain erupted through his body so intense stars burst at the edge of his sight.

The woman patted his face, forcing him to open his eyes which he had clenched shut. "I warned you about that. Sorry. You'd have tested it anyway. They all do. Don't keep trying. It'll get worse every time until it kills you."

"Why have you done this? Who are you working for?" Jarand demanded as soon as the wave of pain subsided enough for him to breathe again.

The woman ignored him and turned away. The crunch of gravel underfoot announced the arrival of more people. Someone unlatched the back of the wagon and grabbed Jarand by the feet. Before he could brace himself, they dragged him from the cart and let him fall to the hard ground. The sudden shock made him retch into the dirt.

A thick shouldered man with a drooping eye loomed above him and pushed up his sleeves. "We'll take him from here."

A leaner man joined the first and eyed Jarand. "He's a beefy one, isn't he? Good thing he's tied up."

"Shut up and grab his knees. The sooner we get him in, the sooner I can get back to my drink." The droopy eyed man grabbed Jarand roughly under his arms.

"Now listen," he said into Jarand's ear. "I don't want to hurt you, but I have a job to do. Don't fight me and things will go much smoother."

Jarand couldn't fight back. Not until he regained some of his strength and knew what he was up against. When they lifted him, his body convulsed as his wound stretched and pulled. They carried him through a series of doors and down a flight of stairs. By the time they set him down in the dank cell, sweat dripped down his face and he couldn't stop shaking.

An escape plan would have to wait until the thought of moving didn't bring with it a wave of nausea. If the blade had been created by Regulus, any strength he wasted would not return. He patted his pockets. Bremin's vial had to be there. His fingers brushed against the hard tube. Bless the man. With the medicine he might stand a better chance. He dripped four drops on his tongue.

A square of light from the cell's door slid along the floor. At times, the light didn't move at all, at others it jumped. With each jump of the light Jarand worried another day had passed, another day where he had failed to find a cure for Mirelle. With each jump he found he was weaker, drawing breath grew more difficult. The bar of light finally disappeared leaving the room dark and gray.

A bar slid back on the door. Jarand heard voices in the hall. A different guard from the two he saw before entered, followed by a woman dressed in a low cut, tight-fitting dress. She spoke to the guard. "You say they bladed him?

"He wouldn't come willingly otherwise, I'm told."

Something about the woman bothered Jarand, something in the way she moved sent shivers down his spine. She reached down to inspect him, placing her fingers around the wound. Jarand stiffened as a pulse of power ran through.

He growled at the sudden intrusion. "What do you want with me?"

"Don't speak unless I say you can. Do it again and I will be forced to punish you." She slithered into the chair next to the bed, draping herself over the arm rest. "I am Wrothe," she said. "Surasio did well luring you here, General. The world is changing, and I need the strongest men and women. If you join me, you'll have a part in the glory of my new world. What do you say?"

As she spoke, the power of her words forced their way into his mind. His mouth went dry.

A demon.

It was insane. Impossible. Bremin, with all his theories and secret sources had never considered a demon being involved.

Her pull caught him like a vise, his body screamed at him to want her, to do anything to be with her. He focused on his pain, the one thing he knew was real.

"Never. I won't have a part in your madness."

"Oh, really?" She ran a finger along his bicep.

He flinched away. Her touch made his skin crawl.

"You're more handsome than the legends would have me believe." She bit her lip and continued tracing her finger down his side. "If you join me, I'll make your eternity blissful. You'll want for nothing."

Her promises rang through his head. He could taste her skin, feel the pulse at her throat. He would not give in. He couldn't. "You'll have to kill me first."

"Killing you is too easy. If you don't join me willingly, I'll break you." She traced her finger back up his body and ran her fingers through his hair. She gripped a fistful and yanked his head back. "I have that girl you've been hiding away. She worked well as bait. You'd follow her to the ends of the earth to ensure her safety, wouldn't you?

Jarand growled and jerked his head away from her probing hands. It was one thing for him to be caught in a demon's trap, but to know Katira was caught as well snapped something inside him. "Don't you dare touch her."

"I won't have to. Not if you choose to join me, at least." Wrothe bent close enough that Jarand could look in her too dark eyes. "I wonder how long you could watch me torture her before you change your mind.

Jarand forced himself upright and stifled the groan threatening to escape. "Stay away from her."

She slapped him across the face. The blow made his ears ring. "Join me and I will. You'll be healed and given a place of power. Your girl won't be touched. The world has forgotten the power of demon spawn. I'll show them we're a force to be reckoned with and I'll do it with the very power used to hold me back."

The High Lady was right. A threat was growing on the horizon. The attacks, the abductions, were all part of a coordinated attack to destroy the Stonebearers and possibly the world. Just as she said. Jarand had a responsibility to the Order to be on the front line and organize the defense against such a threat. It was his duty to serve and protect the High Lady.

And now that threat stood before him and threatened his family. Wrothe coordinated the attacks. She had members of the society hunted down and killed. She used Katira as bait. Kill the head, and the body will die. She needed to be brought down.

"So help me, I will kill you and put an end to this." Jarand lunged for her throat.

She seized Jarand with the power, lifting him off the ground and squeezing him like an olive in a press. "Before you do anything else foolish, let me explain what a nasty situation you are in. *I* decide whether you live or die. I can make your every minute the worst hell you can imagine. I will torture your family as you watch on, helpless to save them."

Jarand clamped his mouth shut. He couldn't give in. He couldn't risk speaking and angering her more. Her power clenched around him tighter, forcing the blade deeper, pushing the breath from his lungs.

"Know me, Jarand. I am Wrothe." She stood before him in awful glory, eyes aflame with a hunger that would only be sated when she destroyed everyone who ever opposed her. "Join me or I'll hurt your precious Katira. Think carefully. You have until tomorrow to decide. If you don't fight against the blade, you'll live that long, but not much longer."

Wrothe turned and left the cell, slamming the door shut behind her. The heavy bar fell into place, locking him in. The invisible bonds evaporated and dropped Jarand to the floor gasping for breath. He clenched his fist. She would not win. Not while he lived.

Chapter
13

The sound of footsteps echoed louder and louder down the other hallway as they came closer. Isben yanked Katira into their cell and closed the door with a soft thud.

"Sit down, act normal," he whispered as he peeked through the bars.

Katira settled on the stone slab that served as a bed. Nothing about that day could be described as normal. With so many changes, she had no idea what normal meant anymore. "What about you?"

He put a finger to his lips. The footsteps approached their cell. She clutched her hands together to keep them from shaking. They had left their cell. Katira had no doubt Wrothe could kill Isben for it, should they be discovered.

Isben stepped away from the door and leaned against the wall moments before the footsteps passed in front of the door of their cell.

Isben stood there, acting bored, as the footsteps faded away down the hall. The outer door to the dungeon opened and shut.

"What was that about? What were you so intent on seeing?" Katira demanded.

He sat next to her and rested his hand on her knee. "I wanted to know if these guards were Stonebearers."

"Why does it matter?"

"If they are Stonebearers, it means Wrothe has turned them to her cause. They would all be like Surasio."

Katira shuddered. "Was he?"

"I don't think so."

Katira ran a hand over the surface of the stone bed leaving a path in the dust. "We can't stay here. Is there another way out that doesn't walk us into the guards?"

Isben slid down the wall and sat on the floor. He nibbled at the edge of his fingernail. "We tried to escape before. It didn't go well."

"That was different. We were with Surasio. Here we aren't being watched or even listened to." Katira wiped the dust from her hands on her dress and joined Isben on the floor.

Isben leaned his head back. "The death oath creates a link between the user and his victim. All Surasio had to do was follow the connection. It led right to us." He sighed. "I spent all day trying to figure it out."

"And now Wrothe has that same connection to us."

Isben nodded. "She has one with Master Regulus as well."

"We can't leave." Katira rubbed her hands together. As the light faded, the cell grew colder. "We can't just sit here."

"To do nothing is death." Isben muttered to himself.

"What's that?"

"Something Master Regulus taught me." Isben took Katira's hands in his. "Means we shouldn't sit here and wait for something to happen. Means we consider all options."

"Papan used to say the same."

"You know where he learned it from, right?" Isben chuckled to himself.

Katira sighed and smiled before growing serious again. "I can't help but think we've run out of options."

"Thinking like that will paralyze you, make doing anything impossible."

She gave his hand a squeeze. "You're thinking the same."

A man's shouts rang through the dungeon. They sounded familiar, too familiar. Katira jumped up from the floor and stood on her toes by the door to hear better.

Papan couldn't be here, not in the dungeon. Katira refused to believe it. The shouts came again, unmistakably his. Her knees wouldn't hold her. They bent against her will and she slid to the cold floor.

Isben hurried to her side. "What is it?"

The silence following the shouts was more terrible than the shouts themselves.

Katira tried to convince herself that what she heard was her father shouting in anger, that she didn't hear the anguish in his voice, the pain. Her pounding heart and the sharp stab of fear in her belly told her different.

"My father's here. They have him." She scrambled to get the cell door open.

He wrapped his arms around her, holding her back. "Wait for the halls to clear."

More footsteps charged through the halls. Isben waited for the outer door to close before sliding back the lock.

"Are you certain it's him?"

Katira nodded, her throat had clenched tight.

"We'll find him," Isben said. "I swear it."

They found a barred cell at the end of the dark hall. Isben opened the door.

Papan lay on his side with his eyes closed. He barely breathed. As the light from the hall reached him, he blinked.

He reached forward, toward Katira. "Please." The word emerged gravelly and quiet.

She knelt on the floor and took his hand in hers. He stared at her in such a way, she wasn't sure he recognized her in the dark.

"It's me." She pressed his hand to her face. "What's wrong? What happened?"

"Shhh ..." He patted her cheek. "Everything will be okay." He tried to push himself up but fell back with a groan.

Katira placed her hand on his forehead. He burned with fever. "Are you sick?"

He shook his head.

Something else had happened. She looked him over more carefully. Even in the darkness it didn't take long for her eye to catch on the wet stain spreading on his back. Her breath caught in her throat and she pulled back his shirt from the wound.

"I need a healer like Mamar." The effort to speak left him panting.

Katira had to do something to help him. She would not give up.

"I'm here. She's not." Katira paused as a new worry sprung into her mind. "She's not here, is she?"

"No, she's not." He drew another ragged breath.

"Thank the Stonemother." Katira sank back on her heels. "She knows you're here. She'll find a way to help us, right?"

His hand trembled in hers. "She's dying." His breath became more labored.

Katira's hands fell to her sides. "How?"

"Surasio." He stopped to take a breath. "He struck her with a poisoned weapon."

The words struck Katira like a physical blow. She fell back, stunned and shaking.

"Where is she?"

"Somewhere safe." His words came slower. He had exerted himself too much. "Have they hurt you?"

She set to creating a makeshift bandage using a piece of Papan's shirt. "Don't speak."

He gripped her hand once more, harder this time. "Are you okay?"

"I'm fine. But ..." She ran her hand over his, unsure how to tell him what she had learned about herself. "I have the marks, Papan. They made me touch a stone and wielder's marks shone through."

With an effort he rolled up his sleeve, revealing the scroll like patterns circling around his hand and wrist. "I've always known."

"Why couldn't you tell me? At least some sort of warning?" Her despair fueled the anger to her words.

"I couldn't. Not until you came of age. It's how it had to be." He released his grip on her hands and sagged back against the stone. His eyes closed.

"Papan?" She shook him gently. "Stay with me. Please."

The heavy thud of a door opening echoed out in the corridor.

"Go," he mumbled. "Don't let them catch you."

"I will return when I can." She placed a gentle kiss on his brow and ran from the room, back to their tiny dark cell. Once inside, she sank to the damp stone floor.

Isben lowered himself next to her and wrapped his arm around her shoulders. "Don't give up. Not yet. He's alive. You're alive. That means there's a chance. There's hope."

"At what cost? This is my fault." She gripped her wrists and brushed against Elan's bracelet. At least he had survived Surasio's blade. Small mercies. "I should have been more careful. Had I been paying better attention, I wouldn't have been taken in the first place."

"What's done is done. Tell me, what can be done to help your father?"

"We have to keep him still and warm. Judging by the fever, his wound is infected." Her hands trembled. There was so much she could do had she been back in the healer's cottage. Herbs, gut for stitching, clean bandages. There was none of that here.

Isben held her tighter. "It's okay. This is a start."

The last of the light from the hall dwindled away to nothing, leaving them in darkness.

Katira set to figuring out else what she could do to help her father. She shrugged off the cloak from her shoulders. It was thick and long. It was a good start. More footsteps started down the hall, she would have to wait to give Papan the cloak. Hopefully not too long.

Their cell door swung open. Surasio walked in.

He nudged her foot with his toe. "You. Come with me."

Isben jumped to his feet and put himself between the two of them. "No."

"Shall I tell that to Wrothe?"

Isben shied back. "If you take her, I come too."

Surasio gripped his stone. "I can hurt you without the oath. Perhaps I should start by turning your blood to stone?"

"I'll go. Leave him alone." Katira pushed the cloak into Isben's hands. Her eyes met his, hoping he understood what she meant for him to do. If she didn't return, Isben was all her father had left. He took the cloak with a slight nod.

"What are you going to do to her?" Isben demanded as Surasio grabbed her by the arm and led her from the cell.

Surasio ignored Isben and escorted her back to the same room from before. Wrothe draped herself over the chair behind the table.

"Did she come willingly?"

"Willingly enough." Surasio shoved Katira forward. "That boy's a problem though. Do we need him?"

Wrothe tapped her fingers on the table. "It's not for you to decide. Leave us be."

"But Mistress?" Surasio sounded like a spoiled child having a toy taken away. Whatever Wrothe had promised him the evening before, she hadn't given it to him. Katira tucked the bit of information away, it might come in handy.

"Out." Wrothe's tone left no room for argument. "I'll call for you when I'm finished." When he had gone, the demoness stood and walked around the table.

"I take back what I said yesterday." Wrothe examined Katira's face. "In this light you are quite pretty."

Katira studied Wrothe in return. The woman could have easily been mistaken as human, but her eyes betrayed her. Katira had seen those black, beady eyes once before, when the shadow hounds attacked her. Wrothe must be a shadow creature as well. The thought made Katira shiver.

"You must have so many questions." Wrothe reached for her face. Katira flinched away. "I want to set your mind at ease. Do you know why you are here?"

"No."

"No, what?" Wrothe prompted.

Katira struggled to recall what she was supposed to say. "No, Mistress."

"Better." Wrothe nodded her approval. "You see? It's not so hard." She motioned for Katira to sit on a tall backed wooden chair and pulled another chair close.

"Ages ago, I came to your world. People like your father felt I didn't belong here and locked me away. It took years to figure out how to escape and even longer to put my plan into action." Wrothe looked out the window to the nighttime sky, out toward the sea. The sound of the waves sounded so foreign to Katira's ears. She found herself being soothed by them and by the calm cadence of Wrothe's story. Her eyes grew heavy.

"I must seem a monster to you. Some things must be done, regardless of the discomfort they cause."

Katira nodded. How could she have seen the woman as a monster? The cheery fire in the hearth warmed her cold hands and feet.

"I need you because your father is stubborn. I want him to help me organize my army. He isn't convinced my goals are honorable ones. Those with power shouldn't have to hide. I want to change that."

She turned her attention back to Katira. "Do you feel he's being unreasonable?"

Katira felt so comfortable, so at ease, it took a moment to think through what Wrothe had said. She was finding it too easy to agree. Wrothe had hurt her father and now she was talking about how she needed him. Alarm bells sounded in Katira's head. She pressed her fingers to her temples to clear her thoughts.

Her reply needed to be honest, it wouldn't help to lie or agree. "I don't know, Mistress. These are things outside my experience."

"He won't see reason even when it's clear as day. Perhaps if you explain the situation to your father, he'll get it through his thick skull. Being loyal to me is his best choice." A hint of Wrothe's frustration leaked into her voice. She returned to the window.

Katira touched where Surasio's ropes had left scabs on her wrists. He was working on Wrothe's orders. Her father was stabbed on her orders. The comfort she felt wasn't real. It was some trick Wrothe was playing on her to get her to do her bidding. Katira couldn't let Wrothe know she was on to her. "Tell me about his situation, Mistress. Perhaps I can."

Wrothe regarded her for a moment as if assessing how sincere she might be. Katira would have to be careful how she played the game.

"It's simple, really. If he doesn't join me, I let him die. And you don't want that, do you?" She turned back to face Katira. "It's in your best interest to convince him."

Katira gave a slight bow of the head. Her mind raced for a solution. There was no way Papan would agree to join this woman. He would let himself die if it meant protecting innocent people. Especially if those innocent people included herself. It would be foolish to argue with Wrothe. The best Katira could do was delay Wrothe until they found a way to defeat her.

"I'll do what I can. Mistress." The honorific came a moment too late, earning Katira a sharp look from Wrothe.

Wrothe returned to the chair next to Katira. "Give me your hands." Her tone turned almost motherly, enough to put Katira back on her guard. "It won't hurt this time. I promise."

"Please, no." Katira whispered. The memory of the last time Wrothe touched her was too fresh, she couldn't bear the thought of it happening again.

Wrothe grabbed her hands.

The dark lines on Wrothe's arms shone and Katira could feel an awareness open, just as she had felt with Isben. In an instant, she saw Wrothe's dark intentions and what she hungered for. Katira fought to pull away but Wrothe gripped her hands tighter.

A familiar heat ignited within Katira and flowed across their joined hands. Wrothe's expression changed to one of ecstasy as she drank the warmth in.

A cold tremor built in Katira's spine and she grew sleepy. Wrothe couldn't kill her, not like this, not when they had reached an agreement. This forced exchange wasn't because Wrothe was displeased in her; Wrothe wanted it.

The flow slowed and stopped and Wrothe released her grip. "That'll be enough for now." She licked her lips as if having savored some rare delicacy. "For that alone, you're worth keeping around."

She turned and opened the door with a flick of her hand. Surasio entered.

"Take her back to her cell. We're finished here."

Surasio gave a small bow before grabbing Katira's arm and half walked, half dragged her back to the dungeon.

JARAND WOKE when he heard footsteps close to his cell door. It had only been a few hours since Wrothe left him, she shouldn't be back for him. Not yet. He took a moment to assess his situation. He needed to know what his remaining strength would allow him to do, how much he could still fight if it came down to that.

Even with Bremin's medicine, he knew his time was running out. He could scarcely lift his hands and each breath took effort. He could manage one last surge of exertion. One well-timed lunge might be enough to kill whoever came for him next.

The heavy door creaked and eased open a fraction. Jarand steeled himself for the worst should it be Wrothe or her minions. If it was his time to die, he would die with honor, and if the opportunity presented itself, he would take her down with him. He uttered another prayer to the Stonemother for Bremin to come in time to save Katira should he fail.

To Jarand's relief, a young man shuffled in, carrying a bundle under one arm. The youth looked familiar but Jarand had trouble pinning down where he had seen him before.

The boy looked up and down the corridor before pulling the door shut behind him.

"Who are you?" Jarand whispered.

"Thank the Stonemother, you're awake. I'm here to help you. I'm Isben."

The memory of the stable at Burk's Gap flooded into Jarand's mind. This was the boy who had hauled Katira away. A bubble of rage burst within him. Jarand growled and grabbed Isben's arm, yanking him down so they were face-to-face. "Give me a good excuse to not kill you right now."

The boy flinched back. "I'm Master Regulus's apprentice." He dug in his pocket and pulled out a ring.

Jarand released his grip in surprise. Master Regulus's ring. The boy tumbled backwards. "Why did you take my daughter from me?" Jarand demanded.

"I had no choice. I did my best to protect her. Something horrible has happened with Master Regulus, with this demon. He didn't mean to. It was an accident." Isben spoke quickly, his words rushing out. He trembled as he fished a cup from his bundle and filled it.

A wave of weakness struck Jarand. He fell back gasping for breath. "Tell me what happened, tell me everything."

Isben related the events of the night Regulus used the relic they found in the ruins, when he came out bloodied and broken, when he asked Isben to kill him.

"Does Wrothe know you are helping me?" Jarand asked, his voice dry and raspy.

"No, and I hope she doesn't find out." Isben lifted a mug of water. Jarand wasn't sure if his stomach would be willing to hold it. "Drink,

Master Jarand. As long as that blade is in you, the Khandashii will continue to drain away. All you have is your life force to stay alive. That requires food and water."

"You're no healer."

"No, but Katira is." Isben glanced out the cell door. "She thinks the wound has become infected."

Jarand grunted. He knew he burned with fever, but assumed it was from the compounds in the blade, the same as Mirelle. He hadn't considered infection, but it made sense. "Probably is. Master Regulus's mishap doesn't explain your involvement in the kidnapping of my daughter."

"He sent me to you with his ring. For help. Surasio caught me before I could reach you. He placed a death oath on me and made me help him." He stood and paced the small cell. "I had no choice. I knew I couldn't stop him from taking Katira, but I could do whatever I could to protect her." He spared a glance to the stain on Jarand's back. "Otherwise she might have ended up with one of those blades in her as well."

Jarand obediently drank, emptying the cup. To his surprise he wanted more. "Then you have my gratitude. Where is she now? Why isn't she here?"

Isben went silent and stopped what he was doing. "After she told me what she needed to find to help you, Surasio came for her." The boy looked as if he wanted to say more but it was too hard to say the words.

The news made Jarand's skin prickle. Another wave of helplessness rushed over him. His daughter was alone with that monster, and he could do nothing. "Will Wrothe harm her?"

Isben unrolled a cloak and draped it around Jarand. "I wish I knew."

"Tell me more about this Disk Master Regulus was searching for."

"The Tower Historian tasked us to seek out the Disk of Shaldeer, a repository of the ancient Dashiian magic. When we found it,

Master Regulus was too eager to test it. I begged him to wait, to return to the tower." The boy hit the cell wall with his fist. "He refused. I think Wrothe had a hold on him, even then."

"It wasn't the right Disk."

"That's the only explanation I can think of."

"Where's Regulus now?"

Isben pointed toward the hall. "Here, in one of the other cells."

"Is he well?"

Isben closed his eyes and exhaled. "No. Wrothe is bound to him somehow. She's tortured him."

Noises in the hall silenced them both. Isben gathered up his things. "I have to go."

"Thank you." Jarand whispered.

Chapter
14

The sound of the lock sliding in its bracket on the door roused Jarand from a deep sleep. Several hours had passed since Isben left him. Morning light eased through the bars on the cell door. Thanks to the boy's kindness, Jarand didn't feel any worse than earlier, which wasn't saying much.

Wrothe glided in, her silken robe floating like water in the still air. A man followed her, keeping to the shadows.

Something about the man caught Jarand's attention, something familiar in the way he stood, the way he moved. Could it be? Jarand wanted him to speak. At least then he would know for certain.

Instead, he waited. He had to. He couldn't survive another of Wrothe's attacks.

Wrothe knelt next to him and pushed the hair from his face, her fingers alarmingly gentle. A longing for more of her touch rose from the depths and he shoved it back down. She took joy in manipulating him. He wasn't about to give it to her.

"You're strong. You'd do well with me, Jarand. I'd make you a leader among men. You'd be adored, worshiped even." Her probing fingers trailed down his back to where the blade sat. "Let me take this pain away. Nurse you to health. All you need to do is join me. Say yes."

Her voice coated his mind like sweet honey. He teetered on the brink. He wanted to give in, give up, and put an end to the relentless pain.

"No, Jarand." The voice from the man in the shadows broke through the demon's spell. "Think of Mirelle. Of Katira."

Jarand blinked and strained to focus his eyes. Master Regulus stepped forward into the light—his hair unkempt, his clothing haggard and torn, his skin streaked dark with dried blood.

"Shut up, fool!" Wrothe twisted one hand up into the air and a glyph flashed in her palm. Regulus collapsed to the ground, whimpering. She returned her attention back to Jarand.

"You've had the night to consider my offer. It's time to decide, Stonebearer." The full brunt of her influence pressed on him heavy and warm. "Will you join me?"

It wasn't enough. Seeing Master Regulus, hearing his voice, steeled his resolve against the demon. He wouldn't let his master down, not now.

"Never." Thoughts of Katira and Mirelle flashed into his mind. If he joined the demon, he would be destroying the world he worked so hard to protect. "You'll have to kill me."

Wrothe ripped her influence away from Jarand, leaving him shaking and cold. "Oh, I will. But first I'll hurt everyone you care about. Starting with him." She pointed to Regulus who lay curled up on the ground. "Stand, Regulus."

Regulus struggled to his feet.

"Please, don't." Jarand steeled himself against the pain and pushed himself to sitting.

Wrothe drew a jagged knife from under her robe and smiled. "Say 'yes' and I won't have to." She set the blade against the man's cheek, too close to his eye for comfort. Regulus stood firm. If he was afraid, he didn't show it.

"Step away from him, demon!" Jarand gathered up his resolve. "Your fight is with me."

Wrothe's eyes flashed dark and her grip tightened on the hilt. "Make me."

Jarand lurched to standing, ignoring his weakness, ignoring the pain making his vision swim, and he lunged for Wrothe's throat. He couldn't use his power against the demon, but the strength of his arm would be enough.

He moved a fraction too slow. A glyph flashed between Wrothe's hands and she flung it out in front of her. An invisible blow struck him solidly in the gut, forcing the breath from his lungs, sending him gasping to the floor. He could not back down, not this time. If he could end this here and now, he would. He forced himself to stand once more.

He seized the chance and lunged forward again.

She lifted her blackened stone. Three glyphs sprung to life between the demon's hands. They seized his arms and lifted him into the air. More wrapped around his feet and stretched him. The edges of his wound ripped open. Hot blood flowed down his back, down his leg. The bones of his back shifted and cracked.

Stars burst across his vision. Sounds of Master Regulus pleading with Wrothe echoed through the sudden crushing pain. He couldn't hold on, couldn't stay awake, not any longer.

Blackness enveloped him.

Katira rubbed at where Surasio gripped her wrists when he dragged her upstairs. The rope burns and scrapes from being so tightly tied during those first days on the road hadn't healed. The scabs cracked and bled.

Isben hadn't left her side ever since she returned. Her head ached. She didn't want to talk. She wanted to sleep.

He wouldn't leave her alone. "It's important, Katira. What did she do to you?"

"I told you, I don't know. She told me how she wanted me to help her and then she grabbed my hands." Katira pressed her eyes closed, she was so tired.

Isben pulled out his tiny stone, his eyes darted toward the door checking for guards.

Katira shied back, the thought of anyone else touching her with the power made her skin crawl. "Please Isben. No more."

"I have to know what she did. This won't hurt, I swear." The lines on his arms glowed. He pressed the stone in his palm. "Trust me."

She looked into his face, into those clear downcast blue eyes, the soft curves of his lips. He would never hurt her, not on purpose. She knew it. She had always known it. She nodded and braced herself for his touch.

Her breath caught as his hand brushed against the skin on her neck. The warmth of his fingers helped calm her before a different warmth swirled and danced through her body. The warmth lingered near her heart for a moment before withdrawing.

Isben sighed in relief. "You're safe, thank the Stonemother. She drained away some of your Khandashii. It could have been much worse." He sat on the far end of the bed and motioned her to come closer. "Lie down for a while. You can rest your head on my lap."

Katira let him guide her to him in the dark. Let him stroke her hair. Let herself fall asleep.

KATIRA BOLTED AWAKE. It was too early. First light had only barely started to pour through the high windows at the end of the hall.

Sounds of a commotion echoed through the dungeon. Her father's familiar voice carried through the noise. Wrothe was supposed to give Katira a chance to talk to him, to help him under-stand. Why couldn't they leave him alone?

Isben had fallen asleep sitting up. His head rested at an uncomfortable angle on his shoulder. Katira patted his leg.

He jerked awake, arms flailing forward. "What is it?"

More shouts echoed through the hall followed by her father's agonized cry. "By the Stonemother's throne, they're killing him!"

Isben dragged her into the corner of the cell, well out of sight from the door and wrapped his arms around her. "Wrothe is in a rage. Stay out of sight. If she comes after us, we're dead."

"What is she going to do?"

"Quiet. We can't let her find you."

A door slammed open, its wood splintering against the frame. A woman shrieked. Tense moments of silence passed before the footsteps returned to the hall.

Isben held Katira fast until the door leading out of the cells banged shut. The second he loosened his arms, she hurried out into the hall and toward her father's cell.

The door on Lady Kala's cell looked as if it had been ripped from its hinges by a wild animal. Isben rushed into the broken cell first. Lady Kala lay on the floor, eyes wide, hands twitching, and her breath coming in sharp gasps. He knelt beside the woman and cradled her in his arms.

Katira clung to the fractured doorway. If Wrothe had done this to Lady Kala, she didn't dare imagine what might have happened to Papan. The thought brought a rushing need to run, to find him. No, she would stay, for Isben. She would honor this woman.

Isben smoothed away the hair that had fallen into Lady Kala's face. When he spoke, his voice choked with emotion. He wiped his eyes on his sleeve. "I swear I will do everything in my power to stop her."

A slight smile crossed the woman's face. "Good boy," she murmured. "Regulus would be proud." With one last labored breath she was gone.

Katira bit her knuckle. It wasn't fair. Wrothe shouldn't have this kind of power. "What did Wrothe do to her?"

He balled his fist. His face filled with rage. "She stripped her power bare. There was nothing left to sustain her but the residues in her blood. There was nothing we could have done. A proper Stonebearer with his stone could have saved her. He could coax his own power into her heart enough for her to recover. But this ..." He bit his lip. "That is far beyond what I know how to do." He gently laid Lady Kala's body on the floor.

Papan.

Katira bolted down the hall. The door to his cell stood open. Papan lay motionless on the floor. A trickle of fresh blood ran down the side of his face. More blood soaked through the hasty bandages she had applied earlier.

Katira felt at his neck for a pulse, seeking any sign he lived. Isben laid his hands on him, his lines alight.

A weak pulse fluttered under her fingertips. Katira collapsed to her knees.

From the hall they heard more heavy footsteps and shouting. Doors slammed.

"We have to leave," Isben said. "They can't find us in here."

She didn't look up. "I can't let him die here alone. I don't care what they do to me."

"You can't help him or anyone else if you're dead." Isben paced the cell, running his hands through his hair. "We have to go."

Katira crouched protectively over Papan. "No. Not this time."

"But, if we are found ..." Isben left it unsaid. He didn't need to. The constant threat of being hurt, being tortured, being killed had been used so often, Katira wasn't even sure what it meant anymore.

"Close and bolt the door. Then help me get him off this cold floor." She couldn't let Isben see the fear racing in her heart, couldn't let him see how much her hands shook. She had to take control of this moment.

Isben stopped his pacing and took a good long look at her before nodding and closing the door. "To do nothing is death," he murmured to himself. "Let's hope it doesn't come to that."

"It won't. I won't let it." Katira showed Isben how and where to lift Papan so they wouldn't hurt him further. Wrothe would stop at nothing. Katira wouldn't give up. Papan would pull through. Katira wouldn't rest until she had exhausted every option.

EACH HOUR WATCHING over her father dug itself deep into Katira's raw and aching heart. He would wake, in time. Katira had carefully checked his eyes and the bones of his head to make sure he wasn't bleeding into his skull. Until he did wake, she'd keep that monster away from him.

She adjusted the cloak over him, wanting so much to do more. Without the proper supplies it was too dangerous to remove the blade from his back. There was no way of knowing what the blade had damaged inside. She risked him bleeding to death.

More noise came from the far end of the hall. Wrothe was making her next move.

Metal screeched on stone as each door was wrenched open, getting closer and closer to them. Katira's time had come.

Hushed voices came from outside the door, hurried and urgent.

Isben squeezed Katira's hand. "Whatever happens, I'm here. We face this together."

The door swung open revealing a gaunt man silhouetted in the light of the hall. Katira squinted, she knew that lanky frame, that tattered scarf.

The man took a cautious step into the cell. "Katira, is that you?"

For the first time since they had been brought to the ruins, she allowed herself to grasp this new shred of hope. Her fears fell away.

She freed herself from Isben's arms. "Bremin?"

"It is you!" Bremin reached out and cupped her face in his trembling hands. "I promised your father I'd find you." His forehead creased as he looked her over. "Have they hurt you?"

She grasped his hands and pulled them away. "I'm okay. But ..."

She stepped back, letting the light from the hall fall onto her father's unconscious form. "Can you help him?"

"I caught sight of him as they were hauling him away." Bremin ran a hand over his face. "I had hoped the wound wasn't as bad as it looked then. I brought help anyway, just in case." He stepped closer to Papan's side and gently touched his shoulder. "Glad I did."

Isben stepped into the light near the bed and cleared his throat as if he had something he wanted to tell Bremin.

Bremin's gaze flicked up at the sound. Before Isben could utter a word Bremin grabbed him by the shirt and hefted him onto his toes. "Do you know what trouble you've caused?"

"Stop!" Katira grabbed at Bremin's scarf, anything to get him to put Isben down.

Bremin released his grip a fraction so Isben could breathe. "He kidnapped you!"

Katira dug her fingers deeper into the fabric bunched around Bremin's neck. "This is Regulus's apprentice. Let him go."

Bremin narrowed his eyes and studied Isben's face before dropping him. "Explain later." He then leaned out the cell door. "He's in here. Hurry."

Heavier footsteps rushed down the hall in response to the call. A thick shouldered man ducked inside the cell accompanied by an impressive woman wearing armor.

Bremin was quick to make introductions. "This is Cassim. He's a Tower Healer and a friend of your father's. And this is Issa. She's Cassim's companion."

Issa gave a curt nod at hearing her name before positioning herself to guard the doorway.

More footsteps hurried down the hall and a familiar curly-headed boy stepped into view.

Katira felt faint, her mouth went dry. She blinked. Could it be? Was her mind playing tricks on her? "Elan, is it really you?"

He didn't answer. Instead, he swept her into his arms. "By the stars, we found you."

Katira held fast to Elan. The last time they had touched had been at the harvest festival. It felt like months had passed since that night. He was real, he was there. He was so very much alive.

NOISE IN THE HALL, screeching of doors, and new voices echoed through Jarand's dreams. Katira had been with him, had watched over him. Something new was coming. He needed to be awake. She was so young. He couldn't let her face it alone.

A new set of hands was touching him. Efficient, capable hands. "I'm here. Help is here."

Jarand cracked open an eye and was surprised to see Bremin bending over him. "What took you so long?" The words caught in his throat.

"Never mind that. I'm here now." Bremin pulled back the cloak covering Jarand and made a face when he saw the wound. "I've brought help from the Tower. Looks like you need it."

"Miss me already?" Cassim scooted closer and sucked air through his teeth as he peeled back Katira's makeshift bandage. "You have a knack for making people angry, don't you?"

Jarand clenched his teeth. "Just ... fix it."

Cassim put his hands on Jarand's head and chest. "Patience. Delving first." A stream of small symbols sprung to life and a warm wave of power surged through Jarand's body. When Cassim finished, he dropped his hands to his sides.

"What? What is it?" Bremin asked.

"His whole body is shutting down." Cassim spoke with care. "His blood is tainted. He has so little energy left, I'm surprised he's able to speak. Had we been delayed, he would have died." He paused for a moment. "The good news is neither the blade nor its taint is reacting to the power. I can heal him."

"That is good news. Possibly the best news I've heard in a long while." Bremin sighed and leaned against the wall of the cell.

"Jarand, I need to strengthen you before I dare do anything. Okay?" Cassim rolled up his sleeves. "Issa, could we get some light?"

Issa formed a simple glyph, creating a white sphere of light that hovered over Jarand.

Jarand could only nod. Darkness pressed in on him again.

Bremin extended his arm. "Transfer my energy to him. Save yours for helping the others."

"But, your condition ..."

Bremin rolled his eyes. "Only happens when *I* try to use it."

"If you're wrong, Lady Alystra will have my head."

"If your strength fails, we won't live to see the day."

Cassim thought a moment before shaking his head. "Give me your hand."

Bremin placed his hand on Cassim's who rested his over Jarand's heart. The marks on both men's necks and arms glowed in the dim light of the cell.

Cassim formed a red glyph and eased the power into Jarand's chest. Instead of warmth, it shot bolts of pain through him like lightning. He arched and gritted his teeth against the sudden shock.

Cassim pulled his hands back. "It shouldn't hurt. Did any of the energy take?"

Jarand shook his head. "The blade. Take it out first."

"Is there nothing else we can do?" Bremin asked.

Cassim looked to Bremin and spared a glance toward Katira. He returned his attention to Bremin. "Hold him steady."

Bremin shifted closer and grabbed hold of Jarand's hands. "Hang on. This is going to hurt."

Jarand held fast to Bremin. This wasn't the first time he'd had a blade pulled. Knowing what would happen didn't help. He pressed his eyes closed and sought that place deep within where he could distance himself. He let the rushing sound of each of his breaths fill his head.

Cassim dug in, coaxing the blade's edge out far enough to get a good grip. Jarand clung tighter to Bremin's arm. He was being torn in two again. His breaths came short and hard.

"Hang on, he almost has it." Bremin stayed near Jarand's head. "Hurry Cassim, he can't take much more."

When enough of the blade had emerged, Cassim grabbed hold of it and pulled it with a quick yank. Jarand's world went white, as if the pain had ripped his soul free. He floated upward as the scene unfolded beneath him.

"Come on, stay with me." Bremin slapped at his face to rouse him.

Cassim summoned glyph after glyph, slamming them into his quiet body lying on the stone platform. Elan held Katira by the waist to keep her back as she fought to go to him. What was left of him.

Bremin watched on, eyes filled with the anguish of loss.

And then the Stonemother stood before Jarand, her arms outstretched. "Come home, Jarand. It's time," she said. "You've suffered enough."

Her peace filled him as it had before in the quiet glade. It was his time. She had come to take him home. His trial was over. His suffering had come to an end. He wanted to take her hand, walk with her, and allow all the burdens he had been carrying to fall away.

He couldn't accept it, not yet. "I can't. They need me."

She took in the scene beneath them and lowered her arms. "So much pain. Are you sure?"

He nodded grimly. "I have work to do."

The Stonemother nodded. "Know this, Jarand of Pathara. I will only allow you to cheat death once. The next time I come for you, there will be no going back."

"I understand." He cast a glance to Katira. He couldn't leave her, not yet. "Please, let me return."

She approached his still form. Light gathered between her hands. She pressed the light into his body and then faded from view.

One of Cassim's glyphs took hold. A bright warmth spread

through him pulling him back. The pain of all Jarand's injuries crashed down on him again. He gasped and coughed as life returned.

Cassim fell back against the wall behind him. Sweat soaked through his shirt. He fought to catch his breath. "That was close. Too close. Remind me why I offered to come again?"

"Because you are the best Master Firen could spare." Bremin chuckled. "And you volunteered. For that I'm grateful. Not many could have done what you did. Trust me, I know."

Jarand opened his eyes and patted Bremin's arm. "Remind me not to get stabbed again."

"Try not to do anything stupid like walking into a trap again." Bremin said, wiping his face with a handkerchief.

Cassim chuckled to himself. "Don't think he can."

"Is it done?" Jarand gingerly tested his back and was rewarded with splitting pain up and down his spine.

"That was the worst of it, thank the Stonemother. This kind of blade might have left slivers. I've got to get them out as well or you'll never heal. Then there's the matter of putting the important bits back together. Can you hold any power right now?"

Jarand cringed at the thought of letting Cassim continue to work. Knowing what had to be done didn't make it easier. "Not sure."

"Try. It'll ease the next part." Cassim placed his hands around the wound again, "Let me know when you are ready."

Jarand steadied his breathing and sought the place deep within once more. He bid his power waken, but it kept pulling away.

"I can't," Jarand said. "It keeps pulling back. You'll have to do it without."

"Bremin, keep him still if you can." Cassim formed an intricate pattern in the air and fed it down into the wound. Even with Bremin pinning down his shoulders, Jarand couldn't help but stiffen and twitch as each of the fragments surfaced and fell to the floor.

Cassim's lines faded. He removed his hands. "Try again, Jarand. I need to know they are all out."

Jarand closed his eyes and took a slow breath before letting it go.

This was his power, it would obey him. He bid it wake and was rewarded with a slow steady glow stretching through his body. He would need time to recover before it grew back into the roaring fire of power it once was, but it was a comfort to have it back under his control.

"Good, it's done. You'll live," Cassim said as he tucked away his stone.

"Let me through," Katira demanded.

Elan kept a hand on her arm, holding her back. She pried his fingers away to get him to let go.

"It's okay. Let her in." Bremin told him. "We can't stay long. Anyone with an inkling of the power will feel what Cassim did. I expect we'll have company soon." He turned his attention back to Jarand.

"Jarand, what are we in for?"

Jarand gave a dry chuckle. "I was right. Master Regulus isn't responsible."

Bremin scowled. "Then who is?"

"Wrothe. The demoness." He coughed with a wince.

Bremin sat up straight. "I guess I owe you a drink." He brushed off his hands. "It also means we leave as soon as possible. We're not prepared to take down a demon."

"We don't leave without Master Regulus." Jarand held Katira close, she needed more reassurance than anyone right then. "He's Mirelle's only hope."

Bremin agreed with a bob of his head. "Where is he?"

Isben pointed toward the door. "Wrothe sometimes keeps him down the hall, when she's not using him. But he can't leave this place. Master Regulus is tied to her somehow. It hurts him if they get too far apart."

"That Stonemother twisting demon." Bremin spat onto the ground.

Cassim stood and straightened his shirt. "I might be able to break him free."

Bremin issued orders. "Fine. Cassim, go with Isben. Just in case."

The two ran down the hall and returned just as quickly. "He's not there," Isben said. "He must be up in the great hall with her."

"Does anyone have any good news?" Bremin asked, rubbing at his temples.

The outer dungeon door slammed open. From the end of the long hall they heard hurried footsteps.

"Well, we're dead." Bremin said, rolling his eyes again. "Can we make it to the back exit before they see us?"

"If we move quickly, yes." Issa answered.

Jarand knew he couldn't go fast enough, not against running guards and rogue Stonebearers. "Go without me. Save yourselves."

"Not after saving your skin, we won't." Bremin scanned the scene. "New plan. We defend the cell, send the kids away."

Issa unsheathed the sword from off her back and gripped her stone. Cassim stood near her, a knife in hand. Both glowed with power.

"Elan, take Katira and Isben out the way we came in." Bremin instructed. "Stay out of sight. With luck, most of the guards' attention will be drawn down here to the dungeon. The way will be clear for you to make it to the protection of the cliffs."

Elan took Katira by the arm, but she pried his hand off. "I can't leave."

Elan reached to grab her arm again. "You can't fight against this."

Isben put himself between Elan and Katira and seized Elan's hand. "It's true, she can't. I can't either."

Jarand strained to hear what the problem was, why his daughter wouldn't leave. He prayed it wasn't because she didn't want to leave him. He had seen Wrothe's violent side. Katira needed to be far away.

"It'll be okay, Katira. Go. Get to safety." Jarand tried to make himself heard over the commotion.

Bremin seized Isben and Katira by the collar and shoved them out into the hallway. "Get out of here before things get ugly. That's an order."

Katira struggled against Bremin's grip.

Isben grabbed the man's hands. "We can't leave here, Bremin."

"Why?" Bremin demanded. "Give me a good reason."

Katira looked too tired to fight against Bremin. She stood her ground, panting. "Wrothe. She forced us under an oath. If we try to escape, it'll trigger and kill us both."

"Is this true?" Bremin asked Isben.

Isben gave a solemn nod and ran a hand through his hair.

Bremin pushed the three of them into the corner of the cell, close to the head of the stone bed where Jarand rested. "Stay out of sight."

Issa watched at the doorway. "There are two, perhaps three, coming."

Bremin unsheathed his hunting knife. "If we take them by surprise, we might be able to subdue them."

Issa closed the door without a sound, preparing the trap. Bremin and Cassim pressed their backs to the wall, out of view from the barred window.

A ball of light leapt through the bars and hovered in the center of the room.

The guard with the scar crossing his face peered in. "I thought you said Wrothe had her way with him. How'd he get back on the bed?"

"Open the door," a familiar voice ordered. Surasio.

The door creaked open. The guard entered the cell first. Bremin signaled for them to move. Cassim's and Issa's power crackled to life as they attacked. Issa grabbed the guard and threw him to the floor face down and pinned him there, her sword glowing at his throat.

Cassim sprang for Surasio a moment too late. Surasio sidestepped him and delivered a powerful punch to the back of his head, sending Cassim sprawling to the floor.

"It's a shame, Jarand." Surasio's voice slid around the cell like oil.

"Your rescue party wasn't up to dealing with me." He stepped closer to Jarand.

"One step closer and your friend here tastes my blade." Issa pulled on the hair of the guard, raising his head and bringing the edge of her sword against his throat.

"He's not my friend." Surasio nudged the guard with a toe. "Do it. Save me the aggravation. In fact ..." In one swift motion Surasio brought his foot down on the back of the guard's head, forcing his neck onto Issa's blade.

The guard clawed at his ruined throat, his shrieks gagged by his own blood. After a moment he fell still.

Issa dropped the dead man and leveled her sword at Surasio's chest. "Don't you bloody move, you stone twisting twat."

Surasio ran his finger along the top of the blade, across the red slick of the guard's blood. "I don't do well with orders." The lines on his hands flashed bright and three glyphs formed in the air.

Issa acted quickly, forming her own glyphs. She threw them into action as Surasio's glyphs exploded through the air with an immense crack of energy. Issa's glyphs shattered and fell as Surasio's glyph wrapped around her, Bremin, and Cassim, holding them fast.

Surasio pushed Issa's blade out of the way and drew closer to her. "Issa, Issa, Issa. It's a shame we didn't meet under different circumstances." He stuck his probing fingers down the top of her breastplate and then pulled them free and smelled them. He grinned and leered at her. "Under all that metal you are still a woman. I would very much like to do more interesting things to you."

Cassim grunted in his bindings. Surasio's glyph caught him stuck halfway between kneeling and standing.

"Don't mind me, Cassim. I wouldn't hurt her. In fact, I think we would rather enjoy our time together." Surasio pulled Issa's sword from her hand and tested its edge. "But for now, I have business to attend to."

Surasio approached Bremin next, leaning close and resting the point of Issa's sword against the notch at Bremin's throat.

"Hello again, Bremin. It seems you can't stay away from me, can you?" Surasio played with the sword, running the edge of the blade across Bremin's chest and close to his neck. Bremin stared the man down.

"Leave them alone," Jarand said, forcing himself upright. Surasio had not bothered to bind him with his glyph, most likely assuming he wasn't a threat. He was probably right.

"Why should I?" Surasio stopped short and turned to face Jarand. He tossed Issa's sword on the ground. "I have been charged to protect Wrothe's interests. These friends of yours are interfering. Wrothe sent me to bring you to the main hall. Your girl, too." His gaze darted to the corner where Katira hid. "Thanks for making it easier. Now I don't have to fetch her from her cell."

Jarand weighed the options. They outnumbered Surasio. Once his holding glyph failed, it would be easy to subdue him. He needed to stall. "If Wrothe wants me, she'll have to come get me herself."

"Why must you always make things difficult?" Surasio pulled three small darts from his pocket and cupped them in his palm. "Now we have to do things the hard way."

Jarand eyed the darts. They were the same as the ones killing Mirelle. He swallowed hard and coaxed the threads of his power to wake. The effort made him shake. He couldn't let anyone else fall to this man's cruelty, not if he could help it. "Wrothe's interests border on insanity and you know it."

"Sanity is overrated. I'd rather have myself a little fun." Surasio summoned another glyph. The darts floated into the air.

Jarand calculated what it might take to keep Surasio from releasing his weapon. He'd have to act fast and hit hard. He wasn't sure if he was strong enough. "You call torturing and killing fun? You're no more than a monster."

Surasio's eyes flashed dark. "Oh, you have no idea how much of a monster I am."

"Let them go. They aren't involved." Jarand fought to keep a steely calm in his voice. He would win no battles by losing his temper. Binding glyphs required a huge amount of energy to maintain. It couldn't be much longer before it failed.

"Since they're here, I might as well use them as leverage. If you come with me, I won't kill them. Refuse and they'll die, just like Mirelle." The darts spun in the air, faster and faster.

"Mirelle will survive this, you won't." One glyph was all Jarand needed. One glyph at the perfect time.

"Do you really think threatening me is a good idea right now?" The darts spun even faster. "Time is running out, Jarand. Are you coming with me or not?"

In a blur, Isben rushed at Surasio from the corner, catching the man off guard and knocking him to the floor.

Jarand formed and released his glyph, seizing the darts midair, preventing them from striking their targets.

Surasio's head struck the floor, and he released the binding glyph. Cassim, Issa, and Bremin fell as if their puppet strings were cut.

"You insignificant brat!" Surasio shouted, his face turning red with rage. "You'll pay for this."

"No. I won't." Isben yanked one of Surasio's throwing knives free and plunged the blade into the man's chest. He struck over and over again, inarticulate sobs breaking from his mouth with each blow.

Bremin grabbed Isben under his arms, pulled him away, and locked him in his grasp until he stopped fighting. "Enough, boy. It's done."

Cassim touched the body, feeling for any trace of life. He shook his head.

Isben trembled in Bremin's arms. He lowered the youth to the floor and gently pried the stained blade from his hands.

"I killed him," Isben whispered.

"I know." Bremin cupped Isben's chin in his hands. "You saved our lives."

Bremin turned his attention back toward Jarand. "Can you walk?"

"I'll need some help."

Cassim offered Jarand his shoulder and hoisted him to standing. They took a step forward before Jarand's left leg buckled out from beneath him. "It's no use," he said, clutching his thigh. "I can't lift it."

Cassim set him back onto the stone bed. "The blade must have damaged your back. It's beyond my skill. We'd best get you to the Tower."

Bremin peered out into the hall. More guards were sure to be on their way, and possibly Wrothe herself. "Damn demon shadow. We're trapped like rats if we stay here." He adjusted his scarf and checked his knife. "It will be too difficult to get Jarand out the way we came in. Anyone have any other ideas?"

Issa gathered her sword from the ground and studied the blade before slipping it into its sheath. "If we move quickly and quietly, there is a chance we might slip through the main hall before they can mount a defense."

"She's right." Jarand added with a grimace. "From what I've seen, they aren't prepared for a fight. It might work. It also gives us a chance at finding Master Regulus. If he's not down here, then he has to be up there somewhere."

"Do you think it wise? We might run into that she-devil." Bremin's face wrinkled at the possibility.

Jarand gripped the door frame of the cell to steady himself. "We aren't leaving without Master Regulus. It's worth the risk."

KATIRA CLUNG to Papan's confidence as he made his way through the corridor, using it to bolster her own. The weight of the blade in her pocket brushed against her leg as they walked. If the broken blade was enough to bring down her father, it might be enough to make a difference should there be a fight. If anything, it gave her much needed reassurance that she wasn't completely helpless.

She worried about Elan. He hadn't left her side. He was so out of his element here. The brave face he wore would break the moment Wrothe touched him.

Isben hadn't said a word since he struck out at Surasio. He walked down the corridor, his eyes vacant and glassy, his mind still locked on what he'd done. Katira longed to comfort him as he'd done for her, but this wasn't the time.

No guard sat in the room outside the dungeon door. Issa darted up the spiral stairs. Cassim waited at the base of the stair, his lips pressed together so tightly they had gone white. A moment later they heard the distinct sound of a body hitting the floor.

Papan turned to Katira. "When we get to the hall, stay out of sight." Even with one arm around Cassim, Papan winced with each step. He could barely use his leg, could barely stand. Katira knew he was in no shape to face anyone, let alone a demon.

Katira gave a small nod but promised nothing. She wouldn't abandon him, not after all that had happened.

Issa called down the stairs. "The main hall is empty, at least for a while."

Cassim released a sigh of relief. "Let's get this over with."

Sweat dripped down Papan's face as they made their way up the steep stairs. They slipped through the door and into the shadow of a tall column. He swayed and stumbled.

"You okay to make it out of here?" Bremin asked in a low voice.

"I'm getting too old for this," Papan answered.

Bremin patted his shoulder. "Aren't we all?" He walked Papan to the stump of a large broken column. "Do you need a moment? We can wait."

Papan leaned against the column. It took him a few moments before he could speak. "No, we can't. She's close. I can feel her."

Bremin quickly checked the hall before ducking back into the shadows. "We best get a move on then. Can you manage a bit longer?"

Katira stepped forward. "We can't leave. Not without killing that monster." She gripped the blade of the broken knife hidden in her skirts.

"Killing is not something to consider lightly." Bremin flashed a look at Katira that made her feel like a little girl being lectured.

She held out her wrist. "The death oath. Isben and I are connected to Wrothe." She looked at her father. He couldn't fight Wrothe. Not until he was well, but there were three Stonebearers there who could. "If you leave, you leave us to die."

Papan's eyes widened. "Is there a way of breaking them free without engaging the demoness?"

"Death oaths are tricky. One wrong glyph and it will trigger. It's too risky." Bremin pressed his knuckle to his mouth. "Katira's right, we have to eliminate the source."

"Then we do it. Now." Papan hobbled forward. Bremin hurried to get under his shoulder. The great hall echoed with their steps.

Two guards rounded the corner in front of them. They spotted Issa, with her marks shining and her sword drawn, and turned and ran.

Halfway across the room, Wrothe's familiar draw filled the air. "Well, well, well. What have we here?" The demoness's voice caressed Katira. "I expected Surasio to bring just you and the girl. I didn't know we had unexpected guests."

Cassim shoved Elan back down the dungeon stair, slammed the door shut, and slid the beam into place. Katira held her ground next to Papan. This monster had hurt him. She wouldn't let it happen again.

Papan pushed her behind him and squared his shoulders to face the demoness.

Issa pivoted on her heels and darted forward, forming a barrier between Papan and Wrothe, her stone held ready.

Bremin tried to pull Papan and Katira toward the safety of the massive columns flanking the hall. Papan shook the man off.

"What are you doing?" Bremin demanded.

"For whatever reason, she wants me alive. I may be able to use that."

"Or she might kill you and be done with it."

Papan took a step toward the demoness with his good leg. "This is my fight."

Bremin let go, holding his own blade at the ready. He fished out another blade from under his coat and handed it to Papan. "Together then."

Wrothe walked out from behind the throne and laughed. The sound chilled Katira's blood as it bounced around the room surrounding them.

"I'm ready to talk." Papan sounded stronger than Katira knew he felt.

Wrothe's eyes widened, a curious smile spreading across her face. "You continue to surprise me. Why give yourself up?"

"I want Master Regulus freed and my daughter and the boy released from that oath. Three lives for one. It's worth it."

"What are you doing?" Cassim whispered.

Papan didn't answer him. Katira prayed to the Stonemother that whatever he had planned, it didn't involve him doing something stupid.

Wrothe stepped closer. Behind her, in the shadows, someone groaned. Master Regulus shuffled into the light. His eye had been blackened since Katira had seen him last. He reached for Papan, his face pleading but silent.

"You have me intrigued. Why are their lives more important than your own?" Wrothe patted Master Regulus on the head the same way someone would pet a dog.

A bead of sweat rolled down Papan's face, his breath grew labored.

"No one dies because of me. If I can save them, I will. It's that simple."

"You don't honestly expect me to believe that, do you?" Wrothe stepped down the two steps and onto the tile floor of the great hall. "There's something else, isn't there?"

Papan touched the stone beneath his shirt. "It is that simple. If you free those three, it means the people I care most about will be safe."

"Interesting." Wrothe took a sauntering step toward him, a mirthful grin gracing her cruel face. "You realize once I have you, I will use you to hurt the same people you're trying to save."

"I'm buying them time and a fair chance." Papan swayed. Katira propped him up. "Until now, you've attacked those of the society without warning. It needs to end."

"Be careful, Jarand." Bremin warned under his breath. "Our glyphs might prove useless against her."

Papan waved him off and continued. "You can't kill all of us. And you can't make me do it for you."

"You're right, and I don't want to. Any who swear loyalty to me will be spared." She crooked a finger at Katira. "Come here, girl."

Katira froze at the command, her hand tightened around the hidden blade.

Papan held her back. "You promised you wouldn't hurt her if I agreed."

"Oh, I won't hurt her. I want to show you something." Wrothe gestured for Katira to come closer. "You doubted my influence. I can make anyone do anything. Isn't that right, Katira?"

Katira didn't know what to say. If she denied it, she would trigger the oath and put everyone in jeopardy. "Y-y-yes, Mistress."

"You're hiding a blade in your skirts." Wrothe leaned forward. An evil smile crossed her lips. "I'll ignore your intention to harm me if you do exactly as you are told."

Katira started to sweat. Wrothe would ask her to do something terrible and she'd have no choice but to obey. "Yes, Mistress."

"Be a good girl and kill the warrior woman. I don't like the way she's looking at me."

Katira's steps faltered. Issa was innocent. Katira couldn't bring herself to think about plunging the knife into her chest. Wrothe held up her wrist, reminding Katira what would happen should she refuse.

"What are you waiting for?" Wrothe's tone turned syrupy sweet.

"Yes ... Mistress." Katira's voice faltered. She didn't want to do this, there had to be a way out. She turned toward Issa, hoping the woman could see the struggle in her eyes. The hand holding the shard trembled.

"No!" Cassim cried out and fell to his knees. "Don't do this, Katira."

Issa faced Katira, her sword held ready to defend herself. "You don't have to do this. Don't make me hurt you."

Katira walked closer to Issa, mind spinning. Any action she took against Wrothe would trigger the oath. If she was to save Issa, she'd have to sacrifice herself.

"That's a good girl." Wrothe spun a massive glyph into the air. "I'll make it easy for you."

Issa and Cassim both threw shield glyphs forward. Wrothe's power slammed into the ground and raced across the floor in an ever-widening circle, shattering both shields and extending to the corners of the hall. The glow faded into the shadows.

The hair on Katira's neck prickled. Nothing changed. Nothing moved. What had the glyph done?

"I don't like this." Bremin said as he shifted around to see what had happened.

Growls and hisses came from the shadows. Dark things, shadow creatures, hundreds of them, spilled from every shadow and surrounded them, each showing gleaming lethal teeth. Katira flinched back as one passed inches from her knee.

"I see you are familiar with my pets." A great wolf bounded to Wrothe's side. She set her hand on its head. "If any of you intercede, they'll tear you apart." She turned to Issa. "And you, my dear, make any move against Katira to defend yourself and my pets will destroy both of you."

"Don't do this. She's only a child." Issa shifted back and stopped short when a creature hissed at her heels. She turned her attention to Katira. "You don't have to do this. Fight it."

Katira gritted her teeth. The blade rattled in her hand. She knew what needed to be done, but she didn't know if she was strong enough to do it.

The expression on Issa's face softened and her shoulders relaxed. "It's okay, Katira." Issa spoke softly, without fear. She looked to Cassim and lowered her sword, leaving her neck exposed. "Strike true. Be quick."

Cassim fell to his knees. "No, Issa!"

Katira raised the knife. Issa's breaths came short and fast. With a cry of defiance Katira twisted on the balls of her feet and made a mad dash for Wrothe. The net of the oath seized her with such force it lifted her off the floor and threw her back. A hoarse yell ripped from her throat as hundreds of burning fibers pressed through her skin. She gripped the shard and forced herself to stand. No matter the cost, she would plunge the shard into Wrothe's breast. Katira charged forward once more.

Wrothe pulled the net of the oath tighter. The edges of Katira's sight went white. Her legs buckled out from under her. She couldn't breathe, couldn't move, couldn't hear. The shard fell from her hand.

Jarand watched on in horror as Katira fell screaming to the tiled floor. He reached for the sword that should have been at his hip. Wrothe had to be cut down and fast. It was the only way to free Katira from the oath. His hand came away empty. Issa didn't waste a second. In a blur of motion, she flung a dagger, striking the demon in the dead center of her chest.

Wrothe let out a wild shriek. A crimson mist sped around her in wide ribbons, catching at the hem of her dress and tossing her hair into her face. The knife's handle glowed red hot and slid from her body, falling to the floor.

The shadow creatures went wild, snarling and swarming toward any target they could sink a fang into.

"What's happening?" Issa yelled over the noise.

"She's losing control. Her demon half is overtaking the human half." Bremin shouted back.

Through the noise and chaos Jarand only saw one thing - his daughter succumbing to that monster's cruel power. Katira's eyes pressed tight as her body trembled, her hands clenched and unclenched.

Jarand hobbled closer. He had to do something to stop it. The hounds swarmed them, teeth snapping at anything they could get their mouths around.

Issa slammed a shield around the three of them. "Protect her. Stay back-to-back with me. Kill as many as you can."

On the other side of the hall, Cassim slammed down his own shield around himself, Isben, and Bremin, accidentally catching two of the creatures inside. Bremin made short work of them, but not fast enough. A dark stain spread across the fabric of his sleeve.

"Cassim, my daughter! Can we do anything for her?" Jarand swung his knife at the nearest hound, opening a wound across its snout.

"Not until we've dealt with the shadow creatures." Cassim shouted back.

Cassim and Issa hurled power-wrought weapons, felling shadow creatures. As soon as one fell, two took its place. It was a losing battle.

"Fools, all of you." Wrothe spat, her voice changed to a raspy piercing howl. "You wanted this wretch of a man?" She raised an arm toward Master Regulus and he moaned as the lines on his arms burned an angry dark red. A stream of his power flowed toward her and she drank it in. "Then watch as I break him." Regulus's hands clenched into fists and he stumbled against the wall.

"You'll kill him!" Jarand lurched forward. His leg gave out, sending him to his knees.

"A good demon knows how much she can take from her host."

Wrothe laughed and drank in more of Regulus's energy before releasing him and letting him sink to the floor. With renewed energy, another glyph flew from her fingers and their shields exploded away.

The shadow creatures leapt forward. Too many, too close, they slipped in between Jarand and Issa faster than either of them could stop them. Katira had stopped moving. Bloody bites marred her arms and legs. Jarand redoubled his efforts, blocking the hounds from reaching Katira with his own body. His head swam, he grew dizzy, more and more hounds piled on him.

"Enough of this!" Cassim roared and charged forward, belt knife swinging, hacking his way through the sea of shadow monsters. Issa screamed at him to stop, but he was beyond listening, beyond anger.

Wrothe formed a force glyph between her fingers and released it at the healer rushing toward her. He flew back, striking the rubble with a sickening crunch.

Issa dropped her guard long enough for several shadow creatures to strike her. A pack of hounds broke free and set down the hall toward Cassim.

"Go, Issa. You have to protect him," Jarand ordered.

Issa gave a brief salute before running to the back of the hall, the only barrier between the hounds and the unconscious healer.

Another creature jumped at Katira, long teeth bared and snarling. Jarand slashed it with his blade. Katira lay still, too still, no whisper of motion showed she continued to breathe. The oath was taking her away from him. He had run out of time. The blade fragment rested on the floor in front of her.

He seized it and concealed it in his palm. "Wrothe! Call your creatures off. You want me, you have always wanted me. I'll be your prize."

Wrothe cocked her head to the side as she considered his offer. The creatures fell back, snarling. "How sweet. A sacrifice to save your friends?" She walked closer. "I admit, I do desire you for my own. You have so many admirable qualities."

"You can have me, I give myself to you. I'll do whatever you ask."

Jarand continued, the sound of defeat echoing through his teeth, he had to make it sound real, sound convincing.

Wrothe licked at her top lip and came closer. "You'll be mine for the freedom of these few?"

"Yes."

Wrothe reached for him, the glyphs forming between her hands. Before she could touch him, he thrust the shard forward with all his strength, burying it in her stomach. She gasped and staggered back, surprised to see blood on her hands.

"What have you done?" She screamed as she stumbled to the ground. The lines on her arms flickered out, and she screamed again, this time in abject panic.

"What are you without your power now?" Jarand sagged down to the floor, near Katira. She had to be alive.

Wrothe's eyes widened in horror. She tore at her belly, trying to rip the shard free. The lines on her arms flickered. Crimson ribbons of mist flowed and puddled around her. They jerked and flared, almost as if they were searching for something.

"Get away from there." Bremin yelled over her screams. "She's seeking a new host."

Jarand collected Katira in his arms and dragged her away on his hands and knees, avoiding being seized by the flailing tendrils.

Wrothe took a final gasping breath, her eyes wide with surprise. Her body convulsed. Her eyes rolled back. She threw her head back and a black mist shot from her mouth into the air. The mist swirled and formed the true form of the demoness. Great horns stretched from the sides of her head, her too-long face all sharp angles and sharp teeth. Her too-large eyes burned from a fire deep within.

Her harsh voice pierced everyone in the room. "You'll pay for what you have done to me, every last one of you."

Wrothe's incorporeal form shrieked again before shooting down and disappearing into the floor.

The room plunged into a sudden, startling silence.

Chapter
15

Jarand clutched Katira to his chest, refusing to believe he was too late. Wrothe was gone. The oath should have broken. He held his daughter tight, willing her to breathe, praying for the smallest mercy.

She didn't move, didn't wake.

He summoned his power and opened his awareness to her, searching for a pulse, any spark of life. He'd tried so hard to protect her. The dimmest glow hung around her, nothing more. He formed a life glyph and eased it into her. He didn't have much to give, but what he had, he would give to her.

Still no pulse. No breath.

Jarand pressed Katira to his chest and rocked her back and forth. He had come so far, had tried so hard, and he was losing her.

Isben drew near, hand outstretched.

"Leave us be." Jarand didn't move to look at the boy. "There's nothing you can do."

"Please, let me try. I ... I love her, too."

Jarand wanted to push him away, to force him to leave him in his anguish. But, if there was a chance, he would give it to her. He nodded.

Isben laced his hand into hers and his lines glowed to life. He formed no glyphs, yet the glow from Isben's hand passed through to Katira, running up her arm, filling her. She took a shallow breath, then another. The gray around her mouth faded. Light clustered around the wounds left by the hounds as the venom burned away.

Her eyes fluttered open. A smile bent her lips when she saw Isben holding her hand. "You saved me."

Isben kissed her knuckles. "I couldn't let you go."

Jarand watched on in stunned silence. This untested boy had brought Katira back from the brink of death. It shouldn't have been possible, he was only an apprentice. Tears of gratitude ran down Jarand's face. He held Katira tighter to him, unwilling to ever let her go again.

Over by the toppled throne, Master Regulus groaned from where he had collapsed on the floor. The sound took Jarand by surprise. He had believed Wrothe's anger had killed the man. He wasn't ready to face that truth, not yet. Not while Katira was in danger. Master Regulus was Mirelle's only hope, and he had survived. The cold blade of fear that had pierced Jarand once when Katira was taken, and once again when Mirelle fell wounded, eased back, allowing him to hope again.

Isben's eyes widened and he stood to go to his master. Jarand took hold of his hand as he went, stopping him. "Thank you."

The boy accepted the thanks with a bow of his head and hurried to his master's side.

Bremin limped up to Jarand, lines on his arms still shining. "You two had me worried. Is Katira okay?"

Jarand placed his hand over Katira's heart. Each beat pulsed against his palm like a victory. Her eyes were closed in peaceful sleep. "I think so. Did Cassim live?"

Bremin gave a slight nod and sat down. "Big fella's hard to kill. Especially since he's got an Issa."

"What about you? Are you going to be in trouble once you let go?"

"Probably. Needed to let you know Alystra is on her way." He sighed and laid himself on the floor. "Don't let her get too angry with me." His lines faded. "Promise to tell me everything when I wake up. Make me sound like a hero."

Before Jarand could answer, Bremin's eyes rolled back as the shaking fit took him. His price for using the power.

Hours passed in quiet before the great hall filled with a rush of new voices.

Lady Alystra knelt at Bremin's side. He had shown no signs of waking. The tremors shaking him had slowed but hadn't stopped. She placed her hand on Jarand's shoulder.

"How long?" she asked without looking up.

Jarand studied the shadows on the floor. "Nearly three hours."

"You promised me you'd take care of him."

"I promised I'd do my best. He lives."

She straightened and signaled for a pair of men dressed in tower robes to come over before returning her attention to Jarand. "I expect a full report once everything is settled. These two will escort you and Katira back to the tower."

JARAND FELL into the chair at Mirelle's bedside. He kissed her forehead and intertwined his fingers with hers. Her hands felt like clay, cold and soft. In the three days since he had left, she had grown thinner, the bones at her neck more pronounced, her cheeks hollower. She didn't move when he touched her. Her fingers didn't flex or show any sign she knew he was there. In death-like sleep, she lay as if suspended in time.

He opened himself to her and allowed her pain to wash over him, to mingle with his own. The poison had spread as he had feared it would. Its fiery breath consumed her from within. Even still, an impression of her smile flitted past.

The infirmary door continued to open and shut as white robed healers brought in more victims from the ruins. Issa half-carried, half-dragged a cursing and sweating Cassim to the nearest bed. A tiny healer woman chased after them, protesting with each step.

Katira lay in the neighboring bed, resting from her ordeal. Jarand reached for her hand.

Her eyes opened halfway. Her gaze traveled past Jarand to her mother. "Is she suffering?"

"Master Firen keeps her asleep, so she doesn't feel the pain."

Katira sniffed and wiped the corner of her eye with her sleeve. "What about you?"

"Once things have calmed down, I imagine Master Firen will want to take a look at me."

The infirmary door swung open once more, Master Firen entered issuing his orders to the other white robed healers following in his wake. He glided over to Jarand and Katira. "You know how to get the tower's attention, don't you?"

"I can't take all the responsibility. As I recall, there was a demoness involved this time." Jarand glanced across the chaos of the infirmary. Wrothe had hidden far more Stonebearers in that dungeon than he'd realized.

Master Firen collected a stool and sat on the other side of the bed. "Who is this lovely girl?"

"This is my daughter, Katira."

Master Firen bowed his head in an apology. "My, my. I didn't know so many years had passed." He extended a hand to her. "A pleasure to meet you, my dear."

Katira gave his hand the barest of shakes before hugging her arms back to her chest. The dark hollows under her eyes looked like bruises.

"I imagine things won't calm down in here for a few hours and your father and I have a lot to discuss." Master Firen caught the attention of one of the tower staff. "Would you like someone to help you get a bath and fresh clothes? After that they'll find you a soft warm bed away from all this noise."

Katira hugged her arms tighter to herself. "I should stay."

"It's okay. Go." Jarand reassured her. "I'll find you."

An attendant in sage green robes, a girl perhaps a year or two older than Katira, stepped forward and beckoned Katira to come with her. Katira gave one last, longing look toward her mother before gingerly getting up and following the girl.

Master Firen returned his attention to Jarand. "I saw Master Regulus down in the courtyard. They'll bring him up shortly." He patted Mirelle's bed. "Until he gets here, did he say what needs to be done?"

Jarand leaned forward with a wince. "The poison clings to the power. If the power is drained off, the poison will come with it. He described a stone used to draw away power like a magnet draws steel, do you know of it?"

"Did he mention what it was called?"

"I believe he called it a fire something orestone, or something like that."

Master Firen's brow wrinkled in thought. "Would it be the fire-blossom lodestone?"

"That's it. Do you have one?"

Master Firen called to another of his assistants who looked to be heading back to the courtyard. "Please summon Master Ternan here immediately."

The woman gave a curt nod and hurried away.

Master Firen turned back to Jarand. "Have you ever met the Master Artifact Keeper?"

"If I've had the pleasure, it's been ages."

"He's an odd one. Best not to distract him or he'll talk for hours."

Jarand stroked Mirelle's hand. "Any word on Bremin?"

Master Firen ran a hand over his chin. "Lady Alystra has taken him to her quarters. He hasn't regained consciousness since the ruins and might not for some time yet. What in the world did the man do this time?"

"Fought off a demon and her hoard of shadow creatures hell-bent on ripping everyone to pieces. He saved Regulus's apprentice from having his throat torn out."

Master Firen's eyes grew wider and wider with each new detail. "You must be joking."

"I wish." Jarand wiped a hand over his face and looked at in in disgust. He had forgotten it was covered in blood. "It's been a hard day."

Chapter
16

I ntricate carvings bordered the floor along the corridors. Katira didn't look up any higher to see more than the heels of the girl's embroidered slippers. She was too tired, too numb, to pay attention to much else. After a handful of turns, she stopped keeping track.

"I guess things got intense at the ruins, right?" the attendant asked, her voice curious and upbeat.

Katira didn't respond. Answering the question would force her to relive what had happened. She wasn't ready for that. Not yet.

They walked along in silence for the length of another hall before the girl stopped and pushed open a heavy oak door. "This is the mess hall. Get yourself something to eat while I round up some clothes for after your bath. Shouldn't take long."

She waved Katira inside before turning on her heel and heading back the way they had come.

Katira had seen many inns and tavern halls over the last few days, all the same. The long heavy tables, huddled groups of strangers, and a crackling fire. Any second Surasio would come around the corner to drag her away.

No. He was dead. Isben had killed him. She took a steadying breath. This was no ordinary inn. All these people were Stonebearers like Papan and Mamar.

A row of large windows along the wall at the end of the room revealed a panorama of familiar peaks and valleys. They looked so much like the mountain ringing Namragan, it hurt. She wanted to go home.

Tears welled up in her eyes. She slid out the door of the mess hall and into a quiet corner where she curled up on the ground and wept.

The fine carpets and tapestries of the tower disappeared. She lost herself to pain and heartache.

Someone sat next to her and set a warm hand on her shaking shoulder. He said nothing, asked nothing. She wanted to scream at him to go away and leave her in peace. When the racking sobs had run their course, she looked up.

Isben stroked her hair. "It's okay. Let it all out."

They sat there in the quiet, neither speaking, until the shadows stretched across the floor.

The attendant turned a corner, arms full of neatly folded clothes. "There you are." She bent and offered Katira a hand. "From the looks of it, I'd say you need that hot bath more than ever."

Isben brushed the hair from her face. "It's okay. Let them take care of you."

JARAND KEPT his vigil beside Mirelle into the evening and through the long night, hoping and praying a lodestone would be found. He couldn't sleep, and despite Master Firen's efforts to get him to eat, the thought of food made him sick. His one consolation was that Katira had been cared for. Despite her protests, he knew she hadn't recovered fully yet. She needed sleep.

It wasn't until the next afternoon when the door to the infirmary burst open and Master Ternan, the Artifact Master, came hurrying in carrying a box inlaid with amber and silver. Dirt streaked his unruly white hair, and he smelled of dust and mold. Deep bags lined his eyes and his shoulders drooped forward.

"I had to search seventeen different vaults, but I believe this is what you are looking for." The historian set the box on Master Firen's desk where Master Regulus sat writing. "As for you, Regulus, I have another assignment."

Master Regulus set down his pen being careful not to let the ink drip. "With all due respect, Master, I'll need at least a month to recover from this assignment. Thank you."

Master Ternan patted Regulus on the shoulder. "Don't be too long. I've got work for you to do."

Master Firen lifted the lid off the box and pulled back the thick blue cloth. A smooth polished sphere the size of a man's fist nestled deep inside. Within the sphere's depths shone an orange burst of color, like the petals of a flower.

Master Regulus let out a low whistle and leaned close to examine the specimen. "Jarand, if you would touch its surface. We need to be sure this is what we are looking for. If this is a lodestone, it will draw off your power into itself."

"Why don't you?" Jarand suspected he knew the answer. His master had been acting odd ever since the ruins.

Master Regulus shrugged. "I haven't had the use of my power since Wrothe mucked about with it."

Master Firen rounded on him. "Don't you think you should have mentioned that?"

"It's not urgent. There are far more pressing matters at hand." Master Regulus pointed to the lodestone. "Jarand, if you would."

Jarand placed his hand over the stone. At his touch, a warm light glowed from the center of the blossom. A streak of heat raced up his arm and seized the power lying dormant deep inside of him and pulled it back into the lodestone. He yanked his hand away back, cutting the connection. "It works."

Master Regulus nodded. "Good. We best get to it then."

Master Ternan bobbed his head and smiled. "I'm glad this is the right one. You never know with relics."

Master Regulus paused at the statement, his eyes narrowed in thought as if he was considering saying something else. "Thank you, Master Ternan. You're welcome to stay."

The artifact master waved his hand. "No, I have work to do. Send me word when all is done." Without further ado he turned and wandered out of the room.

"He did well." Master Firen examined the lodestone closer, taking care not to touch it. "If all is ready, it's time to wake Mirelle. Jarand, will you?"

Jarand laid a hand on her shoulder and opened the connection between them. He urged her to wake, to return to him, that he had news. Her consciousness rose through the thick layers of sleep. Her eyes opened a crack. He folded her hand into his.

"Katira, where is she?" She tried to sit up and look around. Her brow wrinkled with fear.

"She's here in the tower, safe and sound." Jarand guided her back down.

Mirelle squeezed Jarand's hand as a wave of pain flowed through her. "How long did I sleep?"

"Not long." Jarand tried to give her a reassuring smile, tried to mask the unease he felt about what needed to be done. "We've found a way to cleanse the poison from your blood."

Mirelle looked to Master Firen who nodded in agreement. "The poison clings to your power." Master Firen pointed to the lodestone. "By using a lodestone, we can coax your power through it and filter out the poison without triggering a more severe reaction. You'll be left clean."

Mirelle squeezed Jarand's hand. "Without any power left, what will keep me alive?"

Master Firen placed the box next to Mirelle. "Jarand will be ready to infuse you with life energy."

Jarand held her shaking hands in his and pressed them to his lips. "I'll not let anything happen to you."

She smiled. "I know."

He placed her hand onto the sphere and held onto the other. He opened his awareness to her and felt the tug of the lodestone setting to work. Its flame-like glow returned, only a fraction as bright. Despite her outward calm, inside her fear was a raging torrent. She clung to the last threads of power as the lodestone worked to pull them away.

He held her hand tighter to soothe her, giving her permission to let go, that he would be there. Slow minutes passed, her breathing grew labored and shallow. She struggled to remain awake.

The essence of Mirelle was slipping away, like sand through a sieve. There were so few grains left. The last speck of her power teetered and fell away in to the depths of the stone. He pulled her hand away. She lay pale and motionless. Jarand felt a vast void within himself where she usually was. "Master Firen, is it enough?"

Master Firen laid his hand over her heart and closed his eyes. Light glowed around his fingers. "It's hard to say. Infuse her now. If there is any remaining poison, it will react."

Jarand summoned a life glyph and eased it into her. Its light and warmth resonated within him. Mirelle took a sharp breath. The color crept back into her cheeks.

"Is she clean?" Master Firen asked.

Jarand could only nod. Mirelle was safe.

He wove himself into her once more, allowing her to fill him and him to fill her. Again, he felt her pain. It felt different, less angry. The steady beat of her heart and the even rhythm of her breath brought him more comfort than anything Master Firen could have told him.

THE MIST of early morning curled around Elan's feet as he walked out into the courtyard. Katira watched him from the shadow of a doorway. So many things had changed since the night of the harvest festival.

Elan stood taller, his boyish slouch gone and replaced with the squared shoulders of a man ready to face anything. His eyes, which had always showed a charming vulnerability, radiated with fresh confidence. He tugged the woolen gray cloak closed to ward off the chill. Dressed in the fine clothes of the tower, he could have passed for a prince.

She stepped into the light and put on her bravest smile.

"Hello, Elan."

He turned toward the sound of her voice. "I wasn't sure you would come."

Their breath misted in front of them and Katira shivered. Elan pulled her heavy cloak closed around her shoulders.

"I'm worried about you." He brushed his hand against her cheek.

She shied away from his touch. "Don't be."

He led her to a stone bench to one side of the immense courtyard. Tall statues to either side stared down at her, making her feel small.

"What happens now?"

"I need to return home, tell the town what happened." He chanced a glance at her. "I'd like for you to come with me."

She pulled her arm free of the cloak and rolled up her sleeve. Beneath the skin, silvery lines hid, invisible unless she woke them. She wished there was a way to make them go away, make everything go back to how it was. She had been happy then.

It felt like ages since she and Elan first seen Papan's marks. So much had changed since then, had he changed as well?

She collected her thoughts, working to tell him what she was in a way that wouldn't hurt him, that wouldn't scare him. She took a deep breath to calm her racing heart and steeled herself to meet his gaze. "I bear the marks. I've seen them."

He set a small kiss on her wrist. "I know." He pulled her hand into his lap and met her gaze. "Your father thought it would be easier if I knew the truth before. Said something about being able to prepare my heart."

Her heart burned as if it would melt from her chest. "Do you still love me, even knowing what I really am?"

A cold breeze swept through the courtyard, stirring the leaves into a dance at their feet. Weeks ago, they had danced at the harvest festival and dreamed of a life together. Elan pressed her hand between his as if he struggled to find his answer. "I've loved you ever since we were children. Nothing will change that."

Her throat caught on his words. She knew he would say them, knew he would never give her up. It made what she had to tell him press heavy enough to crush her. "We can't be together, Elan. You deserve to spend your life with someone who can grow old with you."

Elan traced his finger around the back of her hand as if imagining the lines there. The warmth of his touch brought back memories of their time in Namragan.

"Do you still love me?" It was a gentle quiet question, soft like a baby's kiss, hard like Papan's anvil.

It wasn't fair. How could she hold this much feeling inside and not burst? "Of course I do." Her throat ached with emotion she couldn't swallow. The next part is what had shattered her the most when she learned it herself. "I can never give you a child."

Elan pressed his eyes shut. His head fell to his chest.

She swallowed down the words and they were bitter. "We can't be together. You deserve happiness, deserve a family of your own."

Elan's voice became hoarse, his eyes misted. "What about you? What about your happiness?"

Katira hugged her arms around her knees, holding in the vast emptiness echoing inside of her. "I watched you die once, and it nearly destroyed me. I can't watch you die again." She gave his hand a reassuring squeeze. "If the Stonebearers can find happiness in this way of life, I'm sure I can as well."

"No matter what happens, I won't stop loving you." Elan stared out across the courtyard and toward the massive spire of the mountain tower looming above them. "Promise me something."

She could feel him pull away, accepting the truth. Part of her wanted to scream at him. How dare he give her up this easily? The other part of her felt relieved they could part ways without destroying their friendship.

"Anything. Ask."

"Promise you won't disappear from my life. Whenever you venture north and near home, promise you'll come visit me."

She felt her throat tighten again. "I promise."

A woman dressed in a simple dark green cloak entered the courtyard carrying a travel bag over her shoulder. A tall fellow accompanied her, dressed in simple village clothes, most likely her companion. At first glance, the woman could have passed for a woman close to the same age as Mamar, only barely entering her fortieth year. As a Stonebearer, though, she would be decades older, perhaps even centuries. The woman glanced toward the two of them and gave Elan a nod before crossing the courtyard to the traveling post.

"Lady Alystra is sending me with a new healer for Namragan." He tugged her close, like they used to do back when they didn't have a care in the world. "I swore to bring you home." Their foreheads touched and Katira felt the warmth of his breath on her neck. Had things not changed she would have stolen a kiss. She longed to have her heart flutter at his touch, like it used to, but it remained steady.

"My place is here." She reached into her pocket and withdrew a small parcel. "Something to remember me by."

He hesitated to take it. "I have nothing for you."

She touched the bracelet he had given her. "Consider this my belated Harvest Festival gift."

Inside the parcel was a locket of fine silver. He opened it with a thumb revealing a perfect picture of her.

"I had it made when I learned you'd be leaving." She lifted a chain from around her neck and showed an identical locket. "I had one of you made as well. That way I'll always have you with me."

He hugged her close once more, nuzzling his nose into her hair. "I'll never forget you as long as I live. Thank you."

"Nor I, you." She found herself wiping her eyes again. "You best not keep your healer waiting."

He clasped the locket in his hand. "Until we meet again?"

"Until then. Stay safe." She watched as he walked away and entered the traveling post, watched as the light washed over him and took him far away.

Then she turned and walked back into the fortress. Alone.

Hours slipped by. Jarand knew it was best for Mirelle to let her own powers take control of the healing process, but he worried. He snuck his hand into hers and joined their consciousness.

He had expected her own natural energies to rebound. Master Firen was counting on them, fueled by the Khandashii, to heal what had been damaged by the poison. However, none had returned.

Despite their efforts, the only thing keeping her alive was the life glyph he gave her hours before, and it trickled away one grain at a time. It wouldn't be long before there would be none left to sustain her. After all they had done, he was still losing her.

Master Firen put his hand on Mirelle's chest. He drew it back after a moment and turned to his assistant. "Get Lady Alystra. We need her to administer the last rites."

The assistant's eyes went wide, and he fled from the room.

Master Firen gripped Jarand's shoulder. "Somehow the poison has damaged her ability to retain power. Infusing her will sustain her, but I'm afraid she will never heal. The pain will never leave her."

Jarand pressed both hands over his heart. He had tried so hard. "What if she needs more time?"

Master Regulus appeared next to Master Firen. "This was always a possibility, Jarand. Time was our enemy from the beginning."

The words passed over Jarand like sharp claws, ripping at his senses.

He balled his fists, the nails biting into the flesh of his palms. He wanted to smash something, make something else hurt as much as he did. Jarand allowed his power to flare within him and welcomed the surge of pain as it coursed through. He pulled so much it felt as if his markings were on fire.

"Jarand, stop!" A brilliant flash filled the room. Lady Alystra stepped out of the light, her markings glowing brightly against her skin. She threw a shining blue glyph at him and it wrapped around him as if he were encased in ice, his skin burned with the cold.

The fire of his anger dimmed as the cold continued to press in on him. His sorrow returned, dagger sharp.

He stopped struggling, all the anger had burned out of him. Lady Alystra released her hold, and he fell to his knees, struggling to catch his breath.

"Come." She stood with her hand outstretched. "It's time."

Jarand took Lady Alystra's offered hand and found strength there he hadn't expected.

Red edged her eyes. The many deaths from her tower had taken a great toll.

Jarand found his feet again and released Lady Alystra's hand. "How's Bremin?"

She leaned on the rail at the end of the bed and bowed her head. Her knuckles went white. "It might be several days before we know for sure. He woke a few hours ago."

Jarand looked to Mirelle and then to Lady Alystra. Had their roles been reversed, he wouldn't leave his companion's side, not when they needed him. "You should be with him."

"I want to be here. Mirelle has earned her last rites. Her soul deserves to find peace." Lady Alystra pulled the nearby stool close to the bed and sat close to Mirelle's head.

"Child," she said, placing her hand on Mirelle's pale cheek. "Do you know why I'm here?"

Mirelle nodded, her eyes heavy. "I'm ready," she said in a whisper.

Again, the urge to fight back filled Jarand. He gripped his fists into knots. He struggled to breathe against the tightness wrapping around his chest. He wasn't ready. He'd never be ready.

Lady Alystra shot him a chilling stare, a warning of what she was willing to do if he couldn't calm himself.

"Connect with her Jarand. I'll guide her, you are to follow. This is Mirelle's time to find peace, not yours. Don't interfere."

Jarand took a steadying breath. He wove his hand into hers and allowed himself to sink into her consciousness.

When Lady Alystra joined in, it was as if the two of them were bathed in her light. She spoke the ancient hallowed words of the ceremony, foreign and strange in this space. The words formed patterns that raced around and through their combined minds.

The pain wracking Mirelle's frail body lifted and disappeared into Lady Alystra's light. Mirelle released a pent-up breath. With the pain gone, her thoughts became clearer and sharper.

Lady Alystra guided them both through the greatest joys of Mirelle's life, reliving them again with Jarand. A sunlit meadow filled his mind. Mirelle danced in the flowers, holding Katira as a baby. The meadow faded, replaced with the joyful noise of a music-filled celebration in the mountain tower's feast hall. He and Mirelle had just been joined as companions, the world was theirs that night. Some memories he wasn't a part of, like the day Master Firen accepted her into the sept of Master Healers and arrayed her in the white robes of the tower.

Lady Alystra did the same with the sorrows and Jarand shared each pain of loss with her. As each of these memories lifted, Mirelle's spirit grew lighter, freer. One tiny tether anchored her to her failing body.

Lady Alystra laid a hand on Jarand's shoulder and he realized he had been weeping. He brushed the tears away hurriedly to hide them.

"Embrace your tears, Jarand." Tears streaked down her own

cheeks unchecked. "Find joy in the memories you have shared together."

Lady Alystra leaned in close to Mirelle. "Do what you must, then go in peace." She placed a kiss on Mirelle's brow and left the room without another word. The others followed suit, leaving Jarand and Mirelle alone.

Jarand slid next to her on the bed and cradled her as he would a child. She had become so light, so frail in these past few days. She leaned into his chest.

As he held her, he fought to find the right words to comfort her.

She touched his face. "Stop thinking you've failed."

"I was supposed to protect you." His tears flowed freely down his rugged face and into his neatly trimmed beard.

She wiped his tears with a thumb. "You did everything you could. There is nothing to be ashamed of."

Jarand fought the urge to think of the hundreds of things he could have done differently, all the mistakes he had made that led them down this path. While he knew he had her forgiveness, he would never forgive himself. None of it mattered now, what was done, was done.

"There was one thing during the rite, one last thing holding you here. What was it?"

She pressed her lips together and touched his face. "My one regret."

It caught Jarand by surprise, of their whole life together he couldn't think of a single thing that would cause regret. It was true she never liked his beard. Perhaps she regretted never asking him to shave it. "What have you to regret?"

"I can't tell you." She took a breath, and her eyes wavered. Her time was fast running out. "Not until you make me a promise."

He'd do anything, promise anything, if it would grant her peace in her dying moments. "Anything, please."

"Once I'm gone, you'll move on." Her smile held the warmth of a sunrise after a cold night. "You won't spend an eternity grieving for me."

"I don't know if I can do that." He held her tighter and kissed her hair, breathing in her scent. "I would follow you if it were possible."

"Katira needs you." She whispered fiercely. "Promise me! Swear it!"

Jarand traced his finger down the outside of her face. She looked so beautiful, as if the angels had already left their mark. Her pain and cares were gone. All except this one.

He blinked back his tears. "I swear it. I'll not grieve you forever. I'll move on."

She looked at him straight in the eyes. "I have always loved you," she said between shallow breaths. "My regret is that I've never told you before."

They had never said those little words to each other, even after all these years. It was always a secret touch, a quick smile, or one of hundreds of little gestures.

Choking back the sobs he answered, "And I have always loved you, my dearest."

Mirelle smiled and sighed. The last threads of her life energy slipped away, and she was gone.

KATIRA ROAMED the labyrinth of the tower, not caring if she got lost.

Her wanderings took her to a balcony overlooking the jagged mountains and the steep-sided canyon leading up the tower. In the slim moon light, the scene was painted in grays and blues.

Quiet footfalls rose from the carpet behind her. She turned to see Isben, who looked as tired and worn as she felt. It was as if some great weight was holding him down, some great pain had him locked in its grasp.

"I've been walking the whole tower to find you." There was something about the halting way he spoke.

"Isben, are you okay?"

He ran a hand through his hair. "Master Regulus asked me to find you and be the one to tell you." He sniffed. His hands were trembling.

She held his hands in hers to steady him. "Tell me what?"

Tears spilled over the corners of his eyes and streamed down his face. "They couldn't save her. Your mother died a few hours ago. I'm so sorry."

Katira sank to the floor. Mamar was gone? But ... hadn't they saved her? Papan had summoned her after using the lodestone, had told her everything would be okay. What could have happened?

She never had a chance to say goodbye. It wasn't right. Sharp anger pulsed through her, vivid and intense, and she felt a burning ache within. The lines on her arms flared to life and shone brightly in the dim light of predawn.

Isben tried to speak to her, tried to reach her through the pain and the fury, but she was lost in a void beyond hearing, beyond speaking. The walls of her fragile and broken world came crashing down and buried her underneath. The energy within her lashed out unbidden, fighting against the misery within.

He grasped her hands, like he did before in the glade, harnessing her power, holding it, letting the heat and anger of it run through him, letting it run its course. His presence filled her mind, wrapping her in layers upon layers of warmth and comfort, his comfort. He wanted nothing more than to take the ache away, to be there for her.

Katira wiped her eyes. "Why does that happen?" Her thoughts returned to the shrine when she discovered that his feelings for her had grown into something more. The ache of her power faded away within her.

He released an unsteady breath. "It's how Stonebearers comfort each other. When two people holding the power touch, they can feel what the other feels, understand their pain." The light from the lines on his hands faded.

Isben lowered his head toward her. "What you're feeling," he pointed to her heart, "this ache, this anger at the loss of your mother, is a real pain and will hurt. The least I can do is carry some of it with you."

She leaned into him. Having him so close and feeling once again the intensity of his love for her filled a part of the vast emptiness left by losing Mamar. She'd have him comfort her again, but deep inside she knew no magic could mend a broken heart. Only time could do that.

She craved the gentle touch of his lips on hers. Their faces drew close, his breath warmed her cheek. He would always be there for her.

Their lips met, cautiously at first, almost by accident. Warmth spread through Katira, soothing and gentle as it blossomed in her belly. She pressed her lips to his once more, tasting him, longing to feel close, longing to feel whole.

Isben returned the kiss gently, allowing his lips to linger a few moments before pulling away. "What was that for?"

"I made you a promise that if we survived, I'd give you a kiss." Katira could feel the blush spread across her cheeks. "I always keep my promises."

TIME SLID by as Jarand sat curled on the bed with Mirelle in his arms. She looked as if she slept.

The last light of evening faded, and the stars trailed through the sky. Through the long night he stayed with her. It wasn't until the first light of morning warmed the sky far to the east that he laid her down and carefully smoothed her hair.

He didn't want to leave her. It didn't feel right, but he supposed it would never again feel right. As he limped toward the infirmary door, two attendants appeared at his side.

"We will take good care of her."

He didn't see who had said the words, it didn't matter much. Jarand's body was a wrung-out rag.

The attendant let Jarand lean on him as he led him away down a corridor, thankfully empty at this time of morning, to a small guest room. The bed was made with fresh sheets and a covered tray rested on the small three-legged table. His pack and sword rested in the corner.

He sank onto the edge of the bed, craving sleep, fearing the night-mares that would come, needing release from the gnawing pain of loss.

The attendant directed him toward the table. "Eat first, then sleep. Master Firen's orders." He pulled back the cloth and folded it neatly alongside the tray.

Jarand's stomach knotted at the sight of food. He wasn't sure if he could keep it down. The attendant waited, no doubt charged by Master Firen to see he did as instructed. A thick aromatic stew steamed from within a crockery bowl. Next to it sat a warm loaf of dark bread. He pulled off a piece of the bread and dunked it into the stew before chewing it. The attendant gave a short bow and left.

Jarand ate mechanically, he didn't taste anything. Someone tapped at the door before it opened. Lady Alystra entered and shut the door behind her.

"Good, you're eating." She sat on the other high backed wooden chair. "Master Firen wanted me to make sure."

Jarand didn't look up. This was his pain. He didn't want to share it. "Leave me be."

"I won't be long." She regarded him carefully. "Mirelle's cere-mony begins at sundown. I'm here to grant you a dreamless sleep until then. Will you accept my gift?"

"Does Katira know?" He had promised Mirelle to care for Katira. He intended to fulfill that promise.

"She knows."

He rose and made for the door. "She needs me."

"She's sleeping." Lady Alystra caught Jarand's sleeve. "And you need rest too. She's stronger than you think."

Jarand fell back into the chair. He knew Katira was strong, but he had made a promise to take care of her. One he was already failing.

"If you want to care for your daughter, you must care for yourself." Lady Alystra stood and gestured to the bed. "She'll understand."

Jarand held out his hand, it trembled with fatigue. Curse her for always being right. He hobbled to the bed.

She placed her hand over his forehead. Bittersweet memories of the countless times Mirelle had cared for him drifted through his mind. Lady Alystra's deft flows pushed him into a deep restful sleep - the first real sleep he'd had in a long time.

KATIRA ALLOWED Isben to guide her back to her room through the haze of grief blinding her. She didn't remember getting into the bed or covering herself with a blanket. All she could remember was Isben's warm hand in hers.

When she woke later, he had gone.

A light tap sounded at her door. Papan stuck in his head.

"May I come in?"

She turned her back to him. "Go away."

He stepped into the room and shut the door behind him with a soft thud. "We need to talk."

"Leave me alone." She pulled the blanket tighter across her shoulders as if it would make her invisible.

He sat heavily on the edge of the bed. "I think out of everyone I can understand how you feel."

Katira threw off the covers and sat up to face him. Instead of his usual drab shirt and vest, he was dressed in a brilliant royal blue tabard. A shining breastplate covered his chest, emblazoned with the tower sigil - a hand with a symbol held in the palm. A great sword hung from his hip. In his hand he held two roses.

"Why are you wearing armor?"

He patted his chest. "It keeps my important bits from being stabbed. Why else?"

Katira rolled her eyes. "Since when do blacksmiths need armor?"

Papan ran his palms over the cane between his knees. "Perhaps the real question here is, why would a war general take up black-smithing up north in a tiny village?"

Katira scooted further away. Her Papan was nothing more than a skilled blacksmith. This war general was a different person, not her Papan. He used a sword, but that was it. "You are not making any sense."

He studied his hands. "Katira, I'm over four hundred years old. I've lived many lives, including this last one as a blacksmith and father, which has been more challenging than I ever expected."

Katira had never thought of Papan living a Stonebearer's long life, had never considered what it meant. He wore the armor well; it was clearly meant for him. But a general? She wasn't ready to accept it, not for a while at least. "How many of those years were you with Mamar?"

He passed a hand over his face and rubbed at his beard. "We would have celebrated our two hundredth anniversary next summer."

Thoughts of Elan swirled through her mind, followed by the growing desire to be with Isben.

"Where there any others?" she asked, suddenly desperate to know. "Did you love anyone else?"

"Of course there were others. And I loved them all. Or at least I thought I did until I met Mamar. There is a profound difference between simple love and what two bonded companions feel for each other. When you finally find your match, you feel complete."

"Is that what Mamar was to you? A bonded companion?" The words felt foreign and awkward in her mouth.

"Yes, she completed me." He looked out the window. The silence hung heavy in the room. "I've brought you clothes for the ceremony tonight."

Katira fidgeted with the embroidered hem on the blanket. "I don't belong there."

He pushed the sky-blue robe into her hands. "You are my daughter. You belong there more than anyone else in the tower. Get dressed."

GREAT HORNS SOUNDED, filling the tower with a tremor that resounded in Katira's bones. The time had come to bid farewell and send Mamar's body back to the Stonemother. Papan took her by the hand and offered her a rose to carry.

Tidy lines of long-robed Stonebearers had gathered in the great colonnaded courtyard of the mountain tower.

Mamar lay on a stone platform chased through with green stripes of what Katira now knew was motherstone, dressed in fine white healer's robes edged in silver.

Master Firen, along with those of the healer's sept, stood in a line along the right-hand side of the stone platform bearing her body. Their long white robes rippled in the breeze.

On the opposite side, a line of guardians in gleaming armor stood at attention. When Papan crossed the threshold leading into the courtyard, the captain of the guard barked a sharp command and the guardians raised their swords in unison.

Lady Alystra stood at the head of the raised stone waiting for them with Bremin by her side. Katira almost didn't recognize him. His red tattered scarf and long coat had been replaced with deep purple ceremonial robes of the tower. His ordeal at the ruins had left him unsteady. He kept one of his arms threaded through the High Lady's.

The great horns sounded again, this time somber and melancholy.

Four drums, one on each corner of the courtyard beat a steady slow pulse.

Lady Alystra stepped forward and unfastened the delicate chain and green stone from Mamar's neck and placed it into Papan's hand.

"Her stone, by right, is yours to keep. With it, she will always be with you." Lady Alystra laid her hand over his, sealing the stone between them. "Present your final gift to her."

Papan took slow halting steps toward the platform. He laid his flower on Mamar's chest, next to her heart, and gently kissed her for the last time.

Katira placed her white rose alongside her father's and lingered there for another moment. How could she say goodbye to the woman who'd held her when she cried from heartache and pain? Who taught her all she knew and guided her along her path? Papan put his hand on her shoulder.

If he could say goodbye, she could as well.

She let him guide her back to his side.

Lady Alystra raised her hands into the air. The drums beat faster, and the horns sounded once more. Bright light collected between her palms like a brilliant star. One after another, the assembled Stonebearers raised their arms. Their radiance competed with the setting sun for both beauty and power.

When the assembled host had raised their light, Papan pressed his cane into Katira's hand before raising his arms. His own brilliant star formed between his fingers. Together each of the stars rose in unison and converged together into a small sun hovering over Mamar's body.

This sun lowered until it had encased the body, turning it into a fine powder.

Lady Alystra formed another symbol and a great spinning column jetted the ash to the dome of the sky, spreading it in a great arc and filling the darkening night with a golden light.

The drums and horns fell silent, leaving a hard, unyielding quiet. Tiny flakes of snow fell. The light faded, and the assembled

Stonebearers filed from the courtyard, returning to their quarters for the evening.

When Papan finally spoke, his voice was husky and quiet. "I couldn't save her. But one day, I'll find that demon and put an end to her."

Katira leaned into his chest and he wrapped his arms around her.

"I want things how they used to be."

"I know." He held her tighter. "I can't tell you how many times I've wished for the same thing. But things have changed. It's time we move forward."

Katira followed as his eyes drifted over to where Master Regulus leaned against a massive pillar with Isben at his side. Learning at the feet of these respected Stonebearers would be a rare privilege, but that's not what she wanted.

Perhaps, though, it could be enough.

For now.

Acknowledgements

No act of creation is done alone. I am so grateful for the team of people who added their insights, knowledge, and support during the creation of Stonebearer's Betrayal.

The first thank you goes to my wonderful husband who has been my number one supporter and test reader since the beginning. If it weren't for him, none of my writing career would have been possible. I'd also like to thank my kiddos who let Mommy have working time at her computer, sometimes.

The next thank you goes to the Immortal Works Press crew, especially my editor, Melissa Meibos, who bravely plunged into my pile of ideas, plucked out the diamonds, and tightened the loose threads. Also, a special thank you goes to Ashley Literski of Strange Devotion Designs for my beautiful cover.

A huge thanks to my writing groups: The League of Utah Writers, American Night Writers Association, and the Wednesday Writers Whatchamacallit. They all enabled me to make important connections and gave me the confidence to finish writing this book.

To Candace, Laura, Nicole, and Eliza, thanks for being the best cheerleaders a girl could have.

To Mom and Dad, thanks for encouraging me to follow my dreams, even when you thought they were crazy.

And finally, to you, dear reader, thank you for lending your imagination to make my words take flight.

About The Author

Growing up, Jodi L. Milner wanted to be a superhero and a doctor. When she discovered she couldn't fly, she did what any reasonable introvert would do and escaped into the wonderful hero-filled world of fiction and the occasional medical journal. She's lived there ever since.

These days, when she's not folding the children or feeding the laundry, she creates her own noble heroes on the page. Her speculative short stories explore the fabric of dreams and have appeared in numerous anthologies and SQ Magazine, while her novels weave magic into what it means to be human.

She still dreams of flying.

This has been an
Immortal Production